BY TANANARIVE DUE

The Between
My Soul to Keep

The Black Rose

TANANARIVE DUE

ONE WORLD
THE BALLANTINE PUBLISHING GROUP • NEW YORK

A One World Book
Published by Ballantine Books

www.randomhouse.com/BB/

Library of Congress Catalog Card Number: 00-109927

ISBN 0-345-44156-7

Manufactured in the United States of America

Cover design by Dreu Pennington-McNeil
Cover photo of Madame C.J. Walker: Photographs and Print Division, Schomburg
Center for research in Black Culture, The New York Public Library Astor,
Lennox, and Tilden Foundation

First Hardcover Edition: June 2000
First Trade Paperback Edition: January 2001

10 9 8 7 6 5 4 3

To my grandmothers

Lottie Sears Houston
and
Lucille Graham Ransaw
(1911–1992)
(A Madam C.J. Walker School of Beauty Culture graduate, 1941)

for planting the seeds

Based on the research and writing
of acclaimed author

ALEX HALEY

ACKNOWLEDGMENTS

This project was a tremendous opportunity and gift, and for that I must thank the Estate of Alexander P. Haley and my agent, John Hawkins, of John Hawkins & Associates. Also, thanks to my editor, Cheryl Woodruff, for her encouragement and her role in bringing this book to life.

Special thanks to the Indiana Historical Society, where the Madam C.J. Walker Collection is housed and open to the public, and the Madam Walker Theatre Center in Indianapolis, which is definitely worth a visit. Thanks also to Bethel AME Church in Indianapolis and the Vicksburg and Warren County Historical Society. For small favors that meant a lot, I also thank E. Ethelbert Miller and Charles Johnson.

For teaching me to cherish my history, I thank my parents, John Due and Patricia Stephens Due. And for much-needed emotional support, as always, thanks to my sisters, Johnita Due and Lydia Due Greisz, and my dear friend Luchina Fisher. And lastly, thanks to my wonderful husband, Steven Barnes, for believing in me even during those moments when I forgot to believe in myself.

Yellow Jack

O my body's racked wid de fever
My head rack'd wid de pain I hab. . . .
—SLAVE HYMN

Sometimes I feel like a motherless chile,
Far, far away from home,
A long, long way from home.
—NEGRO SPIRITUAL

*N*o one had seen a car like it.

Delta was not a rich town, mostly an assemblage of weather-beaten country stores, banks, and feed shops beneath faded, hand-painted signs. Residents sat on barrels in the shade and engaged in their cheapest town entertainment, which was watching the episodes of the day: a hitched horse trying to rear up, the parade of cotton growers' wagons on their way to market, or a motorcar owner cursing in the middle of the street, working up a sweat as he cranked furiously, trying to coax the engine of his stalled Tin Lizzie back to life.

So when a long, sleek black convertible touring car glided its way into Delta that day, driven by a somber-faced colored chauffeur in black cap and uniform, the entire street took notice. The car seemed to stretch forever, with room for at least seven or eight people to sit. And who was the primly dressed colored woman in a black suit and white shirtwaist who sat in the backseat with a smile fixed on her face, waving to people as she passed?

Before long, colored and white children, and a few older people, were chasing the car. When the car slowed and the woman inside invited a few children to climb in beside her for a ride, excitement rippled through the town like fire through a field of summer wheat; colored people began to pour toward the car, clamoring for a ride themselves. Soon there was no room on the street for passing traffic, and whites could only stare at the scene with bafflement. Was this woman the wife of a king or chief somewhere in Africa?

Virtually unnoticed, another colored woman walked through the crowd passing out yellow notices to any of the colored onlookers who would have one: MME. C.J. WALKER HAIR PRODUCTS, the advertisement said, and careful observers noticed right away that the likeness of the woman affixed to pictured products called Wonderful Hair Grower, Glossine, and Vegetable Shampoo matched the face of the woman inside the beautiful car. This was Madam C.J. Walker!

"That's her?" A barely concealed, excited whisper.

"Reckon so. That's her face, all right. Seen it on the shampoo box!"

The car came to a stop, and the Negro woman expelled a huff of air as she stepped down from the car, betraying her bone-weariness, but the crowd of on-lookers didn't hear it. Sarah Breedlove Walker had been traveling for months. In the past three weeks alone, she had visited five cities and spoken to hundreds of Southern agents and customers. Last night she'd stayed up in her boarding-house writing letters long past midnight. On mornings like this, she awakened with leaden arms and legs, her back aflame, restful sleep a distant memory. Headaches seemed her daily companions, and at times her heart raced in her chest for no good reason at all. Her doctor's nagging words plucked at her memory like prophecy: You'll work yourself to death, Madam Walker. Your blood pressure's sky-high.

But as usual, when Sarah saw the huddled people waiting to greet her, their faces glowing with anticipation, energy suffused her bones and flesh, lifted her spirits, cleared her mind. Especially here, and especially today. She was home.

Sarah's heart fluttered with a strange mixture of exhilaration and dread as she stared at the pebbled roadway beneath her delicately laced shoes. This wide clay street had once touched her family's feet, long ago. The road now carried shiny automobiles alongside the horses and buggies she remembered from child-hood, but many of the same clapboard homes still stood, older but little changed. She'd been born here nearly fifty years ago, and now she was back.

And there was so much work to be done! The folks who used threepenny words like ostentatious to criticize her fur coats, diamond jewelry, and fifty-dollar shoes just didn't understand. She wasn't putting on airs. In fact, truth be told, in this Louisiana sun she'd just as soon be wearing the threadbare cotton dresses she'd worn in her days as a washerwoman, without her starched white shirtwaist and heavy skirt to trap the heat against her skin. But she had more to think about than her own comfort. How many Negroes in towns like Delta had ever met one of their race who spoke, walked, and dressed as she did? How often could someone stir their imaginations into thinking they might make a good wage working for themselves instead of cleaning houses or sharecropping for white folks? Who could believe that a woman, born poor like them, might grow wealthy selling products to other Negroes?

Well, if ideas were bread, Sarah figured she could feed her whole nation. And if the good Lord would just keep firing her words with inspiration, or let her capture her people's attention through the finery of her car, then, Sarah decided, yes, sir, it was all right. The travel and the fatigue, the long years, the work and the sacrifice . . . it was all worthwhile. Only one life that soon is past. Only what's done for God will last.

Sun or no sun, bone-tired or not, she was going on. Especially today, in Delta. And especially now, when the Lord had guided her to more fortune than any other woman of her race in the world.

"Lady . . . you got a million dollars?" a boy blurted out. "Lemme see it!"

The boy's mother swatted him across the cheek, too hard. Sarah's aching back tensed when she saw anyone strike a child, and her heavy arms grew taut in anger. All too easily, she recalled the beatings from her brother-in-law, when she was just a child herself.

"Who you talkin' to?" The boy's mother shook his arm. "This ain't just no lady. This is Madam." Sarah could hear her parents in the young woman's country accent and cadences, and for a moment the woman's features blurred into her mother's, a long-ago dream. " 'Scuse his manners, Madam Walker, ma'am. I mean, if chirren ain't got a mule's sense!"

Sarah nodded at the woman, smiling. Not a happy smile, just bittersweet and knowing. I've got my own mule, by the name of Lelia, she thought. She knew that mother's fear of balancing too much love with not enough discipline, and the dangers only increased with money and status. That thought, the first hint of self-pity, was banished as the crowd penned Sarah in, flurrying for her attention. There were even some white folks vying to shake her hand. Oh, yes. White folks had even come to hear one of her lectures in Jackson last week, praise the Lord, and those were some ornery, Negro-hating folks over in Mississippi! Seemed like her skin color mattered less all the time, so long as her money was green.

"Please, Madam, you just sign me up, an' I'll be a good agent!"

"Madam Walker, I'm a washerwoman jus' like you was—"

Sarah touched as many as she could, distributing handshakes and hope with equal measure as she walked through the crowd. "That's right," she said, her voice pitched to rise above the din. "I started out just like you. My sister and I were here without a thing to call our own, in a shack not far from where we're standing now. The Lord showed me a way through hard work and faith, and he can show you, too."

One old white woman caught Sarah's eye, standing in the shade of the awning of the church where Sarah was scheduled to speak. The woman's bright eyes watched Sarah's every move, a smile lighting up her gently wrinkled face. Recognition eluded Sarah, but not the conviction that she had met this woman before.

Seeing Sarah's hesitation, the woman stepped toward her into the bright sun, her smile widening. "Sarah?" she began, then quickly corrected herself. "Madam Walker. Do you know me?" Her thin lips were trembling slightly. Sarah guessed she must be at least sixty-five, but it could be so hard to guess with white folks, what with the way their skin aged so fast.

"I'm Anna Burney Long," the woman said. The name resonated straight to Sarah's soul, momentarily stealing her words. "Your parents . . . worked for my father." There was a world of meaning within that carefully inflected word. Sarah flinched, but hid it well. "I remember you when you were an itty-bitty li'l thing, out on the farm. I'd like to invite you out to the house for a cold drink today, if you have the time. That cabin where you grew up is still on the land."

Now the memory of the woman's face was clear, washed of the years in between. Yes, Sarah had known this woman. Before the war, Sarah's parents had belonged to the woman's father.

"Mrs. Anna Burney Long," Sarah said, drawing out the name. Without being obvious, she evaluated the scuffed shoes, the dull purse, a dress worn at the hem, and realized that the Longs were poor folk compared to her. The people who had owned her parents did not have nearly what she did. Sarah had to conceal a smile. She would have loved to know what her father would have to say about this. Funny this woman being named Long, because Sarah's journey had been long, indeed.

"Lord, Lord," Madam C.J. Walker said, squeezing the white woman's hand. "I accept your invitation, Mrs. Long. We've got lots to talk about, and a cold drink after my speech would do me good."

From the beatific smile on the woman's face, Sarah knew Mrs. Long felt honored. "How did you do it, Sarah . . . ? I mean, Madam. All the Negroes I see seem to have such a hard time, but you! How did you ever come so far?"

Sarah smiled sadly. "To tell you the truth, Missus Anna . . ." Sarah said with a sigh, naturally lapsing into the form of address she had used as a child, "some days, I don't know myself."

Already, as the years began to blur away, Sarah could scarcely believe her journey.

Chapter One

The slave-kitchers couldn't get her. Not so long as she stayed hid.

Stealthily, Sarah crouched her small frame behind the thick tangle of tall grass that pricked through the thin fabric of her dress, which was so worn at the hem that it had frayed into feathery threads that tickled her shins.

"Sarah, where you at?"

Sarah felt her heart leap when she heard the dreaded voice so close to her. That was the meanest, most devilish slave-kitcher of all, the one called Terrible Lou the Wicked. If Terrible Lou the Wicked caught her, Sarah knew she'd be sold west to the Indians for sure and she'd never see her family again. Sarah tried to slow her breathing so she could be quiet as a skulking cat. The brush near her stirred as Terrible Lou barreled through, searching for her. Sweat trickled into Sarah's eye, but she didn't move even to rub out the sting.

"See, I done tol' Mama 'bout how you do. Ain't nobody playin' no games with you! I'ma find you, watch. And when I do, I'ma break me off a switch, an' you better not holler."

A whipping! Sarah had heard Terrible Lou whipped little children half to death just for the fun of it, even babies. Sarah was more determined than ever not to be caught. If Terrible Lou found her, Sarah decided she'd jump out and wrastle her to the ground. Sarah crouched closer to the ground, ready to spring. She felt her heart going *boom-boom boom-boom* deep in her chest. "Ain't no slave-kitcher takin' me!" Sarah yelled out, daring Terrible Lou.

"Yes, one is, too," Terrible Lou said, the voice suddenly much closer. "I'ma cut you up an' sell you in bits if you don't come an' git back to work."

Sarah saw her sister Louvenia's plaited head appear right in front of her, her teeth drawn back into a snarl, and she screamed. Louvenia was too

7

big to wrastle! Screaming again, Sarah took off running in the high grass, and she could feel her sister's heels right behind her step for step. Louvenia was laughing, and soon Sarah was laughing, too, even though it made her lungs hurt because she was running so hard.

"You always playin' some game! Well, I'ma *catch* you, too. How come you so slow?" Louvenia said, forcing the words through her hard breaths, her legs pumping.

"How come you so ugly?" Sarah taunted, and shrieked again as Louvenia's arm lunged toward her, brushing the back of her dress. Sarah barely darted free with a spurt of speed.

"You gon' be pickin' rice 'til you fall an' drown in them rice fields downriver."

"No, I ain't neither! You the one gon' drown," Sarah said.

"You the one can't swim good."

"Can, too! Better'n you." By now, Sarah was nearly gasping from the effort of running as she climbed the knoll behind their house. Louvenia lunged after her legs, and they both tumbled into the overgrown crabgrass. They swatted at each other playfully, and Sarah tried to wriggle away, but Louvenia held her firmly around her waist.

"See, you caught now!" Louvenia said breathlessly. "I'ma sell you for a half dollar."

"A half dollar!" Sarah said, insulted. She gave up her struggle against her older sister's tight grip. Louvenia's arms, it seemed to her, were as strong as a man's. "What you mean? Papa paid a dollar for his new boots!"

Louvenia grinned wickedly. "That's right. You ain't even worth one of Papa's boots, lazy as you is."

"There Papa go now. I'ma ask him what he say I'm worth," Sarah teased, and Louvenia glanced around anxiously for Papa. If Papa saw Louvenia pinning Sarah to the ground, Sarah knew he'd whip Louvenia for sure. Louvenia and Alex weren't allowed to play rough with Sarah. That was Papa's law, because she was the baby. And she'd been born two days before Christmas, Sarah liked to remind Louvenia, so she was close to baby Jesus besides.

"You done it agin, Sarah. Got me playin'," Louvenia complained, satisfied that Papa was nowhere near after peering toward the dirt road and dozens of acres of cotton fields that had been planted in March and April, sprouting with plants and troublesome grass and weeds. Still, her voice was much more hushed than it had been before. "You always gittin' somebody in trouble."

"I ain't tell you to chase me. An' I ain't tell you to stop workin'."

"Sarah, see, you think we jus' out here playin', but then *I'm* the one got to answer why we ain't finish yet."

Seeing Louvenia's earnest brown eyes, Sarah knew for the first time that her sister had lost the heart to pretend she was a slave-kitcher, or for any games at all. Right now, Louvenia's face looked as solemn as Mama's or Papa's when the cotton yields were poor or when their house was too cold. And Louvenia was right, Sarah knew. Just a few days before, Louvenia had been whipped when they broke one of the eggs they'd been gathering in the henhouse. It had been Lou's idea to break up the boredom of the task by tossing the eggs to each other standing farther and farther away. They broke an egg by the time they were through, and Sarah hadn't seen Mama that mad in a long time. "Girl, you ten years old, almost grown!" Mama had said, thrashing Louvenia's bottom with a thin branch from the sassafras tree near their front door. "That baby ain't s'posed to be lookin' after you! When you gon' get some head sense?"

Louvenia's eyes, to Sarah, looked sad and even a little scared. Maybe she was remembering her thrashing, too. Sarah didn't want her sister to feel cross with her, because Louvenia was her only playmate. In fact, although Sarah would never want to admit it to her, Louvenia was her best friend, her most favorite person. Next to Papa and Mama, of course.

Sarah squeezed Lou's hand. "Come on, I'll help. We won't play no mo' 'til we done."

"We ain't gon' be done 'fore Papa and them come back."

"Yeah, we will, too," Sarah said. "If we sing."

That made Louvenia smile. She liked to sing, and Papa had taught them songs he learned from his pappy when he was a boy on a big plantation he said had a hundred slaves. Sarah couldn't sing as well as her sister—her voice wouldn't always do what she told it to—but singing always made work go by faster. Mama sang, too, when the womenfolk came on Saturdays to wash laundry with them on the riverbank. But Papa had the best voice of all. Papa sang when he was picking, and to Sarah his voice was as deep and pretty as the Mississippi River on a full-moon night. Papa always started singing when he was tired, and Sarah liked to watch him pick up his broad shoulders each time he took a breath before singing a new verse, as if the song was making him stronger:

> O me no weary yet,
> O me no weary yet.
> I have a witness in my heart,
> O me no weary yet.

Sarah and Louvenia enjoyed the uplifting messages in Mama's and Papa's songs, which were mostly about Jesus, heaven, and Gabriel's trumpet, but they also liked the sillier songs Mama didn't approve of, the ones Papa sang on Saturday nights after he'd had a drink from the jug he kept hidden behind the old cracked wagon wheel that leaned against their cabin. Sarah and Louvenia thought those songs were funny, so that was what they sang that afternoon as they crouched to chop weeds from Mama's garden:

Hi-ho, for Charleston gals!
Charleston gals are the gals for me.
As I went a-walking down the street,
Up steps Charleston gals to take a walk with me.
I kep' a-walking and they kep' a-talking,
I danced with a gal with a hole in her stocking.

Together, as Sarah and her sister yanked up the stubborn weeds that grew frustratingly fast around Mama's rows of green beans, potatoes, and yams, they sang their father's old songs. Finally, the boredom that had felt like it was choking Sarah all day long in the hot sun finally let her mind alone. Instead of fantasizing about slave-kitchers Papa had told them so many stories about, or fishing for catfish, or the peppermint sticks at the general store in town she was allowed to eat at Christmastime, Sarah thought only of her task. Her hands seemed to fly. She'd chop the soil to loosen it with the rusted old hatchet Papa let her use, then pull up the weeds by the roots so they wouldn't come back. Chop and pull, chop and pull. Sarah didn't stop working even when the rows of calluses on her small hands began to throb in rhythm with her chopping. By the time they saw Mama's kerchief bobbing toward the house in the distance, followed by Papa's wide-brim hat, their weeding was finished, and they were lying on their backs in the crabgrass behind their house, arguing over what shapes they could see in the ghostly moon that was just beginning to make itself visible in a corner of the late-afternoon sky.

The cabin's windows, which were pasted shut with paper instead of glass during cooler months, were a curse in the winter, since they were little protection against the biting cold even with the shutters tied shut. But now, in spring, when the bare windows should have been inviting in a cool twilight breeze, the air inside the cabin was so still, so stiff and hot that Sarah hated to breathe it. It felt to her like hot air was trapped in the wooden walls, in the loose floorboards, in every crooked shingle on the drafty roof. Sarah watched the sunlight creeping through the slatted cracks in the walls and ceiling where the mud needed patching, wishing dark would hurry up and come and make it cool. Hungry as she was, Sarah wished Mama didn't have the cookstove lit, because it only made the cabin hotter. And it wasn't even summertime yet, Sarah thought sadly. By summer the heat would be worse, and the sun would bring out the cotton they would have to pick come the first of September.

Papa swatted at the big green flies and skeeters hovering above the table. Mosquitoes always seemed to know when it was suppertime, Sarah thought. Papa's arm moved lazily in front of his face as he shooed the insects, as if he were hunched over the table asleep. Sarah knew better than to try to talk to Papa too soon after he'd come back from the fields, especially close to June. Sarah and Louvenia were both too small to help in the fields in late May, because that was when Papa, Mama, and Alex pushed plows to break up acre after acre of soil to tend the cotton plants properly. Sarah and Louvenia did weeding, or on some days carried water and corncakes out to the croppers. Papa hated plowing those deep furrows between the rows, and Sarah could see how much he hated it in the lines on his frowning, sunbaked face as he sat at the table. Papa and Alex were barebacked, so slick with sweat they looked greased up.

Papa and Alex spoke to each other with short grunts and words uttered so low Sarah couldn't make out what they were saying, man-talking that came from deep in their throats. She'd heard men speak that way to each other in the fields, or as they rested on the front stoop and shared a jug and rumbles of laughter. Papa grunted something, and Alex smiled, muttering husky words back. Sarah knew her brother was nearly a man now, and she'd seen the change in the way Papa treated him. It was the same way Mama was treating Louvenia like a grown woman, expecting her to cook and mend and do a bigger share of fieldwork. Everyone was grown-up except her.

Sarah knew she could go to her pallet and play with the doll Papa had made her out of cornhusks wrapped together with twine, but she wanted to be more grown-up than that. She walked across the cabin—she counted twenty paces to get from one side to the other; she'd learned numbers up to twenty from Papa—and stood by the cookstove on her tiptoes to watch Mama stir collard greens in her big saucepan while Louvenia sat on the floor and mended a tear in her dress. Mama had one kerchief on her head and one knotted around her neck, both of them gray from grime. Her cheeks were full, and she had a youthful, pretty face; skin black as midnight and smooth like an Indian squaw's, Papa always said. Gazing at her, Sarah wondered if her mother would ever become stooped-over and sour-faced like so many other women she had seen in the fields.

Sarah expected Mama to tell her to get from underfoot, but she didn't. Instead she gave Sarah a big, steaming bowl. "Pass yo' papa his supper," Mama told her, and Sarah grinned. The smell of the greens, yams, and corn bread made her stomach flip from hunger. Papa's eyes didn't smile when he took his food from Sarah, but he did squeeze her fingers. Sarah knew that was his special way of saying *Thank you, Li'l Bit*.

Outside, Papa's hound barked loudly, and Papa and Alex looked up at the same instant. They all heard the whinny of a horse and a heavy *clop-clopping* sound that signaled the arrival of not one horse, but two or more. An approaching wagon scraped loudly in the dirt.

"Who'n de world . . . ?" Mama said, leaning toward the window.

"Not-uh," Papa warned her, standing tall so quickly that his chair screeched on the hard packed-dirt floor. "Don' put your head out. Git back." Something in Papa's voice that Sarah couldn't quite name made her stomach fall silent, and it seemed to harden to stone. His voice was dangerous, wound tight, and Sarah didn't know where that new quality had come from so suddenly. She had never heard Papa sound that way before.

Silently, Mama took Sarah's hand and pulled her back toward the stove at the rear of the cabin. Louvenia was still sitting on the floor, but her hands were frozen with her thread and needle in midair. Alex stood up at the table while Papa took long strides to the doorway, where he stood with his arms folded across his chest.

"Whoa there!" a man's voice outside snapped to his horses. It sounded like a white man. Sarah felt her mother's grip tighten around her fingers, her face drawn with concern.

Papa's whole demeanor changed; the shoulders that had been thrust so high suddenly fell, as if he had exhaled all his breath. He shifted his weight, no longer blocking the light from the doorway. The dangerous stance had vanished. "Evenin', Missus," Papa said, nearly mumbling.

"Evening, Owen," a woman's voice said.

A frightening thought came to Sarah: *I hope they ain't here to take our house away.* She didn't know why the visitors would do something like that, but she did know that she'd heard Mama and Papa talking about their payment being late. And she knew that their house, like everything else—including the land as far as they could see, Papa's tools, their cotton-seed, and even the straw pallets they slept on—belonged to the Burney daughters. Time was, before *'Man-ci-pa-tion* and the war that ended two years before Sarah was born, and before Ole Marster and Ole Missus died in '66 ("Of heartbreak," Mama always said, because of their land being overrun by Yankees and their crops and buildings burned up), the Burneys owned Mama and Papa and a lot of other slaves besides. Some of those slaves, like Mama and Papa, still worked on the land as croppers. But some of the other slaves, Mama told her, were so happy to be free that they'd just left.

Where'd they go? Sarah had asked, full of wonder at the notion that the other freed slaves had crossed the bridge to go to Vicksburg, or even beyond. The only other places she knew about were Mississippi and Charleston, like in the song. Had they gone away on a steamship? On a train?

They went on they own feets, pullin' every scrap they owned on wagons, Mama said. *And Lord only know where they at now. Might wish they was back here.* Now Sarah had a bad feeling. She wondered why Mama and Papa hadn't pulled a wagon with every scrap they owned and left on their own feet after freedom came, too. If they had, they wouldn't be late on their payment, and these white folks wouldn't be coming to take their house.

" 'Scuse the hour, Owen, but we were on our way from an affair in town." The woman's voice floated from outside. Despite Sarah's nervousness, the stranger's voice sounded like music to Sarah as her words rose and fell in the breeze. *An affair*, Sarah repeated to herself. She didn't know what the elegant word meant, but it intrigued her.

"It's just Missus Anna," Mama said, relieved. "Go sit down at the table, Sarah."

Quickly, Sarah did as she was told, climbing into a chair that rocked back and forth on uneven legs. Her attention was riveted to the doorway. Visitors to their cabin were rare, and white visitors were unheard of except, rarely, to leave their washing.

Daddy was mumbling the way Alex did after a scolding. "I figger I know what you callin' after, Missus. . . . Soon as we git the eggs to market, we can pay—"

"No business tonight, Owen. I know you'll pay. You always do. Hope I'm not disturbing supper," she said, then her voice changed, growing slightly softer as she addressed someone else: "I'll just be a moment, George. I'm going on in."

The man outside muttered something, but Sarah couldn't hear him except for two words: One was *hoodoo*, which Sarah knew meant magic; the other was *niggers*. He didn't sound happy.

Papa stepped aside, and the woman ducked through their doorway to walk inside. She was tall and thin, like something that might break, with chocolate-colored hair pinned on top of her head in feathery rings. Gentle strands of her hair bobbed above her brow. What would it feel like to have that soft, pretty hair? Sarah was also captivated by the woman's marvelous white dress. Gold buttons glistened up and down her lacy breast, and beneath her thin waist, the dress flared out into graceful layers that floated above the floor. Faint, lovely patterns were woven across the fabric like something sewn by angels. Sarah's mouth fell open as she stared. She had never seen such a dress! She could even *smell* the dress's crispness from where she sat.

"Evening, Minerva. Oh, you *are* sitting down to eat! I feel so badly about the hour, but it couldn't wait another day," the woman was saying, sounding nearly breathless. "Oh, my goodness, look how all these young'uns have grown! I just don't believe it."

The woman walked directly up to Sarah and leaned over to look at her face. She cupped Sarah's chin in her hand, and it was the softest hand Sarah had ever felt. A touch so soft and buttery it could melt clean away. "Don't even *tell* me this is the baby! You remember me? How old was she when I last saw her, Minerva . . . ?"

" 'Bout three o' fo', I think," Mama said. She had pulled her rag from around her neck and was twisting it in her hands, shifting her weight from foot to foot. Mama looked troubled. " 'Tain't tidied in here, Missus Anna. . . ."

Wasn't tidied! Sarah wondered why her mama would say such a thing. Sarah and Louvenia took turns sweeping the bare floor each morning with a brush-broom. The table, the chairs, two footstools, and some crates were the only furniture except Papa's rocker on the porch, but all of their belongings were in neat piles. Mama always said any house that worshiped God should stay as neat as if Jesus himself were calling at suppertime. "That ol' table look like it 'bout to break, an' dem pallets on the flo' full of flies. . . ." Mama said, mumbling like Papa.

Then, gazing back at the splendid newcomer, Sarah understood. Their cabin was too . . . *raggedy* for a woman in a dress like that. Sarah couldn't imagine this woman curling up on the floor to sleep on one of their pallets, or sitting at the table in one of the chairs that might stain her dress with sweat. Mama was ashamed, Sarah realized, and suddenly she was, too. The foreign feeling slapped her face hot.

Sarah knew she had been to this woman's big plantation house called Grand View when she was little, but she didn't remember the visit. And she didn't remember this woman, although she wondered how she could have forgotten her. The woman's soft fingers lingered at Sarah's chin a while longer, then slipped away. "Oh, 'Nerva, stop talking nonsense. Let me look in my handbag, because I know I have something this little one'd like."

"Me, too, Missus Anna?" Louvenia blurted suddenly, and Mama gave her a harsh look.

The woman laughed. "Oh, of course, little Lou. I wouldn't forget you."

To Sarah's amazement, the woman produced a wrapped piece of brown candy.

"You like taffy, Sarah?" the woman said, holding the candy close to her face.

Sarah nodded eagerly, although she had no idea what in the world *taffy* was. She'd seen candy in jars when Mama shopped for flour and sold their eggs in town, but the only candy Mama ever bought her was a peppermint stick at Christmas. Her taste buds pricked. "Yes'm."

"Now, you may have this piece if you know what to say," the woman told her.

Sarah's heart tumbled with panic. Her fingers were already twitching to take the candy dangling before her nose, but suddenly her mind was wiped blank. What did this lady want her to say? Did she want her to tell her what a pretty dress she had? Or how nice her hand felt because it wasn't rough like Mama's? Sarah didn't know what to say to a white lady! Her eyes darted over to Louvenia, who was gazing at her with envy, then to Mama, who looked impatient, as if it were clear as day what the answer was.

"Sarah, what you say?" Mama said crossly. Then, seeing Sarah's confusion, Mama made her voice gentler. "Like what I tol' you the other day 'bout that molasses? 'Member?"

Sarah didn't remember a thing, and the stinging behind her eyes warned her she was close to tears. The candy was right in front of her, but now she'd never have it at all!

"It starts with a 'P' . . ." the white woman said instructively, coaxing. More perplexed, Sarah began to blink fast, trying as hard as she could to keep her tears away.

"She don't know what that mean, Missus Anna," Papa said, and Sarah felt her chest loosen with relief even as the shame she'd felt earlier flared again. "She ain't learnt spellin'."

"*Please!*" Louvenia finally hissed at Sarah. "You s'posed to say *please*."

Was that all? Even though her mouth had become suddenly dry, Sarah forced herself to speak as loudly as she could: "Kin I . . . please . . . have it?"

"Of course!" the woman said. Her face lit up as if Sarah had said something extraordinary, but Sarah knew *please* was a regular word Mama told her to say when she asked for something. How could she have guessed this lady wanted her to say a plain word like that?

"Kin I please have one, too, Missus Anna?" Louvenia said.

Papa spoke up in a voice more like his own: "I don' know if you need to be spoilin' 'em with that store-bought candy, Missus Anna. It's much 'preciated, but . . ."

"Oh, come now, Owen, one piece won't hurt them." She said it as if that were the end of the matter, even though she was talking to *Papa*, and Papa made the rules. Sarah looked at Papa, amazed he didn't speak up and tell her *that was that*, but he didn't. Instead, he shoved his hands in the pockets of his scuffed pants and let his face go hard.

"Not before you eat your supper, all right?" the woman said after both Sarah and Louvenia had the treasured pieces of candy in their possession, and they nodded. Sarah tried to say *thank you*, but the words were stuck in her throat because she was sure Papa was about to tell the woman to take the candy back. But he never did.

"Anna!" the white man's voice outside called impatiently above the horses' snorts.

The woman pursed her thin pink lips together, standing upright again. She spoke hurriedly, fanning a fly from her face. "Oh, have mercy, George is as impatient as Daddy was. George says it's blasphemy to cotton to Negro hoodoo, but all the same, here's why I'm calling: The town was buzzing today about Yellow Jack. Vicksburg, too, I hear tell."

Yellow Jack? Sarah knew of no such man, but she imagined he must be pretty remarkable if white folks were interested in him all throughout

Delta and Vicksburg, and if this lady would call on them just to ask about him. She'd never known white folks to get excited about any nigger, black or yellow, except the ones Papa said played music and sang in the minstrel shows.

"Yeah, I heard sump'n 'bout that, ma'am," Daddy muttered.

"Well, I don't mind telling you both, I won't sleep a wink tonight. You remember what poor Mama and Big Pa went through in sixty-six, God rest them both, and so many others besides. And it seems like the doctors can't do nothing about it. So it would put my mind at ease if you'd go out to see Mama Nadine and tell her to make me a potion against Yellow Jack. I want her to bring it to me come morning. I'll give you three dollars to go to her, and that ought to help you meet your debt. Tell Mama Nadine I'll pay whatever she says."

Sarah saw Mama and Papa look at each other, and she knew what they were thinking: *Three* whole dollars just to go out and see the witch doctor, Mama Nadine? She wasn't much more than a half-hour's walk away, out in her brick house in the woods. Mama had taken Sarah there once, long ago, when she had a cough that had lasted for a month. Mama Nadine made her drink something that tasted awful, and that cough sure was gone a week later.

But what kind of yellow nigger could be so evil white folks would need a potion against him? He must have some powerful magic, Sarah thought with a surge of fear.

"Dark's comin' on," Papa said, still looking at Mama. "I better git movin', if I'm goin'."

The white woman's face brightened with a wide smile. "Thank you kindly, Owen! I sure hoped you'd do it! I've known you and 'Nerva so long, you're like kin. You're good folks, and I told Mama and Big Pa I'd look out for you. I hope you'll be here with us a long time."

"Well, now, I don't know 'bout that. . . ." Papa said, speaking more slowly. "Nex' year, maybe, Missus Anna, I been thinkin' 'bout goin out west, maybe up nawth. I figger me an' cotton seen enough of each other by now. I hear there's good wages workin' on the railroad."

Tonight was full of surprises! Sarah had never heard Papa talk about moving away, but the thought excited her. She could imagine her entire family hitched up to a wagon and rolling across hills and valleys to places she'd never seen. Maybe the days wouldn't be so tedious in a new place, and she'd have more time to climb trees and play marbles, slave-kitcher, hopscotch, and "Hide the Switch" with Lou.

"Out west!" the woman said, dismayed. "Owen, that's no place for civilized folk, what with the Injuns running wild. They'd just as soon eat your young'uns as look at you. And you don't need to go north. Don't we treat you good here? Freeing y'all is one thing, but then how can you feed yourselves? That's the biggest price of the war, to my mind. Did you already forget how many Negroes died in the riot in Vicksburg in December? At least thirty-five, all told. And there's babies starving on the streets there today."

"Yes'm, we done heard that," Mama said quickly. "Sho' did—"

"We heard it, Missus Anna," Papa went on, "but that don't mean we gon' starve, too. I also done heard 'bout whole towns full o' nothin' but niggers. An' they ain't starved yet."

"What the hell is all this about?" Suddenly the room went silent, and a broad-shouldered white man in a long black coat stood in the doorway. It must be the lady's husband, Sarah thought. Sarah barely noticed his fancy clothing because she was so frightened by the anger in his eyes. Mama and Papa always told her the surest way to trouble was to make a white man mad, so she mustn't ever even look one in the eye. She tried to look away, but not before she saw the rider's crop in his hand.

"Did I hear you right, Owen Breedlove? You in here starting a damn debate?"

"George . . . your language . . ." the woman said weakly, her face changing colors, but then she was silent under his gaze. Sarah saw her brother fold his arms across his chest, imitating Papa's earlier stance that had seemed somehow dangerous. She also noticed that Alex was staring right toward the white man's face without blinking, despite Mama's warning.

"No, suh, Mr. Long, I ain't doin' nothin' like you said," Papa told the man. "Niggers sho' don't know nothin' 'bout no pol'tics an' such. I was jus' tellin' Missus Anna a story I heard 'bout some niggers out west."

"Well, east, west, or south, seems to me niggers were happier when they were looked after. We never had these troubles before the war. Wish someone else was responsible for feeding and clothing *me*. Is your business finished here, Anna?"

"Yes, it is," the woman said, opening her tiny handbag again, and she pulled out three gold-colored coins that shone in the lamplight. She gave them to Papa. "Three dollars, Owen."

"Might as well throw that money in the river and make a wish," the white man muttered. "I swear, Anna, sometimes . . ."

"Thank you again, Owen," she said, ignoring the man. "Y'all have a good supper and a good night."

The white man and woman walked out the door, leaving the excitement of their visit hanging in the air. Sarah didn't even mind that the white man had seemed so cross, since at least his presence had been a novelty. "Ooh, Mama, did you see that lady's *dress*?" Sarah cried.

"I seen it," Mama said, but kept her voice low. She and Papa both seemed to be listening; Sarah wondered what they were listening for, until she heard the man shout for the horses to *git*, and they could hear their wagon driving away. Mama and Papa didn't want to talk about them until they were sure they were gone, Sarah realized. She wondered if the visitors were driving one of those fancy carriages she had seen in Vicksburg, sleek and black and pretty.

"Come askin' after that hoodoo at *suppertime*, when she know you tired an' hungry," Mama said. "Her mama woulda knowed better manners'n that."

"Sho' glad for this money, though," Papa said, shrugging. He picked up his bowl and began to scoop food into his mouth with a spoon. "This'll go a long way to what we owe 'em."

"Y'all see how Mr. Long come in here all haughty 'cause he liked them Rebs?" Alex said, laughing as he imitated the white man's barrel-chested stance, his hands planted on his hips. "Them Rebs ain't do nothin' in that war but lose. Papa, I seen him jump away scared o' dat nigger still goin' roun' wearin' his blue coat on Sundays. You know who I mean, that cropper was with them Yankees way back?"

"Yeah, I know 'im," Papa said. "They say Simon crazy, but don't none of them buckras bother 'im, neither. They hate that blue like they hate the devil. Scared, that's why. Simon was jus' a-poundin' on his drum in the war, tol' me he didn't even git no gun with that blue coat, but white folks roun' here think he done kilt a mess o' buckras an' liked it."

Mama *humphed*, exhaling loudly through her nostrils. "Scarin' 'em ain't gon' do no good. That's why them Vicksburg niggers gettin' kilt now. Seem like ain't nothin' changed."

"Sho' ain't," Papa said. "Talkin' 'bout Mis'sippi done sent a nigger to the Senate, but ain't nobody better fo' it but him. Niggers out here still workin' theyselves to death like befo'," Papa said, and Mama and Alex murmured their agreement.

Sarah mustered enough nerve to creep to the window to try to peer after the woman in the white dress to see if she was indeed riding in a shiny carriage. By then their visitors had already vanished behind the thick stand of trees. All she could see was a low cloud of dust left by their departure. She knew Papa hadn't told the truth when he told the white man he didn't know anything about *pol'tics*, because that was his favorite subject with the men who came to visit him on the porch. He talked about *Re-con-struc-tion* and the *Freed-men's Bu-reau* and *Wa-shing-ton*. Those days, Papa was like a preacher, and every time his voice rose up, the men called back to him *Tell it!* and *You ain't lyin'!* They had come to talk to Papa a lot before Christmastime, when all those people got killed in the race riot in Vicksburg. Mama said she was tired of all their talking, and on Christmas Eve she just about had to chase all those men home. She said they shouldn't be talking about so much ugly so close to Jesus' day.

"But we gon' go west or nawth, come spring," Papa said, eating a spoonful of food. "If there a way, Lord know I'ma find it."

"Tell you what, if Missus Anna give me a hunnert dollars, I'll mix up a

potion my *own* self," Mama said with a laugh. "*That'll* git us west and whatever else we want, too."

"Mama, you don't know no hoodoo like Mama Nadine!" Louvenia said.

"I ain't said I did. But Missus Anna ain't got to know I don't."

"Woman, you so wicked," Papa said, but he was grinning. The grin
changed his whole face, as if he weren't tired at all. "Who wanna walk
with me down to Mama Nadine's?"

Sarah jumped up and down. "Ooh, Papa, I does! Me!"

"You ain't scared o' that witch woman, Li'l Bit?" Papa said, and Sarah
shook her head. Papa rubbed the top of her head, his fingers sifting
through her plaits. "Come on, then. You an' me's on a errand tonight."

Sarah couldn't believe her luck! She closed the palm of her hand
tightly around her candy and vowed to save it until later. The white lady
had told her not to eat her candy until after supper, and besides, she might
try to wait until tomorrow or the next day, or even longer, before she ate it.
She wanted to save her candy for a special day.

"Take a lamp, and y'all hurry back," Mama said, then she sighed. "I
sho' hopes Missus Anna ain't be bringin' none o' that Yellow Jack roun'
here."

With Mama's worry in their minds and a low-burning kerosene lamp
to light their way, Sarah and her father began their journey along the rutted road in the twilight. Stalks of high grass swept across Sarah's thighs as
she walked. She could hear the bathing creek gurgling a few yards away
from them, which made her wish she could jump into the water and splash
the heat away. Insects followed them, and Sarah scratched at a new bump
on her wrist from a bite.

"Papa," Sarah said, "who Yellow Jack is?"

Papa laughed. "Yellow Jack ain't no *who*. It's a fever makes white folks
turn yellow."

"Yellow like a nigger?"

"Nah, not like that. But they'd sho' be scared o' that, too, maybe mo'
than they scared *now*. Yellow Jack'll kill 'em, though, lots o' time. That be
what kilt off Ole Marster and Ole Missus, use to own all this land. Ole
Marse Burney got the fever in April, then his wife went sick in fall, near to
Thanksgivin'. That was a awful year roun' here, Li'l Bit. I only stayed here
on 'count Mr. Burney had axe me to, cuz he done me a good turn long time
ago. Ain't for that, your papa woulda been runnin' to the Yankees, too.
Then the crop went bad in sixty-seven, and I ain't pull myself out of owin'
since. Only good thing to come out o' that year was *you*. But 'til we leave
roun' here, we still be slaves, every one o' us, don't matter what po' Abe
Lincoln writ down."

Papa was silent for a long time after that, and Sarah enjoyed the sight
of their long shadows walking alongside each other on the road. Papa

usually didn't talk to her like she was one of his grown men-friends, and she didn't want to say anything stupid to ruin it so he'd remember she was still the baby, only six years old. She looked up toward the sky, and saw that the sun was ready to dip out of sight inside the tree line to the west. It would be dark soon, and they'd need the lamp for sure. Sarah knew the bugs would follow their light and bite them the whole way.

"Papa . . . where do Yellow Jack come from?"

"You git it from touchin' and breathin' on folks that's gots it, I reckon, or maybe the air git dirty. When somebody die from it, they burn up the bodies so won't no one else kitch it. I figger it's like one o' them plagues on Egypt the Sunday preacher be talkin' 'bout. Plagues take the good an' wicked alike. I sho' would hate for Yellow Jack to take Missus Anna. I knowed her since she was born."

Swatting away a cloud of gnats flying close to her head, Sarah looked up at her father's bearded face and sharp chin, feeling at once very small and very safe. Her feet stumbled in the deep, muddy ruts, but she struggled to keep pace with him. Her bare foot splashed into a thin puddle of muddy water left over from last night's storm, and she hoped she hadn't stained her dress. There were still three more days until Mama did washing.

"Papa . . . only white folks git Yellow Jack?"

"That's what they say, Li'l Bit, but plenty niggers git sick, too. Jus' don't be breathin' on nobody who sick, an' you be fine. But know sump'n? I figger God ain't got no plagues in mind for a sweet li'l one like you."

Sarah hoped Papa was right. He smiled down at her, his teeth glowing bright in the waning sunlight, but this time Sarah didn't feel warmed by his smile. Her stomach felt tight suddenly, and she wished she'd eaten before she'd left for such a long walk. Maybe she was scared to see Mama Nadine, after all.

"Bugs think you eatin' good tonight, huh? No, you ain't," Papa said, slapping at a skeeter on his neck. When he moved his hand away, Sarah could see the tiny smear of blood left behind. "I got 'im?" he asked her, cocking his head like he did when he shaved his face clean each summer. Sarah nodded, gazing uneasily at the blood spot on her father's neck. Blood always made Sarah feel queasy.

Owen Breedlove smiled, satisfied. Soon, as he walked, he began to hum the song about dancing with the Charleston gal with the hole in her stocking, and Sarah hummed right along with him until the queasy feeling went away.

Chapter Two

By the time Sarah reached Mama Nadine's sturdy brick house nestled between old, thick oak trees, she was soaked through from the sudden downpour. Droplets that felt as big as her fingers splashed her clothes, thunder roared above the trees, and lightning seared the cloud-darkened skies in flashes that made her vision dance. Sarah's teeth were chattering, but although she was wet, she wasn't cold. The chattering was because of fear.

Tentatively, Sarah strained to reach up to knock on the smooth wooden door with the iron knocker that had turned green from time. As she did, she felt disbelief tickling the back of her neck, reminding her that Papa had used this very same knocker only two weeks before, when she could smell simmering stew from Mama Nadine's supper wafting from underneath the door. Oxtail stew, and red beans and rice. She and Papa had eaten well that night, which was so few days ago but already felt like a make-believe memory.

Please, please, please, please, Sarah thought, wrapping her arms tightly around herself. She heard a fiddle's deep strains from inside the house, the music growing more rapid and then slowing down until it almost sounded as mournful as Sarah felt. Certain her knock hadn't been heard, Sarah rapped the knocker sharply again. This time the fiddling stopped.

Sarah recognized the lanky, curly-headed man who opened the door; he looked almost like a white man, except for his lips and broad nose that reminded her of Papa's. He held his fiddle by the neck in one hand, the bow in the other. He looked surprised.

"Well, lookie what the storm blew in," the man said. "*Salut, chérie.* You here for Mama Nadine?" To Sarah, he sounded exactly like a white man, too, except for the words she couldn't understand. Cajuns always talk funny, Papa said. Besides, Papa had told her this man was Mama Nadine's son, who was being schooled up north by his rich white daddy. He had a strange-sounding Cajun name Sarah couldn't remember, but he'd been nice to her when she was here last.

Silently, Sarah nodded.

"Come on inside then. You came all this way your lone self?"

Again, Sarah nodded, stepping out of the rain and flinging droplets of water from her face. Her dress, which was clinging to her tightly, dripped on the straw mat. Sarah's teeth clicked uncontrollably. "I g-gotta see M-Mama Na—"

"And you will, little one, soon's I find you a blanket. Looks like that rain caught you unawares. *Un moment.*"

Mama Nadine's house had three rooms, or maybe even more, Sarah guessed. This room in front had a small table and soft chairs for sitting, and a shelf full of books. Mama had only one book—an old Bible Ole Missus had given her a long time ago, even though Mama didn't know how to read the words in it—but Sarah had never seen so many books in one place. There were big candles everywhere, most of them lit to give the room light. There was a strange scent around her; something sweet was burning in the air.

"Somebody out there at my door?" Mama Nadine's voice called from the back.

The man, who draped a sour-smelling blanket over Sarah's head, called something back to her in Cajun, then he began to gently push Sarah toward another brightly glowing room. Sarah was eager to see Mama Nadine, but her feet didn't seem to work the way they should, dragging and half stumbling as she got closer to the other room.

He was taking her to the kitchen, Sarah realized. She and Papa had eaten in here when they came last time, and the thought of it made Sarah's eyes grow misty. The small kitchen smelled smoky. It was an entire room with nothing in it except a cookstove, a washtub, shelves filled with jars, and a smoothly sanded wooden table with four chairs. There were strings of garlic, feathers, and some trinkets hanging on the wall from nails. And, of course, there were candles. Candlelight made overlapping shadows on the walls.

And here sat Mama Nadine. She was a honey-colored woman younger than Mama with thin, birdlike limbs. She wore her head wrapped in a colorful scarf that dangled to her breast. She was sitting in a chair, and a dark-skinned girl about Louvenia's age sat cross-legged on the floor between her thighs. The girl's hair was spread across her shoulders, and Mama Nadine was running a strange-looking comb with metal teeth through it. Inexplicably, when the comb touched the girl's hair, it sizzled with smoke. Mama Nadine was performing some kind of magic on the girl, Sarah decided.

"Who down buried in that blanket, Bertrand?" Mama Nadine said.

Her voice, too, sounded smoky and somehow far away. Her fingers worked gracefully with the comb, pulling the girl's strands of hair, and the girl's head fell back and she gritted her teeth as if it hurt. To Sarah, the girl's hair looked like Papa said an Indian's did, hanging straight and black.

"Owen Breedlove's girl, one come here two weeks back," the man answered.

"Sarah?" Mama Nadine said, pulling the name from memory.

Sarah nodded, sniffling this time.

"What drive you out in this storm to see Mama Nadine, *ma chérie?*"

Sarah knew it was time to tell, but her lips felt stuck together, and her tongue was swollen thick in her mouth. She'd planned out what she would say, down to promising Mama Nadine all the eggs in the henhouse if only she would come. But with the storm so fierce outside, Sarah suddenly felt certain the witch-lady would laugh at her. Or worse, she might put a curse on her, if there weren't one already. After all, a curse was probably the reason all the bad things had happened so fast.

Papa got sick first, on Monday the week before. He came back from the fields complaining he had a fever and a backache, and he worked only a half day on Tuesday before he dragged himself home. Sarah and Louvenia gave him wet rags to keep on his forehead like Mama said to, but Sarah was shocked when she touched the skin on Daddy's face and felt how raging hot it was. Hot as burning kindling, it seemed. It looked swollen, too. And even though Papa was sweating, he was shivering on his pallet as if it were the middle of wintertime.

Fever, Sarah knew. And maybe, just maybe, whispered a voice far in the back of her head, Papa had Yellow Jack. She went to bed at night praying Missus Anna hadn't brought Yellow Jack to Papa.

Then Mama got sick, too. One morning Mama just woke up retching on the floor. She said she wasn't strong enough to go to the fields, but she was scared of losing wages, so she sent Louvenia with Alex instead. Louvenia complained about it so much, sticking out her lip, that Sarah wished she could hit her. Sarah would have gone her own self if she could, since she hated Mama and Papa to be worried about wages when they might have Yellow Jack, but she knew she was too weak for listing. So she stayed and nursed Mama and Papa.

Yellow Jack. The word played in her mind constantly, and two days, then three, went by without either of them getting better. In fact, truth be told, they seemed to be getting *worse*. Sarah gathered firewood and boiled water for oatmeal, but neither of them could keep any food in their stomachs without throwing up. They were always thirsty. And since they were both too weak to go to the outhouse, Sarah brought them a bucket to use for a toilet, and she cleaned up after them if they made a mess like she did some nights when she woke up with a full bladder and discovered she was spilling warm urine all over herself. Late at night, Mama would wake up calling out the names of people Sarah didn't know.

But this morning had been the worst of all. This morning, when Mama threw up, the sickness that came out of her mouth was *black*. And after Alex and Louvenia had already gone out to the fields, Papa sat up for the first time in three days and told Sarah she'd better go get Mama Nadine. He said he knew this wasn't an ordinary fever like the chills they got sometimes in the summer when they stood out in the rain too long. He said they had Yellow Jack for sure, and he'd had a dream Mama was about to die.

Go on, Li'l Bit. You know where Mama Nadine at. You follow that road, then veer off by where that big tree done fell, an' walk straight 'long the creek 'til you see her house.

And Sarah had done just fine until the rain, but then she'd started running and nearly lost her way, and all she could think about was Mama at home dying because she was out lost in the woods. But she'd found the house, sure enough. She'd made it.

"Devil he took your tongue, *chérie?*" Mama Nadine said, still combing.

"M-my mama and papa sick," Sarah said, finding her voice. "They gots Yellow Jack."

Mama Nadine stopped combing, giving Sarah her full, wide eyes. Sarah felt the man behind her take a step away from her. He coughed gently into his hand as if he were embarrassed because she'd said a cussword.

"How you know this for a fact, little one?" Mama Nadine said at last.

And so Sarah told her everything, about the fevers and the sweating and the black sickness from Mama's stomach. But, more important, she told Mama Nadine about Papa's dream.

At this, the woman nodded and sighed. "That sound like the fever to me," she said. "Where your brother?"

"Plowin' them cotton fields," Sarah said. "Him and my sister both."

"Nobody with your *maman* and papa but you?"

"In the day," Sarah said, sniffling again. "An' sometime Missy Laura, my mama friend, she bring food by. But she gots to work, too."

Mama Nadine made a clicking sound with her teeth and sighed again. Sarah's heart thumped, because she was afraid Mama Nadine was about to tell her to go back home, that there was no help for her here. "You m-made a p-potion fo' Missus Anna," Sarah reminded her.

"Missus Anna ask me for potion, yes. But like I say to her at her big, grand house, it not that simple. Not that simple, *belle*. This fever has a demon's ways. You want Mama Nadine to go to your *maman* and papa?"

Overjoyed, Sarah nodded her head vigorously. Water shook from her hair into her face. "Yes'm," she said. "We g-got eggs what to pay with."

Mama Nadine nodded, barely listening, as if she heard voices somewhere else in the room. "*Maman* and papa both *malade*. That very bad, *chérie*. Very bad. This a hungry fever, but we try to keep one parent for you, eh? Every girl need at least her *maman*."

Keep one parent for you. Mama Nadine's words raked Sarah's stomach. What did she mean by that? She needed her mama and papa both!

"I give you some red snakeroot I get this spring, full of sap. You take that home, you boil it, make tea. Both you parents drink tonight. They drink as much tea as you make. Tonight, I light my altar and pray. I come morning-time to you. I come."

Sarah nodded, feeling a sharp twinge of disappointment. She was grateful for the tea-root, but she wished Mama Nadine's remedies sounded more powerful. Sarah had been praying night after night herself, and praying hadn't helped a bit. What if morning was too late?

"Bertrand, ride her home when the rain is finished," Mama Nadine said. "But you don't go in that house, no? You don't go near that fever."

"No worries, *maman*."

The girl with the straight black hair was gazing at Sarah with her head to one side, the way someone looks at something that breaks her heart. The girl's gaze made Sarah feel angry, then petrified. What if she would never have another chance to sit between her mama's soft thighs and have her own hair combed and plaited again? Sarah's scalp always burned and itched in the sun, and only her mama's combing seemed to help. In that instant, Sarah hated the girl and everything about her, especially her Indian hair that hung down past her shoulders.

"My mama and papa ain't gon' die," Sarah told the girl defiantly.

The girl's pitying expression didn't change.

"With the help of the gods, we see, *chérie*," Mama Nadine said. "We see."

Papa drank two cups of Mama Nadine's root tea before he went to sleep for the night, but Mama took only two sips and then shook her head. "Cain't," she whispered.

"Mama Nadine tol' you to," Louvenia said.

"Please, Mama?" Sarah said, squeezing her hand. Mama's hand felt damp, and her lip had split open so that it was peeking blood through the crack in her skin. In the lamplight, her mama was beginning to look like somebody else, like one of those old ladies who sat at the riverbank and tended babies while the younger women worked. Right before sunset, Missy Laura had brought some briers she'd strung together and hung around Mama's neck, saying it was a remedy for fever she'd learned from her grandfather, but the briers didn't seem to do anything except make Mama scratch weakly where they touched her skin.

"I'se gon' drink it by an' by," Mama said in the same tiny voice.

Sarah was aching to tell Mama about Papa's dream and how she would die for sure if she didn't drink the tea, but she couldn't bring herself to say it. If she actually *said* it, she reasoned, that might make it come true. Sarah decided she would just wait until Mama started mumbling nonsense words like she had a few hours ago, and when her mind was asleep, she'd give her the tea. She'd drink it and wouldn't even remember.

Suddenly Mama stared up at them with frightened eyes. She clung to Louvenia's dress. "Lou? Sarah?" she said, as if she was afraid they would walk away. "That y'all? I thought y'all was both here befo', but then the thunder came, an' wasn't nobody here 'cept me. An' Owen, but he was 'sleep." Speaking seemed to make her breathe harder, and Sarah heard a gurgling from Mama's chest she'd never heard before. The harsh sound nearly stilled Sarah's heart.

"We here now, Mama," Louvenia said.

"Lord," Mama said, amazed. "Lord, seem like I been gone. Seem like I don' know where I'm at no mo'."

"You at home," Sarah told her cheerfully. "And Lou and Alex and Papa, too."

"It's day or night?" Mama asked.

"Night," Louvenia said. "I made supper."

At that, Sarah made a face; Louvenia had *tried* to make supper, but she'd overcooked the green beans, and she'd burned the biscuits besides. Sarah was still hungry. She'd felt a little hungry ever since Mama got sick, except when Missy Laura brought a basket of corn bread and fried chicken for them. She wished Missy Laura had brought them some food today when she brought the necklaces of scratchy briers, but she hadn't.

"Oh, Lord, Lord." Mama gasped. "Owen still sick, too? We losin' wages."

"No, we ain't, Mama," Louvenia said, although that was a lie. Mama always told them never to tell lies, but Sarah figured it was all right now. Lies would make Mama feel better, maybe. "An' Papa gettin' better. He 'sleep now, but he was sittin' up today."

That part, at least, was true. Papa had even felt well enough to argue with Missy Laura when she put the briers around his neck, telling her he thought it was an old wives' tale.

"Lou," Mama said, licking her dry lips, "you go run an' find me that Bible-book Ole Missus give me." This time she almost sounded like she wasn't sick at all.

Louvenia must have forgotten Mama was sick, too, because she sucked on her teeth just like she did anytime she was asked to do something she didn't feel like doing. Except usually Mama would cuff her if she did that, and now Mama didn't do anything except lie shivering on her pallet. "I don' know where that ol' book at," Louvenia complained.

"Chile, go find it. Quick, now, 'fore . . ." Mama paused for a long time, then she sighed. ". . . 'fore I forget."

"I'll find it, Mama," Sarah said.

Suddenly Mama's hand was tight around Sarah's arm. The grip was so strong it almost hurt, and Sarah was shocked Mama still had so much strength. Maybe Mama was putting all the strength she had into holding on to her, she thought, and that thought made Sarah feel better. "No, Sarah. You stay. Stay."

The way Mama was looking at Sarah reminded her of the doleful gaze from the girl sitting between Mama Nadine's legs, with her eyes full as if she were seeing something big, terrible, and sad, something she wished she didn't have to see. Tears sprang to Mama's eyes.

"The baby . . . Ain't even quite seven years old . . ." Mama whispered, then she began to speak so quickly that Sarah almost couldn't keep up with her words. "Seem like you was talkin' 'bout as soon as the midwife slap you to life. . . . You could 'member all them words an' numbers . . . 'an you could make Owen laugh, chile. . . . You brighten that man life so . . . yes, you did . . . time you took that stick in yo' hand, wavin' it an talkin' . . . you 'member? You was so little. . . ."

Sarah listened as hard as she could, but she was afraid Mama's mind was going to sleep again. She didn't understand what she was talking about. Then, just that quickly, Mama seemed to be praying. Her eyes drifted away.

"Lord, I promised I'd learn to read all them words in yo' Good Book . . . or one of these chillen would read it to me . . . an' I thought it'd be Sarah, 'cause seem like she could do it . . . an' me an' Owen talked an' said we'd take her out the field . . . put her in one of them freedmen schools . . . but we needed her back 'fore long. Lord, we ain't have the chance. Fo'give us, Lord. . . ." Mama's eyes snapped back to Sarah's, seeing her. "Sarah . . . you hear me?"

"Yes'm," Sarah said.

"When Lou bring that Bible-book . . . you keep it, hear? That's the Lord's book. All them words in there . . . I want you to read 'em. I want you to read His word. . . ."

Sarah didn't know anybody who could read, except for white folks, or maybe Mama Nadine and her son with the Creole name. She'd learned the letters in her name when Mama and Papa let her go to the school in the woods when she was little, but that was all. She'd stayed in school for only three months, then she'd stopped because Mama needed her help. Sarah had flipped through the pages of Mama's Bible many times before, but the tiny symbols on the pages were a mystery. "Mama, how I'ma . . . ?"

"Shhhh," Mama hushed her. "You go to school. Tell Alex and Lou I say you goin' to school, hear? They gon' take you out them fields . . . an' you gon' learn to read all them words. Jus' like I promise God . . . Jus' like I promise . . . You hear me, Sarah?"

"Yes'm," Sarah said. "I'ma read all them words."

"An' then you come read 'em to me. You come back, hear? Come see me."

Come see her? What did Mama mean by that? Was Mama sending her away? Even though Sarah suspected Mama was speaking foolishness again, she felt flames licking inside her throat. Her eyes burned, too.

"The par'ble of the seed and sower, like Preacher say . . ." Mama said, her whisper more faint. "One seed. Owen say seem like you the seed, Sarah, an' I knowed it, too. I always knowed it, chile."

Then Mama closed her eyes, breathing fast. She let go of Sarah and clutched at the briers around her neck, trying to pull them away.

"Don't do that, Mama," Sarah said, taking Mama's hands gently. "Missy Laura say that gon' make you well. An' you gots to drink this tea now, jus' like Mama Nadine say."

But Mama had gone to sleep. Sarah watched the rising and falling of her mother's chest, terrified it would stop like the sick goat they had when Sarah was little. When the goat's stomach stopped moving up and down, Papa had stooped over and said, *He dead, Sarah,* even though Sarah had been staring straight into the goat's wide-open eyes and was sure he would jump back to his feet at any moment. But he hadn't. That was how Sarah learned what *dead* meant.

Up and down. Sarah sat at her mother's side, watching her breathing, listening to the menacing gurgling sound from deep in her chest. Up and down. Was Mama Nadine praying for Mama and Papa right now in her brick house, kneeling in front of her candles? Sarah hoped so. Even after Louvenia came and quietly slipped the black Bible-book in the crook of Mama's arm, Sarah was afraid to let her mama out of her sight.

Mama was still breathing when Mama Nadine came to their cabin with the morning light. But Mama was in a deep sleep, and she wouldn't wake up even when Alex shook her hard and Mama Nadine said her name so loudly that her shrill voice rang from end to end of the cabin. Mama Nadine sighed and said she was very disappointed Mama hadn't drunk the tea, then she lit four candles, two at Mama's head and two at Mama's feet. With her eyes closed and her face vacant, she began to chant words Sarah didn't know.

Papa woke up then. Much to Sarah's surprise, he brought himself to his feet and walked very slowly out of the front door without saying a word to anyone. He wobbled when he walked, but he never lost his balance. Sarah followed him, and she found him sitting on the porch in his rocking chair, fumbling to light his pipe. His hand was shaking so much he nearly dropped the match. The brier necklace from Missy Laura still hung from his bare neck.

"You well now, Papa?" Sarah asked, relieved despite her worry for Mama.

He shook his head slowly back and forth, finally reaching the pipe with his match. The tobacco in the pipe lit up in red, and smoke floated from Papa's nose. "Crazy woman makin' all that noise . . ." he muttered. "Cain't sleep."

"Mama Nadine ain't crazy. She makin' Mama well!" Sarah said.

"No, she ain't," Papa said flatly, his voice full of knowing, and Sarah felt like he'd just hit her in the stomach as hard as he could. "She sho' ain't."

Sarah walked around to stare at Papa's face then, to see if he was awake-Papa or asleep-Papa. His eyes were dark red, and his face was angrier than Sarah had ever seen. He'd lost weight since he'd been sick, because she could see his sharp cheekbones above his beard. He was slumped so low in his chair that he looked like he might slip out of it and crumple to the floor.

"I ain't gon' let it . . ." Papa said, muttering again.

"What, Papa? You ain't gon' let what?"

He nodded curtly, taking another draw on his pipe. He coughed this time, but he stubbornly kept the pipe in his mouth. "I ain't gon' let it take me," Papa finished finally, although he was looking out toward the fields instead of at Sarah. "Not like this. No, suh."

Let what take you? Sarah was going to ask him, but stopped cold because she realized she knew perfectly well: Yellow Jack.

Owen Breedlove sat on his front porch all through the day, and even after it got dark, when Alex and Louvenia came out crying, telling him their mama's breathing had stopped. He wouldn't come inside to look at his wife's body, even though he'd jumped the broom with Minerva Breedlove nearly twenty years ago, he'd cried in her arms without shame when he heard the news that no man owned him but *himself*, and he'd never touched another woman in his life.

And he didn't return his youngest daughter's hug when she stumbled outside, climbed wailing onto his lap, and wrapped her arms around him so tightly he had to strain to breathe. As if she thought she could pull him away from Yellow Jack's hands all by herself.

Chapter Three

Every night before she went to sleep, Sarah tried to strike a new pact with Jesus. Sooner or later, she was convinced, she would find the right way to make him happy. If she gathered firewood. If she swept up both the floor inside the cabin and the front porch. If she churned butter in Mama's churn, even though it was such terribly hard work that it made her arms ache for days. If she pulled weeds for six hours straight, maybe even seven, without resting for food, water, or play. If she prayed for a full hour until she went to sleep. If she washed clothes all day Saturday and again on Sunday. If she tried very hard not to get cross with Louvenia, even if her sister cuffed her or cursed her first, or if Louvenia refused to get out of bed the whole day. If she said a blessing every time she ate even a bite.

One day, she knew, Jesus would be happy with her. One morning she would wake up from the bad dream he was giving her and Mama and Papa would be back.

In fact, every morning she lay very still before opening her eyes and reminded Jesus of all the things she had done to please him. How she hadn't eaten the taffy Missus Anna gave her so many weeks ago because she was waiting for Mama and Papa to come back. How she had not used His name in vain. How she had not mussed her clothes or stepped on any ants or clapped her hands to take the life of a single mosquito. Clutching Mama's Bible-book tightly to her chest, Sarah would whisper, "Please, Jesus? Please? Ain't I done good?"

Then she would wait, listening for sounds that would tell her if her wish had come true. Many mornings, in fact, she was *sure* she heard the sounds: Mama's feet whispering across the floor near the cookstove, or Papa's whistling breathing while he slept and then a grunt as he rolled over on his side. Those mornings, she would wait as long as she could, her heart thumping against her naked breast, holding her breath and wishing so hard that her forehead pulled tightly across her skull. Then she would sit up and open her eyes to see if it was real this time, or simply in her head like so many mornings before. *Chile, yo' head sho' tells some stories. Seem like you anywhere but in dis room*, Mama used to say.

Or was she saying it right now? Was she *really* hearing Mama's voice this time?

Sarah felt a stinging kick to the soft of her hip. When she opened her eyes, Louvenia was standing over her, not Mama. Louvenia's plaits were wild in the air because she hadn't combed them out in so long. There was a crust on her face, running from her right eye all the way to her nose. And her dress was filthy; she hadn't washed it, or herself, in as long as Sarah could remember. Louvenia was making no efforts to please Jesus at all, Sarah thought.

As if she'd heard her thinking the words, Louvenia suddenly swooped down with her arm and snatched the Bible-book from Sarah's hands. "Hush all that prayin'! They ain't comin' back," Louvenia said. She rarely spoke now, but when she did, her voice always startled Sarah because it sounded so much older. "This book ain't gon' help you, neither."

Sarah sat up, but she didn't grab at the book out of anger even though she wanted to so badly that her muscles twitched. Jesus might see, and that would ruin a whole day's promises. "Give it back, Lou," she said as calmly as she could.

Instead of answering, Louvenia whirled around and broke into a run. She forgot all about Jesus and promises and goodness as she watched her sister running off with Mama's book. *"Give it back!"* she shrieked, and this time it was her own voice that startled her, so loud and big that she was sure she would wake people for miles. "Gimme M-Mama's book!"

But neither running nor screaming helped, because Louvenia was fleeing from her so fast that she seemed to be flying, even when she stumbled and nearly lost her balance. Sarah heard her sister sobbing, and she sobbed, too, realizing she couldn't catch her no matter how fast she ran. Louvenia was growing smaller and smaller as she ran ahead, disappearing in the shadows of trees. Finally Sarah fell and tumbled to the ground, scraping her knee against a rock until it bled, and she could only watch her sister's retreating form as she ran along the creek, her dress flying behind her. Louvenia had gone crazy, Alex had said. Maybe he was right.

Sobbing so hard she could barely breathe, Sarah made her way back to the cabin, where it seemed like Mama and Papa should be waiting. She surveyed the things that belonged to her parents: Papa's rocker on the porch, Mama's churn and rusty washtubs out front, Papa's plows leaning against the side of the cabin. Not even realizing why she was doing it, Sarah crawled behind the wagon wheel leaning against the house, smelling the sweet, dry earth, and felt around for Papa's jug. Wasn't it still here? She couldn't see anything but dried-out corncobs, stones, a big ham bone, and a bent spoon. No jug. Papa must have moved it. But where?

"*Papa!*" Sarah screamed, momentarily daring to believe that if goodness and promises didn't work, then maybe Jesus would send her parents back when He saw how angry she was.

But there was no answer except the hound's far-off barking. Papa's hound had run off after they didn't have anything left to feed him. He was half wild anyway, Alex had said, but Sarah found herself wishing the dog would come loping up to her now to lick her face. No one came; not Papa, not Mama, not the hound.

Sarah's chest heaved and her entire frame shivered with sobs. She climbed up the porch to go inside the cabin, which was so empty it felt profane. Her eyes roved quickly around the room, looking for . . . *something*. Mr. Long had hired some Negro men to come burn the bodies up, and they'd taken Mama's and Papa's clothes to burn, too. They had to burn out the fever, they said, or else someone else could catch it. Nothing was left but shrunken bodies charred beyond recognition, which Alex had dug a hole for and buried. Then Missy Laura and the other croppers had come out, lit a fire near the buried bodies, and sung sad songs all night. But it wasn't the same. Sarah had seen funerals before, and a burned body wasn't the same as watching someone put at peace under the ground. A burned body meant they were just . . . gone.

Her parents *were* gone, Sarah realized as she stood in the middle of the empty cabin. Jesus wasn't going to send them back, no matter what she promised or how hard she worked. And Alex was gone, too, over to Vicksburg because he said they couldn't make enough wages cropping without Mama and Papa. Mama would have been very worried about Alex over in Vicksburg, what with all the foolishness she said was going on. But he'd left anyway, and he'd visited only once so far, on Sunday, bringing them fifty cents, and he'd left at dawn on Monday morning, like he'd never been back. Sarah gasped for air as her sobs pummeled her insides.

Then something on the shelf above the cookstove caught Sarah's eye: Behind Mama's near-empty jars of flour and meal and rice, there was a picture she'd seen Mama admiring before. Feeling a tiny sense of relief from her sobs, Sarah dragged a chair to the shelf, stood up on it, and reached for the photograph as carefully as she could, so she wouldn't tip over.

It was Papa. He was younger than Sarah had seen him look before, maybe in his twenties, and he didn't have his beard, but Sarah could tell it was him from his eyes, which were twinkling with life even though his face had no smile. Ole Marse Long had let Papa pose for that photograph before the war, when his whole family sat for portraits, and Mama had been busy washing clothes that day. Mama had said many times she wished she had a picture of her face, too. She said she had nearly forgotten what her own mammy and pappy looked like, and she wanted to leave something for her children to remember her by.

Sarah hadn't understood how important remembering was, until now.

She climbed down from the chair, her sobs nearly gone, and slid the precious photograph of Papa under her pallet. She might not ever get Mama's Bible-book back from Louvenia, she knew. Louvenia might give it back to her if Sarah told her about the reading promise she'd made to Mama, but she also might not. Louvenia was so contrary! Besides, her sister had been acting half crazy since Mama and Papa died, and Papa said crazy folks would do anything. She'd thrown the book in the creek, maybe, just to show God how mad she was.

So Sarah made a new vow, not to Jesus, but to herself: She would keep Papa's photograph, always. And this time she didn't make the vow as a bargain to try to bring Papa back, either. This time she figured if she kept that vow, no matter how much time passed, her father wouldn't really be gone at all.

Sarah never did see the Bible-book again, but Louvenia's "crazy" spell seemed to pass just in time for her to fall silently industrious so that she and Sarah could somehow make do on their own. Food was the constant struggle, since Mama's garden had begun to fail without her expert touch. Within a month, the food their neighbors had brought for them after the funeral had dwindled to nearly nothing except some salt pork and a sack of black-eyed peas. In the beginning, Missus Anna stopped by the first Sunday of every month with a pail of milk and a treat, like a jar of sweet-tasting marmalade or a delicious candy she called peanut brittle. Sarah looked forward to those baskets from Missus Anna more than she'd ever remembered anticipating even Christmas, but they stopped after a while.

Sarah and Louvenia rarely ate even chicken anymore, since the chickens had become more valuable than ever for their eggs. Louvenia let some of the eggs hatch so they'd have more chickens, but it took time for the chicks to get big enough to be much use either as food or as laying hens. When three of the growing chicks vanished, probably killed by the wild hound who hunted nearby, Sarah cried about it all night. *Seem like we can't git nothin'*, she thought bitterly, and that thought flung her into a dark hopelessness for days.

Delta, Louisiana, was not a friendly place for two young girls trying to survive on their own. It was a very small town with most of the colored folks scattered throughout the farmlands, and they were struggling too much to consider taking in two more children. Most of their neighbors, like Missy Laura, were too poor to be of any help except occasional visits to hold their hands for prayers and to tell them God would provide. There was a man-size hole in their roof after the summer rains for nearly three months, until Alex saved up enough money and fixed it with two of his Vicksburg friends during one of his visits. Alex had found work on a dock, and Sarah noticed that he'd bought himself shiny black boots and a pair of denim blue jeans.

Meanwhile, Louvenia became very earnest about her sewing, using the money she got from Alex, the hens' eggs, and the washing to buy material for winter clothes. Sarah helped her, counting out coins on the table by lamplight at the end of the day, trying to guess how many they would need to buy what. Many times their guesses fell short of the prices at the store and they had to leave with less than they'd wanted. When Louvenia realized she would not have enough material to make coats for both Sarah and herself, she just went to work on Sarah's. "What 'bout chu?" Sarah asked her, realizing that the coat's sleeves were too short for her sister. At that, Louvenia just shrugged.

For Sarah, there was no more time for games of any sort during the workdays. The endless cotton fields saw to that.

The cotton began blooming in dots of white by the middle of August, and picking began in September. Sarah thought longingly of the time when she'd been so small that Mama let her ride on her sack while she picked, and she didn't have to do any work, dozing to the rhythm of Mama's movement up and down the rows. This was the first time Sarah would be expected to work as hard as any other grown-up cropper, just like Louvenia. With a sack around her shoulder that dragged the ground, Sarah went with her sister to their field at dawn, where the downy white cotton plants they'd planted in spring had opened up in a sea.

We gon' pick all this cotton? Sarah asked herself in amazement, since the task looked as fruitless as trying to collect snowflakes. Yet she started at one end of a neat row of plants and slowly worked her way to the other side, her hands yanking to pull off the cotton bolls while the sun bullied her from above. She knew she had to pick the soft cotton free of the clinging bolls and throw only the cotton in her sack; *that* was the most important thing, Papa used to tell her. She cried out and sucked on her fingers when the bolls pricked her, but she couldn't pause long because she knew she had to fill her sack. Papa told her he'd been whipped as a boy when his *oberseer* saw him tossing bolls in the sack with his cotton. Sarah also remembered figures Papa had told her, that every acre of a cotton field grew about one bale's worth of cotton, and that he said he could pick two hundred pounds of cotton in a day. The more cotton she and Louvenia picked, she knew, the more they could catch up on their lost wages so they wouldn't have any debts to Missus Anna they couldn't pay. If they couldn't pay their debts, they couldn't stay in their house. There were no games to make of that.

It seemed to Sarah that as soon as she and Louvenia dragged their feet home at night and surrendered to their pallets, morning was already glowing outside and it was time to go back to the fields. She never felt rested, and her muscles ached. She was so sore from reaching for the plants that it hurt to stand up straight.

And even on days they weren't picking, they had to work just as hard on the washing. The night before washing day, they walked to collect the dirty clothes from two nearby white families who paid them fifty cents each week to do their wash. By the time they got the clothes and returned to their cabin, it was after dark, so they ate whatever food they could find for a hurried supper and went to bed. If any of the clothes looked particularly dirty, they soaked them overnight. Then, in the morning, they dragged the clothes, two washtubs, and as much firewood as they could carry to the river. They filled the tubs with water from the river until they could barely carry them even between the two of them—one tub was for washing, one for rinsing—and began their work. They had to boil the clothes, wring them out, rinse them, and wring them out again. Then they brought the damp clothes home and hung them on the line outside their cabin, hoping it wouldn't rain overnight.

All along the riverbank, other Negro women like Missy Laura were there washing, too. Often the women were singing, but Louvenia and Sarah rarely sang along, their brows knitted with concentration as they scrubbed and beat out the dirty spots in the laundry so their customers wouldn't complain. Any complaints, no dollar. Sometimes Sarah rubbed fabric against the washboard so hard that it felt like it was grating her hand, and she especially hated the hot job of tending the clothes in the tub of boiling water they used to clean the huge bedsheets and table-cloths. She also hated the stink of lye soap, which stayed on her hands and arms for hours after all the washing was done.

Sarah missed the naps she used to take. She missed sitting in the shade watching the riverboats pass with all their majesty. Now, when riverboats went past on washing day, Sarah glanced at them for only the barest moment, watching their paddles churning the water white and the steam hissing from their long smokestacks. They were no longer magical; they were an annoyance. The boats made her angry now; she envied the people she could see on board whose lives on a Saturday afternoon afforded them the luxury of a boat ride. She envied that they could go anywhere they chose, when she could go nowhere at all.

Then, mysteriously, as if God had heard Sarah's complaints, one day the river simply went away. In April of 1876, in the midst of rainstorms, the Mississippi River flooded over portions of Missus Anna's lands and retreated from its bank as if it had been sucked out of sight. When Sarah, Louvenia, and their neighbors emerged the next morning, they all stood in huddles staring up and down the sandy, deserted landscape with fear and wonder in their eyes. The river had left behind only ridges and deep puddles in the damp ground, hills of sandy soil and dead fish whose scales glinted in the sunlight. No more steamboats, no more washing place, no more fishing.

No river.

"Where'd it go, Lou? Where'd it go?" Sarah asked her sister in a panic, tugging on Lou's arm. Louvenia shook her head, unable to speak. During that first impossible instant, as she surveyed the land that had been a riverbed only the day before, Sarah's young heart once again tasted the lonely realization of how small and fragile her life was, how little she could control the world around her. *I wanna leave this place,* Sarah thought fiercely, clinging to her sister. *If even the river's done left, how come we can't, too?*

Sarah realized later that the mighty Mississippi River had simply changed its course, flowing a few miles away. But her desire to go somewhere else, anywhere else, remained firm.

A little more than two years after her parents died, Sarah thought her wish was about to be granted. Alex came to visit them, clean-shaven, wearing a fresh Sunday shirt and pants with suspenders. Sarah thought maybe he'd met a girl and was getting married, but he said he'd decided there wasn't enough steady work in Vicksburg. Life had changed dramatically since the previous year's flood, he said, since Vicksburg had been cut off from river traffic, too.

"Durn river's lef' Vicksburg high an' dry," Alex said. "Them wharfs where people was workin' ain't nowhere near a drop o' water. You should see 'em now, 'bout a mile an' a half inland when the water use to come right up on 'em. They done built a new pier, but there's so much mud the wagons is gettin' stuck. So them boats is passin' us on by, an' all them crews an' travelin' folks is goin' someplace else. I ain't never seen it so quiet at the hotel I work at, Chamber's. Time was, the place was *full* of folks. The boss man say he can't keep all us porters on when he got so many empty rooms."

Sarah had also heard Missus Anna complain about how Delta had been cut off from the river, leaving the former river town hidden behind a sandbar and wildly growing young willow trees. To Sarah and Lou, the change meant they had to struggle to fill their tubs with water from the shallow bathing creek not far from their cabin, which seemed shallower all the time, or else beg a ride on Missy Laura's mule-drawn wagon to travel several miles to the river.

"So I'm leavin' today," Alex announced brightly. "Goin' west like Papa wanted to."

"We goin' out west?" Sarah shrieked, no longer the least concerned with the Mississippi River and its fickle course. She was so full of joy, she thought she might faint.

Alex's buoyant face deflated. " 'Til I got a good job, don't make no sense me tryin' to feed y'all," he said. "Shoot, I may need to come back. We can't be givin' up this house."

At first the disappointment threatened to drown Sarah—even small disappointments still drove her to tears much more often now than when her parents had been living, since she couldn't help thinking that any setback might not have happened if Mama and Papa had been there—but she swallowed back the bitter taste in her throat and clung to her brother's sleeve. He had grown so much taller, he was probably taller than Papa by now. "But you gon' send after us when you gots a good job? You promise, Alex?"

"I'ma do my best, Li'l Bit," Alex said, but it didn't gladden her to hear her brother call her by her favorite pet name because he did it so rarely, and only when he was trying to convince her not to argue with him. Even when he *did* make promises, he couldn't always be held to them. He'd promised them new shoes last spring, and they were still waiting for their shoes in the fall. Sarah's shoes pinched her growing toes so badly that she usually went without them, preferring to chafe her bare soles on rocks and soil.

"Don't be callin' her Li'l Bit," Louvenia said to Alex, annoyed. "She ain't little no mo'. 'Sides, that's Papa's name. An' you ain't Papa, cuz Papa woulda took us all."

At that, Alex looked hurt. Quickly he swiped at his brow and turned his eyes away. "If Papa woulda took us, wouldn't none of us be here now, would we?" His voice was low, but the words were like a gunshot.

Louvenia snorted, *humph*, sounding like Mama. "Sound like you think you a man jus' cuz you big like one," she said. "If you goin', then git. You ain't gon' stand here in Papa's house talkin' bad 'bout him."

"I didn' mean nothin' by that, Lou. . . . When you gots young'uns an' such, you gotta be where you *know* you gots work, even if it ain't much. But I got a chance to look roun' an' see what else a colored man kin make o' hisself, not jus' haulin' an' pickin'. I might even go out to them Dakota lands an' find me some gold like the white folks, since them Injuns that kilt that Gen'ral Custer done give up. Folks gittin' rich out there! Papa couldn't do that, see? I promise I'll send y'all money through Missus Anna," Alex said. "Now . . . do I git a hug good-bye?"

Louvenia cast him an evil look, then she walked to him to give him a weak hug. Many times Louvenia had complained to Sarah that Alex had so much more freedom than she did because he was a man. Men didn't have to be careful and stick close to home the same way women did, she said. Louvenia's envy was naked in her jutting lower lip as she hugged her brother good-bye, and Sarah could guess what her sister was thinking: *Maybe a colored man can make something of himself, but what about a colored girl?*

Sarah hugged her brother tightly, even though tears gleamed in her eyes. To her, Alex smelled like the river, sweat, and the promise of a new life far away, hidden from her. In all the time since their parents had died,

Sarah was no closer to fulfilling her promise to Mama to learn how to read. She hadn't had time to learn even a single new letter of the alphabet; and even if she had the time, where would she learn it? She didn't know any colored children who went to school. But maybe if she went out west . . .

"You promise, Alex? You gon' send fo' us?" Sarah said.

"Promise," Sarah's brother said, and Sarah closed her eyes. Sarah gave Alex a long, hard squeeze, remembering how she'd hugged Papa on the porch the day Mama died. Already she'd forgotten what Papa had smelled like that day, and she hadn't wanted to forget a single thing.

As infrequent as Alex's visits had become, she and Louvenia still relied not only on the money he brought, but the comfort of having a brother in the cabin to tell them stories of Vicksburg, with all its people and excitement, and help them with heavy work they couldn't manage on their own. Besides, with Mama and Papa gone, Alex was the only family they had.

"Y'all take good care of yo'selves, hear?" Alex said, tugging at the rim of his dusty cap. "Treat each other good."

When Alex Breedlove set out west, he was eighteen years old and Sarah wasn't yet nine. Sarah would be a grown woman with her own child before she would see her brother again.

By the summer of 1878, a new plague had begun.

No matter how much the sharecroppers frantically picked at the little pink worms nestled in the plants' blossoms, mashing them dead between their fingertips, the bollworms kept coming back, feasting on the cotton-seed in the bolls. So, despite ample rain and sun during the growing season, by the time the fields should have been awash with white cotton ripe for picking, there were only occasional spots of white in acres of empty, worthless bolls. Day after day, no matter how long Sarah picked, her bag dragged virtually weightless behind her because it was so empty. She and the other croppers walked listlessly through the fields like grave robbers looking for trinkets to steal. "Lawd, what we gon' do?" she heard the croppers agonizing. Many, in fact, had already left in search of other work in hopes of paying off their debts to the growers.

The yield was everything to a sharecropper. If there was no yield, there was nothing.

Sarah was ten and Louvenia was fourteen, but their hardscrabble lives had given their eyes an ageless quality defined by their toil. The cabin had slowly fallen into disrepair because Alex wasn't there to mend it and neither of them had the time or the spirit to keep it tidy. Able-bodied men nearby who might have cleaned the chimney or nailed new wall planks where the old ones sagged had families of their own to care for; besides,

Sarah had noticed their women neighbors had cooled off toward Louvenia ever since her face had lost its baby fat and her chest was sprouting breasts already the size of grapefruits. *'Fraid they gon' lose they man,* Louvenia had explained to her with a hint of pride.

Alex sent them money three months after he left—it was only two dollars, granted, but it was welcome—and they were sure they could expect a letter from him again soon. Missus Anna told them whoever had scribbled her address on the envelope for Alex had not enclosed any note inside with a return address, or any news of his doings. Still, Sarah and Louvenia hoped Alex's next letter would say something about when he would be sending for them, and they especially hoped he would send more money. A lot more. They hoped there would be enough to pay their rent and help them buy the seed they would need for the next planting season, which was bound to be better than this year's. As she gazed helplessly at the naked cotton plants that seemed to mock her, Sarah began to realize that Alex was their only hope.

For the first time in a long time, Sarah felt vivid pictures stirring in her imagination: She saw Alex married to an Indian squaw, swinging a pickax against a rock until he threw his cap in the air and hollered, "*Gold!* I done struck gold!" She imagined Alex mailing them a box full of money, and new dresses besides. And Alex's big house with two stories, just like Missus Anna's, where Sarah would have her very own room.

Louvenia might have been having the very same fantasies, because one afternoon she said cheerfully to Sarah, "Time to go over Missus Anna's an' see if she heard from Alex."

"Same thing been on my mind, too," Sarah said, and they set out on their mile-long walk.

It was late August, and the full heat of the summer sun slowed their progress. As they made their way up the neatly bordered pathway to Grand View, they could see Missus Anna sitting on her huge porch with the whitewashed wooden rails (her *ve-ran-da,* she called it) in a white summer dress with short sleeves. This dress wasn't nearly as fine as the one Sarah remembered from Missus Anna's visit to their cabin, but it was still much daintier and prettier than any dress Sarah had seen on a colored woman. Missus Anna was sipping from a glass.

"You think she drinkin' lemonade?" Sarah whispered as they approached.

"I hope so. I want me some, too," Louvenia said.

Grand View, to Sarah, was like a house in a made-up story about kings and queens and princesses in faraway kingdoms. It stood sturdy and tall, with all its windows glistening. The back part of the house had been burned by Yankees, Papa had told her, but Mr. Long had fixed it up again. Luckily Missus Anna was on the porch in front; otherwise they would have gone to the kitchen door in the back and talked to her cook, Rita, who never let them even peek inside. Rita just passed the messages, or gave them Missus Anna's laundry, and never cracked a smile. *Biggity house-nigger, think she better than us cuz she ain't a cropper,* Louvenia complained. Sarah was glad they wouldn't have to talk to Rita, not with Missus Anna out in plain sight. But Sarah didn't stay glad long.

Missus Anna watched them approaching without moving. As they walked closer to the porch steps, Sarah could see the expression on her face she despised so much: pity and sorrow. Before they said a word, Missus Anna was shaking her head.

"You ain't heard from Alex, Missus Anna?" Louvenia said.

Missus Anna sighed. "No, Lou. I think you two had better come take a seat. I'm glad you came by today. George was going to send someone out to you in the morning, but I told him I'd rather talk to you myself. I feel I owe that to Owen and Minerva, God rest them."

To Sarah's astonishment, she saw tears in Missus Anna's eyes. Louvenia took Sarah's hand, squeezing so tightly it hurt, and led her to the white bench in front of Missus Anna's chair. Louvenia didn't let go of Sarah even once they were seated, waiting in silence for bad news.

"I know it's not your fault the crops were lost. Everyone worked so hard, and it just breaks my heart. But I can't keep you on the land, girls. George says we just can't afford . . ."

She talked on and on, but for a moment Sarah felt as though a steamboat whistle had sounded in her ears because she could no longer hear what Missus Anna was saying. She didn't even realize she was holding her breath until she suddenly felt a need to take a big gasp of air, and then the noise in her ears seemed to vanish. ". . . hard on everyone. I wish I could keep you here, especially little Sarah, but it's just out of the question."

"Missus Anna," Louvenia said, surprising Sarah with the business-like calm in her voice, "you ain't got no work roun' here? We both can cook, an' we could clean up—"

"Sweetheart, I already have a cook, as you know," Missus Anna said, still looking forlorn. "And neither one of you has ever worked in a house, even if we could afford it. And the fact of the matter is, girls, we *can't* afford it. I know we may look rich to you, but we're struggling alongside everyone else. These cotton worms have made a big mess of everything, and we had the flooding on top of that."

Now there was a hard silence that tugged on Sarah's throat. She couldn't move. How could Missus Anna say she wasn't rich? What did she think *rich* was?

"You can stay until the end of the month—that's two more weeks—but then I really think the best thing for you is to go to Vicksburg. Rita wants to give me some names of Negroes there who might be able to help you find work doing washing. She's always saying how you're *so* good and thorough with the wash, both of you. And I'll see to it you have those names before you go. I won't send you away empty-handed, neither. I'll give you some money to start, and it's a *gift*, not a loan. That means you won't have to pay it back. It's not much, but I think you'll be able to make do."

"How Alex gon' find us?" Sarah blurted, forgetting to address Missus Anna by her courtesy title. Mama would have cuffed her for that.

"Believe me, girls, any letters I get from your brother will be kept safely for you. Y'all can come back anytime and ask me if there's been any word. I owe you that, too." Suddenly she paused, breathless. "Oh, my, I forgot my manners. You girls want some lemonade?"

Sarah looked at Louvenia, who was slowly shaking her head. "Thank you, ma'am, but no," Louvenia said in a scratchy voice. "We got to go now."

"Are you sure? After that long walk—"

Louvenia had already stood up, tugging on Sarah's hand. Sarah gazed at the cool, sweet yellow liquid in Missus Anna's glass, which was beading through in fat droplets of water. Sarah would have given just about anything, in that instant, just for one tiny sip. Missus Anna had offered them lemonade on a visit once before, and she thought maybe it would have made her feel just a little better. But Louvenia was ready to leave, and Sarah had no choice but to follow.

Louvenia was walking swiftly, nearly running, and it wasn't long before Sarah heard sobs catching in her sister's throat. The awfulness of the sound reminded Sarah of the few times she'd heard her Mama crying, a sound that had made the world stand still.

"Guess that ol' biggity Rita do too like us, huh?" Sarah said, trying to make a joke.

It didn't help. Louvenia sobbed on, inconsolable, wiping her face with her arm as she walked. She nearly stumbled into a tree trunk, until Sarah guided her past it. Louvenia was murmuring the same helpless words she'd heard falling from so many other croppers' lips: "What we gon' do now?" The words tried to burrow into Sarah's heart and make her cry, too, but she refused. Wouldn't make any sense for both of them to be crying all the way home.

"But jus' think, Lou. What if we do really good in Vicksburg? You know how you been talkin' 'bout gettin' out the fields."

"Not with no damn money!" Louvenia screamed at her.

"But Missus Anna say she gon' give us—"

"An' how long that gon' last? Girl, we 'bout to go to that city with *nothin'*. You heard Alex say he couldn't find no good work. An' now we don't even . . ." Her words were interrupted by an anguished sob. ". . . we don't even know where *he* at."

Maybe Louvenia was right, Sarah realized. She'd been imagining life in Vicksburg as a grand adventure, a chance to change their lives for the better, but maybe the same cold and hunger and endless work were waiting for them there. Maybe they would starve.

The more she thought about it, the more Sarah's heart began to plummet with terror. What if they hadn't heard anything from Alex because he was out starving somewhere, too? Louvenia was crying because she was *scared*, she realized, not because she was sad.

In her mind, Sarah could see the fear rolling toward her, she could hear it like a cold drumbeat, and she thought about the first time she jumped in the river over her head when she was little because Louvenia had dared her; how she couldn't hear anything or see anything, hardly, and she'd never been more scared in her life, but she knew if she screamed she would drown. So she hadn't screamed.

She'd looked up toward where the sunlight was glowing above her, and she'd kicked her legs and flung her arms alongside her just like Papa had shown her, and she kept doing it even though she'd felt like she wasn't moving, she'd kept doing it even when she was *sure* she was about to die because her lungs were tight with hot air, and then just as she'd felt like giving up, her head had broken above the surface and been kissed all over by the air. She could breathe.

Maybe going to Vicksburg would be like that, Sarah thought. Maybe it would seem like they were drowning at first, but they would be just fine if they kept swimming. The thought brought a tiny smile to Sarah's face even as Louvenia sobbed. Sarah wished she could explain it to her sister to help her stop crying, but it was hard for her to explain the pictures and ideas in her head sometimes.

Instead all she said was, "We ain't got to be scared, Lou."

And she believed that, even as their cabin appeared in the distance and they both stopped walking as they gazed at it, realizing simultaneously that they would have to leave their memories of Mama and Papa inside those ramshackle wooden walls. If new people came to live there, they wouldn't know how Papa had cussed every time he tripped over the loose board just inside the doorway, and they wouldn't know how Mama had once had a fit of anger and thrown a whole kettle of stewed tomatoes against the wall, leaving stains that had never gone away. And the new people wouldn't remember how Mama giggled late at night when Papa sneaked over on her side of the pallet and they woke everyone up even though they thought they were being so quiet, Papa saying, *Hush girl, hush girl* as his panting voice grew louder all the time. Once when Sarah had asked Louvenia what Mama and Papa were doing, Louvenia had shushed her and whispered back, "That be how grown folks love." The new people just wouldn't know. And maybe one day she and Louvenia wouldn't know anymore either, Sarah thought. Maybe Mama had forgotten so much about her mammy and pappy because she'd left their house and all the memories inside it.

A single tear wound its way down Sarah's cheek, but that was the only one she allowed. Crying might let the fear in, and Sarah was determined not to drown.

Chapter Four

"Sarah? It's your turn."

Miss Dunn's voice broke into Sarah's thoughts. Until she heard her name, Sarah had been transfixed by the portrait of Jesus in prayer hanging behind Miss Dunn on the wall, with his eyes gazing piously skyward and his flowing light brown hair cascading across his shoulders. She'd been gazing at the portrait for more than six months now, but it still captivated her; in all the years Mama and Papa and Preacher had talked about Jesus, the blue-eyed man in the painting on the wall was nothing like she'd imagined Jesus to be. It was hard to believe any white man would love her so much he would die for the sins of a colored girl.

"Sarah, did you hear me?"

Miss Dunn was sitting primly on the bench at the front of the tiny basement room, which was barely bigger than the cabin she and Louvenia had left behind in Delta. Sarah liked Miss Dunn, and hated to hear her sound cross. Miss Dunn talked prettier than any colored woman Sarah had ever met—she was from up north, she'd told them, from a city called *Phil-a-del-phi-a*, where there had been no slaves before the war. Her hair was always pulled back tight behind her head in a bun, and the simple gingham dresses she wore were perfectly neat and clean. Miss Dunn was a very young woman, younger than some of the grown men and women who came to her class, and her cocoa-colored face looked as smooth as glass. If she ever smiled, Sarah thought, Miss Dunn would be truly beautiful.

"It's your turn to read. Come on up here."

"To . . . read . . . ?" Sarah said, nearly choking on the words. She sat frozen on her bench, and she heard two boys behind her snicker. Sarah shook her head. "N-no, ma'am, I can't. . . ."

"No back-talking, Sarah. Everybody has a turn."

Walking on legs that threatened to betray her at any instant, Sarah made her way to the front of the class. She glanced at the watching students; there were at least fifty of them of every age, from children younger than her to old men and women with gray hair who needed canes to walk, and they were all crammed on their benches with their eyes on her. Some of the students in the back, who'd arrived late, had to sit on the floor, and they shifted uncomfortably as they fanned themselves. Sarah couldn't remember a time when so many people had been watching her.

And expecting her to read! She *couldn't* read. That was the whole reason Sarah had asked Louvenia if she could take time off from her washing in the mornings to come to the school held every weekday in the basement of the African Methodist Episcopal Church on Washington Street. She told Louvenia she'd promised Mama, and Louvenia had asked their colored employer, Miss Brown, who said it was fine with her, so long as Sarah made up for the lost time in the evenings. Louvenia had told Sarah not to expect any fancy school clothes, so Sarah wore the same simple clothes she wore when she did washing and wrapped herself up a sandwich for lunch, which she kept in her lap. In this way, she'd been going to school each day, trying to pay close attention to every word Miss Dunn said.

Sarah *loved* school, much more than she had the few months she attended the Negro school in the woods not far from the fields when she was very little. Miss Dunn was a better teacher; her old teacher, Sarah remembered, could barely read herself, and she'd been painfully slow at her figures. But not Miss Dunn. Miss Dunn had been to a *college*, and she read without any pauses or having to sound out her words one letter at a time.

And Miss Dunn knew a wealth of information Sarah was sure her other teacher had not. She taught them about the battle in the Civil War that had taken place in Vicksburg before Sarah was born, and how people had hidden in the caves. If they looked carefully, Miss Dunn told them, they could still see the caves, trees that had been split by cannonballs, and even a few exploded bombshells. She taught them about the president of the United States, the leader of the country voted on in the election, whose name was Rutherford B. Hayes. He lived in Washington, D.C., which Miss Dunn had told them was a thousand miles away. And President Hayes was a *Re-pub-li-can*, she'd told them, which meant he was from the party that had fought to end slavery, just like the last president, Ulysses Grant, who had been the general of the Union Army that had come to invade Vicksburg.

In fact, every day it seemed Miss Dunn had a fascinating new piece of information to share that made Sarah realize how little she really knew about anything except cropping and washing. And Miss Brown, their employer, was always telling her and Louvenia they barely knew anything about washing, either. "Washing clothes in water straight from the river!" Miss Brown had exclaimed when they told her about their experiences in

Delta. "That water wasn't proper. Didn't y'all see how gray and brown the clothes got? Might as well have been using bathwater!"

Sarah didn't want to disappoint Miss Dunn, so her hands were shaking when Miss Dunn gave her a small square chalkboard and told her to read the first word written in white chalk. Although Sarah didn't dare disobey, in that instant she felt she would rather run off and never come to school again than shame herself in front of Miss Dunn and the class.

With unblinking eyes, Sarah stared at the letters Miss Dunn had written on the board in neat block letters. S-K-Y. F-L-Y. M-O-R-N-I-N-G. She sighed and started to sound them out the way Miss Dunn was teaching them, beginning with the first letter, then blending the first letter to the second and third.

"Sssssss . . . kyyy?" she said at last, faintly.

"Louder, Sarah," Miss Dunn prompted. "And don't say it like a question."

Sarah took a deep breath. Her fingers were so sweaty she was afraid she would drop Miss Dunn's board and break it in two on the floor. "Sssss . . . kyyy."

"Next word."

"Ffffffff . . . lllyyy," Sarah said.

"Next."

The third word was a long one, with a lot of letters. "Mmmm . . . oooorrrn," she said, then licked her dry lips.

"Go on," Miss Dunn said.

"Mmmmmooorrrrn . . . ing?" Sarah said, relieved to be finished. She couldn't help saying the word like a question, even though Miss Dunn had told her not to. The sounds felt awkward in her mouth, and she was sure Miss Dunn would correct her now that she'd finished.

But instead, her teacher was gazing at her with a tiny smile. Just as Sarah had suspected, the smile made Miss Dunn look angelic. "You see that? And you've been coming only a couple of months. You can too read, Sarah Breedlove, so read with confidence. Now go sit back down."

You can too read, Sarah Breedlove. Drinking in Miss Dunn's words, Sarah felt as if she'd been lifted from the floor and was floating high above the room. She didn't remember walking back to her seat, because she kept turning the idea over and over in her head: *You can too read, Sarah Breedlove.* She was so ecstatic, she barely even heard one of the boys whisper "Li'l ol' nappy-head, country pickaninny" as he walked past her. Usually his words would have upset her, but not today. Sarah sat, her heart trundling inside her chest with joy. Miss Dunn had said she could read! Was that all reading was? Sounding out the letters? She'd been doing that at home, borrowing Miss Dunn's books.

She couldn't wait to go tell Lou she was reading! Maybe she could teach Lou, too.

When Miss Dunn dismissed them for the day, Sarah practically ran up the widely set cobblestones on Washington Street, no longer cowed by the sight of so many people walking in a midday flood, or the parade of carriages and mule-drawn wagons that had shocked her so after she and Louvenia first came to the city. On cotton market day, despite the disappointing crops, there had been so many wagons with bales of cotton clogging Vicksburg's streets that Sarah could see nothing else. She'd been nearly afraid to walk by herself, convinced she would get swallowed up in so much activity and chaos. And Washington Street, where the small church was nestled next to a colored eating-house called Dolly's, was always in a flurry of excitement. She saw white folks and colored folks, men and women, some dressed in finery, some dressed in rags, everyone with fixed expressions as if they were on their way somewhere important.

There was also joy and relief in Vicksburg, since the shadow of last year's epidemic of Yellow Jack had finally lifted. It had seemed to Sarah and Lou that as soon as they arrived in their new town, Yellow Jack enveloped them as surely as if it had followed them to create more heartache and terror in their lives. All over the city, reports of Yellow Jack had begun first as cautiously muttered fears, then as confirmed reports of mounting deaths. Killing white and colored alike, Yellow Jack had swept through Vicksburg until Sarah had seen wooden coffins piled up outside carpenters' shops awaiting new corpses from the undertakers. Newsboys shouted out new death tolls each morning, the devil's messengers. Sarah and Lou had left their room only when necessary, avoiding contact with anyone who might give them Yellow Jack. At night, Sarah had woken up sweating from nightmares about Mama and Papa, reliving Papa's hollow-eyed look as he sat on the front porch the day Mama died, and how Mama had retched up black sickness. By the end of the epidemic, which had lasted from July until November, Sarah heard that at least a thousand people had died from yellow fever in Vicksburg, and more in other parts of Mississippi.

But now that was over. Sarah's nightmares had stopped, and Vicksburg had come to life with the promise of a new frontier. Sarah had noted that town folk walked faster than country folk, so she dodged out of the path of riders on horseback, men arguing over newspaper articles, browsers gazing into shop windows, or ladies strolling with parasols. Sarah especially liked the well-dressed colored hotel porters who smiled at her as she walked past, proud of their uniforms. Sarah wondered if Alex had worn a uniform, too, when he was a porter.

Carpenters carried lumber, draymen drove their loaded carts, and bricklayers stacked bricks onto new walls. Sarah had learned to enjoy Vicksburg's sights and sounds, although she was sure to walk very carefully and steer clear of whites she might accidentally offend. If she accidentally splashed a shiny shoe with mud or brushed her shoulder against the wrong person, she had learned there were quick penalties. "Impudent little

Negress!" an old white woman had practically spit at her two months before, when Sarah lost her balance and bumped against her. The woman lunged before Sarah could utter an apology, flinging her handbag across Sarah's cheek so hard that Sarah wondered if she was bleeding. "Never thought I'd live to see the damned streets full of niggers."

Miss Dunn had already explained that the colored population of Vicksburg was swelling as more sharecroppers and their families sought better lives in the city because of poor cotton crops. Whites didn't like it, she said, because now Negroes weren't competing only with each other for jobs, they were competing with whites, too. Folks were slow to change their thinking and ways, Miss Dunn said. She said salaries for Negro teachers were less than for white teachers, and they were still being lowered.

Sarah could tell by the sun above her that it was high noon—almost time for her to be back at Miss Brown's—but she quickened her pace so she could walk a block west out of her way, to the wharves. The water had risen, as it did each spring, so the riverfront was even more intriguing to Sarah's senses; she inhaled the briny, fish-scented air from the water and watched seagulls wheel in the skies and gather in noisy groups whenever fishmongers tossed away raw fish that weren't fit to sell. She also enjoyed watching the sailors and their fascinating cargos of furniture, livestock, and large crates she imagined were filled with jewels or gold and silver.

Barely sated by her meager noonday meal of dried pork and corn bread, Sarah felt her stomach growl when she walked past the colored fish lady frying fish on an open fire on the street. The price was only a nickel, but Sarah rarely had money to spend. She and Louvenia spent practically everything they earned to pay their keep at the boardinghouse where they lived, which provided dinner and the room they shared. Anything extra was saved for hard times.

Lingering near the fish stand full of longing, Sarah finally noticed a crowd of young Negro men causing a flurry near the pier. Many of them had sacks slung over their shoulders, and they were fidgeting with excitement. "Who they?" Sarah asked the fish lady. She didn't know the woman's name, but they knew each other's faces. In town, Sarah had learned, folks didn't always greet each other by name but could still be friends.

The fish lady grinned, exposing her missing front tooth. "Goin' off to Kansas, chile."

"Where that is? That in America?"

"Sho is," the fish lady said. She flipped over a catfish until the brown side was up, and the oil sizzled and popped seductively in her grill. "Kansas in what they call the Midwest. Men passin' 'round papers talkin' 'bout how pretty it is, an' how much land they got. I speck those colored men think they gon' get their forty acres an' a mule at last. 'Fore that, it was a colored man, Reverend Collins, goin' 'round talkin' 'bout boats to Africa. Seem like folks wanna be everywhere but here. But white folks ain't likin' it. That's how come there's all the fuss."

Sure enough, when Sarah looked more closely, she saw three white men standing in front of the group, apparently in the midst of a shouting match with two very large colored men. The sight nearly made her gasp; she'd never seen a colored man talk back to a white man. The boldness of the colored town men both excited and frightened her.

"What they care for?" Sarah said. "Seem like white folks don't want us 'round nohow."

"Sho, some of 'em don't. But look like plenty of 'em do. They been writin' 'bout it in the newspapers, callin' it the Exodus. See, they figger if they ain't got niggers to work for 'em, who gon' do it?" With that, she cackled cheerfully, and Sarah smiled, too. "I hear 'em always talkin' 'bout bringin' them Chinese coolies over here to take the place o' niggers. They say Chinamen don't eat but once a day, and say niggers got too many complaints. But 'til that happens, I guess they stuck with us. Oh, Lord—we better keep a distance, chile."

The rumble from the crowd turned to a roar, and Sarah took a frightened step back when she saw half a dozen white men rush toward the Negroes with sticks in the air. As shouts erupted, the white men began to strike at the Negroes, who either threw up their hands to try to defend themselves or immediately began to run and scatter. Although the turmoil was more than thirty yards away, Sarah clearly saw a Negro man knocked unconscious when a heavy stick landed squarely at his temple. A white man had hit him from behind. From where she stood, Sarah even saw a spurt of blood from the man's head. At the instant of the impact, she'd felt all of her nerves pinch tight, as if she'd taken the blow herself. Her mouth fell open, soundless, as the man crumpled to the ground.

"You see that?" the fish lady said. "An' the sheriff ain't gon' do nothin' 'bout it, 'cept lock up what niggers they can find an' say they's vagrants. No suh, they don't want us goin' nowhere yet. Chile, you stand out here sellin' fish long enough, you'll see plenty o' blood spillin' in these streets. An' you know the worst of it?" At this, the woman leaned closer to Sarah and spoke to her conspiratorially, and Sarah could smell the spruce gum on her breath. "I know a fella come back from Kansas cuz he missed his mama. He say there ain't nothin' out there for niggers, neither. The Promised Land ain't nothin' *but* promises, he say."

Sarah realized her hands were shaking. Watching the Negro man lying motionless, unattended, it occurred to her that Alex might not have written to them because he'd gotten himself killed somewhere. She hoped the man on the street wasn't dead.

"I don't unnerstand . . ." Sarah whispered, near tears.

"What you don't understand?"

"How come . . . they don't want us to get nothin'?" Sarah said.

"What you said?" the woman said, cackling again. Her laugh, which had seemed pleasant to Sarah at first, had turned ugly to her ear. "Go find yo'self a mirror one day an' take a look. You a nigger, that's why. That's all we ever gon' be to white folks, cuz if we ever get sump'n, that's less for them. You better learn that quick."

But Miss Dunn and Miss Brown *did* have something, Sarah thought stubbornly. Miss Dunn was a schoolteacher, the smartest colored woman Sarah had ever met. And Miss Brown was a Prize Medal washerwoman with her own laundry business, and four women worked for her, including her and Louvenia. With that thought, Sarah suddenly realized that her diversion had made her late to work. Nothing made Miss Brown madder than workers who weren't *punc-tu-al*, as she always put it. She'd told Sarah more than once that if she couldn't make it back from school on time, she'd better stop going to school.

And nothing was going to stop Sarah from going to school. Nothing and nobody.

"I read three words today in class," Sarah announced over her shoulder to the fish lady before she turned to run back toward Miss Brown's house on Pearl Street.

"Good for you, chile! I read ev'ry newspaper that come out in Vicksburg," the fish lady called after her. "You bes' read, to keep up with the plans them white folks got for you!" Sarah could hear the woman's cackling mingling with the seagulls' cries and the curses of frustrated men even as she turned the corner and ran well into the next block.

America Brown was a woman with a heft to match the grandness of her name. She was the big kind of woman Sarah's mama used to call *meaty*, with rolling thighs and a protruding backside underneath her bustles. She kept herself very neat, with a collection of two-piece, floor-length dresses called *suits* for each day of the week, the likes of which Sarah had never seen on a colored woman; her navy-and-sky-blue seersucker dress for Mondays, her rose-colored chambray dress for Tuesdays, and all through the week until she made her way to the gray cashmere dress with ornamental cords running across its length she wore on Sundays. The suits must have been special-made for her size, Sarah thought. And Miss Brown loved hats: she had a different hat to match each of her seven dresses.

Sarah was relieved Miss Brown wasn't in sight as she slipped beside Louvenia in the oversize kitchen where the washerwomen worked. The room was steamy because of the two large cast-iron pots boiling over the stove fires, stirred by Miss Brown's seventeen-year-old cousin, a gangly girl named Sally who worked in exchange for room and board.

Miss Janie, one of the other washerwomen, nodded at Sarah and went on with her wringing and scrubbing as water splashed in the tub and flies buzzed near her face. Miss Janie was older and had her own family, but she had trouble walking because of a bad leg; if not for that, she'd told Sarah and Lou, she'd go find her own customers instead of working for Miss Brown. Miss Janie had told them Miss Brown's laundry business was making thirty-five dollars a month because she was so prized by her customers. Of that, Miss Janie got eight dollars a month because she had worked with Miss Brown for so long, but Sarah and Lou shared only five dollars a month between them. That was less than they would have made in Delta! But Sarah and her sister were grateful for the work, and Miss Brown had promised that if they continued to work hard, she would raise their pay soon.

There was no singing in Miss Brown's kitchen, only work. Miss Brown prided herself on finishing her wash assignments faster than any other colored washerwoman in Vicksburg, and she promised her customers that their clothes would never be borrowed or damaged. Some washerwomen were shameless about wearing their customers' clothes to church or Friday-night fish fries, and Miss Brown had told Sarah and Lou that they would be dismissed on the spot for that kind of foolishness. Miss Brown's policies had made her so popular that she had more customers than anyone else, but that also meant a long day for her four employees.

"You lucky Miss Brown ain't come back here an' see how you was late," Louvenia said, not looking at Sarah while she worked. "What I tol' you 'bout that?"

Sarah ignored her sister's rebuke. "Know what I did today, Lou? At school, I read three words. Sky, fly, and mornin'."

At that, Louvenia glanced at Sarah sidelong. "You tellin' the truth?"

Sarah nodded, grinning. "Miss Dunn said I ain't made no mistakes."

"Durn, Sarah," her sister said, with real awe in her voice, "that real good, huh? You mus' be learnin' quick."

Sarah glowed. Louvenia was usually too tired or distracted to give her many words of encouragement, so the compliment from her sister carried weight. Lately all Louvenia seemed to care about was the man she'd started meeting behind their boardinghouse in the evenings, when Sarah could hear them laughing and talking through her window. Sarah had never seen the man, but his voice sounded old to her, like Papa's. All Sarah knew about the man was that Louvenia had met him near the dock one day. Sarah asked questions about him, but her sister usually just mumbled in response. *Ain't nothin' you need to worry 'bout,* Louvenia said.

"I'ma teach you, too," Sarah said. "Soon as I learn my readin' good."

At that Louvenia only shrugged, but Sarah knew her sister would like to read, too. Miss Brown read newspapers just like the fish lady, and Sarah had seen Louvenia gazing at her with envy. Lou envied a lot of things about Miss Brown, especially how she had money for clothes and owned her own house. Sarah had even heard white folks who came by call her

Miss Brown, not Auntie-this or Mama-this or by her first name the way white folks talked to colored women.

Miss Brown was a curiosity, and Sarah never tired of studying her, even if it meant stealing quick, shy glances when her back was turned or as she was instructing somebody on how long to soak the linens, which temperatures were appropriate for which clothes, how to properly make starch from wheat bran, and how to add bluing to the wash to make white clothes brighter. Oh, she knew something about washing, all right!

Anytime Sarah tried to talk to Miss Brown, her mouth threatened not to work right, but she forced herself to speak anyway because her curiosity burned so strong. Louvenia accused Sarah of trying to win favor with their boss so she wouldn't scold her the way she did the other ladies, but that wasn't true. There were just so many things Sarah wanted to know about her, and the only way she knew to find out was to ask. *Aft'noon, Miss Brown. That's a purty dress—what you call that cloth it's made of?* ("Girl, you don't know what cashmere is? Feel it, then.") *Miss Brown, how long was you washin' clothes 'fore you got to hirin' these womens?* ("I was washin' in my massa's big house since I was younger'n you, and I opened my own business six years ago Monday.")

After three o'clock, Louvenia and most of the other women left to make deliveries in wooden carts. Miss Brown promised customers they could have their washing back in two days, so the deliveries were as important as the washing. The clothes were pressed, folded, and covered neatly in the carts so they wouldn't catch any dust or dirt during the journey. Louvenia was assigned to deliver to a fancy section of town in the southeastern ridge tops, which meant she had to do a lot of walking before she got home for supper. Louvenia complained Miss Brown ought to hire some men with mule carts if she wanted the customers to get their clothes back so quick. Miss Janie had laughed at that, telling Louvenia they were lucky they didn't have to carry the bundles of clothes on their heads like most washerwomen did. Louvenia said some of the white customers' homes were quite a sight, bigger than Missus Anna's in Delta.

Sarah's task in the late afternoons was to stay behind and tidy up, or to press and fold the clothes that weren't scheduled for delivery until the next day. It could be lonely, tedious work—Sarah missed Louvenia and the other women as soon as they were gone, because at least Miss Janie was prone to make witty comments about Miss Brown or one of the customers, giving everyone a soft, secretive chuckle while they washed—but working alone gave Sarah one advantage she cherished: She could sometimes talk to Miss Brown by herself.

That afternoon, as Sarah stacked the washtubs neatly on their rims so they could dry, she heard the floorboards outside the kitchen creak and thump, which told her Miss Brown was on her way. To Sarah, Miss Brown didn't walk, she *thundered*; she had footsteps Sarah could hear on the floor-boards long before she entered a room.

In she walked, perspiring slightly beneath her heavy clothes. Still, to Sarah she looked as noble as the pictures of the white women in the pages of the outdated magazines Missus Anna used to give them to paste up on their walls to keep the cold out of their Delta cabin in winter; she'd called the magazine *Godey's Lady's Book*. Miss Brown's clothes weren't nearly as fancy as those many-layered, frilly costumes in the pictures, but Miss Brown's presence always made Sarah feel shabby in her own rough, home-spun dress.

"I got pressin' for you today," Miss Brown said.

"Yes'm," Sarah nodded, not betraying in her face how much she hated pressing. More often than not, she singed her fingertips trying to keep the iron hot enough in the stove to smooth away the wrinkles in the clothes. But pressing was better than picking cotton, she reminded herself. She thought about the cotton fields almost every day, and how much better it was to work under a roof, at least.

"You should be finished by six, and then you can go on home."

"Yes'm."

Then Miss Brown did exactly what Sarah had hoped: Instead of whirling back around to leave the kitchen, she sauntered inside, checking the room for neatness, making sure there weren't any puddles of water on her floor. Watching Miss Brown's inspection, Sarah worked up her courage to speak: "I read three words at school today," she said.

"Glad you learnin' *somethin'*," Miss Brown said, not turning around to look at her.

That wasn't the enthusiastic response Sarah had hoped for. Miss Brown walked past her, her hips bumping against Sarah in the narrow opening, and Sarah inhaled the woman's sweet scent that was part rose-scented perfume, part powdery. Miss Brown never smelled like sweat.

"Miss Brown, how long it took you to read good?"

At that, Miss Brown stopped to look at her. Her skin was so dark her Papa would have called it *blue*, and her round cheeks made her look cheer-ful even when she wasn't smiling, which she usually wasn't.

"They don't teach y'all grammar at that school?"

"Ma'am?" Sarah said, confused.

Miss Brown shook her head as if Sarah had displeased her. "You don't read *good*, you read *well*. There's a difference, and I pray you'll learn it one day. How long did it take me to read well? Years and years. Anything really worth doin' always takes time. When the little missy where I grew up went to school, she taught me, too. When she learned, I learned. 'Course, when the master found out, that was the end of that." Sarah saw a shadow pass across Miss Brown's face, and she understood why. In school, her teacher had told them how much the slave owners were afraid of their slaves learn-ing to read; then some of the grown folks in the class had told stories about things that had happened to them when they'd tried, how they'd gotten whippings or been sold away from their families. The oldest woman in Sarah's class had said her baby *son* was sold away from her as punishment when her master, who was the baby's pappy, found out she was learning to read from a preacher.

"That ol' marse did somethin' bad to you, Miss Brown?" Sarah asked.

Miss Brown shrugged. "A few licks, and I couldn't play with the little missy after that. But by then it was too late. I already had what I wanted. An' I went back and taught my mammy and pappy both." At that, Miss Brown smiled, but it wasn't a happy smile; it was a smile of triumph.

"Miss Brown, how come yo' mama name you America?"

Miss Brown laughed merrily, a sound so loud and unexpected that at first Sarah was afraid she was in pain. Miss Brown took a deep breath and steadied herself by reaching for the table behind Sarah. "Named me . . . ?" Miss Brown said. "My mama didn't name me America!"

"Then, who . . . ?"

"Let me tell you somethin' 'bout white folks," Miss Brown said, still laughing in her eyes. "The last thing in the world they wanna do is give colored folks any respect. You see how they talk to men and women old enough to be their own mammies and pappies, call 'em *boy* an' *girl*, or Auntie, or call 'em by their Christian names like they were horses—'Whoa, Mary!' Now after the war, when I figgered I wanted to come out to Vicksburg with the little money I'd saved an' start takin' in wash, I knew I had to find a way to stand out from all these other washerwomen or I'd make nary a cent. An' you think this child was gonna keep the name of the man that owned me? No, Lord! So I said I'd come up with a name for myself folks would remember. I looked down at my skin an' said, 'What color is that?' Ain't black, it's *brown*! An' the Christian name . . ." At that, Miss Brown began laughing again. Finally she paused long enough to go on. "Well, these folks were so mad at the Union Army, the way they marched in here an' blew things to bits an' freed up their slaves, and I named myself America after the U-nited States of America. What hap-pened is, white folks couldn't cotton to a Negro named America. Seemed to them like I didn't have the right to it. So you know what they did?"

Eagerly, Sarah shook her head. Miss Brown's story had her mesmerized.

Miss Brown leaned closer, practically whispering in Sarah's ear. "They started to callin' me *Miss Brown* rather'n have to say it! Lord's my witness!" Then she shrieked with laughter, until she had to dab at her eyes to dry them. "I just stuck by the name after that."

Laughing with Miss Brown, with their voices echoing against the walls in the empty kitchen, Sarah was as happy as she could remember being in a long time. She felt a sudden longing to give the woman a hug, but she didn't dare.

After a moment, Miss Brown was silent, and she gazed back down at Sarah. Her smile vanished, and she slowly shook her head. "Oh, child, Lord have mercy . . ." She tugged gently at the plait hanging near Sarah's face, then she flicked at Sarah's scalp. Sarah saw a flake of dandruff float down, landing on the tip of her nose. "You've got all this dander showing. You don't go out looking like this. Don't you know how it shows up? It's ugly."

"But it itches me, Miss Brown."

"So you scratch it *out*. Doesn't your sister scratch your head out?"

Sarah shook her head. She wanted to say her mama used to sit her on the floor and scratch the itching dandruff out of her head when she had time, since the dryness was so uncomfortable in the hot sun that Sarah had felt like her head was on fire, but that had been a long time ago. And Mama used to braid her hair, too, winding tight braids across her scalp that stayed neat for weeks and weeks. But Sarah felt too embarrassed to open her mouth, as if she were sinking into the floorboards.

Miss Brown went on. "These plaits look like they ain't been tended to since the days of Methuselah. You're a right mess, Sarah. It's a shame. There's no need for all you colored children to be runnin' 'round looking so homely. You aren't monkeys in a tree. Don't you know you're gonna be a young lady soon? What man will want to look at this? Put some cornrows in here, or *somethin'*. Don't you move, hear? I'll be back."

But Sarah couldn't have moved if she'd wanted to, hearing Miss Brown's hurtful words ringing in her ears. A boy at school said hurtful things about her hair all the time, but it was far worse to hear the criticism from Miss Brown. Slowly, Sarah felt her eyes growing hotter until they began to sting. She prayed Miss Brown wouldn't come back and find her crying.

Sarah heard thumping and then the swishing of Miss Brown's dress as she made her way back into the kitchen with several small white ribbons in her hand. "My little niece left these here," Miss Brown said, and she began pulling on Sarah's braids, grouping them together, then tying them with the ribbon. "Now, this won't help much, but at least it's somethin'. My niece is bright-skinned and got that good hair from her Creole daddy, so her hair doesn't get like this. But that's no excuse for you not to look neat. Why do you want to look like you got dragged headfirst through a brier patch? You have to work with what God gave you. You hear?"

Sarah nodded, hoping her throat would loosen enough to make a sound. "Yes'm."

"An' I don't want to hear any cryin' or foolishness, neither. Somebody's got to teach you or you won't know any better."

"Yes'm."

"See there?" Miss Brown thrust a hand mirror at her, and suddenly Sarah was staring at herself face-to-face. She saw her shame-reddened eyes, her face that looked older than she remembered, and, finally, the white bows Miss Brown had tied in her hair. Although her heart was still smarting, Sarah saw herself begin to smile.

"That's right," Miss Brown said. "You've got a pretty girl buried down there somewhere. You're not in the cotton fields anymore, Sarah. Out here in the world, folks try to look nice. An' even if menfolk don't, womenfolk *better*." At that, Miss Brown patted her sharply on her backside. "Now, you better get to that pressin'. An' don't expect to leave 'til it's done, even if you have to stay late. I'm not givin' you any special favors."

"No, ma'am," Sarah said, smiling more widely. Her eyes were still drawn to the image of herself in the little mirror, and the bows Miss Brown herself had placed in her hair.

It was after dark when Sarah got home, and she found Louvenia sitting in their room with their lamp and several candles burning, making the room bright as day. Their room at the boardinghouse wasn't nearly as nice as any of the rooms in Miss Brown's house, which were so scrubbed and neat, filled with store-bought furniture and rugs. The furniture in their boardinghouse was ramshackle and dreary, only a table and one chair, shelves for their clothes, and a mattress on the floor hardly big enough for both of them to share. Louvenia called their boardinghouse a *chinchpad*, one of the city words she'd picked up from her beau, although Sarah was glad she'd never encountered a single chinch bug in their bed the way she used to in their Delta cabin. Besides, the roof didn't leak, their window overlooking the alleyway had glass in it, and they always had plenty of blankets when it was cold.

"How come you got all these lights burnin'?" Sarah asked.

Louvenia grinned, holding up a letter. "They said this was for us, from Missus Anna Burney Long!" she said. "Alex sent us twenty dollars!"

Alex was alive! With a shout of joy, Sarah ran to her sister and gave her a tight hug that nearly pulled Louvenia out of her chair. Twenty dollars would be enough for them to buy new coats and heavy clothes for winter. Maybe even shoes, too!

"He sent a note?" Sarah said eagerly.

"Sho' did. Can you read this?"

Lou thrust the folded piece of paper into Sarah's hands. The letter was surprisingly official-looking, written on fancy printed stationery, but the handwriting was small and difficult to make out. Sarah saw the word L-O-U at the top, along with her own name, S-A-R-A.

"It's to me an' you," Sarah said, excited.

"Well, we *know* that, dummy. Who else it gon' be for? What else it say?"

Your bruther Alex aksed me to write to you. He hopes this letter will find you well. He is fine. He has setled in Denver Colorado and is a porter at the Hamilton hotel which he says is bigger then any hotel you could ever beleive. Denver is very buetiful but he was sick all winter long and would have starved exept for friends. He is sorry it took him so long to find work but times are hard and he is geting on his feet at last. Pleas write back to him at the above adress and let him know if you are fine too. They say the cotton crop was not good and he sends this money to help pay rent.

Prayers and love, Alex.

Sarah shook her head, frustrated, as she studied the note in her hands. There were too many words she didn't know, and the challenge scared her even though she could pick out words here and there—*hhheee, iiissss, ffffiiiinnnne.* She felt pressure under Louvenia's stare.

"He say he doin' fine," Sarah said slowly. "He gone out west and say he done made some money. An' he say he miss us both. An' he love us, too, an' think 'bout us every day."

"He tol' us how to come where he at?" Lou asked eagerly.

Again Sarah scanned the words to try to recognize anything familiar. Finally she shook her head. "Uh-uh. Not yet, he say. He say he ain't made enough money to be feedin' us. 'Sides, he say he fightin' off Injuns with them Buffalo Soldiers. A tribe o' Injuns tried to take off his scalp while he was diggin' for gold."

"What?" Louvenia said, skeptical. "Sarah, that's a baldhead lie. You ain't readin' that! Bet you can't read it nohow."

"Can, too! He said it right here," Sarah insisted, pointing, feeling guilty for lying but unable to stop herself. It *might* be true, she thought. At school tomorrow, she would ask Miss Dunn to read the letter to her, so she'd know what it really said.

Maybe Alex had found his gold and was sending for them, after all.

Chapter Five

"It don't seem real, do it?" Louvenia said in a hush, smoothing out the lovely fabric of the white dress she'd sewn, which hugged all the burgeoning curves of her body. To Sarah, Louvenia had never looked prettier. Her sister was sixteen, but this was the first time Sarah had really noticed how much she looked like a grown woman. She had a full bust like Mama's, and rounded hips. Louvenia's dress was plain cotton, but it still reminded Sarah of the magical white dress Missus Anna had been wearing when she came to their cabin that night because she was afraid of Yellow Jack. Six years ago. The memory made Sarah's stomach squirm.

"Sho' don't seem real," Sarah said. She'd tried to sound cheerful, but couldn't.

"Sarah, I'ma be Missus William Powell. *Me* a missus!"

Sarah and Louvenia were in Miss Brown's bedroom, and Louvenia stared into the mirror over the table Miss Brown had called a *vanity*; the table's wood was so shiny Sarah had touched it when she first saw it, wondering if some of the shine would come off on her fingertips, but it hadn't. Miss Brown's neatly made bed, draped in an intricately sewn quilt that looked old, was built very high off the ground and seemed like it was big enough for four people. Their feet sank into the lovely, plush rug that covered most of her hardwood floor.

"But Lou . . . you don't even hardly *know* this man," Sarah said.

Sarah had met William Powell only twice; once when Lou took her to see him working at the blacksmith shop, and another time when he went with them both to the big summer picnic across the river in Delta, where colored folks from all parts had gone to eat, dance, laugh, and talk about politics. Sarah hadn't known how many people were there; she stopped counting at two hundred, delighted with watching their loud laughter and dances where they flapped their arms, swaying and bucking to the fiddle players' music. But Missy Laura had been there, and lots of other croppers she and Lou knew. Sarah had a good time that day, one of her finest times in years—she'd eaten her fill of fried chicken, catfish, pound cake, candied yams, and chitterlings, more food than she could remember eating in a single sitting—but she hadn't thought very kindly of Mr. William Powell.

First of all, like all the men Louvenia favored, he just seemed *old*. Lou said he was thirty, which was old enough, but he seemed older to her. He had a bushy mustache that grew all the way to his cheeks and nearly covered his lips, and the whites of his eyes looked red and runny. He also had tobacco-yellowed teeth and breath that smelled of smoke, which Sarah didn't like. Mr. William Powell and his men friends had sat around their jug at the picnic, laughing more and more loudly as the day went on, and by late afternoon the tip of his nose had turned purplish and he was slurring his words. If Sarah hadn't known he was the one who had paid their fare across the river, she would have forgotten Mr. William Powell was accompanying her and Lou at all that day. Sarah had noticed the way the other "courting" couples danced together and leaned close to each other, and she decided her sister was not being properly courted at all.

She'd been as surprised as Louvenia when, two weeks later, Mr. William Powell had told Lou he wanted to get married. He'd told her the date and the church, as if it were all settled.

"I know enough," Louvenia answered Sarah, her face unchanged in the mirror except for slightly rigid lines that appeared at her jaw. "I know he got a house, so we won't be on top o' each other in that chinchpad no mo'. I know he work hard, which mean we all gon' have more money. An' I know I'm full up with worryin' 'bout how we gon' get by. I'm tired, Sarah. I'm tired through an' through."

Sarah remembered once asking Papa what he had felt when he first met Mama. Colored people didn't get legal-married in those days, not like Louvenia and Mr. William Powell were going to. Papa had told her jumping the broom was the only way most slaves were allowed to show their love. *Yo' mama? First day I seen her in the field, I knowed she'd be my wife. I couldn' sleep the whole night through for thinkin' 'bout her. She b'longed to a man 'cross the way, an' Marse Burney axe to buy her special fo' me.*

Sarah was pretty sure her sister had never had a sleepless night thinking about Mr. William Powell, and she felt even more certain he'd never stayed awake thinking about *her*. Still, Louvenia was gazing at her image in the mirror with dancing eyes, admiring her dress she'd made from the fabric Miss Brown had given her as a wedding gift, as if Mr. William Powell had promised her all the world.

"Things gon' be better fo' us, Sarah," Louvenia said, locking her eyes to Sarah's in their reflection in the mirror. "We gon' have a good home now."

And for the barest instant, despite her gnawing reservations about making a life with a stranger, Sarah actually believed her.

By the winter after Sarah and Louvenia began living with Mr. William Powell, Sarah began to think Louvenia's optimism on her wedding day had been well placed. As the sky filled with dreary gray and the wind began to bite through her clothes, Sarah was grateful for the heavy coat Mr. William Powell had bought for her with his own money, and pleased with the gleaming, sturdy ankle-high shoes on her feet that fit just right. Finally the dark, hard corns she'd grown on her toes from so many years of wearing too-tight shoes throbbed less all the time, and walking was no longer painful. And instead of having a single good dress, she now had three, all of them made of calico, and only one of them handed down from Lou. Sarah cherished her dresses, and she was careful to wear a long apron when she worked at Miss Brown's so she wouldn't accidentally stain or tear her precious clothes. Miss Brown even smiled at her when she noticed the hair bows Mr. William Powell had bought for her when he took a train trip to St. Louis, a big red one, a white one, and a sky blue one that brightened up her hair.

Now Miss Dunn had begun to take a special interest in Sarah, since there were only two or three other students in her class who had been coming almost every day. Mostly the class was filled with new people who were far behind; Miss Dunn tried to catch everyone up, even if it meant she had to begin with the ABCs, but most students didn't stay long. Either their families moved away or they had to go out to the plantations for picking or planting. But not Sarah. Hard as it was, Sarah had been coming to Miss Dunn for more than a year.

One day after class, Miss Dunn called her aside just as Sarah was about to make a dash through the door so she wouldn't be late to Miss Brown's. Miss Dunn's manner was much softer than Miss Brown's, and she smiled at Sarah often with those familiar warm eyes. "You're at a second-grade level, Sarah," Miss Dunn said. "It might not sound like much, but you've been learning fast, compared to where you were when you started. And your penmanship is glorious."

"Thank you, ma'am." Sarah worked hard on writing her letters in script, practicing late at night so that her writing matched the letters Miss Dunn had written on paper for her to mimic.

"If you're ever a teacher one day," Miss Dunn went on, "you'll understand what it means to have a student with both determination and intelligence. Believe me, some people in my family don't understand why I ever came to Mississippi, but you make me glad to be here."

At that, Sarah lowered her eyes shyly, still smiling.

"Did you think you might ever be a teacher?" Miss Dunn said.

Sarah shook her head. She couldn't imagine herself ever being like Miss Dunn, speaking so proper and knowing so much. "No'm," she said. "I ain't thought 'bout nothin' like that."

"Well, I think it's about time you did. How old are you now?"

"Twelve," Sarah said softly, still feeling too bashful to look back up at Miss Dunn although she knew it was impolite to avoid her teacher's eyes. "I be thirteen come Christmas."

"You'll be old enough for high school soon," Miss Dunn said. "Have you ever heard of Campbell College?"

Sarah shook her head. Then Miss Dunn explained that the African Methodist Episcopal Church had established a school for Negroes called Campbell College in 1887, with one branch in Friar's Point and the other right in Vicksburg. Even though it was named a *college*, she explained, the school taught many students at the grammar-school level. It wasn't public like a free school, and Campbell College didn't have much money because it wasn't supported by any white organization, Miss Dunn said, but she thought she might be able to help Sarah attend at a fee she could earn through her washing.

"They've already asked me about my promising students, and I mentioned you," Miss Dunn said. "I don't think you're quite ready now—I'll need to give you some special instruction—but you will be soon. And the best part is, you could learn a trade, something other than washing and domestic work. I'll probably be teaching there myself after next year. Would you like to go to Campbell?"

Sarah's senses swam into a blur. Miss Dunn thought she could go to a college! Sarah knew Miss Dunn had attended a college somewhere, but the only other people she'd heard about who attended college were the children of the white families they delivered laundry to. Sarah's heart was suddenly pounding so loudly that she felt dizzy.

"Well?" Miss Dunn said, and Sarah realized she'd forgotten to answer.

"Yes, ma'am!" Sarah said, nearly shouting.

"Fine, then," Miss Dunn said with a pleased laugh. "I'd like that, too."

Sarah's head wasn't any more clear when she got to Miss Brown's and began her washing alongside Louvenia, watching her hands disappear into the soapy water that devoured her arms up to her elbows. *You could learn a trade, something other than washing.* She'd been so happy to be free of cotton that she'd never imagined a life beyond washing. All the colored women she knew, except for Miss Dunn, were either washerwomen, croppers, cooks, or maids. In her most fanciful imaginings, the most she'd hoped for was that one day she would make so much money washing that she might have other washerwomen working for her, like Miss Brown. What had Miss Dunn meant when she said a *trade*? That she could learn to be a teacher? And what else?

"Sarah, where yo' head is at?" Louvenia hissed at her. "Didn't you hear me jus' say I got sump'n to tell you?" For the first time, Sarah noticed her sister, who was smiling girlishly the way she'd been smiling the day of her wedding. "I'ma have a *baby*," Lou said in a loud whisper.

Stunned, Sarah lifted her sister's apron to gaze at her slim belly. Lou had looked a little rounder in the cheeks since she married Mr. William Powell, but she didn't look big like women who were expecting. "How you know?" Sarah asked.

"I ain't had my monthly since October," Lou said, more privately this time. "William say it look like we gon' have a baby. He so happy!"

Even though Sarah hadn't started bleeding between her legs yet, Lou had told Sarah about the monthly, so she understood how women's cycles worked. She even thought she understood how women made babies, from watching the roosters, hens, and horses when she was younger. And she had certainly heard Lou and Mr. William Powell making the same late-night sounds as Mama and Papa, even though she slept clear on the other side of the house.

"I'm happy too, Lou," Sarah said sincerely, with only the smallest tug of disappointment. Suddenly her news about going to college one day seemed very small.

It was dark outside when Sarah walked through Mr. William Powell's front door, and she was surprised to find him waiting for her, sitting on the sofa she slept on as her bed at night. His leg was crossed over his knee, and he held his gold pocket watch in his hand, the one he'd paid $10 for when he went to St. Louis. He was still wearing his clothes from the blacksmith's, his worn work pants and a gray shirt spotted with mud. He was also smoking his pipe, which Sarah hated because the sharp smell lingered in her nostrils when she was trying to sleep. "Evenin', Mr. Powell," Sarah said uncertainly, wondering why he was sitting in the front room alone, without Lou. He didn't usually pay her any attention, except obligatory conversation.

"It sho' is evenin'," he said, lifting his watch closer to the lamp burning on the small table next to him. "It's 'bout . . . five after seven o'clock, 'cording to this here." He was so pleased with his pocket watch that he constantly recited the time, a habit that annoyed Sarah to no end.

"Yessir," Sarah said, fidgeting. "Miss Brown tol' me I had to—"

Mr. William Powell thrust up his palm, a gesture Sarah knew meant she should be quiet. She and Lou couldn't talk when he wanted to talk. "Lou done fixed supper, but she ain't feelin' good so she went to lay down. She tol' you she havin' a baby?"

Sarah nodded.

"Well, we gon' have some changes," he said, and Sarah's heart quickened. Changes, in her experience, were rarely good ones. "Lou need help back in the kitchen. She ain't as good a cook as you, an 'sides, don't make no sense for her to have that burden all her own."

"Yessir," Sarah said quickly. "I can git up early in the mornin's an' . . ."

But Mr. William Powell was shaking his head, and Sarah knew what he was going to say before he spoke again; somehow she felt she'd known it since she first walked in and found him waiting: "I won't have you comin' home this late. You gon' go early to washing like Lou an' come back with her to help cook an' tidy. An' that's all."

For an instant, Sarah couldn't speak. Mr. William Powell's eyes were unblinking as he gazed at her, and they seemed to hold her silent. Still, somehow, she opened her bone-dry mouth. "But Mr. Powell, I gots school in the mornin'." Sarah rasped the words.

Suddenly Mr. William Powell was on his feet. "I said that's all," he told her, his voice angry, and he turned to walk away.

The sight of his back turned, and the thought of how easily he had dismissed her, both infuriated and frightened Sarah. "But my teacher say I kin go to college! She say—"

"College?" At that, he stopped short and turned to look at her. Instead of softening, his face seemed to have grown harder. "What the hell a li'l nigger gal gon' do in a college?" he said, practically spitting, and Sarah felt as if her heart had been shorn in half. "I knew it! One o' them yellow niggers from up north fillin' you up with nonsense, wastin' yo' time. Lou say you wants to read—well, you readin'! You read better'n me, better'n Lou. What you want next? What you think gon' happen? You think you read 'nuff, you won't be a nigger no mo'?"

Sarah's face was coated with stinging, sticky tears. "N-no," she choked.

"Well, you damn right," he said. "Niggers can't hardly feed theyselves, but they talkin' 'bout college an' walkin' 'round dressed like they got a hunnert dollars in they pocket, thinkin' they's white folks. Well, you ain't. An' *here's* what you gon' do: You gon' do yo' washin' like I say an' come home an' help Lou so you can earn yo' keep under this roof, an' I ain't gon' hear another word 'bout you goin' to school or college. You lucky you got a damn home."

The pain burning in Sarah's chest and midsection nearly doubled her over. Miss Dunn had believed Sarah *could* have something different, but now Mr. William Powell was taking it all away. He was taking Miss Dunn away.

"You ain't my papa!" Sarah shrieked at him suddenly. "You jus' some man Lou married! You don't own me, and I'ma go to school if I want!"

At that instant, Mr. William Powell's eyes felt like fire, too, but his face held no emotion at all. He quickly walked away without a word, toward his bedroom. Sarah watched his purposeful strides as he left, her shoulders heaving with deep, silent sobs. Her heart drummed loudly. Had she convinced him? Was it over?

No, Sarah, a certainty-filled voice inside her said. *Run, Sarah. Run right now.*

But she couldn't move, even when she saw Mr. William Powell walk back into the room with that strangely vacant face and his thin razor strop dangling from his hand. In a mere instant, it seemed, he'd grabbed her arm and was tugging at the buttons on the back of her dress so roughly that she felt them popping. Panicked, Sarah screamed.

"I don' know who you think you talkin' to," Mr. William Powell said, pulling the dress off her back, until she could feel cold air against her bare skin. He yanked the dress down one of her shoulders, exposing her chest and one of her budding breasts, and Sarah screamed again, mortified, wriggling with more strength than she knew she had.

But her strength couldn't match Mr. William Powell's. His grip on her arm never loosened, until she thought he might pull it from its socket.

Then Sarah felt the strop sear into her back with a loud snapping sound. This time Sarah didn't scream so much as yelp. Mama, Papa, Alex, and Lou had all hit her with a switch before, but she'd never been hit with something that *bit* into her skin. She'd never felt a bright, lingering glow of pain.

"*Next* time," Mr. William Powell said—*snap!*—emphasizing his words when he brought his lashes down, "you gon' keep yo' mouth *shut* an' do what I *say.*" Instinctively, Sarah tried to turn her back away from him and succeeded, so his last lash landed across her chest, setting her nipple afire. Sarah did scream then, from unexpected pain.

"You *hear* me? You answer me, girl. *Answer* me." He never raised his voice, but his blows landed as if they were accompanied by shouts.

Sarah couldn't answer him; her throat was clogged with sobs. She paid for her silence with a rain of lashes that came in silent succession across her back until she was sure Mr. William Powell was ripping away her flesh.

"Yes . . ." she whispered, surrendering.

"What you *say?*" *Snap!*

"Yes!" Sarah screamed, and this time when she tried to yank away from him, she lost her balance and fell to the floor, where she curled in a ball and tried to cover the parts of her that were naked. Her torn, ruined dress lay crumpled at her waist. She heard herself wailing, in part from her whipping, and in part because she felt so helpless to control her life, like always.

Sarah heard Lou's voice then, alarmed and somehow distant. "William, what's—"

"Yo' sister got too much sass. Li'l niggers like her need to be broke," Mr. William Powell said, breathing hard from his exertion. His voice grew louder. "An' you gon' pay me fo' that dress, too. You hear me, girl? Every cent it cost me."

Sarah felt as if she would suffocate as long as Mr. William Powell was still standing in the same room with her. If he said another word to her, she might curse at him and get another whipping. She held herself tight, barely breathing at all, waiting for the sound of his retreating footsteps. Finally, thankfully, she did hear him leave. Sarah wished Lou would leave, too.

But she didn't. Lou knelt beside Sarah on the floor, and Sarah whimpered when her sister put her hand on her back. "Sssssssss," Sarah said, drawing away. "Don't."

"Sarah, what 'chu say to make him act like that?" Lou asked, concerned. "You can't be back-talking William. He don't like that."

"I don't care what he like," Sarah muttered weakly through a sob. "Lou, let's go away. I ain't stayin' here. He don't want me goin' to school. I want it like it was befo'."

Sarah looked into Lou's eyes, which were first incredulous and then sad. This time, when she spoke, her voice was hushed. "Sarah, you can't go no place. Me neither. It ain't like befo', cuz I got a baby comin' now. He my legal-wed husband."

Sarah felt something inside of her give way, tumbling inward, and suddenly she had no strength to try to explain to Louvenia that Miss Dunn had thought she could go to college, that she might have learned a trade or become a teacher. Lou probably wouldn't think any better of it than Mr. William Powell. Sarah couldn't ask her sister to choose between her and her husband.

Sarah examined her chest, where a long, red welt was already rising, capped by tiny pricks of blood. Her back must be a mess, she thought. Then, sighing miserably, Sarah curled her head in her arms. Her temples pounded with a headache, she was cold, and she felt sick to her stomach. She never wanted to move from that spot.

In a moment, Lou did walk away, but she soon came back. A soft blanket floated on top of Sarah, bringing warmth and the vague smell of cedar, but Sarah didn't look up at her sister.

"You know, I *wuz* gon' save this for Christmas . . ." Lou said in a too-cheerful voice, "but you seem like you so sad, I speck I better let you have it now."

Sarah only sniffled in response. Lou couldn't give her anything now that would make the hollowed-out feeling inside of her fill up again. She didn't even want to see what Lou had brought, because any gift would probably make her feel only worse that she couldn't enjoy it.

Lou sighed. "I know you 'member how after Mama and Papa passed, I went out my head fo' a while. I can't 'splain it, 'cept I was so wretched an' mad an' sad all at once. But seemed like one day I jus' woke up an' all the crazy wuz done with."

"I 'member . . ." Sarah mumbled, her face still hidden away.

"Well, one thing I feel bad 'bout to this day is how I run off with Mama's Bible-book. I snitched it from you an' tore up all the pages an' threw 'em out in the wind. If I hadn't of did that, I would'a gave it back to you. But I can't. So Mama's book is gone."

New tears pushed their way through the old ones, wetting Sarah's eyes as she listened. That was an old hurt, one she tried not to think about. And although she hadn't realized it until now, Sarah had held a secret hope that Lou had kept that book safe, and one day she would return it to her. A new sob formed in Sarah's throat, forged by her anger and loss.

"I wants to mend it, Sarah. An' I don' know if you gon' like this, but it wuz so purty. . . ."

Curious despite herself, Sarah peeked from behind her arm, and she saw a black leather-bound book in Lou's hands. The gold-colored edges of the pages gleamed in the lamplight.

"The man at the sto' said this wuz the Holy Bible. Is that what those letters say?" Lou held the book up to Sarah with the cover facing her, and the gold-colored letters glowed, too. H-O-L-Y B-I-B-L-E, it said. Gazing at the book, Sarah's grief gave way to rising awe. "See, way I figger it, you promised Mama you was gon' read it, so now you can read it all you want. Maybe you don' know all the words, but . . ."

Slowly, Sarah reached for the book and grasped the soft, textured cover in her own hands. Unlike other books she'd had, which she'd borrowed from Miss Dunn, this one was her very own. She could keep it as long as she wanted, and she would never have to give it back. This time, when her tears came, Sarah knew she was no longer crying from sadness. She reached over to hug Lou, ignoring the pain that flared across her back as her sister squeezed her. "Thank you, Lou," she whispered. "It's the best present I ever got."

"What it say on the first page?" Lou said, excited. "Lemme hear it."

With trembling fingers, Sarah flipped open her fine book. Her eyes scanned over the first letters, past the strange word that began with G, until she saw something familiar. "Chap . . . ter one," she said, and took a deep breath so she could read the next part, feeling her sister's breath against her neck. "In . . . the . . . beeee . . . ginnn . . . inng," she read, "God . . . creeee . . . aaaaated . . . the . . ."

The words were hard, Sarah realized, and reading them would take a long time. But Lou was leaning against her ever so patiently, just listening in still silence, and Sarah had a feeling her sister wouldn't mind if reading the first page took her all night.

Chapter Six

1882

Sarah Breedlove was fourteen when she met a man who called himself Moses.

After watching the fish lady earn good money frying fish, Sarah had started doing the very same thing on her day off, choosing a busy bluff where she could attract customers on their way to and from the railroad yard. She had become a familiar sight, her head wrapped in a bright red scarf similar to the towel the raw fishmongers waved so they could be spotted from a distance. Amid the spirited cries of "Freeeessssssshhhh fish!" and other calls from the boys selling newspapers, Sarah stood over her fire in silence, hoping the scent of the cooking fish would carry in the wind. She bought her fish early in the morning and prepared them with deft hands, chopping off the heads and tails and flicking off the scales and fins. After she shook the fish in a sackful of cornmeal she'd seasoned with salt and red and black pepper and other spices she'd experimented with until she'd found the right taste, the fish went into her skillet and cooked in the hot grease. Then Sarah would wait and hope, watching people pass.

Moses was one of the people who walked by, and one of the few who ever acknowledged her. He had a brilliant smile, his white teeth contrasting sharply with his deep complexion. And he was so tall and wiry he was unusual, generally standing nearly a foot above even the tallest men around him. *He like to be six and a half feet tall, maybe mo'*, Sarah thought when she first saw him loping along the street. *He belong in that Barnum circus show.*

He said hello to Sarah every day he saw her, even though her eyes immediately busied themselves somewhere else whenever he came near. His presence was imposing, and he frightened her despite his smiles. "You ain't gon' speak, is you?" he'd said during his last visit, with a lulling deep voice. "Well, I go by Moses. You gon' tell me yo' name when you ready."

Today, already feeling slightly warm in the wave of heat from her fire despite the temperate spring air, Sarah found herself searching for Moses in the stream of early morning risers. She nearly jumped when his voice startled her from behind: "So . . . you sellin' much o' them fish today?"

Sarah glanced around at him and found she was standing at eye level with his bare rib cage, where his dark skin cleaved to the clearly defined bones and muscles. She looked quickly away. She was standing so close to him, she could smell his personal scent, which seemed sweet and sour at the same time, the smell of a stranger. She'd intended to tell him her name today—what was the harm in that?—but her voice was locked away tight in her throat. She wasn't accustomed to speaking to men she didn't know.

"Hope you don' mind me sayin' it . . ." Moses said, hitching his thumbs to his pants, "but it's a wonder to me you makin' as much sellin' these here fish as it costs you to buy 'em. 'Less you go out an' kitch 'em, too."

Sarah felt her face burning. That was the same complaint Mr. William Powell made, even though the money she earned from selling fried fish was all hers. He had no claim on it, unlike her washing money. She exaggerated when he asked her how much she'd made each day, saying she'd earned a dollar or two when most days she was lucky to go home with twenty-five cents above what the fish had cost. She would have quit long ago, except she was so desperate to save any pennies so she could move from under his roof. The notion of going to college felt like a hazy dream compared to her immediate goal of moving away from her brother-in-law, even if it meant trying to find work as a live-in maid for a white family. He'd whipped her three times while she'd been living with him and Lou, always ripping off her clothes in a way that felt more demeaning than the whippings themselves, and she was beginning to fear that if he ever laid a strap on her again, she might lose her senses and make her sister a widow. She would not hold still for him, not again.

"I ain't axed what you think," Sarah said, still not looking at the man. Now that he'd annoyed her, it wasn't hard to speak to him at all.

Moses laughed. "Well, that's the truth! You ain't axed me nothin' a'tall."

When Moses didn't walk away, Sarah was sorry she'd opened her mouth. Now she'd invited a conversation with him, and she'd rather pay attention to her scaling and cooking. "Ain't you 'posed to be someplace?" Sarah asked him at last, unnerved by his silent staring.

"Uh-huh. I 'posed to be over at that yard washin' train engines. But I jus' been a-lookin' here, thinkin' to myself, see, an' I think I know why you ain't sellin' no fish."

Sarah gazed up at him skeptically. Why was it his business, anyway? But before Sarah could tell him she wasn't interested in his observations, he pointed toward the white fishmonger near the pier. There were three customers clamoring for his attention. "See that?"

"So?"

"So I reckon *he* makin' some money. Know why?"

Despite her irritation, Sarah considered the question. She'd wondered the same thing herself. "I dunno," she mumbled.

"Cuz he been screamin' out here all mornin', an' I ain't heard you make a peep. How come you so quiet? How folks gon' know what you sellin' if you ain't gon' tell 'em?"

"They see me," Sarah said, a pout in her voice.

Moses paused, assessing her up and down, and Sarah felt herself shrinking under his lingering gaze. Mr. William Powell looked at her that way sometimes, and she didn't like it a bit. "Oh, yeah, they see you. They see a li'l colored gal in a red head-rag standin' over a fire. But they can't see all the way in this pan. They can't see this here catfish."

Silently Sarah considered his point. True, the old fish lady who worked on weekdays wasn't shy about yelling out to the crowds, but to Sarah she sounded coarse and mannish. She couldn't imagine raising her voice like that, shouting to strangers.

"Try this here . . ." Moses said, winking, and he heaved his shoulders high, which made him appear to grow even taller. He cupped his mouth with his hands: "*Fishfry fishfry fishfry! Friiieeeeed catfish heeeee-yuh! Friii-ieeeed catfish heeeee-yuh!*" His deep, commanding voice carried in the air and echoed around them.

Sarah's heart jumped. He was so loud, she almost wanted to cover her face. "Why you hollerin' like that?"

"Why . . . ?" Moses looked at her with disbelief. "Gal, I'm tryin' to sell yo' fish! Ev'rybody ain't gon' come over here cuz they think you purty."

"I ain't s-said . . ." Sarah's voice faltered as she felt a wave of embarrassment that was foreign to her when she realized that Moses had complimented her. "*Stop* that," she snapped. She meant she wanted him to stop making her feel bashful, but her words came out more sharply than she'd intended. Moses' face fell slightly as he looked at her.

"All right, then, li'l gal . . ." he said, shrugging. "All I'm sayin' is, seem to me like colored folks 'fraid to raise up they voices. You ain't the onliest one—it's the same with the niggers I work with at the yard. But how I look at it, if you don't raise up yo' voice, don't nobody know what you got to say. What you scared of?"

Sarah didn't have a chance to answer him, because a ruddy-faced white sailor walked up to her and peered down into her pan, her first customer of the day. "Smells good. How much?"

"Ten cents," Sarah answered him, but her eyes were on Moses. He was grinning at her with those striking teeth, which intrigued her even though his front teeth were slightly crooked, growing toward each other instead of straight. Tipping an imaginary hat to her, Moses turned and began to walk away in his long, jaunty steps.

Sarah longed to call out to him and tell him her name, since she'd forgotten to do that, but shyness kept her silent. As Sarah served her new customer, she realized Moses had been right: She'd been afraid to raise her voice, and Moses might never know what she'd wanted to say.

Moses' birth name was Joseph McWilliams, Sarah learned in the coming weeks, but his friends had started calling him Moses because they said he was always preaching. He was twenty-three, his parents had been slaves and then croppers like hers, and he had moved to Vicksburg when he turned twenty-one to look for better wages. His family lived just outside Warren County, he said. He had a mama, a papa, and three younger sisters. He'd never been to school, he told her, and he couldn't read or write, except the letters in his name.

Sarah listened to him, but she barely talked about herself beyond telling him her parents were both dead and that she lived with her sister, brother-in-law, and baby nephew. When he'd asked if she could read, she said, "Not good," which was true in her mind but probably wouldn't be true in his, she knew. In truth, if she really put her mind to it, she could read most of the signs she saw on the street, as long as the words weren't too long, so she didn't have to constantly ask folks, "What this say?" like so many colored people she knew. In fact, most folks asked *her*. But Mr. William Powell constantly accused Sarah of thinking she was superior—in fact, he'd whipped her the second time because he thought she'd tried to shame him in front of his friends—so she didn't want Moses to think she was bragging. Some days she wished she hadn't ever gone to school. She'd be happier with her life if she hadn't had her hopes raised, she thought.

Like Louvenia. Now that Lou had her little baby boy, Willie, she seemed happier than she'd been since before Mama and Papa died. Sarah could hardly imagine ever feeling that way.

Three Saturdays in a row, Moses walked Lou back to Mr. William Powell's street, although she wouldn't let him come close to his house. She didn't want Lou to catch sight of him and begin teasing her about having a beau. Moses, she thought firmly, was *not* a beau. He was so much taller than her, in fact, that she felt self-conscious when she walked beside him, as if anyone who saw them would think they looked odd together.

"Li'l gal, some days I think you got the saddest brown eyes I ever seed," Moses said to her one day, standing gallantly aside so Sarah could walk around a pile of lumber blocking most of their path on the sidewalk. He had bought fresh peaches at a stand, and they were both taking bites into the soft, dripping fruit as they walked. "How come you so sad to go home?"

Sarah didn't answer, simply shrugging.

"Somebody whipping on you?" he asked bluntly, startling her.

She stared up at him accusingly. "Who tol' you that?"

"Ain't nobody had to tell me. You kin tell somebody bein' whipped same way you can tell with a dog, by the way he jump back. I seen lots o' whipped dogs. Yo' sister whippin' you?"

Sarah shook her head, but she didn't answer. Everything inside her suddenly wanted to tell Moses about Mr. William Powell's strop and the way he tore off her clothes, and how his eyes gazed at her while he beat her, but she felt too much shame. After the last time, when he'd pulled her from her bed late at night and whipped her in the kitchen after stripping her completely bare, she'd been too ashamed to tell even Louvenia. She'd struggled not to cry out for fear of waking her sister. Sarah felt her ears begin to prickle, and the skin on her face grew warm. She folded her arms and wrapped herself tight.

For a moment Moses didn't say anything. "Where he from?" he asked finally. "Who used to own him?"

"Who?"

"That man whippin' on you."

"I dunno," Sarah mumbled. She'd never asked, and she didn't care.

Moses took another bite of his peach, and a jagged line of juice dripped from the corner of his mouth. "Why I ask is, some of them massas in slave times was better'n others. But some massas an' oberseers was jus' low-down *mean*, an' treated they niggers worse'n they treated horses an' dogs. An' if you came up with one o' *them*, well . . . that cowhide's all you knew 'bout. Them marks don't never go 'way. An' I ain't jus' talkin' 'bout marks on flesh. There's the other kind, too, marks what come when a man can't be no kinda man."

Sarah puzzled over Moses's words, then she felt a surge of anger when she thought she understood: He was making *excuses* for Mr. William Powell! Her frame went rigid with rage. "You takin' his side!" she shouted, not realizing she'd raised her voice so loud. "You ain't even never met him, an' you takin' his side over me!"

Moses looked surprised and uncomfortable, but his voice stayed calm. "I ain't met *this* one. But I met him, all right, li'l gal." He leaned closer to her, pointing out a scar at his temple that must have once been a deep gash. "I met my pappy, ain't I? So I ain't takin' his side. I'm jus' tellin' you the way I learnt it. Slaves couldn't be no men, but men 'posed to be treated like men. An' when they ain't . . ." He didn't finish his sentence, shrugging. "Well, I'm sho' glad I don't 'member bein' no slave like my pappy do."

Still fuming, Sarah began to walk faster so she could pull ahead of Moses. He didn't seem to feel the least bit bad for her! But Moses, keeping his slower pace, called after her: "I'm sorry you bein' whipped on, li'l gal. That's a crime, whippin' on a li'l thing like you. Maybe this man need somebody to tell 'im to keep his hands to hisself."

At that, Sarah slowed again. Moses had spoken the words she'd been longing to hear. She'd often drifted to sleep at night with the fantasy that Alex had come back to beat Mr. William Powell so badly that he'd be too scared to go near her.

Moses stopped walking at the street corner where Mr. William Powell's slant-roof wooden gray house was visible halfway down the block. Sarah could see the bright red and yellow roses Lou had planted near his porch in full bloom, deceptively welcoming in the late-afternoon light. "Nobody's gon' whip on my li'l gal," Moses said resolutely, nodding as he stared at the house. "You an' me's gon' have to think on what to do 'bout this. That all right, Sarah?"

Sarah nodded, encouraged. She barely noticed when Moses took her hand and squeezed it, except that his palm was so warm and damp. After a moment, feeling uncomfortable with her tiny hand inside his much bigger one, Sarah slipped her fingers away.

"You aren't yet the woman Louvenia was, child," Miss Brown said through the straight pins in her mouth as she fussed with the hem of Sarah's dress. The pins bounced when she talked. Sarah posed, her arms outstretched like a scarecrow as she gazed at herself in Miss Brown's vanity mirror, dwarfed inside the too-big white dress her sister had worn on her wedding day. "I've got to take in the bust, the hips, an' the length, too. *Might* fit then."

Sarah's heart had been pounding steadily harder since she came to Miss Brown's that morning, and the rhythm of her nervousness reached a peak while Miss Brown worked. Sarah licked her dry lips. "I ain't got to have this dress," Sarah said. "I'll wear one o' mine."

Miss Brown sucked her teeth. "Don't be silly, girl. You can't wear one o' those rags. Hold in your breath."

Sarah took a deep breath, and Miss Brown drew the waist in tighter, pinning it in place. " 'Sides," Miss Brown went on, "I assume the boy has somethin' presentable he's gonna wear. He has money, doesn't he?"

Sarah shrugged. She'd never seen where Moses lived, and all she knew about his livelihood was that he was an engine wiper at the railroad yard. He always seemed to wear nice boots, and he'd bought her a beef-stew lunch at an eating house once, but she didn't have the faintest idea how much an engine wiper earned.

"I'll tell you why I ask . . ." Miss Brown said, her voice muffled behind Sarah's back. "One thing I've learned bein' in white folks' business all these years is this: When a girl's getting married and she doesn't *have* to . . ." At that, she patted Sarah's belly, and Sarah flushed with embarrassment. ". . . and if it isn't for *love* . . ." Miss Brown straightened up to gaze into Sarah's eyes at the word *love*, and Sarah couldn't hold her gaze. ". . . then it's always for money. So I assume this here boy—what's his name again?"

"Moses," Sarah whispered.

"Yes, so I assume this here boy, Moses, must have some money."

"Miss Brown, he ain't got no money." Lou spoke up unexpectedly from the bedroom doorway. She was holding baby Willie on one arm while Willie reached for the white lace in Lou's other hand. Thwarted because Lou dangled the lace out of his reach, Willie let out an indignant cry. "He look like he can barely 'ford clothes on his back. He's black as coal, tall and skinny as a willow tree, and got crooked teeth to boot."

"He don't have no crooked teeth!" Sarah said, although she hardly sounded convincing.

"So what is it, then, girl?" Miss Brown said. "It's love after all?"

Sarah nodded, unable to bring herself to lie to Miss Brown. Noting Sarah's silence, Miss Brown pursed her lips and sighed. "I sure hope you aren't about to have no baby."

"Oh, Lord . . ." Lou said. "That's the same thing William said!"

Angry at the mention of Mr. William Powell's name, Sarah forced herself to ignore the doubts emerging in her mind. She tried not to remember what she'd been thinking when Lou put on this very same dress for her wedding, when she was so convinced Lou was not truly in love. Now she wasn't any better than her sister. But she *did* love Moses, didn't she? She loved the way he was so gentle with her, the way he listened to her, the way he told her things about himself, the wise way he seemed to ponder things she never considered. She loved him just like . . . a *brother*, she realized, and she felt nausea tickle her throat.

"All right, Sarah, I'll have this altered by Sunday, since you're in such a hurry. It's a shame! Your little figure hasn't even had a chance to grow in yet," Miss Brown said. "I don't understand why you're in such a hurry to marry these men you scarcely know, jus' looking for botheration. Lou got lucky with that Powell fella, 'least so far. I hope you get lucky, too, Sarah, but it doesn't seem to me like luck runs in your family."

On their way back home from Miss Brown's, Sarah carried Willie, enjoying the gleeful way her nephew's eyes danced above his round cheeks as he stared at her. He gurgled, reaching up to wrap his little fingers tightly into her scalp, and Sarah laughed. It seemed like Willie was the only one who *could* make her laugh anymore. Remembering the scar at Moses's temple, she hoped her little nephew would never have one like it from his father. She wished she could take Willie away with her, too.

"I ain't gon' make like I don' know why you gettin' married," Lou said as they walked, watching Sarah with eyes that didn't blink. "An' I ain't gon' make like I ain't glad you goin', neither. I'm glad fo' both o' us, cuz things ain't right like they is."

Those words hurt despite their truth, and Sarah swallowed hard. In the time since Lou had been married, she and her sister had grown much more distant because Lou was defensive whenever Sarah complained about her husband's violent moods. As far as Sarah knew, Lou had never once said a word in her defense, and she resented it. Was Lou afraid of her husband? And was she jealous of Sarah, too? Probably so, Sarah thought, and she'd be more jealous if she knew how Mr. William Powell looked at her when he tore off her clothes. Unless she knew already.

"You always sayin' how you think William so mean," Lou went on slowly, "but you jus' got to talk to a man a certain way. You know—don't be fat-mouthin' all the time. An' don't be too bossy-like. A man always gon' cuff you if'n you do that."

"Papa didn't cuff Mama," Sarah said. "Not even one time."

"Sarah, you gon' have a sad life if'n you speck you gon' find any man like Papa," Lou said matter-of-factly. "Moses gon' be jus' like William, you watch."

Now, with dread to accompany her uncertainty, Sarah's feet felt leaden as she climbed the porch steps behind Lou and they walked into the house. She could smell the greens Lou had begun simmering that morning for supper, but the other scents in the house made her feel sick. She hated the smell of Mr. William Powell's pipe, of the musk of the dirty old sofa where she slept, and even the roses Lou had cut off to put on the table. She hated everything about his house.

Even if Lou was right about Moses, it didn't matter, she thought. She needed to *leave.*

"Shhh. Put the baby down. William prob'ly back there 'sleep," Lou said, speaking very quietly the way she always did when she knew her husband was taking a nap. "I'ma go to the back an' git you a few dollars. You 'bout to move out, so that money's yours. An' by the look of that man you marryin', you gon' need it, too."

Sarah was alarmed, quickly taking her sister's hand. "No, Lou, don't do that. Don't make 'im mad. Jus' leave the money be."

"*Hush.* It's only right, Sarah."

For the next tense minutes, while Sarah laid Willie on a blanket next to the sofa and tried to keep him quiet, Sarah's heart was in a frenzy of worry for her sister. Mr. William Powell was very particular about the money he kept in the drawer next to his bed, and she couldn't imagine what he would do if he woke up and found Lou fooling with it. She didn't want any more shouting, any more whippings. She just wanted to be gone.

Satisfied that Willie was near sleep, Sarah jumped up and crept to the back room her sister shared with her husband. When she reached the doorway, she saw Mr. William Powell sprawled facedown across the bed with no shirt on, snoring loudly. Lou had apparently finished what she had come to do; she was pushing in the drawer beside his bed, and it made a small scraping sound that made Sarah jump. But Mr. William Powell didn't notice, not stirring. Grinning the way she used to when they were girls, Lou waved several dollars over her head for Sarah to see and covered her mouth to contain a muted laugh. As scared as she was, Sarah nearly laughed, too, reminded of the times she and her sister had broken into their mother's precious molasses jar when they were children.

But Sarah's smile slowly vanished as her eyes went back to Mr. William Powell's sleeping form. She had never seen her brother-in-law without his shirt on, and she tasted something vile coat her tongue when she noticed the crisscrossing dark lines that looked like brand marks imbedded deeply in his back. Scars, she realized with an awfulness so dense that it was a cloud she could not breathe. So many awful scars, nearly a lifetime's worth, just like Moses had said.

Please, Jesus, Sarah prayed earnestly, closing her eyes, *please don't let Moses be like Mr. William Powell even though his pappy gave him marks, too. Please let him be good to me.*

She repeated that prayer and held on to that wish until her wedding day.

Sarah and Moses got married at the AME church by the same preacher who'd married Louvenia and Mr. William Powell, although the only people who attended the ceremony were Lou, Miss Brown, Miss Janie, and Sally. Instead of marrying at the pulpit, she was married in the basement where she'd once attended school.

"You now pronounce man an' wife," the cotton-haired preacher said, and Sarah froze when she saw Moses's face looming above hers, poised for a kiss. She held herself perfectly still as he bent over to press his wet lips to hers, holding her breath until he pulled away. She tried to smile at him afterward, but her heart was flying. Moses would expect to take off her clothes and touch her when they got home, she thought. He would want to fuss with her between her legs the way Louvenia had told her a man would like, and stick his man-part inside her, and it would hurt. It was her *wifely duty,* Lou said, and if she tried to refuse him he might force himself on her because it was his right.

Sarah barely tasted the food Miss Brown fixed for them after the wedding, and she couldn't respond when Miss Brown shook her head and muttered that she wished Moses had at least *pressed* the white shirt he was wearing. "He seems like a nice enough boy, but didn't he notice that rip in his trousers near his foot? You'd think he'd wear his Sunday-go-to-meeting clothes on his wedding day! *You* look lovely, but I swear . . ."

The whole time, Sarah dreaded the time when Moses would say he was ready to go, and then they would be alone. *Sarah, you really done it now,* she thought, feeling dazed as she took shy peeks at this giant who was now her husband. *Why you had to go an' git married 'fore God?*

It was a long walk to where Moses lived south of the railroad, near Cherry Street, and he carried Sarah's meager belongings in a sack on his back: her folded-up dresses, her Bible from Lou, her photograph of Papa, the five dollars Lou had snatched, and the wooden bowls and quilt Miss Brown and the ladies had given them as wedding gifts. He whistled all the while he walked, gently tugging her hand. Sarah could feel Moses' pulse-beats in his long, clammy fingers. Or was that her own heart racing? Moses tried to begin conversations with her about how nice Miss Brown's house was, but Sarah was unable to so much as grunt back at him, so he gave up on talking to her. They walked most of the way in silence, and Sarah felt as though she was moving farther and farther away from everything she knew.

The houses near the railroad were built close together, and they were in poorer condition than the ones where Mr. William Powell lived. Many of the houses had tin roofs, wooden walls with large spaces between the planks, chickens in the yards, and goats tied to wooden posts. There were no sidewalks or gas lamps to light the streets, so it was very dark by the time Moses pointed to a little house at the end of the row of shacks.

"I know this look like catfish row out here, but there it go," Moses said, sounding slightly dispirited. "Mine ain't nothing like Miss Brown's, but it got two rooms, a cookhouse an' outhouse in back, an' it keep warm in wintertime."

The house was built of brick, at least, Sarah noticed, but it also had a tin roof, and the patch in front was overgrown with weeds and wild grass nearly four feet high. Moses had chickens in front of his house, too, behind a wooden fence. Gazing at the house that was now her home, Sarah felt nothing at all. A strange numbness had spread inside of her, which grew as she heard the rumbling of an approaching train and its deafening whistle on the nearby tracks. The noise drove all the thoughts out of her head.

Inside, the front room was small, crammed with a rocking chair, a fire-place, and a pinewood table and two chairs that looked homemade, but sturdy. There was also a small braided rug on the hardwood floor that was very faded, but added a comfortable touch. A well-kept banjo stood against the wall in the corner. There were two windows in the front room, but no curtains. The more Sarah studied the room, the more it reminded her of her family's little cabin in Delta. Feeling nostalgic, Sarah sighed a small sigh.

"I figger on gittin' better work 'fore too long," Moses said, mistaking her sigh for displeasure. "We gon' move to a better street then, not right up on the train yard. I know them big boys is loud comin' through, but you gits used to it."

Next Moses showed Sarah the back room, which was much smaller still, with only room enough for his sleeping-mattress on the floor and a wooden bureau against the wall. This room had no window, so he had to bring in a lamp so she could see. As soon as he followed her inside the doorway of the small room, Sarah felt trapped. The neatly pulled blankets on the bed looked ominous to her.

"This where we gon' sleep," he said, his voice rumbling a bit in his throat.

Sarah didn't answer. Without realizing it, she'd hugged her sack in front of her.

Moses' hands went to Sarah's shoulders, and he began to rub them. Sarah's entire body felt as if it had turned to rock, and her head tensed back. After a moment, Moses pulled his hands away. She could feel the warmth of his body behind her, but he didn't move to touch her.

Moses sighed, and she smelled his breath wash over her. "How old you said you was, Sarah Breedlove McWilliams?" he asked her. Her new name sounded like a lie to her ears.

"Fo'teen," Sarah said, a whisper. It was the first word she'd spoken to him since she'd become his wife.

"Fo'teen, fo'teen . . ." Moses murmured. "Well . . . there's all kinds o' fo'teen. Some girls ready to marry when they's twelve, an' some still ain't ready when they twenty. Ain't that right?"

Not turning to look at him, Sarah slowly nodded. She felt herself bracing for him to touch her shoulders again.

"I know you ain't axe me, but you wanna hear sum'pin I think?" Moses said.

Sarah didn't move or speak in response.

"To my mind, the kinda fo'teen you is ain't ready for no husband." Was he going to send her back to Mr. William Powell's? Sarah turned around to look at Moses, and she saw that his features were gentle, free of anger. His eyes bored into hers. "Naw, you ain't heard me wrong," he said. Very slowly, he raised his fingertips to her chin and rubbed her skin with his thumb. But when he lifted those same fingers toward her hair, Sarah felt herself angling her head away. She was ashamed of her dry, coarse hair, which she'd covered the best she could under the lacy veil Miss Brown had made her. She also couldn't bear the thought of Moses touching her that way.

"Lemme tell you what I'm thinkin' 'bout," Moses went on, moving his fingers back to her chin. "We legal-wed now, an' you belong to me, and can't no man whip on you no mo' 'less he ready to die. That what you wanted, right?"

Sarah nodded, but she felt her eyes stinging. Maybe it wasn't fair that she'd married Moses for that reason, since his eyes plainly told her he wanted much more from her.

"So . . . you gon' live here, an' you gon' cook fo' me an' wash my clothes, an' you gon' work at the laundry fo' Miss Brown 'til I gits better wages. An' I only got this one little room what to sleep in, so we gon' both sleep in here. I'ma let you sleep in my bed tonight, an' I'ma fix myself a spot in the corner, yonder," he said, pointing to a bare spot next to the bureau. "Come mornin', I'll fix sump'n diff'rent so's we both got 'nuff room.

You'll sleep on yo' side, I'll sleep on mine. An' I'll tell you why: You ain't ready fo' no husband yet, an' I seed that from the start. You still too much a child. But I'm a man, see, an' I can't be sleepin' close to you 'cept to think like you a woman. So we ain't gon' sleep close, not to start. An' you keep yo'self covered up, cuz I can't be lookin' at no woman's body I can't touch. You hear?"

Stunned, Sarah nodded, her lips falling apart as she gazed up at Moses. Was this some sort of trick? Did he plan to take her by force after she fell asleep?

But in his eyes, she saw the answer was no. And she also knew, beyond a doubt, that Jesus had answered her prayer and given her a good man, after all. She hoped she could grow to love Moses the way she thought he must love her, even though she couldn't quite explain to herself why in the world he did. Had she ever shown him a single proper kindness?

"You s-sorry you married me?" Sarah asked in a small voice, feeling unworthy of Moses.

Moses grinned. "Course not, li'l gal," he said. "I know you mine, even if'n you don' know it yo' own self yet."

Sarah Breedlove McWilliams finally allowed herself to smile.

Chapter Seven

1885

Once Sarah decided she was ready to be touched, Moses could hardly touch her enough. Her body, which until then had served only as a tool to enable her to accomplish her endless array of tasks, became something entirely new beneath her husband's fingertips. After a year and a half of sleeping apart, Sarah had overcome her childlike timidness one night and slipped inside the blanket beside her sleeping husband, nestling her curves against him. In part, she'd gone to Moses because she'd heard Lou's voice in her head, warning her that a man would always seek elsewhere what he didn't get at home, and Moses had made it no secret that he occasionally visited a saloon or two that had reputations as brothels. But more than that, Sarah was drawn to the dark smoothness of Moses' skin, the mystery of his lanky muscles that had grown taut and solid since he'd begun doing more heavy lifting, and that unnameable glow she felt from him that had ultimately sparked slowly and steadily within her. She'd wanted to feel him lock his arms around her. That night, for the first time, she'd *needed* his touch.

Methodically, with the same patience he'd demonstrated during the time they'd slept apart, Moses ran his fingertips across Sarah's skin and followed their inflamed trail with his warm, broad mouth. His hands, made so rough from the extra work he'd been able to find at the coal yard, never felt rough because he used such a feathery touch. And when he thrust himself inside her, his eyes squeezed tight, Sarah felt a completeness that was bigger than herself, at once ecstatic, comforting, and even frightening. This feeling had been absent so long, how could she bear it if she lost it again?

By the time she was seventeen, Sarah felt she was thriving with Moses. The life she had with him was by no means easy, but it felt good, better than anything she had felt since her parents died. Selling fried fish together—with Sarah's tasty preparation and Moses' loud, spirited calls—they earned nearly half as much on the weekends as they did at their regular jobs the other five days of the week. They'd moved into a bigger house on Main Street farther from the railroad tracks, just as Moses had promised; this one also had only two rooms and a kitchen out back, but the rooms were bigger, allowing for a wardrobe and the rough pine bed frame and headboard Moses built himself to give Sarah a proper bed for the first time in her life.

Their new house was only two streets from Lou's, so Sarah's sister visited much more often. Sarah cherished the evenings when Moses wasn't too tired to pick up his banjo and pluck out cheerful melodies for her, Lou, and little Willie; no sooner than he'd been able to stand up on his own, her nephew had stomped his tiny feet on the floorboards and tried to dance. "Look like he tryin' to do the cakewalk!" Moses said. All the while, Sarah marveled at how he could get his long fingers to move so quickly and with such precision on the cheerful instrument. Moses sang for Willie, too, although his voice cracked when he held a note.

Those were the good times, although there were plenty of bad times, too. Sarah's husband was as opinionated as she was, and they argued freely when their viewpoints clashed, although Sarah had long since figured out that Moses would never raise his hand to her the way Lou had predicted. The worst times, to Sarah, were when Moses found himself out of work. During those times, he sank into brooding silences that could last for days, when he would barely acknowledge Sarah when she spoke to him. He vanished for days at a time in his search for employment, which led Sarah to screaming fits when he returned because his absences terrified her. He avoided answering Sarah's questions unless he could give her the good news that he'd found someone doing some hiring for weeks or months at a time, whether it was at the railroad yard, helping to build roads, driving wagonloads of cargo to neighboring towns as a teamster, or on a distant plantation picking cotton. The work always showed up as if by a miracle because Moses could do so many things, but it could never be relied upon. Sarah and Moses were always just a step ahead of their landlord, struggling to pay their more expensive rent.

Moses told Sarah he'd thought about applying to be a Pullman porter, but he didn't want to spend so much time away from home. "Not with this baby comin'," he said, nuzzling his chin into Sarah's protruding belly. "I hear some o' them porters talkin' 'bout how they don't git no time for sleep, and gotta run 'round after them trains so fast they hardly git home. They young'uns don't hardly know who they is when they come in the door. My son gon' know *me*."

Sarah was expecting her child at any time; she spent at least a couple of hours a day lying on her back because she ached so much from the extra weight, and her feet felt like swollen sausages. "How you know this a son?"

she said playfully. She stroked Moses's short-trimmed hair, envying him for the way his hair felt so woolly and soft beneath her hand.

"Course it's a son! I tol' you I speck six big ol' boys."

"An' one girl," Sarah reminded him.

"I don't 'member sayin' nothin' 'bout that. One purty gal in the house is 'nuff for me." Then Moses' face grew somber as his mind wandered. "My sons ain't gon' live like we is. This town gon' make room for colored folks to make a good wage jus' like white folks do."

"Unh-hnh." Sarah knew Moses was headed toward another of his political rants, and his defiant talk always made her uneasy. She was afraid her husband was setting himself up for useless rage and disappointment, like so many men and women she'd known who ranted for a time and then slowly accepted their lot.

"Slav'ry been dead an' gone since sixty-five. Here we is all these years later—I mean, been *twenty* years, Sarah—an' white folks still actin' like we slaves, like we s'posed to do what they say do. An' niggers still moanin' 'bout they forty acres, waitin' on the gov'ment. Ain't nobody gittin' no forty acres, an' niggers best look to how they gon' get it *theyselves*. They best learn to speak up an' make some fuss." As he spoke, growing more impassioned, the two days' worth of whiskers on his chin tickled Sarah's belly.

Sarah sighed. In the past few months, two or three of Moses's friends had begun stopping by the house after suppertime to sit at the table and complain to Moses about Vicksburg politics. Unfair arrests for vagrancy. All-white hiring policies for hotel porters and railroad mail agents. The beatings of Negro leaders. The lack of Negroes in elected office. Sometimes Sarah heard their angry voices at the table late into the night, long after she'd gone to bed. Their complaints only filled her with hopelessness. White folks had always been running the country, so what could a few Negroes do about it now? It might be a hundred years before Negroes had anything at all, Sarah thought, and they might not have anything even then.

Moses stopped talking, rubbing circles around Sarah's navel, as if he'd heard her thoughts. "You think I'm jus' blowin' wind, huh?" he said. "You think I oughta be happy with what crumbs the buckras toss out? An' speck no diff'rent for that young'un you carryin'?"

"I ain't said that. I jus' don't like talkin' 'bout it." In truth, she wanted to tell Moses she was afraid he might end up in jail, or worse, for spouting his ideas so loudly.

"Don' nobody wanna talk 'bout it!" Moses said. "But tell you what, if you don' talk 'bout it, it ain't never gon' change. Niggers sayin', 'Aw, we jus' got to work hard an' we be fine,' but that ain't true, Sarah. Look how hard we both workin', me drivin' to an' from Natchez an' you still over there washin' when that baby's 'bout to fall out. When you ever seen a white lady big as you out workin'?" At that, his voice trembled with emotion. "Work ain't nothin' 'less you makin' some money. You can work your whole life choppin' down trees, an' then you ain't got nothin' to show but a empty field of grass an' stumps. You gotta *build* sump'n, too. See, like I keep sayin', them washerwomen down in Atlanta had the right idea in eighty-one. *Thousands* of 'em done went on strike so's they could get a *u-ni-form* wage—that mean they all gits the same pay, what *they* thinks they worth. An' I know Miss Brown colored, but she ain't payin' y'all 'cept as much as it suit her, too. She keepin' most o' that money to herself."

Sarah winced every time Moses criticized Miss Brown, who had saved her and Louvenia from almost certain homelessness when they first came to Vicksburg. But it was true that in seven years, they had received only one large increase in pay. Moses insisted they would both be better off finding clients on their own. "She pay us what she can," Sarah said.

"Lemme axe you sump'n, Sarah: Why you keep talkin' 'bout goin' to college?"

"To learn things."

"What for?"

By now Sarah was irritated. She sighed hotly. "So's I can teach, maybe. Or . . ."

"Or what?"

"I dunno. Sump'n."

"Why you wanna teach, then?"

Sarah tried to turn away from him, but her stomach bulged in her way. "Moses, jus' hush, please. I don' feel like all these questions. . . ."

"Well, you best axe yo'self, Sarah. I'll tell you why: Seem to me you don' wanna be standin' up all day no mo', stoopin' over them tubs washin' white folks' clothes. Or maybe you wanna teach these little colored young'uns so's they can go be lawyers an' doctors an' such."

At that, Sarah laughed softly and shook her head.

"Why you laughin'?" Moses asked, genuinely angry. "See? You don't wanna talk 'bout it cuz you can't even see it. But they *is* colored lawyers an' doctors, too, the kind what went to school. How you think they got there? Cuz they said, 'Aw, shucks, I'ma jus' take what the white man gon' give me'? Or you think they had to raise Cain?"

Moses's words lanced into Sarah. In a flash, she remembered the night Mr. William Powell whipped her after she tried to defy his order not to go to school. She'd been so heartsick, she'd never been able to face her old teacher, Miss Dunn; she'd just stopped coming to class without a word of explanation, praying she would never come across her teacher on the streets of Vicksburg to remind her of her dream. Should she have tried to find a way to fight? But how?

Sarah blinked rapidly. "You know what happen when folks want too much, Moses?" she said softly, stroking his hair again. "When they pine for sump'n in they heart they can't git?"

She was going to say, *They die just a li'l bit, deep down where can't nobody see but them,* but she suddenly bucked when she was startled by a cramping pain in her belly. At first she thought the pain had been brought on by the memory of her heartbreak, but as she cradled her middle and felt warm moisture seeping between her legs, she knew her baby was coming instead.

While Sarah half sat despite her fatigue, she watched with alarm as the midwife slipped her fingers underneath a bloody cord wound around her baby's neck like a snake. The sight of that cord, and her baby's reddening, gasping face, nearly stopped Sarah's heart. But Nana Mae's fingers were well practiced, and she flung the life-threatening umbilical cord away from the baby's neck with ease with her gnarled, leathery fingers. Immediately the baby began to wail with lungs full of air.

"*There* we go . . ." the old woman said, smiling. Only then did she glance toward the baby's swollen genitals, in the same instant Sarah did. "Y'all gots yo'selves a baby girl!"

Disbelief flooded Sarah. She had just given birth to her very own child? But despite her joy at having a healthy baby, Sarah felt a twinge of disappointment as she thought about Moses. He wanted a son so badly! She hoped Moses would love this child as she knew she would, as the most precious gift God had ever laid in her hands. "Can . . . I hold her?" Sarah whispered.

But Nana Mae was busily at work, tying a string around the umbilical cord still threading its way from Sarah's insides to the child's belly, cutting it with a small knife close to the baby, and fixing a deft knot at the end of the cord that was left. As she watched Nana Mae at work, Sarah was so exhausted after the five-hour labor that she nearly dozed until she felt something else oozing from her legs. Her body gave a small spasm, startling her. "Nana Mae, what's that—"

"You ain't never seen no baby birthed before?" Nana Mae said, and Sarah shook her head, watching Nana Mae catch the bloody, runny mess in a sack. Sarah had not witnessed her nephew's birth because Mr. William Powell had sent her to the kitchen to cook while Louvenia was in labor. Nana Mae, who was Miss Brown's aunt, had delivered Willie, too. "This here ain't nothin' but yo' afterbirth. I'm glad it come out quick. Sometime it take all night, an' I just sets here an' waits." Putting the sack aside, Nana Mae lifted the baby, who was by now wrapped in a small towel, and laid the tiny bundle on Sarah's breast. "You take hold o' this here girl o' yourn. I gots to go outside an' bury this sack, o' it's bad luck—an' you gon' git mighty sick."

"Tell Moses . . . to come," Sarah said weakly, gazing at the wondrous infant in her arms. The baby's eyes were screwed tightly closed, and her nose wasn't even as big as a marble. Her thin black hair, which was still damp, looked like fine wisps of smoke.

As soon as Moses stood over her, Sarah knew she needn't have any worries about him loving his daughter. He gently picked up the baby and paced the room with her, cradling her in his long, thin arms. "Lookie, lookie . . ." Moses whispered in a voice so soft that Sarah could barely hear him, bringing his face down close to the baby's. "Lookie what we got."

"What you think we gon' name her, Moses?" Sarah asked. She felt herself gaining back at least a bit of her strength as she watched her husband and new daughter. Nana Mae had told her she would come back and rub her female parts with sugar to help her heal faster, but Sarah doubted she could be back on her feet anytime soon. Through the birthing process, Nana Mae had told her she'd been bearing down just fine, much better than most first-time mothers, but Sarah ached like she never had in her life.

"We ain't gon' name her nothin', not yet," Moses said. "In a month's time, that's what my mama say. First thing, after seven days, we cut off the rest o' that cord; next thing, a month from today, we do the takin'-up cer'-mony an' give the baby a name. We can think on it 'til then."

"A month!" Sarah said. Louvenia had named her son right away, by the next morning. Mr. William Powell had ignored most of Nana Mae's instructions, telling her she was too countrified and superstitious. *Niggerish* was the word he'd used, and Nana Mae had just shaken her head with disgust.

"You want her to die?" Moses said, looking at Sarah earnestly.

Willie didn't die 'cause of gittin' his name early, Sarah thought in that ornery voice in her head that liked to argue, but she kept that thought to herself. In fact, she felt a gladness in her heart when she realized how much Moses wanted to give their daughter the best start. They didn't have any money for beautiful clothes or a fancy nursery room like rich white folks did, but they could give their daughter good luck. Maybe it didn't mean anything to Mr. William Powell, Sarah decided, but it meant something to her.

A dozen people came to the taking-up ceremony, the most people Sarah and Moses had ever hosted in their home. Lou and Miss Brown came, and Nana Mae, and all of Moses's family, even some of his cousins Sarah had never met before, all of them traveling more than twenty miles by wagon and horseback in the hot July sun to come see the new baby receive her name. Their guests stood close to each other and filled up every corner of the front room. Nana Mae had dressed the baby in a soft white flour-sack with holes cut out for her arms, which were already growing slightly plump from her mother's milk. The baby was fully alert as she gazed in wide-eyed silence at the new people in her home. All of her limbs wriggled, as if in anticipation.

The taking-up ceremony was one of the few times Moses had allowed Sarah to walk much at all since the baby's birth, and she felt as if she'd become a new person. Following his mother's advice, Moses had not swept their room nor cleaned the sheets or pillows on their bed since the baby's birth. He'd also advised Sarah not to comb her hair during that month ("My mama say it'll all fall out if you do!"), so she'd been grateful Louvenia came early on the taking-up day to help her work through all of her matted tangles and fix her hair so it would look neat. Sarah was also wearing a new calico dress Moses had bought her as a surprise, which was slightly big on her but delighted her anyway. On that day, with so much attention on her and her child, Sarah felt like a queen with her princess in her arms.

"Some o' y'all may ain't come to no proper takin'-up 'fore today," Nana Mae said, gazing squarely at Lou, "since these coloreds is comin' to the towns an' tryin' to forget the ways that's been since they grandmama's time an befo' that. Tryin' to be white, way I see it."

Lou, holding tightly to three-year-old Willie's hand, bit her lip sheepishly. Moses' mother, a stout woman with striking rows of gray cornrow braids and a stern face, said *Amen* loudly enough for the whole house to hear. Everyone in the room was dripping with perspiration, and the open windows, as usual, were little help in the heat. But the guests fanned themselves with any items they could find, listening in a respectful hush.

"Well, I'se so glad we's got chillen who ain't scared o' the old ways," Nana Mae went on, turning toward Sarah and Moses. "Now Sarah, you take this here thimble and hold it in one hand. Take that chile o' yourn in t'other. Then you walk with that chile to ev'ry corner o' this here place— an' that means some of y'all gots to *move*," she added pointedly, bringing ripples of laughter from the guests. "Then you's gon' walk right through that front door an' come back."

And so, with her heart pounding steadily from the importance of the moment, Sarah held her daughter to her breast with one arm and the water-filled thimble Nana Mae had given her in the other hand, making her way through her house: first through the bedroom where she and the child had spent so much time in her first month of life, then easing her way past the witnesses in the front room until she had left no corner untouched. After that, following Nana Mae's instructions, she took the baby outside to the sunny front porch and walked back inside.

A room of smiling faces was waiting for her when she walked back over the threshold. Sarah's eyes caught Moses', and he was beaming at her.

"Well, then," Nana Mae went on, "you can take a sip o' that thimble for luck, then give it to the baby. Make sure she drink it, now!"

Sarah took a very small sip of the tepid water—there was barely enough for one sip, never mind one for her and one for the baby—and then she tilted the thimble carefully toward her daughter's mouth, pouring the dribbles of water into a corner. Much to her relief, the baby drank it eagerly. "What y'all namin' this chile?" Nana Mae said.

Sarah and Moses had considered so many names—Minerva after Sarah's mother, Grace after his, and even Louvenia for her sister—but instead they'd agreed on a name Moses had heard a stranger call her child in town, and Sarah had liked it immediately when he mentioned it to her. It was the prettiest name she'd ever heard.

"Lelia," Sarah said, and she was even more certain of their choice when she heard how beautifully the name flowed from her tongue. "Lelia McWilliams."

After that, there were hugs and clapping, and Sarah thought the taking-up ceremony was finished. The table was full of food that Miss Brown and Moses' family had brought, and her stomach was growling fiercely. But Moses gently took baby Lelia from Sarah's hands. "I got one mo' thing, Nana Mae. My mama taught me this one," he said. "Come on outside, y'all."

Sarah was confused, but she followed her husband to the side of the two-story house where they lived; she and Moses had the bottom floor, and there were stairs running from the ground to their upstairs neighbor's door. When Sarah saw that Moses was about to climb the rickety steps, she touched his elbow. There was no railing, and it had always looked like a precarious climb to her. "Where you goin'?" she asked, alarmed.

"Just up these here stairs," he said. "Don't you fret, Sarah."

Shading her eyes from the bright late-afternoon sunlight, Sarah stood in the huddle at the bottom of the stairs and watched Moses carefully climb one step after the other until he stood at the landing twenty feet above them. He grinned, cradling Lelia in his arms, close to his chest. Watching him standing so high, Sarah realized that her husband was truly like a giant. She was also terrified he might drop their child in his giddiness.

"See where we at?" Moses called down to them. "This the highest-up place we got!"

"What you doin' up there, Moses?" Sarah called back.

Nana Mae chuckled. "Don't git cross with 'im, now," she said. "You carry the baby up to the highest place, that mean she gon' be rich one day."

Rich! Her fears forgotten, Sarah's face broke into a grin. Moses' mother patted Sarah on the back, then hugged her close with one arm; the woman was so excited, Sarah thought she might do a dance. The others, too, laughed and clapped gleefully. The very mention of wealth so close to them, when they had so little themselves, visibly raised everyone's spirits.

"See how high you at?" Moses said to the baby, slowly turning around and around on the narrow wooden ledge where he stood. He spoke with his head close to the baby, as if the two of them were alone. "Anything Lelia McWilliams want, she gon' have it. Hear me? Anything she want in this big ol' world."

His face was so full of confident resolve that Sarah had to wonder if her husband was standing high enough to see God's plans laid out before his eyes.

Chapter Eight

"Ma-ma . . . wha's that?"

Lelia had a favorite phrase, which she recited endlessly, questioning Sarah about everything that came into sight of her wide, wondering eyes. Her stubby index finger pointed in every direction, never satisfied. Lela, as she and Moses had begun calling her, was two years old, and Sarah watched with amazement as she became a more finished person every day, with her own particular tastes, likes, dislikes, and moods. Lela had adopted a self-assured walk as she made her way around their house with questions about their belongings: Moses' boots, Sarah's straw hat, the banjo, the whisk broom, the crude wood carving Moses had fashioned for Lela's birthday in the shape of a bear, the chopped wood Moses had stacked in the corner for the fire. She filled up so much of Sarah's time that it was hard to imagine when she had not been.

Like Lou, Sarah had begun doing the washing for Miss Brown's customers at her own home because she needed to watch Lelia, so their kitchen had been overrun with washtubs and hanging clothes, leaving little room for her cooking pots and foodstuffs. Since Lela could no longer be counted on to take long naps after her feedings, Sarah had found that the only way she could keep her inquisitive daughter still was to stand her in a washtub too high to climb out of. But Lela was already getting so tall that Sarah feared she would topple herself over at any time, and Sarah was especially nervous that her daughter might injure herself in boiling water or swallow some lye soap when she wasn't paying attention, since any objects that made their way into Lelia's pudgy hands were likely to end up in her mouth. Today Lela had given Sarah a headache because she was amusing herself by banging on the sides of her metal washtub with the wooden spoon Sarah had given her to play with.

"Ma-ma . . . wha's that?" Lela repeated.

With a weary sigh, Sarah turned around to try to see where her daughter was pointing *this* time. If she ignored Lela's questions too long, her daughter would get irritable and cry, and Sarah didn't need the extra aggravation when she was already so far behind. Lou had offered to help her by taking Sarah's clothes to Miss Brown's to dry on the indoor lines in her kitchen, but Sarah had to finish washing them first. Like most of the other washerwomen who lived on her street, Sarah had been hindered by the past two days' rain showers, which meant that the clothes she'd hung to dry between the trees alongside her house had stayed damp and gone sour. She'd been forced to wash the entire load again, and Miss Brown had already sent Sally by to ask after it once.

Lelia pointed straight up, toward the ceiling. "Wha's that?"

Sarah didn't see anything, but she heard the steady drumming of raindrops on the tin roof. "That's *rain*, Lela. You hear it? That's the sound rain make."

That's the same rain that's making my life a misery today, Sarah thought with a surge of irritation, tightly wringing the end of the bedsheet she'd just pulled from her tub of rinse water. As she worked, Sarah's fingers and knuckles ached from the monotonous wringing motion she'd been repeating for the past two hours in her hurry to finish the clothes. Wringing out a bedsheet was arduous work, second only to the stubborn denim fabric so many men were wearing now in their Western-style blue jeans. But Sarah knew that if the clothes weren't carefully wrung before they went back to Miss Brown's, she would raise the devil.

Thunder growled across the sky, a sound like heavy footsteps.

"Wha's that?" Lela said, sounding delighted rather than frightened.

Sarah sighed. "Thun-der, Lela. It's up in the sky. It come with the rain."

"*Thun*-der!" Lela repeated. She squealed, obviously pleased with herself. The next time the sky thundered, Lela answered by pounding against the rim of her washtub. Despite her weariness, Sarah couldn't help laughing as her daughter tried to make her own thunder. "Well, chile . . . I'm sho' glad one of us is makin' some fun with this rain today."

With that, a thought about Moses brought a new crease across Sarah's brow. The storm clouds had worried him that morning, too, since he'd been counting on making extra wages on roadwork this week. The weather probably ruined his plans. So where was he, then? Maybe he was off looking for another job to make up for what he'd lost, she thought, or maybe he'd been able to salvage some time working on the road, after all. Sarah hoped so. The past two months had been hard on them. Employers were finding more ways to bar Negroes from jobs, and Moses was in a foul mood.

And no matter how much money the Pullman porters made, Sarah didn't want her husband to consider being away from her so long. That would be almost like having no husband at all. Lela stuck like glue to her daddy, and she was old enough to feel his absence. Two weeks before, Moses had come back home after spending a full month picking cotton with his family for extra wages, and Sarah had been relieved almost as much for Lela's sake as for her own. During the time Moses was gone, Lela had been much more irritable than usual, and she'd let out a shriek of unmistakable joy upon his return, reminding Sarah of the way she'd felt when she saw her father making his way home in the distance after a long day in the fields.

This time, the thunder above them was more a roar than a growl, and the rainfall grew so loud on the rooftop that it drowned out the sound of the water splashing into the washtub from the twisted fabric in Sarah's hands. Glancing out of the open doorway, Sarah saw the misty sheet of driving rain that had enveloped everything in sight. "Lou won't be comin' out in this . . ." she muttered, shaking her head. "Guess the clothes just gon' be late, then."

Sarah didn't immediately notice the dark figure standing in her doorway, and even after she did she stared a moment without reacting because the unexpected appearance felt like a strange illusion. It took her some time to even realize that it was her sister, Lou, standing under a tattered umbrella in a long black coat that must belong to her husband. Lou didn't move. Staring more closely, Sarah saw an indefinable expression written on her sister's rain-drenched face. Lou had come after all? Well, why didn't she come into the kitchen and out of the rain?

"Lou? What you . . ." But the pinched, pained look on Lou's face froze Sarah's mouth. Something was wrong.

"Sarah," Lou said in a clipped voice, "you know where Moses at?"

At the sound of her husband's name, Sarah felt her chest begin to squeeze her lungs like fists. "He . . . went out this mornin' after some roadwork . . ." Sarah said, virtually whispering. Her hands clutched at the apron across her breast. "What—"

"Listen . . ." Lou said, and took a deep breath, ". . . you know a man name of Jake?"

Jake. Sarah knew that name, and for some reason she felt a stab of alarm much deeper than she had only a moment before, when her sister's face had arrested her so. When the thunder above her roared again, Sarah felt it rake inside her bones. "Jake work with Moses," she answered slowly. Jake, a strongly built man who wore spectacles, came to the house several evenings a week to talk politics.

"Sarah, his mama live on the same street as me, and they sayin' Jake is dead. Her house full of folks right now." Sarah couldn't speak, dreading whatever words might come next, so Lou went on. "There was some kinda trouble out on the road, Jake an' them fussin' 'bout not gettin' paid. They sayin' it was some kinda riot. An' somebody axe me ain't I kin by marriage to Moses McWilliams, cuz maybe he was there, too."

Sarah's strangled lungs let out a sound. She could not bear to hear her sister utter another word, or she was certain the earth would open up and swallow her whole, or at the very least her mind would leave her. Even though she didn't fully realize it, the deafening pounding she heard now was no longer the thunder or the rain, but her own frenzied heartbeat.

"Where it happen, Lou?" Sarah rasped.

She heard Lou say a street name, Grove, and something about the levee, and those two words whirled around in Sarah's head, which had become suddenly vacant of anything except the image of Moses ducking beneath the doorway that morning, half waving to her over his shoulder only a few hours before, when it had never even entered Sarah's thoughts that she might never see him again. Now she tried as hard as she could to imagine Moses' kiss, or even just his face, because that might make everything right. But all she could see in her mind was the suspenders crossing his back as he'd turned and gone through the doorway, taking long strides into the rain-gray morning daylight, walking away.

Sarah had never been so drenched with rain. By the time she reached the corner of Grove and Washington, her clothes were so heavy with dampness that they had become a burden, her skirts nearly tripping her around her ankles. The cold fall wind had chilled her skin numb.

On Grove Street, she saw only a few young colored boys kicking at large stones on the unrepaired portion of the road. As soon as they saw her, they told her how they'd heard the colored men shouting, and how the sheriff and some white men had come, but that everyone had run off in the direction of the levee. "We heard they done kilt some o' them colored men, ma'am," one of the smallest boys said, sounding giddy despite his morbid words.

"Moses? Moses McWilliams?" Sarah asked the boys, and they shrugged their ignorance.

As she walked, her face turned toward the ground to protect her from the cold droplets pelting her, Sarah searched for any signs of her husband along the way—a piece of clothing, a shoe, a familiar tool, anything she could claim and hold to her breast to ward off the despair she felt growing inside her. *It ain't nothin'*, she tried to reassure herself calmly. *He jus' got in some trouble, prob'ly got took to jail. He be gone a few weeks an' then he'll be back. An' ain't he gon' have a laugh, too, when he hear how you was out lookin' for him in this storm 'til you was cold and wet to the bone.*

The voice gave her strength, and Sarah kept pressing uphill until she saw the levee ahead of her, with huddled people under rows of umbrellas. As she neared the crowd in a rapid walk that grew into lurching stumbles, she heard the babble of men giving orders and women wailing and shouting. Frantically, her eyes searched for one man standing above the others.

She saw a very tall man in a coat and hat she knew were too fine to belong to Moses, yet she tugged on his arm and felt her heart leap when he turned his head—until she saw that he was only a freckle-faced white man she did not know, and who did not seem to even notice her wild-eyed, desperate gaze. Next, Sarah's eyes were drawn to patches of bare Negro skin near the ground a few yards ahead of her, and after she pushed past the umbrellas blocking her vision, she saw that up to a dozen Negro men, most of them shirtless, were sitting on the ground with their wrists chained together. Afraid to breathe, Sarah's eyes skimmed past their faces in search of the one she needed to find; past beards, noses that were too long or too flat, mustaches touched with too much gray, skin that was too light or dark. She knew some of the men, but she could not register their names, only the faces that did not belong to Moses. Then, even though she would not have missed him, Sarah searched those faces again. And again.

Moses was not there.

"Git back, now. You ain't supposed to be here. You gon' have to claim these boys at the jailhouse," a white man in a sheriff's uniform said to Sarah, taking her arm, and she allowed him to pull her away without taking notice of the roughness of his shove. Her eyes were finally satisfied; Moses was not among the prisoners. He had to be somewhere else, that was all.

The onlookers' conversations swallowed Sarah.

"—tryin' to cheat 'em again . . ."

"—musta kilt three or four at *least* . . ."

"—near 'bout knocked that poor man's head clear off . . ."

There were three sheriff's deputies standing at the edge of the bluff with their arms folded, looking down to where she could hear the shallow water breaking against the craggy rocks below. Sarah didn't know why, but her feet were taking her toward the bluff as if they had their own mind. Her breath become hot and labored as she walked closer and her certainty grew.

And then, as if she had been eavesdropping on the men's words since the moment Lou first arrived at her door, she heard one of the deputies say what she had absolutely expected him to say, spitting out a wad of tobacco that fell into the water: "Hell, his own mama prob'ly wouldn't know his face, not like that. And he's so damned tall . . . how we gon' haul him out? The water's gon' float him out soon."

"Might hafta just let 'im float on away, then," the other man said languidly.

That one's so damned tall. The words stopped Sarah in her tracks, and she began heaving as she struggled to breathe.

She *had* to look over that edge, to see if her husband was down there in the water. Yet her feet would not move any farther, anchored as if they were duty-bound to protect her from the sight. Sarah felt someone take her arm, and she expected to see an irate deputy ready to order her back to the other women in the crowd. But instead, Sarah turned and saw the blood-red eyes of the fish lady, whose face was wrenched with misery.

"Girl . . . a bunch of white men done beat Moses and threw him down there," the fish lady said. "They done kilt him. I seen it. Oh, you poor girl, your man is dead." And then the woman began to sob as if the loss were hers.

Sarah felt herself gingerly take the fish lady's hand, patting it, trying to provide the old woman comfort. "I know," she said softly. "I know they kilt him. I know."

She couldn't make herself stop repeating the awful, unbelievable words no matter how hard she tried. Somehow, she *did* know. And she re-fused to push past the deputies to look down at the corpse that was her husband's, disfigured and flung into the water like useless fish innards.

Rather than seeing Moses broken and bruised, Sarah would not lay eyes on him again. *Float on away, Moses,* whispered the part of Sarah's mind that was not frozen in grief and shock, as the skies flooded across her face. *You done in this place now, my big ol' angel-man. This world don't deserve you nohow. You jus' float on away, then.*

For the rest of her life, Sarah would remember nothing else about that day.

For two weeks, Sarah battled the terrible cold she brought home with her from the levee the day Moses died. Lou moved in with her, sleeping at her side in the bed Moses had built, and in her feverish sleep Sarah sometimes awakened believing the covered figure sleeping beside her was Moses. When she touched Lou and saw her sister's face instead of her husband's, the finality of her new life shocked her anew. She would stare at Lou with blinking, uncomprehending eyes. He was gone. And the sobs racked her weak body anew.

"Ma-ma . . . where Daddy?" Lelia asked every day, as she had when Moses was away picking. Lela had been to the funeral, but her father's body had not been there for her to see, so she had not understood why her grandmother was so beside herself, screaming until she was hoarse, and why there had been so many tears in the house since the day of the rainstorm.

Sarah didn't know how or what to tell her, so she gave her the same answer she had the month before: "In the fields, Lela. Daddy's workin'." Her voice was thin.

"When Daddy . . . comin' home?"

Sarah stroked her daughter's face, peering at her more closely for the features that were Moses', her blunt little nose and closely set eyes. She re-membered Moses carrying Lelia up the stairs for her taking-up ceremony, and the joy in his face as he had proclaimed to her that she would have anything she wanted. What could Lela have now that her father was dead?

"I don't know when, Lela," Sarah told her. "I jus' don't know."

As she slowly recovered and her hacking cough began to subside, giving her more time to think, Sarah made the simple realization that she could not salvage anything of her old life. She could not bear to walk past that levee or see Moses' men friends on the street, reminding her of what she'd lost. She could not live in fear that someone Moses had angered might seek to harm her and her daughter. She was already a month behind in her rent, and she could not afford to keep their house without Moses' income. And she could not move back to Lou's, not even for a day, as long as Mr. William Powell was there. In her present frame of mind, she was afraid she might kill that man just for the sake of it, whether he ever touched her again or not.

Sarah felt her spirit sinking even lower, until it seemed that her body was literally turning to stone, pulling her toward her own grave. *They didn't jus' kill Moses that day, huh? They done kilt me, too,* she thought.

Then the answer came. One morning, as she sat at her table and sipped a cup of sassafras-root tea that Lou had brewed for her, Sarah announced she was going to leave Vicksburg.

"You gon' do what?" Lou asked, stunned.

"I gotta go, Lou. I ain't got nothin' here. Not no mo'." Sarah was wrapped tightly in a shawl to ward off the growing draft in the house. She was only twenty years old, she realized, but she looked and felt like an old woman. "If I stay here, all I'ma think of is what I ain't got. What Lela ain't got. I need to go somewhere an' git somethin' else."

"Sarah, you can find a new man here, too." Lou's words sounded nearly cheerful.

Sarah stared at Lou with disbelief, and she wanted to slap her sister's face. Was that all it would mean to Lou if Mr. William Powell died, that she would just find a new man? Or would she be relieved? Suddenly Sarah felt pity for Lou, who was living with an unloving man who frightened her because she could not imagine living any other way.

"I ain't talkin' 'bout a new man, Lou," Sarah said. "I'm talkin' 'bout a *life*. If I can't make no life for myself, then what I'm s'posed to give Lela for hers?"

Lou stared at Sarah, shaking her head. "No matter where you at, you jus' gon' be takin' in washin'. May as well wash where somebody *know* you."

"Papa wanted to leave," Sarah said, suddenly excited by the memory. "You 'member? He was ready to go, right 'fore he died. And Moses was, too. I know it, 'cept he was so damned stubborn, set on makin' things right here. I wish we'd of gone. Alex was smart to set off like he did. I hear tell there's higher wages in St. Louis, an' lots of folks with rooms to rent. Well, that's where I'ma go." Sarah was making the decision as she spoke, and she felt a gratifying relief awaken within her, as if she could breathe again after having a strong hand clamped across her face. Moses, she knew, would be proud of her if he could hear her words from heaven. Sarah felt a comforting sense that Moses was speaking through her own mouth. "That's where I'ma go make a new life."

"Unh-hnh." Lou sounded skeptical, gnawing on the edge of her fingernail. "You talk mighty big for somebody who ain't got no money. How you gon' pay to go to St. Louis?"

"I'll save 'nuff for a train ticket. An' even if I don't have but a dollar an' some left after that, it don't matter. Least I'll be where I want, away from this damn place." At the end, her voice cracked, but she stanched her flood of sorrow.

Lou sighed, gazing at Sarah incredulously, then with sympathy. She leaned over and gave Sarah a tight hug, rocking back and forth with her as if she were trying to call out a demon. "You talkin' out your head cuz of Moses passing on, girl. You know you can't go to no big ol' city like that all alone with a baby. How you gon' feed her? It git cold up there, too. In yo' heart, you know you can't do nothin' that crazy."

This time Sarah didn't answer. In truth, she'd barely heard her.

Sarah had tea with her sister on a Thursday morning. When Lou came back by Sarah's house to see about her that Sunday, only three days later, Sarah's house was neatly swept, her bed was made, her dishes were washed, and their meager furniture was neatly in place. Even Moses' banjo stood in the corner exactly where he'd always kept it, waiting to be played.

But true to her word, Sarah Breedlove McWilliams had taken her daughter and was gone.

St. Louis Woman

I know why the caged bird sings, ah me,
   When his wing is bruised and his bosom sore,—
When he beats his bars and would be free;
It is not a carol of joy or glee,
   But a prayer that he sends from his heart's deep core,
But a plea, that upward to Heaven, he flings—
I know why the caged bird sings!
                              —PAUL LAURENCE DUNBAR

Invest in the human soul. Who knows, it might
be a diamond in the rough.
                              —MARY MCLEOD BETHUNE

*T*here were no markers on her parents' grave sites. Sarah had found the way to the field behind her cabin from memory, remembering an old oak stump that still stood about twenty paces beyond it, even though the stump had been overgrown with tangling weeds and crabgrass. The fall breeze riffled the branches of nearby trees. Sarah knelt on the grassy ground, running her palm along a small mound of earth that might or might not be her parents' resting place. But she knew their spirits were close.

"Well, Mama, I can't stay long . . . but I made you a promise," Sarah said, reaching into her pocketbook for the tiny leather traveling Bible she always carried with her. "You'll forgive me if I can't sit and read the whole thing. But I've picked out a passage I know you'll like. You, too, Papa. Y'all just listen."

Sarah flipped through the book's tiny pages until she came to the Book of Matthew. She squinted at the tiny numbers to try to find Chapter Thirteen. When she did, she began to read, pacing herself the way she'd rehearsed, delivering the words as if she were addressing a crowd: "The whole multitude stood on the shore. And he spake many things unto them in parables, saying, 'Behold, a sower went forth to sow; and when he sowed, some seeds fell by the way side, and the fowls came and devoured them up.' " Sarah paused here, feeling a stone in her throat, because suddenly she realized that was what had happened to her parents, and to Moses. " 'Some fell upon stony places, where they had not much earth: and forthwith they sprung up, because they had no deepness of earth: And when the sun was up, they were scorched; and because they had no root, they withered away. And some fell among thorns; and the thorns sprung up, and choked them: But others fell into good ground, and brought forth fruit, some a hundredfold, some sixtyfold, some thirtyfold.' "

You're the seed, Sarah's mother had told her on her dying bed, and it had taken her years to understand what her mother had been trying to tell her. Or *had she somehow known all along? Today it seemed to her that she had always known.*

Sarah had nearly forgotten the two onlookers who were watching her from a polite distance while she visited her parents' burial site. Once she bowed her head and thanked her parents for the love they had shown her, Sarah stood up and began to walk toward the two women, who stood in the field beside Sarah's car, their skirts whipping in the wind. One was Anna Burney Long, and the other was her daughter, a spinster in her thirties named Lillie with a wide, girlish smile. "Madam Walker, ma'am," the younger woman said, "Mama and I just want to say again how thrilled we are to spend this time with you."

"I'm so proud I could bust," Mrs. Long said, her face flushing. "I never thought less of nobody just because they cleaned house or washed clothes, Sarah. To me, you felt more like family. And I worried for you and your sister so. . . ."

"It's true," the daughter said, wrapping her arm around her mother protectively. "She's read me newspaper accounts about you, Madam Walker, and she's always so tickled. Why, you're a real-life famous person. And it's like you were one of our own."

Sarah had grown so accustomed to praise that she often had to remind herelf of how awe-inspiring her life must seem to outsiders. It really was a blessing, wasn't it? "Well, you'll both have to visit me sometime in New York," Sarah said. "I have a grand four-story town house there and a beauty parlor like you've never seen. I would be very happy to host you. Then you can meet my daughter."

Anna Burney Long's eyes shone with sadness. "Oh, I don't know if these old bones could take that long trip, Sarah, but Lillie would love to go. Just let us know when she's welcome."

"Madam?" said Lewis, the chauffeur. He had climbed out of the car to open the rear door for them. Lewis enjoyed the formality of his role when he drove Sarah, especially when they were driving through the South, and she didn't doubt he was playing it up just a bit more because of the Longs' presence. He'd been giving Sarah strange looks all afternoon, no doubt because he couldn't understand how she could be cordial to a family that had once owned hers.

"Ooh, I can't get over it!" Lillie Long exclaimed. "Riding with a chauffeur!"

Missus Anna looked slightly embarrassed at her daughter's outburst, but Sarah smiled at her gently to let her know it was all right. "Some days I don't believe it myself," Sarah said. " 'Specially back here in Delta."

"Sarah, you just have to tell me about your hair tonic," Missus Anna said. "How in the world did you come up with it? Was it as soon as you moved to St. Louis?"

Ruefully, Sarah shook her head. She gazed back peacefully at her family's old cabin as Lewis drove the car toward the Longs' home. "Oh, no, Missus Anna. When I moved to St. Louis, I didn't have a thought in my head except tryin' to feed my baby girl. Believe me, I had a long set of trials that had nothin' to do with hair tonic. I was still a washerwoman for the longest part of my life, Missus Anna. I wish the change hadn't come to me so late in life, I really do, but then again, I tell myself I should just be grateful it ever came. . . ."

For many years, Sarah reminded herself, she hadn't believed change would come at all.

Chapter Nine

As Sarah pulled her wooden cart over the ridges on Eads Bridge with a rhythmic *chunk-chunk* sound, the monotone note Lelia was holding with her voice wavered with every bump. Lelia's mouth was open in a yawning "O" to amuse herself as she rode in the cart. The Sunday morning light was faint, the air still hadn't lost its night chill, and only a handful of horse-drawn carriages made their way across the bridge alongside them, easily passing their pace. "Mama, you hear how funny that sounds?"

Seven-year-old Lelia was wrapped up in a thin coat and hat, sitting atop the covered crate of freshly pressed clothes Sarah had promised she would deliver to the home of Mrs. Elise Wainwright, who was hosting a breakfast and needed her tablecloths right away. Usually Sarah delivered Mrs. Wainwright's laundry in the afternoons, once church was finished, but the woman had insisted on having the clothes early today. She was one of Sarah's best customers, so Sarah didn't dare argue with her even though it would take her two hours to deliver the clothes, then walk back across the six-thousand-foot length of the bridge to St. Paul AME Church in time for the eight A.M. service. Never mind that she'd have to make the trip all over again to bring out her other Sunday-delivery clothes after church, once she finished pressing them. If Mrs. Wainwright had planned better and sent the tablecloths out for washing earlier, Sarah thought, she wouldn't have to do all this extra running around on the Lord's day.

"Wait, I'ma do it again!" Lelia said, and raised her voice into a droning *ooooooooohhhhhh* before Sarah could respond. As before, the bumps from the cart sliced into Lelia's voice, chopping it up. Sarah longed to tell Lelia to hush up, but she didn't. Why not let the child have some fun? No sense in both of them feeling miserable today. Besides, Sarah could remember the time when her own playful spirit struggled to find distraction in the monotony of a long working day. *Like playin' slave-kitcher with Lou*, she thought, and smiled.

The smile didn't stay on Sarah's lips long. Sarah hadn't seen her sister once in the five years since she'd left Vicksburg, and she missed her. The only responses Sarah received from the crudely written letters she sent to Lou were even more crudely written responses from Mr. William Powell, accusing her of owing him money. She crumpled his letters and tossed them away as soon as they reached her mailbox. The nerve of him! If he was going to take the time to write, at the very least he could bother to mention whether her sister and nephew were well.

Strangely enough, it was *Alex* Sarah had been in most contact with in the past few years. He was married now, with his own children, and he'd even visited her for three days last year with his young daughter, Anjetta, in tow. Sarah knew time had changed her appearance, too, but she'd still been shocked to see Alex for the first time since his departure when she was eight. He'd been little more than a boy when he left, but when he came to see her he'd been a thirty-three-year-old man with a slight paunch, a weathered face, and a recurring cough he blamed on the pipe smoking he'd taken up in Denver. Seeing his eyes reminded her of Papa for an eerie instant, but when she blinked he was only Alex again. He was still a porter and said he made a livable wage; they both laughed over his boyhood dreams of digging for gold in Indian country.

Alex's visit had been a blessing—and little Anjetta, who was younger than Lelia, had been a pure delight—but Sarah had felt a deep sense of sadness after she rode a streetcar with her brother to the train station and then watched him wave good-bye, feeling as if she no longer knew him. Would she ever see him again? Desperation had scattered all three of the Breedloves, and they had gone their own ways. Sarah felt the growing fear that time would keep pulling her and her sister apart until they could no longer remember facing the world together, on their own. *Maybe that's jus' what growin' up feels like*, Sarah thought, reflecting on her sister. But it gave her heart a dull ache just the same. No one was left. In some ways, she realized, Lelia was the only true family she had.

Riding behind Sarah in the cart, Lelia was laughing again in shrieks that seemed to bounce down to the water of the Mississippi River flowing wide beneath them. The sound of her daughter's mirth lifted Sarah's spirits, as it always did.

The Wainwrights lived in a two-story colonial-style house with regal columns at the end of a long block on a street in the midst of an affluent all-white area. The only Negroes who ventured into this neighborhood were domestics, like Sarah, easily recognizable from their maid uniforms, carriage-driver's caps, or baskets of laundry balancing on their heads. Today, dressed in a Sunday hat and her best gray fall church dress, with a real lace collar, Sarah felt like less of an intruder as she made her way along the well-kept street. She'd saved for eight months to buy the dress, and she felt reborn every time she wore it. In fact, she wouldn't be surprised if she was dressed better than Mrs. Wainwright herself this morning, which would be a rare pleasure.

Leaving Lelia in the cart at the end of the walkway, Sarah took the crate and carried it the last few feet to the steps leading to the Wainwrights' glossy-painted white double doors. Standing at her full height, Sarah knocked loudly to announce her arrival. Wouldn't Mrs. Wainwright think she was a sight!

But when Mrs. Wainwright opened the door and peered down at Sarah, she registered no notice of Sarah's Sunday dress. Her hair a bit unkempt, the woman barely looked at Sarah, hurriedly taking the crate. "Yes, it's about time. The guests will be here in two hours, you know," she snapped. "They're all pressed?"

"Yes'm," Sarah said.

Mrs. Wainwright opened the crate, peering down at the fabrics, and Sarah felt no nervousness about the inspection. She'd worked hard on these clothes, staying up half the night to have them finished, and she prided herself on doing good work, just as Miss Brown had taught her back in Vicksburg. Happy customers were loyal customers, she'd learned. They were also willing to pay a little more for the peace of mind that came from hiring a reliable worker.

Miss Wainwright's thin, pointed nose drew more closely to the pile of clothes. "What in heaven's name . . . ?" She flicked at the fabric with her finger, then gazed up at Sarah with unblinking eyes. "Is that *blood?*"

Sarah's heart stood still. Even Lelia, who had been chattering to herself in the cart on the walkway behind Sarah, fell silent.

"I'm talking to you, Sarah. Tell me what this is!"

Nervous and puzzled, Sarah took a step forward to gaze at the fabric Mrs. Wainwright was thrusting at her to examine. As Sarah moved closer to her, Mrs. Wainwright pulled her face back slightly, as if she expected Sarah to smell bad. Sarah's eyes studied a crescent-shaped dark spot that had been invisible to her from a greater distance; sure enough, it was brownish red, the color of blood, almost like a fingerprint.

Then, with a start, Sarah gazed at her fingernails. On her right hand, four fingernails were stained red beneath the nails. She tentatively sniffed at them, and the sharp scent *did* smell like blood! Then a flaring soreness on top of Sarah's scalp reminded her of where the blood had come from: Her head had been itching like the devil all night, and she must have scratched it while she slept until it bled. Why hadn't she noticed the blood before now? And how could she have allowed herself to muss Mrs. Wainwright's tablecloth? She must have been in such a hurry to finish, she hadn't washed her hands the way she usually did before folding the clothes!

To Sarah, it felt as if all color was draining from her face. Her ears were afire.

"Oh, Missus, I can 'splain . . ." she said, so mortified that her voice was whisper-soft.

"*Explain?*" Mrs. Wainwright repeated, staring at her with venom that made her eyes flare. "I have guests on the way as we speak, and you can *explain?* Yes, I'd like very much to know how I should explain how my nigger washerwoman wiped blood on my best tablecloth." Mrs. Wainwright's bottom lip was trembling from rage. Suddenly, as if something new occurred to her, she dropped the crate, spilling the folded clothes to the ground. "Oh, my— Does someone in your house have tuberculosis or cholera? Did they spit up on this?"

"N-no, ma'am," Sarah said earnestly, shaking her head. "It ain't like that. Ain't nobody sick in my house!"

At that, Mrs. Wainwright's eyelids fluttered and she let out a sound that resembled a startled scream. Frantically, she began to wipe her hands on her skirt. "I should have known better! You seemed so neat, not like the rest, but it's all in the papers how *filthy* niggers are. We're inviting nigger diseases right into our homes. And we were going to *eat* on that!" Tears sprang to her eyes. "Oh, my Lord, I think I'm going to faint!"

"I'se so sorry, M-Missus," Sarah said, flooded by equal parts of shame and outrage. "My head was itching me, that's all. Ain't no disease! Ain't n-nothin' like that—"

Suddenly Mrs. Wainwright's face contorted so severely that Sarah could barely recognize the woman standing before her as the polite, quiet client whose clothes she had washed for more than two years. "Get away from this house, you filthy nigger bitch!" she shrieked. Her features were pale from what looked like genuine terror.

In twenty-five years, Sarah didn't think she had ever hated herself and her life as much as she did at that instant. Why hadn't she washed her hands and checked her fingernails that morning? She had no one to blame but herself, and yet Mrs. Wainwright's words felt so unjust that she wanted to spring at her and choke the air from her lungs. She knew whites didn't care for colored folks much at all, except a select few, but she'd tried to convince herself she would change at least a handful of opinions if she conducted herself honestly and well. The Wainwrights had given her two extra dollars at Christmas, and had never given her a cross word. Had Mrs. Wainwright always considered her nothing more than a nigger who washed her clothes?

Sarah's heart ripped even further when she heard the sound of Lelia's muffled sob behind her. In these horrible moments, she had forgotten her daughter was there.

"Missus," Sarah said quickly, "I'se sorry 'bout that blood. My head was bleedin' las' night from where I itched it, an' I didn't know it. It's the worse thing I ever done since I been washin'. You know you been washin' with me all this time, an' ain't nothin' like this happen before. I own up when I done wrong." Sarah took a deep, trembling breath. "But you ain't got no call to talk to me like this in front of my li'l girl. You got no call."

Mrs. Wainwright's eyes narrowed as she stared at Sarah with disbelief. "What did you—"

"Axe yo'self how you would feel if I was you and you was me," Sarah said. "White or colored, you got young'uns, too, an' you know that ain't right."

Out of the corner of her eye, Sarah saw the woman's hand lash toward her, and Sarah caught her tiny wrist before her palm could reach her face. Sarah was *not* going to allow Lelia to see her mother's face slapped by this white woman, even if it meant going to jail. Sarah was strong enough to break Mrs. Wainwright's wrist in two if she wanted to; and from Mrs. Wainwright's eyes, she must have known that, too.

A man's voice came from one of the upstairs windows. "Elise . . . ? What's wrong?"

"Get your goddamn hands off me," the woman said, spittle flying from her mouth. Then she turned over her shoulder to shout for her husband, and Sarah instantly dropped the woman's shaking wrist. Leaving the pile of spilled-over clothes on the porch, Sarah walked quickly to her cart, took the rope she pulled it by, and began tugging her daughter away from the house. She was actually *fleeing*, she realized. Just like a criminal.

She could never come near this house again, she knew. She had been making at least six dollars a month washing clothes for the Wainwrights; through her own stupidity, she had just lost a quarter of her income, and with winter right around the corner. Despite her efforts to keep her emotions hidden for Lelia's sake, Sarah felt herself sobbing in a way she hadn't since Moses died. She could barely see through her tears.

"Mama, don't cry," Lelia begged after a moment, swallowing back her own tears for her mother's sake. "That's a stupid lady. You don't need her stinky clothes nohow."

This time, crossing the huge bridge to go back toward home, Lelia didn't sing a peep as the cart bumped across the cracks.

Sarah almost decided she wanted to go straight home, but as she hurried along Chestnut Street and approached Leffingwell, every step she took seemed to pull her closer to St. Paul A.M.E. Church. She'd had enough money to ride a streetcar up to the bridge on her way to Mrs. Wainwright's, but without her pay she didn't have enough to ride back, so she had no choice but to walk. Instead of feeling tired after walking more than twenty blocks just since crossing the bridge, Sarah felt herself waking up. She needed something at church today. She couldn't put what she needed into words, but the need was as real as the hot breath wheezing through her lungs. It wouldn't matter if her face was puffy from tears or if she was winded and sweating when she walked through those doors, she decided. She was going to church exactly as she'd planned.

When Sarah passed within a block of the grand stone structure of Union Station on Eighteenth Street, which was already hissing and clanging with life from arriving and departing trains, Sarah knew she had only about eight blocks more to go. Her face set in determination, she ignored the cramp in her arm from pulling Lelia behind her and walked faster, passing piles of barrels and large sacks on the sidewalk awaiting delivery, nodding at the colored hostlers tending the horses who pulled dray wagons and trolley cars along the city's streets, and avoiding muddy puddles that had gathered at dips in the road. Lelia, who was ordinarily full of excited observations during journeys through the city, remained noticeably silent.

Po' child, Sarah thought. *Guess she learnt 'bout colored an' white today.*

No white woman would ever speak to Lelia the way Mrs. Wainwright had spoken to her today, she vowed. Lelia was going to school, and Sarah was saving every spare cent she had in a mason jar to make sure she would go to college, too. Lelia wasn't going to be anybody's servant.

Finally St. Paul A.M.E. Church appeared at the corner, sunlight reflecting against the colorful stained-glass windows. Just the sight of the church made Sarah's heart float. As she got closer, she could hear the piano and organ playing inside, the voices of the congregation raised in song, and powerful clapping in rhythm to the music. The sound seeped through the walls and doors and onto the street; it spilled over Sarah like bright sunlight.

"Mornin', sister," the white-clad female usher said at the door, squeezing Sarah's hand with her delicate white glove. As Sarah made her way inside the church, which was packed tight with worshipers in the pews, she felt hands brush over her shoulders and arms, as if she were being bathed, accompanied by whispered greetings beneath the song:

"G'mornin', Missus McWilliams."

"Bless you, sister."

"It's all right, Sister Sarah, it's all right. You're home now."

Sarah's hat was slanted to one side, her nostrils were damp, and she felt large wet spots beneath her armpits and across her chest, marring her beautiful gray dress. But suddenly Sarah felt no concern at all about how she looked, enveloped in the love and song in the church. Her chin held high, Sarah joined the swaying and clapping of the other worshipers, feeling her spirit soar as if it no longer belonged to her alone, but to every other man, woman, and child in the room. Sarah's slightly flat voice was raised so loudly that she was nearly shouting the song "My Lord, What a Mornin'," and Lelia sang with growing rapture alongside her. As the congregation sang, their voices blended like a wind that lifted the entire room from the floor.

For the first time since her husband's death, Sarah felt true joy.

"If one o' those white bitches tried to hit *me*, it'd be the last time, too," Sarah's friend Sadie Jackson said, tugging on the pulley rigged between the trees in Sarah's backyard. Like Sarah, she had changed out of her church clothes and was now wearing a work dress and apron, with a white headwrap. As Sadie pulled, the row of hanging white shirts lurched closer to her so she could check them to see if they were dry. Ropes and pulleys were strung throughout the yard like Christmas-tree decorations, a system Sarah had devised and paid workmen to install so she could fulfill the next-day service claims that had helped her build her clientele in St. Louis.

When Sarah first arrived in the sprawling city, she'd walked from door to door with no luck attracting customers, who either said they already had someone washing for them or didn't want anyone. She couldn't even entice anyone by offering lower prices. The first two months, Sarah had felt so discouraged that she thought she and Lelia would starve just as Louvenia had warned. Many nights she'd had nothing more than warm milk for dinner. Only pride, not a lack of desperation, had kept Sarah from rooting through the garbage in search of food. The woman she roomed with at the time, who was a cook, finally began bringing her and Lelia table leavings from the white family she worked for to help her get by. Sarah had eaten cold rolls and half-eaten chicken parts with a glad and grateful heart.

Then Sarah had come up with an idea: She began offering a free washing with next-day service. A few people took advantage of her offer and then never used her services for pay, but several had been so impressed that they agreed to let her wash for them. Sadie, who had her own customers, worked with Sarah two days a week for extra money, sharing equally in profits for the work she did. Sadie hadn't been scheduled to work today, but Sarah pleaded with her to come home with her after church and help her because she was so far behind. Sadie was a few years older than Sarah, rounder in the hips, with two sons at home who were nearly grown. She had been reared in St. Louis and been schooled through high school, but she still hadn't been able to find any work other than washing.

"I wish you'd hush that cussing in front o' Lela," Sarah said crossly, casting a quick glance toward Lelia, who was on the back step dutifully folding clothes into a basket, the only part of the washing she enjoyed. The fascination Lela used to have for soapy water had worn off by the time she was five; now she hated to get her hands wet. "She done heard an earful from Missus Wainwright already."

"I tell you, she'd of lost that hand of hers. There's just somethin' *wrong* with folks who'll act like that on the Lord's day. Guess the day o' the week didn't make her no difference, since it don't sound like she had time for church. Not with all her *guests* on the way," Sadie said, imitating a genteel accent. Then she laughed.

Sarah sighed, shaking her head as she pulled flapping, dry linens from the line. She'd scrubbed her fingertips with a brush until they were raw to make sure she'd cleaned away the dried blood. "I brung it on my own self, Sadie. That blood skeered that woman half to death. You shoulda seed the way her eyes popped out."

"No, you didn't bring it on, not to be called no names like *that*. I'll never understand why white folks call *us* dirty, when you ain't never seen a sight so pitiful as a bunch o' raggedy poor white young'uns. They're so black from dirt they might as well be niggers."

"Oh, Sadie, stop," Sarah said, but she couldn't help laughing. All washerwomen avoided doing business with "white trash" families because they were notorious for not paying what they owed. Sadie had been shorted more than once, and complained about it loudly.

Sarah's yard was equipped with at least half a dozen tin washtubs, and there were more in her kitchen; she'd made them herself by sawing discarded kegs from nearby breweries in half. Because she had so many kegs, Sarah had enough tubs to keep the water at different temperatures while she washed, instead of having to wait for one tub to cool or emptying them out to fill them again once the water was dirty. Besides that, she was lucky enough that her house was in front of a city water pump, so she could fill buckets of water without even having to leave her yard.

Sarah lived in a squat one-story brick house not far from the church. She was fortunate to have the house, since it was the nicest she'd ever lived in; the street in front was paved, the house was fairly new, and the hardwood floors still had some shine left in them. Of all wonders, her landlord was a colored barber who attended St. Paul. He wasn't any less strict about getting his rent on time than a white landlord, but it tickled Sarah that in St. Louis she could buy her food at a colored grocer's and pay rent to a colored landlord who owned two or three houses on her street. There were even colored doctors, dentists, and attorneys about. Negroes in St. Louis were leaps ahead of Negroes in Vicksburg!

Unlike the Southern houses Sarah was used to, the kitchen was attached to the rest of the house, with a door leading to the backyard, so she never had to travel back and forth from the yard to the table in bad weather. The kitchen was even big enough for a table with four chairs, so that was where she and Lela entertained friends and ate in addition to doing the washing. There were three other rooms—the living room, the bedroom that was large enough to share with Lelia, and a small room off the kitchen her landlord had used for storage; Sarah had been cleaning it out for several weeks because she'd gotten permission to take on a boarder.

Boarding was another way to make extra money, and now that she'd lost Mrs. Wainwright, Sarah knew that finding a boarder would be more important than ever. That day, she'd posted hastily written notices at the church and at the market, advertising that the room would be available by the first of October. CLEEN AND PRYVAT, she'd written, relying on second-grade Lelia to check her spelling.

Something she'd done must have worked.

Sarah heard a rattle at her back fence and she looked up to see a tall, cinnamon-skinned woman standing just within her yard with a suitcase covered in colored stickers. And she wasn't just *any* woman; she was lovely despite the gaudy powder and colors she'd painted on her face. Her curled, shiny dark brown hair hung nearly to her shoulders, and she was wearing a dress that would have been remarkable even if it hadn't been a Sunday, since it clung to her so tightly and displayed the fleshy crack between her breasts at the low-cut neckline. Sadie and Lelia had also stopped working, simply staring.

"Mornin', ladies," the woman said in a singsong voice. No one answered her, but she went on anyway. "I hear there's a room for rent at this address. Is it still available?"

"It ain't ready 'til the first," Sarah said. Unless she was mistaken, she could smell the woman's sweetly scented toilet water even from several feet away. Sarah had seen self-directed, stylish women like this on St. Louis's streets much more often than she'd seen them in Vicksburg, but she'd never had a conversation with anyone like her. She wasn't like the women she'd known who worked in the fields and washed clothes, and she wasn't like the fancy colored women at church, either. She was a different breed entirely. There was something worldly and intriguing about her, although Sarah could already feel her friend bristling beside her.

"Well, a bed's all I need, if you've got one. I'll pay full rent, ready or not," the woman said. Again, she almost seemed to *sing* her words. Where had she learned to speak like that?

Sadie pulled at Sarah's arm. "Sarah . . ." she whispered urgently, scolding.

"Yeah, I gots a bed," Sarah answered the stranger, ignoring Sadie. "Room's full of dust, though. An' I ain't swept up the flo' proper yet."

The woman laughed, flinging her arm dramatically in the air. "Oh, it takes more than a little dust to bother me. Do I get meals, too?"

"The rent 'cludes breakfast an' supper both. One at seven, one at six."

Again the woman laughed merrily. "Oh, I'm rarely up for breakfast! But I do like a home-cooked supper now and again. Is four dollars a month enough?"

"*No*," Sadie spoke up suddenly, and Sarah gave her a harsh look.

"Well, how about six, then? I'd like a quiet room, and this street's quiet as can be."

"That's 'cause there's decent folks on this street," Sadie said.

This time Sarah pinched her friend on the soft of her arm to hush her up. Six dollars a month! Would this woman really be willing to pay six dollars a month just for a tiny room, a meal, and a bed? "Here, lemme show you," Sarah said, straightening up and wiping her hands on her apron. "It's right on through the kitchen . . . Miss . . . ?"

"Just Etta," the woman said, shrugging girlishly. "Everybody calls me Etta."

"I bet that ain't *all* they call you . . ." Sadie muttered just within Sarah's hearing, and Sarah hoped Etta hadn't heard the rude remark, too.

Lelia was frozen on the back step, gazing up at Etta with wide eyes. She and her basket sat directly in their path. "Well, who's this princess?" Etta said, stooping over before Sarah could ask her daughter to move. "Ain't you about the most darling little thing I've ever seen?"

Lelia grinned so wide that Sarah thought her daughter's lips might crack from the strain.

"Go on, girl, let us by," Sarah told Lela.

Instead of moving, Lelia blurted out, "Is that yo' *real* hair?" Sarah thought she would choke from the boldness of her daughter's question. She was curious about the woman's long tresses, too, and on closer examination she'd decided Etta must be wearing a wig.

"Oh, it's somebody's real hair, child. Is that good enough for you? I got it straight out of a mail-order catalog and paid for it with my own money. You wanna touch it?"

Lela nodded eagerly. She reached upward, allowing strands of Etta's silky hair to fall between her fingers. Sarah had to fight the urge to ask to touch it, too. Just thinking about *hair* made her scalp itch again beneath her head-wrap. How much would a wig like that cost?

Lela pointed at Etta's timeworn suitcase. "What's that stuck all over your bag?"

"Well, I keep a memento of every place I've been! You see this one here? That's from New York City. I just come from there. I been all the way to San Francisco, California. I been so many places 'til my head is spinning, and now all I want is my own bed." Etta stretched her hand out to Lelia. "Why don't you show me my new room, honey?"

Much to Sarah's amazement, Lela stood up and clasped the stranger's hand, still studying her with shining eyes. Lela was far from shy, but she had a tendency to be reserved with people she didn't know. Lela had extended Etta her instant friendship. Behind her, Sarah heard Sadie suck on her teeth with irritation.

"It's close to the kitchen, so it keeps plenty warm!" Lelia told the woman brightly.

"Oh, is that so?" Etta said, and she winked at Sarah over her shoulder with her thick black eyelashes. Sarah had seen plenty of men wink, but never a woman. The gesture looked bawdy, giving her pause. But then

Sarah was drawn to the sincerity of the woman's private gaze. "Something tells me you have big plans for this one, huh, Mama?"

"God's my witness," Sarah told her.

"Well, a little extra money never hurts."

"Sho' don't," Sarah said. Six dollars a month would make up for the loss of Mrs. Wainwright. She might actually be able to cut back on her washing and finally start going to night school like she wanted to; her reading and writing skills had diminished since the days in Miss Dunn's class in Vicksburg, and Sarah was embarrassed to see her young daughter's skills already beginning to surpass her own.

She prayed Etta would like the unfinished room.

"Now, I didn't ask *your* name," Etta said to Sarah in that engaging, syrupy voice of hers.

"Sarah McWilliams," Sarah told her quickly. "I'm a widow."

"Ain't we all, honey?" Etta said with a small smile, and her tone offended Sarah at first because she wondered if Etta thought she was like scores of colored women who'd lived with men for a time and then called themselves *widows* when their men moved away. But Etta's smile slowly faded until Sarah saw a gleam of sadness in her eye. "Ain't we all."

At that, Sarah's doubts vanished.

Chapter Ten

"What 'chu said this stuff is called, Etta?" Sarah stared with curiosity at the pasty, clear jelly from a small jar that Etta had smeared on her fingers as they sat at the kitchen table. Sarah sniffed her fingers. No scent. But she'd seen Etta using it before, rubbing it on her kneecaps and elbows to soften them. It had caught her eye, so she'd asked Etta to bring her a jar.

It was after noon, and Etta had just emerged from her bedroom in her wide-sleeved muslin nightgown, her hair bunched beneath a stocking and her face clean of powder or rouge. She'd lived with Sarah for two years before going to New York to work for a year, and it had been a year since her return. Since she'd been back, Etta routinely slept until two or three in the afternoon and stayed out all night long, as far as Sarah could tell. Sarah often thought she heard telltale sounds in the kitchen just before dawn, and she hoped her daughter hadn't noticed Etta's late arrivals, too. What kind of example was that for a girl Lelia's age? Etta had never, *ever* brought a man to the house, at least as far as Sarah knew, but the thought of the peril to her reputation alarmed her.

That morning, Etta stretched her thin arms high above her head, waking herself up before she answered Sarah's question: "The drummers along the levee—the traveling salesmen, I mean—call that stuff rod wax." She yawned. "I've heard it called Cosmoline, Vaseline, all kinds of names. They use it to grease up everything, rub it on cuts or burns. I knew some showgirls in New York using it to make their hair shine. Also keeps dandruff from showing, they say."

"Well, shoot, maybe I kin grease up my head, too, stop all my itchin'," Sarah said.

"Worth a try," Etta said.

Gazing at the jelly, Sarah wondered if it might have any softening qualities. She occasionally ran a fork she'd heated on the stove through Lelia's hair the way her mother used to with her own hair, but Sarah had never been satisfied with the results. A hot fork untangled the hair *some*, but Lelia complained that her hair broke off too easily. She'd tried softening Lelia's hair with lard, too, but that stank and seemed to damage her hair. This new jelly was certainly something to think about! As usual, Sarah found herself delighted by a novelty Etta had brought into her house, like bottles of a sweet, delicious extract called root beer she mixed up in five-gallon tubs to drink, chocolate-cream candies, and exotic soaps that smelled of coconut. *Ain't nothin' like bein' lucky 'nough to travel all over an' see all kinds o' things*, Sarah thought.

"Thank you, Etta," Sarah said, deeply grateful, but she was still troubled by questions of how Etta spent her nights. The subject had come up between them before, and Etta's only explanation had been: *Tell you what, Sarah, honey—you don't ask me questions about things you don't really want to know, and I won't ever shame this doorstep.*

But was that enough? There was Lelia to think about, after all. Lelia adored Etta, eager to hear about her travels and the people she met listening to ragtime music in the Chestnut Valley saloons. Even though Sarah would hate to say it to her friend's face, Etta was not the sort of woman she would want her daughter to be like.

Etta was a dancer by training—a good one, too, Sarah knew from private performances for her and Lela in the front room—and she'd spent several months dancing in a musical show called *Oriental America* in Palmer's Theatre on Broadway. Oh, the stories she'd told when she came back! She'd described the dancers, the singers, the actors, and how all of them had performed for white audiences and gotten written up in the newspapers. *Big-time*, Etta had called it. When she came back to St. Louis, exhausted but happy, she'd breathlessly told them she would be packing her things for good soon because she expected a letter at any time inviting her to dance in the next big show. But no letter had ever arrived for her from New York.

"You ain't heard nothin' from New York?" Sarah asked her again, to be sure.

"You know better than that, Sarah McWilliams. It sounds like you're trying to get rid of me," Etta said, looking Sarah squarely in the eye. "And besides that, I'll tell you the plain truth: Whether it's Broadway palaces or vaudeville houses or even little ol' gin mills, nobody wants brown-skinned dancers. Yellow girls, Sarah—that's all they're after. The lighter the better. Even with my gingerbread skin, I was the darkest girl in my line. That's why I never heard from nobody in New York, and I never will."

Sarah didn't know if she was more upset by the injustice of Etta's words or the nonchalance in her voice. Did that mean she had already given up?

"I ain't tryin' to git rid of you, Etta," Sarah began, hearing Lelia's voice reminding her that it was proper to say *get*, not *git*, even as she spoke the word. "I'm tryin' to help is all."

"Well, some things can't be helped," Etta said with a small shrug. Her eyes drifted, and she smiled. "I know I must tire you out talking about *Oriental America*, but there wasn't anything else like it, Sarah. Black folks on *Broadway*, an' Sissieretta Jones up there singing arias—that's a kind of opera, like I told you before—and I can't even describe the sound of her voice, not in words. She's like an angel, a black angel, as good as *any* white singer. They thought they were coming to a minstrel show to make fun of us running around in blackface paint, but they couldn't in the end. Know why? Because we were *good*, that's why. We took their breath away. They clapped until it sounded like the roof was falling in."

Etta's chest had heaved up high while she spoke, and then she sighed luxuriously, awash in her memories. "And I was *there*—I was a part of it. I'd be a fool not to know it was the highest moment of my life, and I can't spend the rest of my days trying to match something that's come and gone. So I've moved on, and my work now has gotten me through hard times."

In St. Louis, colored men, and even white men, had boldly offered Sarah money on the street if she would "go to their room" or "keep them company," as they put it, until she'd gotten to the point where she kept her eyes cast down when she walked past Union Station or ventured to a new part of town. Even their spoken offers had made her feel sullied; or maybe it was simply knowing she would have done just about anything for money—except *that*. But some days, if she was honest, she might have wished she could.

"Seem like poison to me," Sarah said.

"Oh, yes, it sure can be." Etta nodded solemnly.

Sarah reached across the table and squeezed Etta's hand. Maybe, she thought, something about Etta reminded her of Lou. Her sister had kept company with so many men in Vicksburg, she might have easily walked down the same path if Mr. William Powell hadn't married her when he did, Sarah thought. How could a woman with Etta's intelligence and education have fallen so low? Sarah was convinced Etta was a good woman despite her faults, even if Sadie couldn't see it and the other church ladies wouldn't understand.

"Etta, even washin's better'n what you do."

Etta's face hardened, and she shook her head. "No disrespect, Sarah, but I watched my mama bend over a washtub 'til the day came she could barely walk. You . . ." She stopped herself, sighing. "I won't tell you how to live your life, but I can't do what you do. That's some foolish damn pride, I know, but I can't. So I am what I am. I may not be proud of it, but at least I don't have to drink myself to sleep every night to live with it. Whiskey and cigarettes age you, and I plan on staying young as long as I can." Etta laughed then, sounding more like herself. Her voice brightened. "Hey, look here, there's no man or madam standing over me taking my money like most of those silly girls out there. One day I'll have my money saved up, I'll buy myself a house, take in my own boarder, and my work's done. Now, would you mind fixing a wayward girl a cup of coffee? I need to wake up these bones."

"You goin' to hell, Etta, you keep this up," Sarah said earnestly. She'd wanted to say those words to Etta for a long time, and she felt both sadness and relief when she did.

"Maybe so, but I ain't going today. Any biscuits left, Sarah?"

"Not none that ain't hard as a rock. What you think? It's closer to supper than breakfast."

There was a knock on the back door. Sarah thought it was Lelia coming home from school and wondered why she was knocking, but when the door opened, Sadie peeked her head in. She had a folded newspaper in her hand. Sadie grinned at Sarah, but the grin faded when she saw Etta sitting at the table. "Lord have mercy . . ." Sadie clucked, examining Etta's nightclothes. "If I ain't seen everything now, there ain't nothin' left I need to see. Look at you, late as it is."

Etta dismissed Sadie with a fling of her head. "Afternoon, Miz Sadie. Didn't your mama ever teach you if you can't say anything nice, you shouldn't speak at all?"

"Miz Etta, I don't think you want to hear what your mama should've taught *you*."

The habitual insults between Sadie and Etta usually began with good humor, but Sarah knew it wouldn't take much to spark either lady's temper. She flicked a wood match to light the firewood inside the belly of her stove. "All right, now, both of y'all hush. Sadie, come on in. I'm jus' heatin' some coffee."

"Oh, I just brought over the newspaper to show you. You heard about this Plessy case in New Orleans? They're tryin' to take us right back to slavery days."

"What's this . . . ?" Etta said, reaching for the paper.

"Right there on the front, that case called *Plessy versus Ferguson*. A colored man tried to ride in a white train car and got thrown in jail."

"Ain't that some foolishness?" Etta said. "Now, in New York—"

"You hush, we don't want to hear any more damn stories about New York," Sadie silenced her. "Anyway, Sarah, the highest court there is, the Supreme Court, ruled Homer Plessy didn't have no right to ride on that train. Negroes can be kept separate from whites as long as they're 'equal,' so they say. You remember how Georgia started segregating its streetcars? They're gonna try the same thing here and everywhere else. Just wait. In eighty-nine, Missouri already said whites can only go to school with whites, and colored only with colored. And we all know equal don't mean equal. They're gonna separate us right back to the plantation. Next thing you know, lynching a nigger won't even be a crime."

As she read the newspaper, Etta's brow was creased with a worry that was unlike her. Watching, Sarah envied how well Etta could read; Sarah struggled over a newspaper now and again with Lelia's help, but her reading was still poor and she hadn't gone back to school the way she'd planned. Both of her closest friends could read to her when she needed it, but it just wasn't the same as casually reading the paper herself. It took her so much time to get through one story, she couldn't sit the whole day trying to finish the rest.

"Nobody's treating it like a crime now," Etta muttered in agreement. "Those mobs are running around, and they don't do anything about it."

"Sho' don't," Sarah said. "It's like my husband use to say, things ain't gettin' better, seem like they gettin' worse. An' he 'bout got lynched jus' for sayin' *that*. Makes me so damn mad sometimes I jus' wanna . . ." But she couldn't finish, because once she opened that floodgate of rage, it was hard to shut it. She had too much work left today for that. Etta reached across the room to where Sarah stood at the stove, squeezing her hand.

"Man told the truth, Sarah," Sadie said.

"Yes, he did," Etta added. "There's some hard days for Negroes ahead. No doubt."

At that there was silence in the kitchen. Sarah felt a hopelessness welling inside of her, reminding her of a painful shame so deep she hadn't dared reveal it even to her friends: Lou had sent word that her son, little Willie, had been sent to prison for manslaughter! The boy was only fourteen years old, and Lou said he might spend the rest of his life at Parchman State Farm in Mississippi. Sarah still couldn't believe it. She did not know her nephew well enough to say for certain whether he could be guilty; but she was certain he had not received a fair trial. What poor colored boy in Mississippi could?

Sarah hoped Sadie was wrong about what Mr. Plessy's case might mean for Negroes, but she couldn't ignore her growing feeling that as the days of Reconstruction drew further behind them, Negroes would face more hardships from whites. They weren't still slaves, but they were a long way from truly free.

It was 1896, Sarah thought with some disbelief, only four years from the year 1900. Here she was coming up on a new century, and she was still washing clothes just as she had been since almost the time she could walk. Just like her mother and grandmother had before her, and maybe even her great-grandmother before that.

Sarah was proud of her business, which had kept her so busy she hadn't had time to catch her breath, and she'd even paid a painter to make a neatly lettered sign for her front window—MISS SARAH'S LAUNDRY—NEXT-

DAY SERVICE—which made her beam every time she walked past it. Like Miss Brown, she even had a lady or two, including Sadie, who came to work for her on a part-time basis when she needed extra help.

But washing was washing. Her joints still ached, her fingers and hands still shriveled like prunes after being in water all day, and she still singed herself on those hot irons, just like always. Was she only fooling herself to think she could give Lelia anything better? And to think Moses had not died for nothing, in the end? The idea of it filled Sarah with a terror that she knew would make it hard for her to go to sleep that night.

"You've got a look on your face to beat the devil, Sarah. What're you thinkin' about?" Sadie asked her.

Sarah didn't hear her friend's question immediately. "Jus' the future, that's all," Sarah said softly. "Thinkin' 'bout the future."

"Yeah," Etta said, folding the newspaper. "We'd better all start thinking about *that*."

The small, square piece of plywood had been waiting for a practical use in the backyard for weeks, and Sarah nailed it up on the wall in the bedroom she shared with Lelia, then stood back to decide whether she'd nailed it straight or crooked. Then she scrubbed at a muddy spot in the corner with a rag until it was clean. She was tired and ready for bed, but her mind was abuzz the way she remembered it had often been when she was a child, and the way it had been when she'd been designing her laundry pulleys. She knew she couldn't rest until she was finished.

"Mama, what is *that*?" Lelia said, standing in the doorway. She would be eleven years old in less than a month, on June 6, and she was only half a foot shorter than Sarah, with sturdy limbs. Year after year, Lelia's use of language became more precise and practiced. She constantly brought home grammar corrections from her teacher, and she had tried to ban Sarah's use of words like *ain't*, *cain't*, and *axe*. ("My teacher says an axe is what you chop wood with," she'd told Sarah many times.) Sarah even noted that Lelia had adopted a few of Etta's mannerisms, imitating their boarder's stage-influenced speech patterns, too.

"A Wish Board," Sarah said, thinking of the name as she spoke.

"But it's ugly! How come we can't have pretty pictures in here like in Miz Etta's room?"

"Because this ain't . . . isn't . . . s'posed to be purty, that's why. It's for wishin'."

"Wishing for what?"

"Fo' whatever we want," Sarah told her. "Don't you got nothin' you wanna wish for?"

"Plenty!" Lelia said, bounding beside Sarah to gaze up at the board. "How do we do it?"

Sarah smiled. "Easy. We take pitchers an' stick 'em up on the board. Then we look at 'em ev'ry day 'til we figger out how to git 'em."

"*Get*," Lelia corrected her. "It's an E, not an I."

"*Get*," Sarah repeated, mostly to humor her daughter, but in part because she enjoyed the coaching. After a while, she figured, she would start remembering Lelia's lessons on her own, and she wouldn't feel so self-conscious around the more refined women in her church. She hardly wanted to open her mouth in their presence. "Now, the first thing I'ma do is draw me a pitcher of a schoolhouse, 'cause I'm goin' to night school like I been sayin'. I'ma take me some bizness classes. An' I have to look at it ev'ry day 'til I do it. Now you can wish for somethin', too."

Lelia bit her lip, considering her wishes with wide, shining eyes. "Can I use Miz Etta's Sears and Roebuck pictures of pretty clothes and hats and gold necklaces?"

"If she say you can."

Lelia squealed, sounding exactly as she'd always sounded as a much younger child. "Ooh, Mama, I like this Wish Board! Who told you about it?"

"Ain't nobody tole me. I jus' made it, that's all."

Sarah was warmed by the raw admiration in her daughter's eyes. She'd seen it often when Lelia was young, but these days most of Lelia's admiration was saved for Etta. Sarah hated feeling envious of her well-traveled friend, but sometimes she did. "How do you always know how to make things, Mama?" Lelia asked. Her straight permanent front teeth gleamed white, making her look even more like a little adult.

"Guess God must be whisperin' in my ear," Sarah said, gently tugging Lela's earlobe.

"What's he saying?" Lela whispered.

"Well, first thing . . . he's sayin' we gots lots of wishes to make."

"What else?" Lela giggled.

"Well . . . next thing . . . he's sayin' I best take this jar of rod wax Miz Etta done give me an' scratch out yo' head 'fore you go to sleep."

At that, Lelia's expression soured. She hated to sit still for her mother to scratch the dandruff out of her scalp. Sarah was nearly religious about the ritual, hoping Lelia would have healthier hair that would grow longer than hers. Sarah was eager to try Miz Etta's newest gift on her own hair and scalp after Lela went to sleep. "God didn't say that!"

"Sho' did. Go fetch me the comb."

That night, sitting by candlelight at the edge of the bed with Lelia between her knees, Sarah carefully parted small segments of Lela's hair, scratched out the white flakes of dandruff, then dabbed the glistening rod wax on the scalp with her fingertips. The jelly made Lela's brown scalp shine, and Sarah smiled. *We gon' try this with a hot fork next fo' sho'*, she thought.

"Can I say my wishes, Mama?"

"You can say 'em, but they don't count 'til they up on the Wish Board."

"Well, I want a house with a big, big kitchen for your washtubs. . . . An' I want pretty clothes like Miz Etta, a whole wardrobe so full it can't shut. Oh! An' I want a puppy."

"A puppy, too? We ain't gon' have room on one board for all yo' wishes, girl."

"Yes, we will!" Lelia said, and she continued reciting her list, counting off the endless things she wanted on her fingers while Sarah scratched her head.

Scratch-scratch. Dab. Scratch-scratch. Dab.

Working into the night, Sarah couldn't have guessed how much closer petrolatum and pure imagination would bring her and her daughter to their wishes, after all.

Chapter Eleven

Sarah was so nervous that she could barely keep from fidgeting in the plush cushioned mahogany chair. She folded and unfolded her hands in her lap, stealing quick glances around the pristine parlor so she could remember the details to share with Lelia and Etta when she got back home. The towering grandfather clock was so tall it nearly touched the ceiling! And all the books! One entire wall was nothing but neatly shelved books, within easy reach of an elegant foot-ladder. This was the parlor of Josephine Parkerson, one of the richest colored women in St. Louis, and certainly the richest colored woman Sarah had ever met. Sadie had whispered to Sarah at church one day that the Parkersons were worth two hundred thousand dollars. And Mrs. Parkerson would be back soon to serve her a cup of peppermint tea!

Sarah's heart pounded. Who would have imagined?

Quickly, Sarah checked her dress to make sure it wasn't wrinkled and hadn't hiked up above her knees when she sat down, then she patted her head-wrap to secure it in place. She might be the most ragged-looking guest to ever sit in this chair, she thought. When she'd made the decision to walk past the Parkersons' high, clipped hedges bordering their walkway and knock on their door, she'd never expected to be invited inside. She was taking a collection for her first charitable work with the church's Mite Missionary Society, which she had joined days before.

One of Sarah's first acts since nailing up her Wish Board a little more than a week ago had been to pursue her longtime desire to get more closely involved with her church. *Sho' was a pow'rful wish*, she thought. *I'm here bein' social with Josephine Parkerson, when she ain't so much as said boo to me 'fore today.*

"Here we are . . ." the woman said, and she seemed to glide into the room with her buffed sterling silver tea service, which she set down on the table beside Sarah. Mrs. Parkerson was a pale-skinned mulatto in her forties, with streaks of gentle gray in the hair that was swept dramatically atop her head. "I'm sorry I was so long, Mrs. McWilliams. My help is off today, so I had to dither around in there for it myself."

"Don't vex me none," Sarah said, trying to match her gracious tone. But her words felt flat and heavy, and Sarah suddenly wished she had paid better attention to Lela's corrections. How could she have imagined herself in this situation? After Mrs. Parkerson filled her teacup from a daintily curved spout, Sarah reached for the cup with slightly trembling fingers.

"You were saying earlier, dear?" Mrs. Parkerson said, her face rapt. "Something you read in the newspaper . . . ?"

Don't say ain't. Don't say cain't. Don't say axe. "Yes'm," Sarah said, her throat dry. She sipped quickly from her cup, and was dismayed to hear herself make a slurping sound. She fumbled for acceptable language. "I done read it in the *St. Louis Post-Dispatch.*" Mrs. Parkerson nodded with eager recognition, apparently a *Post-Dispatch* reader herself, though Sarah doubted this woman needed help from her ten-year-old daughter to read the more difficult words. "See, I done read 'bout this po' colored man, an' he havin' some hard, hard times 'cause he got a blind sister an' a invalid wife, and they both dependin' on him."

Invalid. That printed word had confused Sarah at the table that morning, and she pronounced it with special care. Mrs. Parkerson's face fell with genuine concern, so Sarah felt encouraged. "Yes, ma'am, it's a real shame, ai—isn't it?"

"Oh, yes."

"So since I done joined the Missionary Society, I said my first order o' bizness is to try to do fo' folks who's got even less than me. An' it sound like that man sho' do, ma'am. So I figger I'ma go *asssk* all my friends an' other church members, an' see if I can't raise them some money."

"Well, that's a good deal of initiative on your part, Mrs. McWilliams," the woman said.

"Yes, ma'am," Sarah said, though she would have been hard-pressed to define the word *initiative*. It seemed to her that it meant the same thing as *determination*, but she wasn't sure.

Mrs. Parkerson leaned slightly closer to Sarah, lowering her voice. "I hope you don't mind me asking this, Mrs. McWilliams, but . . . when did you learn to read? Weren't you bonded when you were born?"

"Ma'am . . . ?"

"Weren't you born a slave?"

Sarah saw something vibrant and curious in Mrs. Parkerson's eyes, and for an uncomfortable instant it reminded her of the way Lelia's face had brightened when she'd taken her daughter fishing and Lelia finally pulled a trout out of the water. Had Mrs. Parkerson invited her inside as a guest or as a curiosity? But before Sarah would allow herself to get irritated, she decided she would assume the best of the woman and answer her questions honestly.

"No, ma'am, I was born in sixty-seven, two years after the war. But I still been strugglin' with my readin', though. I took a class down in Vicksburg to git where I'm at now, but I done signed up for night school classes in June 'cause I gots a long way yet to go. I'ma take some bizness classes, too, see, 'cuz I gots a laundry bizness. I ain't no way rich, but I makes 'nuff to tuck away so's I kin send my daughter to college when she gits older. An' she don't 'member one single day goin' without no food, neither, so she better off than me already."

"A-men," Mrs. Parkerson said, her face lighting up, and she clapped her hands together. "Well, praise the Lord! That's wonderful, Mrs. McWilliams. Just wonderful!"

"Was there slaves in yo' family, ma'am?" Sarah decided it was her turn to ask questions.

"Oh, no, Mrs. McWilliams, I've been very fortunate. My grandmother was a Virginia slave, but my parents were born free. So were my husband's. Believe me, I know the advantages we've had, and I thank the Lord every day. My husband got both his cattle-shipping business and his training from his father, and I know there aren't many Negroes who can say the same."

"No, ma'am," Sarah said.

"It's women like you who are the future of the race, Mrs. McWilliams," the woman said, her voice so full of emotion that Sarah was startled. "People who came from nothing and build good lives for their children, with education as the basis. It's that simple, really. I believe in us, you know. There are always unfortunate factors to point to, but I believe in us with all my heart."

"Yes, ma'am," Sarah said. "Else there ain't no reason to git up in the mornin' an' stoop over them tubs all day."

"Amen," Mrs. Parkerson said. The woman sipped from her teacup in silence, and Sarah noted the odd way she held her pinky away from the cup. Now this was a true lady, Sarah thought. How many hundreds and thousands of things did Josephine Parkerson know about the world that Sarah would never even learn? "Mrs. McWilliams, you've been noticed at the church," the woman said suddenly. "Your industry. Your good nature. Some members remember you when you were all but destitute, and you've come so very far. That's why I welcomed a chance to talk to you today."

"Yes, ma'am," Sarah said, surprised.

"I'll give you a dollar to help the poor man you read about in the newspaper. But I'd like to also give you something else, if I may . . . and that's a gentle word of advice. There are those who would call me bold, and I hope you won't take offense."

"No, ma'am," Sarah said. "I ain't learned nothin' in life 'cept by either seein' it my own self or somebody tellin' me first."

"Good," Mrs. Parkerson said. But her smile, this time, was thin. "Somehow or other, Mrs. McWilliams, there has been talk that you've made at least some part of your living by some means other than washing. By that, I mean to say, by means that are less than reputable."

Sarah felt her joints stiffen. Mrs. Parkerson could not have shocked her more if she'd suddenly thrown her hot cup of tea into her face. When she didn't speak, the woman went on: "I've been the subject of idle talk in my own past, so I'm never one to give such talk much credence. But if you do have any undesirable associations, it's best to learn this now rather than later—in certain circles, Mrs. McWilliams, whether justly or unjustly, one is most often judged by one's associations. I'm almost certain you'll find the waters here a bit easier to navigate if you always bear that in mind. Do you understand what I'm telling you?"

Her tone was gentle, even kind, but embarrassment burned on Sarah's face, and her eyes flitted around the room for something to gaze at besides the face of her hostess. "Oh, yes, ma'am," Sarah said hoarsely. "I don' know what—"

Mrs. Parkerson patted her hand. "No need to feel ill at ease, Mrs. McWilliams. I just thought it best to advise you. I'm very fond of your landlord, and while I don't think he's been privy to the same suppositions, it could be very unfortunate for you if he ever were. As I said, I've learned better than to pay any mind to idle talk. But he may feel differently, you see."

"Yes, ma'am. Thank you, ma'am," Sarah said dumbly. To her, it felt as if her friend Etta were sitting in the parlor with them, her face covered in paint, her lips drawn up in a lascivious smile. As though Mrs. Parkerson could see her there plain as day.

The next morning dawned with thick, dark clouds, matching Sarah's mood. She'd barely slept that night, puzzling over the dilemma Mrs. Parkerson had laid at her feet. What could she do about Etta? Lelia loved Etta like an aunt. Besides, Etta had been a good and loyal friend for four years, keeping Sarah's spirits up with her wit and stories, sometimes even paying her rent in advance when Sarah was in a fix. If only other people could get to know Etta the way Sarah did, if they could talk to her . . .

But Sarah knew better than that. A whore was a whore, folks would say. She'd been a fool to rent Etta a room in the first place, and a bigger fool to grow to care about her so much. From now on, she would have to be much more careful about her *associations*, she thought, noting Mrs. Parkerson's word.

How could she ever ask Etta to leave? But how could she not?

Bleary-eyed, Sarah climbed out of bed before dawn, dressed in the near darkness without waking Lela, and began heating the tub of water she'd left waiting on the stove in the kitchen. Once the fire was burning hot, she shuffled outside into the warm summer air to check on the dozens of clothes hanging on the lines in her backyard.

As usual, working made Sarah feel better because it kept her mind occupied. Her whole life, it seemed, she'd always had plenty of work to keep her from dwelling on her misery. There were times work had been her best friend, and today was one of those times. Sarah was concentrating so hard on the clothes, testing them for dampness and collecting the ones that were dry, that she barely noticed the sunlight growing brighter through breaks in the clouds.

Then, from the house, Sarah heard the unmistakable sound of her daughter's scream.

The shrill, terrified sound pierced Sarah's skin, bones, blood, and heart. She'd never heard Lelia make that sound; it came from the house like a chilling promise that nothing in her life would ever be the same again. Sarah dropped the clothes in her hands and nearly stumbled over her basket as she ran toward the kitchen door. "Lela!" she shouted.

The scream came again. This time Sarah heard something else inside the house: the low timbre of a strange man's voice.

Her eyes wild, Sarah flung the kitchen door open and barely had time to grasp what she saw: Lela was standing on one side of the table, her arms wrapped around herself to cover her near nakedness in the thin slip she slept in during the summer. And on the other side of the table, not even three feet from Lela, stood a hulking white man in a half-buttoned shirt and trousers. His head, face, and chest were covered in wiry red hair. Seeing him, Sarah let out an outraged cry.

"Okay, now hold on there—" the man began in an accented voice, maybe German. He took a step toward Sarah with a grim smile.

Sarah's instincts acted where her thoughts failed. Her hands flew to the stovetop, grasping the hot handles of the tub heating there, and she had all but lifted it to heave at the intruder when she realized that someone, not Lelia, was screaming her name.

"Sarah, *no! Don't*, Sarah!" It was Etta, wearing a ruffled nightgown, her face drawn with alarm. She stood between Sarah and the stranger. "Put it down! Please, Sarah."

Sarah's bare palms flared with pain, but she didn't let go of the tub's hot handles. She turned around to look at Lela. "He touched you?" she demanded of her frightened daughter.

Wide-eyed, Lela shook her head. "I j-just got up, and this m-man was here—"

"Come on, now. I never laid a finger on her, Auntie. I was on my way—" the white man began, and Sarah cast him such a poisonous look that his tongue fell silent.

"I ain't axed you. You jus' hush," Sarah hissed at him, and she turned her eyes back to Lela, who appeared to be calming. "You tellin' the truth, Lela? He ain't touched you?"

Lela's head bounced up and down as she nodded. "It's the truth, Mama. He only scared me."

For the first time since she'd heard the scream, Sarah felt herself breathe. She quickly pulled her hands away from the washtub, rubbing her singed palms and fingers on her skirt. Her joints were shaking, and she felt weak at the knees. "Git on outta here," she told Lela. "Go back in the room, put on yo' clothes. Don't come out 'til I say."

"Yes'm," Lela said, staring at the floor, and she ran out of the kitchen.

Next, Sarah turned her gaze back to the stranger, who was hastily buttoning his shirt. His smile, which had vanished when he'd seen the tub of water, slowly crept back to his ruddy lips. "See here, this is all a misunderstanding. I was on my way out—"

"An' that's where you best git to," Sarah said, glaring. " 'Fore I change my mind."

The man sighed, glancing back at Etta. Then he stooped over and kissed Etta's mouth, wrapping his arm around her waist. " 'Bye, sweetheart," Sarah heard him say.

But Etta didn't even look at him, Sarah could see. Etta's eyes were locked on hers.

After the man was gone, taking with him his scent of cigarettes, liquor, and perspiration, Sarah and Etta stood frozen in a silence so oppressive it could have made the room shrink. By now Sarah was breathing hard, her mind careening as she tried to make sense of the morning. A part of her was still struggling to believe what she had seen. In that one instant, believing a white man had come into her home and touched her daughter, Sarah had felt as if she had become someone new. She could easily have become a murderer.

"This may not help . . ." Etta began slowly in a soft voice, her eyes red from lack of sleep and sadness, ". . . but he's not a customer. His name is Gregor, and he's a friend. In all the time I've lived here, Sarah, I have never once entertained a man in my room, not until last night. I have too much respect for you. But last night I had a sip too much wine. I know I shouldn't have, and I know it was wrong. I'll tell Lela he was—"

"You ain't got to tell Lela a goddamn thing," Sarah said, speaking at last. The murderer she had very nearly become was still alive in the huskiness of her voice. "You already done told Lela you a no-'count harlot by bringin' that white man in this house. An' it make me sick in my stomach hearin' you talk 'bout *respect*. You don' know what the word mean. You don' respect yo' own self, and nobody else. But that ain't my problem to fix. These the last words you gon' hear from me, Etta, and you best listen good: Anything you got in this house that ain't gone today gon' be thrown out in the street tomorrow. I don' wanna see you near me or Lela never again."

Etta's eyes overran with tears. "Sarah . . . ?"

Somewhere beyond her rage, Sarah felt hidden tears springing inside of her, too. Disgusted both by Etta and her own emotions, Sarah flung one of the kitchen chairs out of her way, toppling it over. Then she went to see about her daughter.

By late afternoon, Etta's room was empty. Etta had found some men with a mule-driven cart and they had taken her clothes, her wardrobe, her bureau, her linens, her lamps, and the canopy bed she'd bought for herself. Once Sarah finished her deliveries, she'd spent her day washing clothes in the backyard with Sadie, avoiding the kitchen entirely because she didn't want any contact with Etta. She stayed outside even though the dark clouds above had thickened, looking nastier than any she'd seen. When she left, Etta didn't come to say good-bye, and Sarah was happy to be spared another painful meeting with her. When she remembered the sight of that man in her house, and the way he'd leaned over to kiss Etta so brashly in her presence, Sarah wished she'd doused both of them with that tub of hot water. The nerve!

"Sarah, child, I hope I didn't bring you no trouble talkin' about that woman around other church folks," Sadie said. "It just got to the place where I couldn't keep it to myself, the way she was taking advantage of a decent Christian family. I've been afraid this would happen, that there'd be menfolk in and out and you or Lela might get hurt. And it was a white man, too? I thought she had *some* shame in her, but I guess not. Ooh, I'm so glad she's gone. I'm glad for you and Lela both."

"Me, too," Sarah whispered. "This ain't nobody's fault but mine." Saying she was glad Etta was gone seemed to be a lie, because Sarah felt more like she was grieving. But for what?

"And you won't have no trouble renting that room out. I'll help you post signs, hear?"

Something made Sarah look up at that instant, and she saw Lelia standing a few feet away from them in the yard, her schoolbooks hugged across her chest. Lelia's face told Sarah that she had overheard her conversation with Sadie. Lelia looked stricken, but there was nothing Sarah could say to her. Without a word to either of them, Lelia turned to march into the house.

Sarah sighed deeply. "Lord have mercy ... this gon' be the hard part. . . ."

"You just got to explain right and wrong, Sarah."

"I knows it," Sarah said. "But folks' hearts don't wanna hear 'bout right and wrong. Look at me! I always knowed I shoulda kept 'way from Etta, but my heart couldn't hear it."

Sarah heard rumbling thunder in the distance. She would have to hang the clothes she could in the kitchen, she knew, because it would likely rain tonight. *Damn it! Can't git the first thing to go right today,* Sarah thought.

After Sadie went home to start supper for her family, Sarah figured she'd better do the same. She wished she had enough money to walk down to the eating house and bring a couple of plates of food home for her and Lelia, but she knew she had to be more careful now that she wouldn't have Etta's rent money. She had some precious beef on ice, so she'd make stew.

Inside, Lelia was sitting at the kitchen table, her head resting on her books. She looked as though she must have fallen asleep while she was crying. Sarah began her supper preparations without a word, chopping the meat on a cutting board with a sharp rapping sound, and she heard Lela stir behind her.

"Help me with supper, Lelia," Sarah told her, but Lelia didn't stand up. Sarah was glad Sadie wasn't there to see Lela's disobedience, because Sadie had told Sarah many times she was spoiling her child. Sadie was a hard parent, just as Sarah's parents had been, quick to find a switch. Sarah had taken a switch to Lelia a few times, but she could hardly bear to hear her daughter cry. She'd cried enough tears as a child herself.

After silence had stretched between them a few more minutes, Sarah said, "It don't make no sense to you, do it? You thinkin', 'How Mama gon' throw her own friend out the house?'"

"I understand," Lela said, surprising Sarah with her straightforward response. She suddenly sounded much older than ten, like a grown woman. "You're jealous, Mama."

Sarah whirled to stare at Lela, shocked. "What I'ma be jealous for?"

"You've always been jealous, 'cause Miz Etta is so pretty, and 'cause she's been places and done something 'sides washing white folks' dirty underwear. That's why."

Sarah would never have believed her daughter could speak such hurtful words, much less that she could actually believe that. Suddenly Sarah wondered if Sadie wasn't right, that maybe Lela had been spared the switch a few times too often. "Well, you wrong 'bout that, Lelia," Sarah said, her anger surging. "I'd rather be washin' shit out of white folks' dirty clothes 'til I go to the grave than spend one night throwin' up my legs like that ho."

The words were too harsh, and Sarah knew it as soon as she'd spoken. Where had those words come from? They had been meant for Etta's ears, not Lelia's.

"That's a *lie!*" Lela screamed at her, leaping from the table. "You're *jealous* you don't got a man, too!" Then, with grief-crazy sobs, Lela ran out of the kitchen.

Let her go, Sarah told herself, tears streaming down her face. *She love that woman, an' you ain't gon' say nothin' now that can ease what she feelin', so you best keep yo' mouth shut.*

Lelia needed patience, that was all, Sarah thought. Time healed everything. In a few days, Lelia would be ready to hug her and climb onto her lap just like before. Then Sarah would be able to explain the rules of decency and indecency, and maybe they could shed tears together.

But Sarah wouldn't have to wait nearly that long for Lelia's next hug.

Within a few minutes, Sarah heard a train coming. Except, she realized after an instant, the train wasn't running on any tracks she knew about; the monstrous sound was on the *street* just beyond her house. She heard her windows shaking, softly at first but then louder and louder, and the ceiling seemed to quiver. Sarah opened her kitchen curtain to peer outside, and she saw that the late-afternoon sky was pitch. The trees and lines in her backyard seemed to be dancing. Oddly, she saw a washtub lift from the ground and sail past her window. "What in—"

Then the glass blew in, spraying Sarah in a shower of cold rainwater and pricking pain.

For the second time that day, Lelia let out a scream. Shrieking herself, Sarah ran toward the bedroom, where she found her daughter crouched on the floor. *"Mama!"* Lelia yelled, her arms reaching out. Sarah nearly fell on top of her daughter, cradling Lelia as she tried to shield her from something she couldn't see or name. She did not realize that she had bleeding scratches on her face; her only concern was holding Lelia, protecting her. The house trembled and groaned, windows crashed all around them, and she heard a howling, chugging sound outside that could have been Judgment Day itself.

Sarah had never experienced a cyclone to rival the one that ravaged St. Louis on May 27, 1896. When Sarah, Lelia, and their neighbors emerged from their homes, dazed and terrorized, they saw rooftops, buildings, and trees littering their neighborhood as if a giant had knocked them over and crushed them beneath his feet. Over the next few hours, they would hear about entire residential streets, factories, hospitals, mills, and railroad yards not far from them that collapsed in the sudden storm. A coachman named William Taylor, someone Sarah knew, had died trying to save his white employer's horse. One hundred thirty-seven people died in

St. Louis that day, and one hundred eighteen more died when the cyclone slammed across the river into East St. Louis.

All night long, as Sarah thanked God she and Lelia still had their lives and a roof above their heads, she worried about her friend and prayed for her safety. After so many years of friendship, why couldn't she have just accepted Etta's apology?

Sarah never saw Etta again.

Chapter Twelve

"Lemme see, Mama," Lelia said, lifting Sarah's chin with her hand so she could study Sarah's hairline as she did each morning. Sarah had to look *up* at Lelia. No doubt because of Moses' influence in her blood, Lelia now stood four or five inches taller than her mother. At sixteen, Lelia was becoming stately, growing out of the gangly limbs that had troubled her so much when her growth spurt first began. She looked like a woman, all right, but Sarah knew better; Lela was still as much a child as ever, in some ways.

Lela washed clothes with Sarah to fulfill her obligations so she could keep the extra room to herself, but that hadn't taught her a bit of independence, as far as Sarah could tell. Lela had no fondness for working around the house; she wanted her food cooked for her, her clothes mended, her hair combed. Sarah was amazed by Lela's lack of maturity; her daughter needed constant reminders to complete her chores and tasks. The woman-child who was her daughter made Sarah marvel at the idea that women had routinely married long before Lela's age when she was growing up. Why, Lela was no more ready to marry than she or Lou would have been at ten! Lela was fascinated by the menfolk, all right, but Sarah didn't think her easily impressed daughter had nearly enough common sense even to begin supervised courting, which she'd been begging to do since she first started attending Sumner High School. She was likely to attach her heart to the first fool who beckoned her, Sarah thought.

Maybe next year, Sarah always told her. But the truth was, she didn't want Lela's immature heart swept away by any young man, not yet. Lela was going to college, and that was that. In college, Lela could meet a man of real standing, not these little pups with few prospects to improve their lives, or hers. Lela had never experienced *real* hardship, not like she and

Moses had faced, and Sarah seriously doubted that her daughter had any talent for it.

Watching her daughter's face that morning, Sarah saw the telltale pity and concern in Lelia's eyes as she gazed at the frayed hairs at Sarah's temples. "Worse?" Sarah asked her. There was a time she might have said *worser*, but her grammar lessons at night school hadn't been completely wasted on her. Words like *ain't* still felt as comfortable as old shoes, and Sarah doubted she'd really learn to say *isn't* or *aren't* except by reminding herself first. Attending classes so sporadically, she probably still couldn't boast much more than a third-grade education, she thought. But she could read the *St. Louis Argus* every week to follow social events and news from the Negro community, and that was better than where she'd been.

Lela shrugged. "A little worse. But it's not too bad, Mama."

"That's a lie and you know it, girl. Now go on to school 'fore you're late."

Lela grinned, and her face looked so lovely that the minor irritations that had been growing between them as Lela got older melted from Sarah's mind, and she gave her daughter a lingering hug. They had their arguments, all right, but Sarah loved this girl like she hadn't known she could love anyone. Maybe it was good Lela was still so childish, because it would be a few more years before she had her own life and family.

Sixteen! Could it really be?

Once Sarah was alone with her work, her mind went back to her other troubles, which occupied her thoughts day and night. For the first time in a long time, it wasn't rent money or loads of wash that concerned Sarah. This time it was her hair.

Sarah's hair and scalp had given her small degrees of grief almost as long as she could remember—and even now, her memory of accidentally bloodying her prize customer's tablecloth still made her cringe—but it was only with the arrival of the new century that Sarah's misery had begun to take over her life.

First, as always, there was the itching. Each night as she tried to sleep, she felt as if the chinch bugs she'd hated so much as a child were crawling beneath her scalp, leaving trails of stinging fire. When she scratched at one spot, the fire moved to another, then came back with renewed pain aggravated by the rawness from her scratching. The back of her head was the worst, to the point where she could sleep comfortably only on her stomach. When her itching woke her up, she scratched as gently as she could, but she could steadily feel her tender skin giving way until her fingertips grew moist with familiar spots of blood. She tried to let the thin scabs heal over time, even sleeping with her hands wrapped in rags to discourage the scratching, but by morning she often discovered that she'd wriggled one of her hands free and scratched herself sore while she'd slept. Sometimes she found thin pricks of blood on her pillowcase. More often she found the dried evidence beneath her nails.

She didn't itch only at night, but that was the one time she wasn't pre-occupied with the business of her life, so it always seemed worse then. Sometimes, no matter what the time, she bundled herself up, climbed out of bed, and went to the kitchen to heat a pot of water so she could soak her head and massage soapsuds through her hair and scalp; warm water gave her small relief, and she hoped fervently that keeping her scalp clean would stop the itching. But it never did for long. More often, the late-night washings gave Sarah a runny nose and sore throat from going to bed with wet hair, especially when it was cold.

Even the rod wax Etta had introduced her to, which Sarah now bought for herself at the pharmacy not far from her house (there, it was la-beled *petroleum jelly* instead), didn't fulfill her hopes for her itching scalp. Sarah had believed she was itching simply because her scalp was *dry*, so she'd hoped the rod wax would provide much-needed oil. But although Sarah had been using rod wax and a hot fork or hot cloth for years to make her and Lela's hair less bushy and easier to braid, it did not help the itching.

Neither did lanolin, nor honey, nor oil from chamomile flowers, nor any number of remedies Sarah used to try to ease her suffering. Sarah and Lela began mixing her purchases together in a bowl in the kitchen, hoping they would luck into a combination that would be more powerful than any of the other ingredients alone, but all they'd made so far was a mess. Her scalp itched on.

To make things worse, Sarah now faced a new horror with her hair: It was falling out. Her hair had never been long, growing with a strawlike spikiness that was hard to pull into a ribbon or rubber band the way Lela wore hers after it had been softened and heated. But lately Sarah's hair looked more blunt than ever. Now, when she ran her hand through her hair, wiry strands of it came out easily on her fingers. She could feel coin-size patches of bare scalp on the spots that itched the worst. And when she glanced at herself in a mirror, which was rare, she saw how drastically her hair had thinned at her temples, drawing high away from her face.

Sarah could barely recognize herself. She had never considered herself *pretty*, not in the way Etta had looked so delicate and comely, because the hardship of Sarah's life had always made the notion of delicacy somewhat of a mystery to her; besides, she was just a little thick in her middle, a little too wide in the face, and a little too sluggish in her gait to draw gazes from the sort of striking, fine-featured colored men she noticed on St. Louis's streets, walking with breezy confidence. Sarah didn't know what sort of women those men pursued, but she knew it had never been *her*.

And she was older now, too; she couldn't forget that. The sassy, slender fourteen-year-old Moses had fallen in love with was a memory nearly as shadowy as her Delta cabin and her long-dead parents. Moses had been twice the man the ones who paid attention to Sarah these days were; grimy laborers with missing teeth, polite widowers with gray hair and frail bones she met at church, and crude-looking roustabouts who swarmed the levee, jockeying for any glance from someone of the female sex. Nearing thirty-five, almost past childbearing age, Sarah had begun seeing herself as she was sure the outside world did—matronly and staid—and she was just grateful she still had a reasonably high bustline and she hadn't let her face fall prey to the ugly creases that so many women her age wore from too many frowns and too little affection.

But this was different. Week by week, month by month, as Sarah's hair rebelled against her and became thinner and patchier, she watched herself growing slowly more hideous, less like a woman at all. Sadie and Lela constantly tried to reassure her that she looked fine as ever, but Sarah knew she'd be a fool to believe them. They were either blind or liars, she decided, and they might even be both. As much as she tried to ignore it, her vanishing hair began to touch a misery in her soul that felt like a bottomless well.

Nappy-head country pickaninny.

She could hear the mean-spirited taunt as clear as yesterday whenever she glanced at herself in a mirror. Hadn't even her beloved Miss Brown, who had taught her much more about washing as a business than even the courses she'd taken at night school (and who, Louvenia had written to her, had died suddenly last winter), told her pointedly once that she looked like a little monkey? *Like you been dragged headfirst through a brier patch.*

Ugly, awful words. But true, every one of them. These days, anyway.

In Sarah's mind, it was bad enough her female organs had been untouched, except by her own hand, in the fourteen years since Moses had died. (She'd discovered, quite by accident, that residual rod wax had a very pleasant slippery effect on her fingers when she ventured to rub them between her thighs.) She'd once felt like a fountain of passion, but now she felt dried, shriveled, and useless. She'd loved Moses, and felt his gazes from heaven every single day, but she'd never intended to keep her body sacred to him. After the first two years of shock and grief, she'd hoped to find another worthy man to marry. But Sadie always complained that Sarah suffered too much from the memory of Moses' good qualities—his hard work, his sly wit, and his serious-mindedness about political ideas—and Sarah had met no man yet who seemed even remotely cut from the same cloth. Sadie had tried her best to interest Sarah in her cousin, a well-built man named John who worked at a brick kiln in East St. Louis, but Sarah could barely talk to the man for the stink of whiskey on his breath.

Still, part of her, at least, had taken for granted that *if* a suitable man passed her way, she could catch his eye. No more. Now, if anything, Sarah felt herself wanting to cringe and hide from the gazes of men, strangers and neighbors alike. No matter how hot it was, she rarely left her house with her head uncovered anymore. She had a collection of white and red kerchiefs she kept clean so dirt wouldn't aggravate her scalp, but even when she wore head-wraps, Sarah felt naked to scrutiny, believing everyone must surely know what she was hiding beneath them.

One day, however, she took off her kerchief because it was damp with perspiration and the itching had become unbearable. Besides, she was hanging freshly washed clothes in her backyard, with a fence and tall papaw shrubs leaving her only slightly visible from the sidewalk that passed behind her house. Sarah rarely paid mind to anyone who passed her while she was working, unless they called out to her. But that day, a young man's voice caught her ear. She was hanging a bedsheet, and she noticed the candy-sweet, lulling voice of a stranger somewhere behind her. He was keeping his voice low, probably deliberately, Sarah thought. He couldn't be more than a few yards away, hidden behind the bush.

". . . as pretty as you should have a beau. Don't you know that?"

A giggle. "You don't really think I'm pretty."

That was Lela! And who was this man talking to her who sounded like he was grown, in his twenties? Sarah bit her lip, fuming.

"Tell you what, if I put you on my arm and brought you down to the Silver Dollar, where I play, there wouldn't be a nigger in there who wouldn't wish he was in my shoes. You ever heard any ragtime?"

The Silver Dollar? Was this a musician? Where the hell had Lela met a musician?

"Oh, I like it fine," Lela's voice said, purring.

"Well, you ain't heard rag 'til you've heard me play, an' I can't think of nothing sweeter than a dance with you. Now, where do you live at? Why don't you march me right on in so's I can meet your mama and daddy?"

"Not-uh," Lela said, the purr gone. She sounded closer to her age again. "I can't do that. I'm not allowed."

"Are you allowed to do this?" the man said in a throaty voice, and then there was silence.

Sarah forgot the bedsheet, casting it to the top of her pile, and whirled around to see what that disturbing silence meant. Over the tall bush, she could see the top of a man's black derby, angled downward. *Does he think this child is one o' his loose little Chestnut Valley tramps? He better think again,* Sarah thought, her face set in anger. She began striding toward the fence, her feet crunching in the grass. Just then, as if he sensed her approach, the man's hat popped up again.

"What's wrong?" he said.

"I can't do that, Johnny," Lela hissed. "Someone might see. . . ."

His voice grew more hushed, urgent. "Who's gonna see? Ain't nobody 'round here but that baldhead washerwoman over the fence. She don't know you, does she?"

Sarah's heart rocked to a halt in her chest. *Baldhead washerwoman.*

There was another silence, then: "No, I don't know her, but . . ."

Crazily, Sarah was suddenly convinced she must have mistaken some-one else's voice for her daughter's. That would explain the musician, wouldn't it? But she'd been so sure! Did another girl really sound so much like Lela? She *had* to, because—

"Then what you worried about, Lelia? Come on, girl," the man went on, and Sarah's knees nearly sagged beneath her. She'd planned to part those hedges, stick her head through, and cuss that man out, but the real-ization that Lela had spoken those words, after all, stole her breath. How could her own daughter deny knowing who she was? Sarah raised her hand to her stomach, feeling a cramping pain that reminded her of her first pain with Lela, right before she was born. Sick to her stomach and slightly dizzy, Sarah turned away from the voices and walked toward the kitchen door. Once inside, she slammed the door behind her with so much force that it made a cracking sound neighbors probably heard up and down the street.

Still, Sarah wished she had broken the kitchen window like the cy-clone had, so Lela would hear the glass shattering. Sarah had been angry at Lela many times, but she had not known, until that instant, how much pain Lela could bring her with mere words.

She's jus' a silly girl courtin', and girls'll say 'most anything to win a man, jus' like men do tryin' to win them, Sarah reminded herself with a rational voice. But the voice didn't help much. Lela was ashamed of her! Sarah had suspected it at times, but she hadn't really *known* it until just then, and the knowledge coiled tight inside of her. Sitting on her bed, Sarah stared up at the mason jar on her bureau, three-quarters filled with coins and bills she had been saving to send Lelia to college. Then her eyes moved to the Wish Board, which was pinned with a dozen or more drawings from newspapers and magazines, many of them Lela's—clothes, jewelry, even a picture of a horseless carriage with a motor, built by a man named Ford. *Automobiles,* they were called, and Sarah had seen a few of the odd-looking contrap-tions chugging along the streets, where they always drew pointing and stares. Lela wanted one of her very own.

She'd done right by Lela, Sarah told herself firmly. She'd given her a good home *and* her dreams, all with the work of her bare hands. What more could she have done?

"Mama?"

Lela stood in the bedroom doorway in one of the school dresses Sarah had sacrificed to buy her from a shop instead of making it herself, since Lela had complained that her clothes looked shoddy compared to some of the other students; it was a lovely sky blue gingham dress with a white col-lar, much nicer than a dress Sarah herself would wear on any day except Sunday. Lela's shoes, too, were buffed to a high black shine. Where did Lela think her nice things had come from, except from washing?

"What you want?" Sarah sniffed, turning her face away.

Lela sighed. She didn't speak for a long time. "You heard me, huh? Outside talking by the fence?" she asked quietly.

Sarah didn't answer.

"Yes, you did," Lela said knowingly. "And you're mad, too."

"You ain't s'posed to be courtin'," Sarah said, still not looking at her.

"Yes'm, I know," Lela said. "And I wasn't—I mean, I didn't know I was. . . . See, he told me his name is Johnny, and he's always at the barbershop 'round the corner, so he sees me walking home from school every day. I never said he could walk me home, Mama, but he—"

"What y'all was doin' behind that bush?" Sarah said. This time she turned around so Lela could see the no-nonsense look in her eyes. "You let him kiss on you, didn't you?"

Lela glanced away, embarrassed, then bravely met her mother's gaze. "Yes'm. I didn't *want* him to, he just . . . and then . . . Well, Mama, nobody's ever kissed me before."

"I don't care how tall and big you are," Sarah said, "if I hear 'bout you kissin' on any other man, I'ma get a switch an' whip you 'til you can't sit down. You hear me? An' I'ma meet you at that barbershop after school tomorrow so I can tell that man he better keep a distance."

Sarah expected Lela's familiar arguments about how other girls she knew were courting, and a few had even received marriage proposals. But Lela only nodded. "Yes'm," she said.

"Well, get on out my sight, then."

Lela didn't move. Her eyes shone brightly with a wisdom Sarah wasn't accustomed to seeing in her daughter, and it made her look more womanly than ever. "Mama, I'm sorry he said that about you. He didn't know. It was such a shock, and it hurt my heart so much. . . ."

Again Sarah was silent, but her gaze didn't waver.

"And when he asked if you knew me, it's . . ." Lela went on, stumbling for the first time, ". . . it's like the words jumped in my mouth from someplace else. Like it wasn't even me talking."

Yeah, those words jumped from your drawers, Sarah thought, but she kept that to herself.

"I wouldn't like that man nohow. . . . He smokes cigarettes and he's got marks on his face. . . ." Lela sighed. "But Mama, I don't know. . . . He said I was pretty, and—"

"But you *are* pretty!" Sarah said, finally shaken from her silence. The part of her that felt like a hurt child herself mended instantly, and she snapped back into her more comfortable role as a parent. "Why do you need some strange man to say that?"

To Sarah's surprise, her daughter's eyes glistened with tears. "I don't feel like it, Mama. Just like you! I w-wish I was . . ." At that, Lela's voice was sliced in two by a sob, and she started a new thought without finishing her sentence, an outpouring. "How come every time I find a picture of something p-pretty to wear, it's always a white lady wearing it? I've never seen no colored lady looking pretty in a magazine!"

"That ain't true, Lela," Sarah said, then she struggled to remember examples. It took her a moment, but then she brightened: "You've seen pictures of those ladies that won that beauty contest, Melanie Macklin an' Gertrude Marshall, an' they're both from St. Louis. Melanie went to Sumner, too, 'member? The papers said they're supposed to be the most prettiest women in the whole country—"

"The only reason folks say they're pretty is because they've got long hair," Lela cut her off impatiently. "White folks couldn't even tell Miss Marshall was colored from her picture, or she wouldn't of won anyway, Mama. And you know which girls colored boys like best? The ones might as well be white, those high-yellow girls with straight hair."

"All boys ain't like that."

"Yes, they are! They're always sayin' how I'm so black! And th-then when that man said you were b-baldheaded . . ." But Lela couldn't finish, covering her face as she cried. She ran to Sarah, sitting beside her on the bed, and Sarah wrapped her arms around her to rock with her. Tears had been running freely down her face as she listened to Lelia, because her daughter's words so thoroughly echoed the fears that had been hounding her. She'd hoped to spare Lela those same feelings, but how could she?

She could deny Lela's observations all day, but that didn't make them less true. Her mother had told her that slave women desperately tried to straighten their hair because that could mean the difference between being sent out to the fields or working in the house. And most colored men *did* prefer light-skinned women, as if they were prizes stolen from the white man's hands, bragging that they had *good hair* free of kinks. Sarah knew of colored women with the same preferences, but men seemed to have so much more disdain for women who were as dark as they were themselves. It would be an outright miracle if Lelia really thought she was pretty, Sarah realized. Why should any colored woman feel pretty?

"You can't pay that no mind, baby," Sarah told her daughter. "That ain't nothin' but folks showin' they're ignorant. White folks got us so trained from slave times 'til we don't even know how to think no more except the way *they* think. Don't you know your daddy thought you were the prettiest little thing he ever did see . . . ?"

At that, Lelia made a sound, half sobbing and half laughing. She savored stories of the way Moses had adored his tiny daughter so much, as she had almost since the time he died—especially the one about how he'd snatched her and taken her to the top of the stairs. To Lela, her long-dead father was like a prince in a fairy tale.

"Colored women don't got to be like white women to be pretty," Sarah went on, speaking to herself as much as to Lelia. She realized with dismay that a part of her believed she was telling her daughter lies. She knew better in her mind, but her heart felt uncertain. Still, the resolve never left her voice. "We've got our own way of bein' pretty. White women don't got no curves like us, do they? They got hips like us? Or these big ol' soft lips?"

After a hesitation, Lelia shook her head against Sarah's bosom. "No . . ." she said.

Sarah patted Lelia's firm backside. "They got rumps like us?"

Lelia laughed ruefully. "Sure don't."

"Believe me, child, back in slave times, white women were scared to death o' colored women 'cause their men was running out to us every chance they got. Wasn't for that, there wouldn't be so many high-yellow folks in the first place! An' if there's colored boys sayin' you ain't pretty 'cuz you ain't yellow, well, those boys just ain't got no sense. They don't know nothin' 'bout where they come from. Tell you what, you don't need to worry 'bout no man who don't want a woman as dark as his own mama. 'Cause a man who don't respect his mama won't never treat you right, nohow."

Lelia sniffled. "Mama?"

"What, baby?"

Looking up at her, Lelia forced a tiny smile through the unhappiness on her face. Her brown eyes glinted with mischief. "Can I start courting, now that you gave me all this advice?"

"Go on an' try it if you want," Sarah said sarcastically. "I'll take a switch to you and those boys, too! Jus' see if I won't."

Lelia laughed, surrendering, and Sarah joined her, the coil of pain in her chest loosening. The sick feeling in her stomach had long passed. Laughter, even bittersweet laughter, always felt so good! Sarah held tightly to her daughter, wondering how much longer Lelia would allow herself to be rocked and hugged before she would finally pull away.

Chapter Thirteen

JULY 1904

"Would y'all hurry on up?" Sarah said impatiently, clapping her hands. "The speech starts at noon, hear? We ain't got to see the whole fair today."

Sarah and Lela had visited the World's Fair three times since President Roosevelt came to St. Louis to officially start the fair's machinery in April, but no matter how many times they came back to sacrifice fifty cents apiece to the turnstile for admission, each visit to the fair seemed more dizzying than the last. Sarah was convinced they would need to come back a dozen times to take in acre after acre that had been transformed, magically, into a wonderland. Every time she entered the fairgrounds at De Baliviere and Lindell, Sarah felt as if she were visiting not only an entirely new city, but a new world. Special fair trains sped past them lightning-quick (twelve miles per hour, she'd heard someone say), an electric bus rumbled along without any horses to pull it, and the giant Observation Wheel towered to the east, blotting out the sun itself while it made its slow, remarkable revolutions and passengers aboard could see the fair from the sky. To say nothing of the endless acres of exhibition halls, glorious statues, breathtaking gardens, restaurants with seats for hundreds or even thousands, entire native villages from around the world, and amazing replicas of cities like London and Jerusalem. Although Sarah knew she would never have the means to visit either of those cities, she had *seen* them at the fair.

But none of that, to Sarah, could compare to the real reason she'd saved extra money to bring Lela to the fair today. She'd posted the real reason on her Wish Board and gazed at it for a full two weeks to motivate herself to get her work done early and budget very carefully; it was an article proclaiming an address by Booker T. Washington himself. A DAY FOR NEGRO UPLIFT, the newspaper's headline had said in bold black letters. The hairs at the back of Sarah's neck had stood up the moment she'd seen the article, and her excitement had only grown each morning as she'd opened her eyes and seen the article displayed high on her Wish Board.

Because it was a special occasion, Sarah had organized a small party to the fair: Lelia, Sadie, Lelia's school friend Hazel, and another church member, Rosetta Grant, who also occasionally washed for Sarah. Together the four of them made their way through the tide of people who were at the fair that day. Sadie, who hadn't yet been to the fair, looked as wide-eyed as a schoolgirl herself as she gaped around her. But Rosetta was shaking her head. "Those folks got to be crazy, chargin' fifty cents jus' to get inside!" Rosetta complained. She had a pretty face, but she was so skinny she looked half starved, even though she could eat more in one sitting than anyone Sarah knew. Like Sadie, Rosetta was slightly older than Sarah, although she hadn't yet found a way to solve her money troubles. She and her family were always on the verge of eviction, and she'd received money from collections taken up at St. Paul more than once.

"Mama, I don't want to go to a speech," Lela said, bordering on a whine that would be unseemly for an eighteen-year-old. "Just tell us where to meet you. Can't me and Hazel see the fair? I promised I'd show her that Electricity House and we'd ride the Observation Wheel. Please?"

That figured, Sarah thought. She'd been pleased when Lela was so eager to hear Dr. Washington's speech, too, but she should have known her daughter had something else in mind.

"Girl, you know nothing here is free, and your mama doesn't have money to waste so you can ride around in a wheel in the sky," Sadie answered before Sarah could. "And even if she did, you'd be crazy to climb up there. All those folks already up there are crazy, too."

Sarah sighed, but she wasn't going to let Lela ruin her mood today. "Lela, I'm s'prised at you," Sarah said quietly. "Booker T. Washington is the greatest colored man in this country—he helped start his own school, an' even President Roosevelt wanted to talk to him so bad he invited him to dinner at the White House. I'd think a young lady jus' finished with high school would want some direction in her life."

"A-men," Rosetta said.

"That's the truth," Sadie said.

"My daddy says he's an Uncle Tom," Hazel spoke up in her prim, practiced way, breaking up their reverie. Her father was a highly respected schoolteacher at Sumner, Lela's former accounting teacher, who had a reputation as a radical.

"Well, I met your daddy, and he's a right smart man, Hazel," Sarah said, vowing to keep her temper although she found Hazel's statement offensive and inappropriate, "so I ain't gonna say nothin' against him. But if y'all didn't come to hear Booker T. Washington, you should've stayed home." It was her end-of-subject voice, which Lela knew better than to argue with.

"Amen," Rosetta said again. Then she grimaced, scratching herself beneath her Sunday hat, which she was wearing a day early in honor of Dr. Washington's visit. "Ooh, Sarah, this sun is 'bout to tear my head up. I thought that Poro was helpin', but not today. You itchin' too?"

For the first time, Sarah realized she'd been so excited that she hadn't thought about her head once all day. A month ago she'd heard women at church raving about a product called Poro Wonderful Hair Grower being sold by a woman right in St. Louis who advertised in the papers, a former washerwoman named Miss Annie T. Malone. In fact, Sarah had begun noticing more and more ads for hair products, but she dismissed them when they disappointed her. Would Poro be different? Sarah's own efforts to make an itch reliever with Lela weren't working, so she'd decided to try the Poro, applying the thick, slippery substance to her scalp each morning. *Was* the itching improving? Sometimes she thought so, but she couldn't be sure. Her hair wasn't growing back, though; that much was certain. As usual, Sarah's patchwork of hair was covered in a scarf, and her scalp was perspiring in the eighty-degree summer sun.

"Ain't nothin' troublin' me today, Rosetta," Sarah said, and she meant it. Her mind was in a fever of anticipation. Most of it, she was sure, was because of Dr. Washington's appearance, and some of it was the hum of the fair itself, with its smells and noises and thronging people. Everyone seemed to be carrying those new little box-shaped Kodak cameras to take photographs, and Sarah understood why. So many sights! The grass on the grounds was greener and more lush than any she could remember seeing, the water in the fountain was sparkling like liquid diamonds, not like the usual brown sludge that passed for water in St. Louis, and the buildings that had been constructed for the fair were so exquisite that it was hard to imagine they'd all been built in three short years. Even the food at the fair was odd; she stared at fairgoers eating tube-shaped sandwiches billed as *hot dogs* and licking ice cream from edible cones.

But there was also something else that crackled in the air, something that felt very much like magic. Whatever it was, Sarah felt a bounce in her step she hadn't enjoyed in years, making her weave through the crowd as purposefully as a hound following a scent in the underbrush. The rest of her party had to walk fast to keep up with her, protesting her pace.

After asking directions from one of the fair's uniformed Jefferson Guardsmen and hurrying past the magnificent statues in the sprawling Plaza of St. Louis, then around the edges of the huge man-made lagoon named the Grand Basin, they saw Festival Hall. Both fatigue and wonderment stopped them as they neared the great hall, which stood before them like a majestic palace from a foreign land, with its columns, statues, and ornate shapes carved into its domed exterior. The dome gleamed brightly in gold leaf, burning like a miniature sun. The gold was mesmerizing.

"It looks like something from a dream," Sadie murmured, wide-eyed.

"This *mus'* be a dream. They lettin' a colored man speak in there?" Hazel asked dubiously, shielding her eyes from the glare. "What about the Colored Pavilion?"

"Come on, y'all. We're 'bout to be late," Sarah said. She'd caught her breath, and now it was time to keep going. She wanted to be close enough to *hear* the man, after all. She was sure she would be more dazzled by what was waiting inside than by anything she could see now.

Inside, the vast hall splintered into several directions, and Sarah was about to ask another uniformed officer where the address would take place when she noticed a stream of well-dressed Negroes making their way toward open double doors she guessed led to an auditorium. Motioning to the others, Sarah followed the group, which began to grow larger in number until they were in the midst of at least two hundred Negroes simply trying to make their way inside. "Is this where Dr. Booker T. Washington is gonna speak?" Sarah asked a woman she recognized from St. Paul, Mrs. Jessie Robinson, whose husband, C.K. Robinson, was a well-known colored printer rumored to own his very own automobile. For an instant, noting Jessie Robinson's wide, regal hat and matching pink chiffon dress, Sarah felt a pang of regret that she hadn't had enough money to buy something she hadn't already worn half to death for this affair. And why had she worn a scarf instead of a hat? But Sarah dismissed the thought when she saw the joyful recognition on Mrs. Robinson's face; she'd taken no notice of Sarah's plain clothes.

"Oh, yes, Mrs. McWilliams, this is the place, all right. What a thrill! Are you going to the National Association of Colored Women meeting later this month? Mrs. Washington is speaking."

Sarah clearly heard Lela click her teeth in bored disgust behind her, but she ignored it and prayed her daughter's insolence hadn't reached Mrs. Robinson's ears. "Yes, ma'am," Sarah said. "I planned on 'em both. I sure hope they've got room inside for all these folks."

"Room?" boomed a man's voice from over Sarah's shoulder. He was a pleasant-featured colored man in middle age with a thick mustache and a wide belly. "I hear there's room enough to seat thirty-five hundred inside here. Even Booker T. Washington can't fill that many seats!"

Sarah savored the feeling of fellowship with so many other Negroes who shared her excitement about the day; the sense of magic was even stronger in here, in the smiles of anticipation on the lips of the people surrounding her. As the crowd grew thicker by the door, Sarah realized this group had *power*. She and her friends were only washerwomen, but surely some of these Negroes, like the Robinsons, had education and their own businesses; and here they were together, all of them bound by their desire for uplift.

Sadie felt it, too, because she was bouncing on the balls of her feet beside Sarah. "Do you *believe* it, Sarah? We're here. We're sure enough here."

We're here. Sarah knew Sadie meant only that they had finally made it to the auditorium, but in her mind it sounded as if her friend were talking about all members of the Negro race. Would she have imagined a day like this for Negroes when she was back in Delta? Or, for that matter, when she was living with Lou in Vicksburg? *Here* meant that they were no longer helpless and pitiful, that they had reached some sort of resting place. No, not a resting place—a *building* place, Sarah thought, and she felt such a tingle that her arms turned to gooseflesh. Sarah yearned to share her thoughts with her friend, but the ideas were too big and muddy in her head. She only squeezed Sadie's arm and she didn't let go.

The auditorium, as promised, was breathtaking. Sarah had never seen a room and a stage so big, designed with the same stately air as the building's architecture. Walking inside, she felt as if she were being swallowed by the room, but she didn't mind. Lela, intimidated, clasped her hand. "Look at all these people, Mama . . ." Lela whispered.

The room was large, all right, but the seats toward the front looked as if they had filled long ago, and the crowd spilled far past the middle rows, nearly to the back. There were mostly Negroes, but Sarah noted with surprise that there were a good number of whites here, too. Sarah motioned once again to her group, pointing toward a row of empty seats closest to them. The seats were much farther back than she'd hoped, but she realized that if they'd arrived any later they might not have found a place to sit at all.

"You'd think it was the president himself come to speak," Sarah said, half to herself.

Soon a white man walked to the stage and said he would introduce the speaker, Booker T. Washington. Sarah ventured a glance down the row at her daughter, and she was glad to see that Lela's spirited conversation with Hazel had come to a halt; her daughter looked riveted.

Despite very good acoustics, which made sound from the stage bounce throughout the room, the man's voice sounded far-off and hollow, and Sarah scooted to the edge of her chair to try to hear him better. He spoke quickly, and Sarah heard only snatches of his words: *Founding principal of Tuskegee Institute in Alabama. Author of* Up from Slavery. *Founder of the National Negro Business League. Honorary degree from Harvard University.*

Then, at long last, he called the name *Booker T. Washington.*

The applause began as a smattering, then grew louder in waves throughout the rows as a second man, with pale brown skin and small in stature, walked to the podium. His head was erect, and Sarah liked his deliberate strides; it was easy to tell he had taken the stage many times before today, and he knew it was a home that suited him well. A shiver of excitement made its way across Sarah's neck. While the audience applauded, the man slipped his hands behind his back and stared toward the floor as if waiting for silence; yes, he was *commanding* them to be silent without speaking a word. Slowly the applause subsided.

When Booker T. Washington began to speak, his voice taking over the room, Sarah forgot everything else. The world, to her, had narrowed to only this man and the words that poured from his mouth in sweeping, dramatic cadences. He was speaking to her and her alone.

"I am sure there are those who thought the planning of this great fair was folly, who insisted a feat such as this could not be done in this great city," Booker T. Washington said. "These are the same voices of pessimism who insist the races cannot live together, or that the Negro will always be cursed to subservience and poverty. But if a world can be built before your very eyes, how difficult is it to then envision something so small as a better way of life?"

Yes, Sarah thought as gently as a sigh, and joined the audience in applauding him.

"Good people, the grandness of this fair brings to mind a story I told at the Atlanta Cotton Exposition in 1895, and it is no less true for this audience. My simple story is this: A ship lost at sea many days sighted a friendly vessel," Booker T. Washington said, and his voice painted the lost ship in Sarah's imagination so clearly she could see it tossing in the waves. "From the mast of the unfortunate vessel was seen a signal: 'Water, water, we die of thirst.' "

Yes, Sarah thought again. She knew that feeling as well as she knew her own soul.

"The answer from the friendly vessel at once came back, 'Cast down your bucket where you are.' A second time the signal, 'Water, water, send us water,' ran up from the distressed vessel and was answered, 'Cast down your bucket where you are.' The captain of the distressed vessel, at last heeding the injunction, cast down his bucket. . . ."

What good's a bucket o' seawater to folks who's thirsty? Sarah wondered, frustrated.

Booker T. Washington's eyes seemed to sweep across the room before he finished, as if he meant to share his conclusion with each member of the audience personally. "And it came up full of *fresh*, sparkling water from the mouth of the Amazon River," he said, and repeated the rescuing ship's instructions with a tremor in his voice: "*Cast down your bucket where you are.*" He said it four times, five times, and Sarah felt herself trembling where she sat, moved to tears.

Booker T. Washington said many things to his audience that afternoon about education, self-reliance, farming, and family, but to Sarah the pearl of his message was in the image of that lost ship full of thirsty, dying crewmen, who'd been floating in enough fresh water to last beyond their lifetimes and hadn't even known it was there.

Nearly two weeks later, meeting at St. Paul for the National Association of Colored Women, Sarah and her friends were still dazed and enthralled by the way the audience had leaped to its feet after Booker T. Washington's speech, Negro and white alike, and how even whites had waited at the edge of the stage to try to shake his hand. Sarah had watched the well-wishers from the back of the auditorium with envy, wishing she could tell Dr. Washington herself how much she had appreciated his message. But how would she have even put her feelings into words?

Wonder what he feels like up on that stage, she thought. *Makin' folks feel so good, like they's standin' in the presence of greatness.*

"The wife of Booker T. Washington must be somethin', too," Sarah said, checking her program. There were several delegates scheduled to speak that day, she noted as she glanced at the clusters of words, so she'd have a fairly long wait before she could hear Mrs. Margaret Murray Washington. "Imagine bein' married to a man like *that*."

Between her excitement over Booker T. Washington's speech and her anticipation of his wife's, Sarah's head was so full that she could barely listen to the speakers who took the podium that afternoon. She didn't even reach over to nudge Lela when she noticed her daughter's head had slumped forward slightly, betraying that she had dozed to sleep. As soon as Mrs. Washington spoke, Sarah thought, she could take Lela home.

But first another speaker took the floor. The first thing Sarah noticed about the young woman who stood up in the front of the room was the thick, neat plaits across her scalp, which Sarah was sure had taken a long time to fix. Speaking in a clear, steady voice thick with the twang of her Southern upbringing, the woman said her name was Cornelia Brown. She was from a school named Mt. Miegs in Alabama, she said. "I agree with Sister Jackson's very moving words about the growing problem of ragtime and coon music among our people," she began, "but I wish to discuss a problem I believe is also as grave for Negro womanhood—and that is the problem of hair-wrapping."

Sarah sat up straight at the mention of *hair*. "I'm sorry to report that this practice of wrapping hair to try to make it lay down straight is becoming more popular all the time. I encourage all you ladies to go to your homes and follow the example of the Anti-Hair-Wrapping Clubs I have organized to keep ladies from going astray."

"Lord have mercy . . ." Sarah muttered under her breath. Anti-Hair-Wrapping Clubs! Sarah had wrapped her hair a few times herself when she was younger, heating flannel by the fire after she had oiled her hair with lard; then she'd wrapped her hair in the cloth and pulled hard to try to straighten the strands. She and Lela didn't like the results much, but it was hardly a sin!

The woman went on, her voice trembling with emotion. "It is foolish to try to make hair straight when God saw fit to make it kinky!" she said, and her passion brought spirited applause and rounds of *Amen* from the dozens of women in the group.

Sarah was so irritated, she felt her heart thundering in her chest. Folks should have just as much right to wrap their hair as they did to comb it, she thought. Did God frown on combs, too? And did this woman also believe folks shouldn't look for relief when their God-given dandruff was troubling them? Sarah nearly shot her hand up so she could respond, but she caught herself in time. She wasn't about to stand up in front of this group and make a fool of herself!

"You should tell her how you're runnin' that hot fork through Lela's hair. She can start a club against *that*," Sadie whispered to Sarah, smiling.

But a faint voice deep inside Sarah's head wondered if Miss Bowen from Mt. Miegs School in Alabama might have a good point. An itching scalp was one thing, but could hair-straightening really just be another way of trying to look white? Some misguided Negroes nowadays were even trying to bleach their skin! Sarah hated to think it, but she didn't doubt that if Negroes could somehow make themselves white tomorrow, the next World's Fair would need a special exhibition on the nearly extinct American Negro.

But Sarah forgot her fear that she might secretly be ashamed of being a Negro as soon as Mrs. Margaret Murray Washington finally took the stage. Mrs. Washington sauntered with every bit of self-assurance as had her husband, yet with the grace and modesty of a woman. She was fair-skinned, wearing gold-rimmed spectacles. Sarah recognized the materials of her black one-piece dress as chiffon and taffeta, and the dress was perfectly creased and complemented by a string of gray pearls that hung from her neck. Her expression was solemn, yet her features were kind. And her hair, not quite straight, but not quite kinky, was pinned with precision atop her head.

"Good afternoon, ladies," the woman began, and her voice reminded Sarah of the tones Etta had used when she was demonstrating to Lelia how actresses delivered their lines on the Broadway stages of New York. "We have so much work before us, and yet we are so lovely a people that my heart swells with pride as I stand before you. We have a problem at hand."

Then Mrs. Washington began to rail against the group's planned visit to the Colored Women's Day exercises at the World's Fair. Despite her husband's speech there so recently, she insisted that the fair was discriminating against Negroes by not offering them employment. "Certain of our race have been refused refreshments and other privileges at the World's Fair accorded to every other group of people, simply on the ground of color," she said, her voice trembling with anger. "So I am introducing a resolution to this effect. I say we should not spend our money to support a fair that does not value our patronage."

Her words caused an explosion in the room. Sarah's fellow church members and others from St. Louis couldn't believe she would try to rob the organization of its chance to see the fair, but the residents from other parts of the country sided with Mrs. Washington. And, though she kept her tongue, so did Sarah. Sarah watched the exchange in silence, more and more impressed by Mrs. Washington's fervor. The woman never once lost her temper, presenting her arguments with convincing logic.

I'd like to be a woman like that, Sarah thought, watching her. What would she give to be so fearless, such a refined beacon to her people, and a partner to a powerful and respected man? But Sarah also felt the growing realization that her distance from the stage where Mrs. Washington stood was so great that she might well be insane to ever hope to cross it.

By the next day, when Sarah was again lugging her cart of clean laundry toward the squalor of the Eads Bridge, a sense of hopelessness had taken hold of her. Her back and arms ached from pulling the cart, and she could no longer attach her spirit to the sense of power and promise she had felt so strongly before. She was just a lowly colored woman with a cart of laundry, in an endless stream of other colored women who carried their laundry bundled on their heads. She'd devised a cart for the job, but that didn't make her superior to the other washerwomen, Sarah reminded herself. Neither did her next-day service. Or her thoroughness. She was still working herself to the bone every bit as much as they were, and possibly even more.

To make things worse, Lela was hemming and hawing about not being ready to go away to school yet, and Sarah was beginning to wonder if her daughter would ever be ready. Maybe Lela *should* start courting and try to find a man to provide for her, Sarah thought, because she didn't know if her heart could bear it if Lela ended up washing her whole life, too.

Those thoughts weighed hard on Sarah's mind as she passed the gritty-looking hay carts, crates, and horse carriages that were crowded near the bridge, looking so drab and awful in comparison to the prettiness of the fairgrounds. Sarah liked the vibrance of city life, but on days like today she also missed the open feeling of the countryside where she'd grown up. Here, smokestacks spewed thick black clouds into the air, irritating her eyes, and she gazed with disgust at the piles of garbage gathering in corners. Was this all life had to offer?

There were puddles left over from the morning's rain, so Sarah had to walk close to the side to avoid flying water and mud from carriages and occasional automobiles that went past her. Drivers didn't pay any mind to a colored woman with her laundry, Sarah thought. *Don't be thinkin' thoughts like that, Sarah. They're jus' like poison to the heart*, she tried to remind herself, but her mind was stuck feeling mean and angry.

Finally, unable to tolerate her aches a moment longer, Sarah stopped walking midway across the bridge, pausing to catch her breath. Where she stood, all of St. Louis was spread out before her—the intersecting streets, rows of homes, factories, alleys. She could even see the fair's far-off Observation Wheel, though it was frozen in the air, not spinning today because it was Sunday and the fair was closed. Sarah felt stuck, just like that big wheel. Even when it was moving, it spun all day long, and for what? It never went anywhere.

A pressing heat began rising in Sarah's chest, and she knew she was close to tears. *All right, then, you jus' stand here an' feel sorry for yourself, Sarah Breedlove McWilliams.*

Why not? She had as much right as anyone. Parents dead before she could even fix them in her memory good, the most loving man she'd ever known stolen from her, a sister and brother far away (and Alex's health was failing, he'd written), a daughter bent on doing things her own way, and aching muscles on top of that. Sarah swallowed back an anguished sob.

You can't think of no more than that? How 'bout you still ain't learned to read as good as you wanted, an' you look 'bout as raggedy as they come? Now you know what a real lady looks like, an' you're only fit to wash her clothes!

This time Sarah's sob broke to the surface of her throat, scraping it raw. But she shook her head hard, trying to prevent any more sobs from escaping. Imagine her nerve to stand up here crying! How could she, after those great speeches she'd heard? Hadn't they meant anything at all?

With that, Sarah gazed down nearly sixty feet into the rushing brown current of the Mississippi River, which had been a part of her life as long as she could remember. Her papa had taught her to fish in these waters, her mother had washed clothes in them, and it was still there running beneath her feet. Still there. So why not do exactly what Dr. Washington had said in his speech? Why not cast a bucket down?

I ain't got no damn bucket, the angry voice inside Sarah railed. *An' that water's so bad you got to let it settle overnight 'fore you can skim off the good parts to drink.*

But Sarah knew that voice was lying to her. The voice was afraid of something. Hard work? Well, she'd been working hard her whole life, so why not work toward something she really wanted? Was she afraid maybe Dr. Washington was wrong? Well, if he was, so be it. It would pain her more to give up than to keep on going, she realized. She could live with failing a lot better than she would be able to live with herself if she tried to smother her deepest hopes.

Inhaling deeply, Sarah tried to come up with a plan for what she needed to put on her Wish Board next, and her mind kept going back to her hair. She wanted to find something that would make her troubles go away, and she wanted to help others with the same problem.

"Poro," she said aloud. She'd bought the jar she was using right from a woman in St. Louis who sold it door-to-door, she remembered. Why shouldn't she do that, too? She had a little extra time, and she could make good money selling something people were so eager to buy. Rosetta wasn't the only friend she had who was using Poro! She'd learn to sell Poro the same way Moses had tried to teach her to sell fried catfish, by raising up her voice and making folks believe they *had* to have what she was selling.

But did Poro really work?

Sarah still wasn't sure. Maybe it did, because she'd heard it said that Annie T. Malone had some chemistry training, and that was how she'd discovered a formula for hair. Chemistry! Sarah had barely finished her business course and was still struggling to read when she'd left school, and she'd certainly never progressed as far as the sciences. Education made all the difference, didn't it? *Maybe* . . .

Sarah knew where that voice was coming from, too. She and Lela had tried a lot of combinations in Sarah's search for a hair formula, with Sarah keeping track of them in her mind like cooking recipes, and none of them had been quite right. *Something* was always missing. What did Annie T. Malone know that she didn't? Was it really *that* hard to find a good formula, with so many ads in the newspaper from others who'd done it?

No, Sarah thought, feeling strangely certain. She could do it, too. Of course she could.

Sarah took the rope of her cart again and gave it a pull to finish her journey across the bridge and get her clothes delivered. Her heart felt nearly as light as it had the day before, and she ignored her aches this time because her mind was in a flurry of thought. She would find out how she could start selling Poro, that was the first thing. She could knock on her neighbors' doors in the early evenings, when her washing was finished. That would give her some extra money to buy ingredients. What was the name for that she'd learned in business class? Those raw ingredients would be her *capital investment*. Then, come hell or high water, she would find her own hair treatment, something she could believe in with all her heart, and start selling that instead.

Now she had a plan! Sarah couldn't wait to finish her work and get back home so she could tell Lela and put it up on her Wish Board. Her Wish Board really did seem to have a way of making things come to life, she thought.

Maybe my bucket's already been cast down a long time, Sarah realized. *An' now all the good water's floated up top so's I can finally start takin' my drink.*

Sarah wasn't sure exactly *how* she would do it . . . but somehow she knew she surely would.

Chapter Fourteen

TWO WEEKS LATER

Dearest Lou,

Word has just Reached me from Denver to say we have lost our brother Alex. I can't find Words for what I feel as I write this. I know we have not seen much of him in these past years in fact we have not seen each other either. But we did not see Alex much since we were young and it feels like a terible Shame. I feel I have lost somthing I did not yet know I had until it was gone. I hope he had Peace. I am sending some money for his Family and I hope you will do the same. I have not met his Wife but she has sent me very nice letters. I was so sad to read this one.

Me and Lelia both miss Aunt Lou!!
Much love,
Sarah

With her hand unsteady and her eyes strangely dry of tears, Sarah wrote the letter to her sister on her kitchen table the same afternoon she received word of Alex's sudden death from pneumonia. The funeral date was long past by the time Sarah received the neatly written note from his widow, and she knew it would be an even more distant event by the time Louvenia received her letter and wrote back to her. All of them would have to mourn alone.

Suddenly Sarah had a vivid image of her parents' bodies being carried out of the Delta cabin, wrapped in the blankets from their bed and then tied with rope around their necks, waists, and feet. Then she remembered a burning, and people singing songs, but she could see little else in her memory. All she really remembered was how she couldn't believe her mama and papa were wrapped inside those blankets, being carried over men's shoulders like bags of seed.

Then, slowly, another image surfaced: Alex hugging her and Lou over the grave site, looking so tall in Papa's hat, betraying no evidence of tears because he was trying so hard to show his sisters that he was man enough to provide for them. Oh, yes, she remembered that!

Today, news of Alex's death seemed far away and long ago, as if it had nothing to do with her or that family of dazed children huddled over their parents' graves. And there would be no hug between her and Lou to mourn Alex, either. That, in some ways, hurt Sarah almost as much as the passing of her brother, her Papa's only son. Almost.

Sarah sighed from her deepest places, but she still didn't shed any tears.

Her thoughts were interrupted when she felt Lelia wrap her arms around her neck from behind, leaning close to her. Lelia stayed there, hugging her mother's neck, for a long, comforting minute, perhaps even two. She didn't say anything, probably because she was old enough to understand that she didn't need to. Sarah grasped her daughter's hand, squeezing tight. In that instant, Sarah was so grateful to have Lela with her that her entire frame gave a violent shudder.

"It's all right, Mama," Lela said softly, at last. "I'll go mail the letter for you. I could've written it, too, if you wanted."

Sarah shook her head. She almost said, *Mama would've wanted me to do it my own self*, but she didn't. Lela wouldn't understand that, and she couldn't even begin to explain.

That night, in the midst of her sadness, Sarah had the most vivid dream of her life.

In her dream, she was standing near her family's cabin in Delta, knee-deep in crabgrass, alongside the rutted muddy roads she'd traveled so often as a child. She even thought she could smell the sweet scent of elderberries in her nostrils, and hear the currents of the Mississippi River rushing just beyond the knoll behind the cabin, the way it had before her parents died. *The river ain't changed course yet*, she thought to herself with amazement, forgetting she was dreaming.

As she gazed toward her cabin, her father suddenly appeared in his rocking chair, gazing toward the sky. Then Mama and Alex were there, too, sitting on the wooden step beside him, telling each other stories as they swatted flies from their faces. Sarah wanted to go hear their stories, but every time she took a step toward them, she felt herself drawing farther away, and a mist began to float in front of the cabin, obscuring their faces.

"Papa!" Sarah shouted.

"Right here, Li'l Bit," her father yelled back, sounding as if he were calling to her from a distant part of a cotton field the way croppers used to shout to each other on the wind to carry their voices. *Calling the wind,*

Papa had called it. Sarah could barely hear him. She wanted to tell him to speak more loudly, but then he called out again, faintly: "Go on, now, Sarah. It's time!"

Yes, Sarah realized, Papa was right. It *was* time.

Then, as much as Sarah wanted to join her family at the cabin, she found herself turning away from them, walking the familiar path toward the shallow bathing creek. This was why she had come, she realized.

A black-skinned man was sitting naked in the creek, his arms folded around his knees. He looked as tall as Moses, but also much broader, built with thick, solid muscles across his chest and arms. His bald head gleamed. In fact, his whole *body* seemed to glisten, either from the creek's water or his own perspiration. He was beautiful. Sarah had never attached the word *beautiful* to a man, but this one was. His skin was the color of midnight. She felt her body glowing warm, drawn to this dark man she realized must certainly be an African.

The man raised his hand, beckoning her slowly with one finger. At first, startled, Sarah shook her head. She couldn't go to him!

What are you afraid of? he asked her, except that he somehow spoke to her without moving his lips. His white teeth were shining at her from his beautiful black face. His teeth were nearly blinding. Suddenly Sarah couldn't think of a thing she was afraid of, not a single thing. Tentatively Sarah took a step toward the creek—and suddenly the creek drew right up to her and she was standing on the bank. Here, standing over the clear water, she could see the man's naked manhood, and her face grew warm, too.

"I know what you seek," the man said, and this time he *did* speak aloud.

"How do you know?" she asked him. Her own voice sounded melodic to her.

"You told me," he said.

Sarah knelt alongside the creek and let her hand slip into the cool water. Sure enough, she felt her hand begin to tingle, and the tingle traveled throughout her entire frame. She shuddered, grateful, relieved, ecstatic. She longed to dive in beside the African and luxuriate in the water with him, but she didn't dare leave the bank. Sarah realized she could no longer see the features of the man's face, only his mesmerizing smile. She had never seen teeth so perfect.

"This is for you, my princess," the man said, and he held between his fingers the thorny stem of a rose. But Sarah had never seen a rose like this one; unlike the red and yellow roses Lou used to grow in Vicksburg to decorate her table, this one was shiny and a deep violet color, almost black. Yes, she realized with wonder, it *was* black. It gleamed like the man's skin.

The mere sight of the extraordinary rose brought tears to Sarah's eyes.

"Look around you," the man told her. His voice was brother, father, lover. "Look all around you, Sarah."

So she did. She lifted her eyes, and her family's little cabin was gone. Instead, stretching as far as she could see, there was a field of roses in full bloom, all of them as black as the one in the African man's hand. They swayed gently in rolling waves, a black ocean, their lovely buds swollen open toward the sky. There must have been thousands! More than Sarah could begin to count.

"Where did they come from?" Sarah asked the man, amazed.

"Come from?" The man laughed, extending the single rose in his hand toward her. "Where do you think they come from? They've always been here."

But I've never seen all these flowers here, Sarah thought in her dream, puzzled. *There was only cotton in this field before. How come I ain't never seen them?*

Then, suddenly, Sarah was awake. The last thing she remembered was taking the stem to raise the flower to her nose and smell it. But then she'd pricked her finger, and the sharp sensation had awakened her with a gasp and a start.

Inexplicably, she was only in her bedroom, and a muted morning light was shining through her curtains, across her bed. Sarah's heart was racing from a quenching exhilaration instead of the awful grief she'd gone to bed with. Feeling groggy, she looked at her hand and blinked rapidly, honestly expecting to find the strange rose in her palm. But it was not there. No prick on her fingertip, either.

"Course not," she said aloud, her voice scratchy. "It was jus' a dream. But they were growin' everywhere, jus' growin' so pretty an' tall. . . ."

Her words sounded like nonsense to her ears, spoken in the delirium that comes from dreams. But even after she was wide awake and working, Sarah kept remembering the startling image of that lovely black rose in the hand of the African man. All day long it flitted back to her mind and made her smile.

Chapter Fifteen

"You listen to this," Sarah said as she and Lelia made their way from the market with baskets of fruit and dried goods. She began to read from the newspaper in her hand. "Her name is Madam Mary McLeod Bethune, she's down in Florida, and she just opened her own school . . . the Day-tona Normal and In-dus-trial In-sti-tute for Girls . . ." she read, hesitating with the more difficult words as she always did.

The fall wind whipped Lelia's scarf around her face. "Mama, I'll finish reading that to you when we get home. You're going to run into someone if you don't look where you're going."

"Just hush," Sarah said, enthralled. The headline NEGRO WOMAN OPENS OWN SCHOOL had caught her eye, and she was too excited to wait three more blocks. "See here? She opened that school with a dollar and fifty cents and five students. And she raises money selling sweet-potato pies! You just imagine that, Lelia. After you go on to college next year, you could start your own school someday, too. I'm puttin' this newspaper right up on the Wish Board."

But Sarah's excitement was forgotten as soon as their house was in sight. Her feet stumbled to a halt, and Lelia stood frozen beside her. Their front door was wide open, and even from where they stood, Sarah could see through the doorway that something inside was amiss. One of her pine chairs was overturned.

"Somebody been in the house!" Lelia gasped, holding tight to Sarah's arm.

Sarah's heart galloped. She dropped her basket to the ground, unaware of the apples rolling around her feet on the sidewalk. Her mind had been stripped of everything except one thought: *Lelia's college money!*

"St-stay here, Lelia . . ." Sarah said, pulling herself free.

Despite Lelia's pleas, Sarah rushed up the steps to the front porch and

ran through the open doorway. As she'd feared, the front room was in dis-
array; small items, including her clock, had been knocked from the fireplace, and there were newspapers strewn on the floor. Sarah didn't even
glance toward her kitchen. Instead she ran straight to her bedroom.

Her father's framed photograph was on the floor, the glass cracked. Her
mattress had been pulled askew. And all of the drawers of her desk were
open—including the one where she kept her mason jar. With a whimpered
prayer, hoping for a miracle, Sarah peered inside the drawer to see if the
money had somehow been kept safe from the thieves' eyes.

It was simply gone. No money, no jar. Nothing.

The room seemed to wheel around Sarah, nearly making her lose her
balance. She leaned on the desk for support, breathing hard, trying to
make some sense of it. They had not been gone even an hour, and the
money had been here when they left. She had counted it only the night
before, as she sometimes did to raise her spirits; she'd had exactly three
hundred dollars. They'd gone without clothes, without treats, without leisure, so she could save that money. That would have been enough money
to buy a house of her own, or enough to buy a piano and suites of furniture
for every room, or enough to buy her own horse and buggy. She could have
used that money in countless ways, but it had always been set aside for only
one thing—so Lelia could go to college. That was all Sarah had been
working for since she'd brought Lelia to St. Louis.

Now it was gone. Someone had come into Sarah's home and stolen
her heart. Her violated house no longer seemed to belong to her. Her life
no longer belonged to her. Sarah was too stricken, shocked, and despairing
even to cry. She stood stock-still in her bedroom for several minutes, listening to her labored breathing, wondering when she would awaken from
this cruel, unexpected nightmare.

"Mama?" Sarah barely heard Lelia's voice when her daughter ventured
into the room. "Who would do this, Mama? Wh-who would do something
like this?" Lelia kept repeating as she walked through their house, gazing at
the intruder's careless damage. Her eyes were also free of tears, but they
were bloodred. "I d-didn't know people did this."

Sarah felt her insides heaving, and she ran for the back door. As soon
as she was standing over the grass in her backyard, she vomited. Hot claws
raked through her trembling body.

She felt Lelia stroking her back. "Mama, don't you worry. It's all right,
hear? We don't need that money. I'll just wait and go to school when it's
saved up again, or maybe I'll marry and I won't need to go at all. We'll be
fine, Mama. You and me both, we'll be just fine."

Lelia's cheerful encouragement sounded painfully naive to Sarah's ear,
and she retched again. Didn't Lelia understand? If something happened to
Sarah tomorrow—if she got kicked by a horse, if she slipped and hit her

head, if she choked on her food, if the Lord called her home while she slept—Lelia would have *nothing*. Sarah wouldn't leave her daughter anything more than Moses had been able to leave her when he was killed, or any more than her own parents had been able to leave when Yellow Jack took them. *Mosquitoes. They're sayin' in the papers how the fever ain't carried by nothin' but those li'l ol' mosquitoes. My mama and papa didn't live long enough to give me nothin' 'cause of damned mosquitoes. And now it's the same with me.*

"Mama, it's all right. Stop shaking. It's all right," Lelia said soothingly. "I don't care anything about that money. I don't care one whit."

Even Lelia's lies couldn't make Sarah's shaking go away.

For the first few days, Sarah avoided even Sadie and Rosetta, since her two best friends were among the barest few people who'd even known the money was in the house. Together she and Lelia made a list of everyone they could think of who might have known—people from church, people from school, people who lived on their street—and they could not find a single suspect they believed could actually have done such a thing.

"After this, I've gotten so I'm thinkin' I better lock my door when I leave my house. But my door in back ain't got no locks nohow," Rosetta said, shaking her head. " 'Fore long, I guess we'll all be locked up tight like the whole street's nothin' but a row o' prison cells."

Sarah never found out who took the money.

But not even a week after the theft, another shock made Sarah nearly forget their loss. She and Lelia were washing in the kitchen in a despondent silence. Out of the corner of her eye, Sarah saw Lelia reach across the stove. The next thing she saw was a startling flash of flame, and suddenly the sleeve of Lelia's dress was on fire.

Lelia shrieked, flapping her arm in the air to try to extinguish the flames. Instead the fire seemed to celebrate, growing brighter. *"Mama!"*

The stupor that had clouded Sarah's thoughts since the theft was magically gone, and she felt more alertness in her mind than she had in days. She grabbed a damp bedsheet she'd just wrung out and wrapped it around Lelia's burning clothes, patting the fire down while she tried to hush her hysterical daughter. Lelia's face was tear-streaked, reminding Sarah of the way she'd looked when she cried as a very young child.

"Lemme see, Lelia. *Shhhh*," Sarah said once the fire was out, pulling the singed sheet away so she could examine her daughter's injury. The fire seemed to have caught near her elbow; the dress was almost completely burned away across her forearm, and she could see raw, red skin peeking through. The burn was bad. Not as awful as it might have been, thank the Lord, but probably too bad for a little butter and a homemade bandage.

"I'll get your coat, baby girl. We're goin' to the doctor. You know that colored doctor, Dr. Wells, just bought that house over on the next street? We're goin' over there right now."

"We don't have any money for a doctor, Mama," Lelia said softly, barely audibly. Her tears and shrieking had stopped, but now she looked crushed. The fire had broken through the facade she'd tried to put on for her mother to soften the pain of the theft.

"Don't you worry," Sarah said, confident again. "Just come on."

It was suppertime at the Wellses', Sarah realized when his wife opened the door to their well-lit, two-story home; the thin, neatly dressed woman was carrying a serving spoon coated in some kind of gravy. Their parlor floor was covered with a lovely Oriental rug, which Sarah couldn't help noticing despite her worry for Lelia. There were also shelves of books visible, and even some sort of bust displayed within her sight. This family might live only a block away, but their home was a glimpse into a much better life, she thought.

Dr. Lincoln Wells was a bearded man in his mid-thirties, nearly as tall as Moses had been. Graciously, he insisted their visit was no inconvenience to him. He led Sarah and Lelia into the kitchen, where he brought out a black bag.

"Let's look at your burn, dear," he said, cutting away what remained of Lelia's dress with a small pair of scissors. While Lelia winced in pain, he cleaned her arm until the visible raw patch looked much less alarming than it had at home. Still, the burn was as large as a soda cracker. The doctor examined it with a furrowed brow. "I've got something for this."

While Sarah and Lelia watched, Dr. Wells opened a box marked *sulfur powder* and mixed it with heated oil. Then, very carefully, he applied the mixture to Lelia's wound. Lelia screwed her eyes tight, her teeth gritted against the pain. "That should fix it up, Mrs. McWilliams," the doctor said. "You take this sulfur home and mix it just like I showed you, then you reapply it every few hours. You'll be amazed at how well sulfur heals. You'll hardly see a mark. The skin will grow back fine. Even these fine little hairs on her arm will grow, I promise you."

"Well, I shouldn't mind if they didn't," Lelia told him, smiling for the first time.

Dr. Wells refused Sarah's offer to wash his laundry in exchange for his medical services. *It's nothing to me except a few minutes away from my table, Mrs. McWilliams. Pay me when you can,* he said. *I'm only happy the burn wasn't more serious.*

So that night at her own dinner table, enjoying chicken stew, yams, and collard greens with Lelia, Sarah felt a wave of gratitude. A thief had entered her house and given her a taste of evil, but God had answered evil with grace. Thank goodness Lelia would be all right, and thank goodness Dr. Wells had been so close by to help. Life *was* just fine, after all.

After a special prayer of thanks, Sarah retired to her bed and felt a smile on her lips as sleep began to wash over her. She'd been restless and angry the past few nights, but she knew tonight would be different. Tonight, at last, she would sleep peacefully.

But just as she began to doze, Dr. Wells's words came back to Sarah's mind, snapping her eyes wide open. *You'll be amazed at what sulfur can do for injuries. Even these fine little hairs on your arm will grow back, I promise you.* She held her breath, excited.

Sulfur! If sulfur could heal a burn, could it also heal her scalp? What was it she remembered about sulfur . . . ?

Still only half awake, Sarah recalled a hazy image from childhood: sitting between her mother's knees with a winter cold, during the months when it was so cold she got sick when she bathed, while her mother used a comb in her head. But it wasn't just a regular combing; this time her mother had stuck a fluffy wad of cotton in the teeth after treating the cotton with . . . sulfur. *Don't want you gittin' wet, Sarah, but this sulfur will clean yo' head without no water.*

Yes, sometimes Mama used lye in the comb, and sometimes she used sulfur. Was that a real memory, or some strange sort of dream-memory? And if she put sulfur in her scalp now, could it help the hair on her head finally start growing back? *Tomorrow,* Sarah thought, feeling her weary mind tugging against her. *I'll ask Dr. Wells tomor . . .*

Sulfur was the last thing on Sarah's mind before she went to sleep.

Chapter Sixteen

DECEMBER 1904
TWO MONTHS LATER

While the smoke fanned away from her face in snakelike wisps, Sarah held her breath, waiting for her image in the handheld looking glass to become clear. The oily scent of the smoke irritated the lining of her nose, and the swath of hair at her forehead was hot and uncomfortable, but Sarah didn't flinch or move. She simply stared, waiting.

She heard Lelia breathing hard beside her. "Ooh, Mama . . ."

Then, instantly, the smoke was gone and Sarah could see. The hair at her forehead was gleaming black, and a tiny section lay in a limp bang, warm and light, hanging nearly to her eyebrows. And it was straight. Not straight and *thin* like a white woman's hair, but straight and thick, with gentle waves. Sarah blinked several times as she stared, barely able to trust her eyes. The hair looked almost like one of Etta's old stage wigs. When Sarah swallowed, she realized there was no moisture in her mouth.

"Mama, it *works* . . ." Lelia whispered, although her voice was edged with disbelief.

Could it be? All from a steel comb?

True to her promise to herself, Sarah had been busy. Since the theft, she'd put her mind on her plan, thinking of little else from the moment she woke up in the morning until she drifted to fractured sleep at night, if she slept at all. *Hair cure.* She'd written the words on a clean white sheet of paper, taking everything down from her Wish Board except that.

She'd easily won a job as a Poro representative, using her persistence and apparent enthusiasm to impress the woman hiring for Miss Malone. Sarah tried to bring the same enthusiasm with her when she knocked on her neighbors' doors, but her secrets made her a poor saleswoman. She tried to sound bright and convincing to women who opened their doors to her, but Sarah knew that the few sales she made were *despite* herself. After all, when customers commented on how lush and healthy Sarah's hair looked, she could only chuckle.

That wasn't from the Poro, no, sir. Sarah had a formula of her own.

She was finally convinced she had refined the hair-growing formula she needed, using variations of familiar ingredients, both old and new. First, there was the rod wax Etta had introduced her to, petrolatum, that served as the base; then burdock (by soaking burdock roots in olive oil the way her mama used to when she soothed their bug bites and skin infections), rose hips (taking a sign from her dream, since she'd heard the old-timers say for years that rose hips could be good medicine), and elder flowers (following a suggestion from Rosetta, who said her mother swore by elder-flower water when her skin was irritated).

But the biggest piece of the puzzle, by far, was the sulfur.

After consulting with Dr. Wells, who told her he believed sulfur would work just fine in a hair grower, Sarah bought a one-pound bag for twenty cents. Then she began mixing it into her hair formula, just to see what would happen. Within only a week, she noticed that she was itching even less than she had using Poro. Then within three weeks after that, Sadie and Rosetta confirmed for her that her hair seemed to be growing back. Just a little, but *growing.*

By now Sarah was *sure* of it. Her hair was thicker and fuller than it had been in years, and it was no longer retreating at her temples. And tonight Sarah felt a giddy premonition that another puzzle had just been solved. Gazing at her treated tuft of hair in the mirror, Sarah felt a growing sense of disbelief: Everything might be about to change, and all because of a steel comb!

"Mama, who told you about this comb?" Lelia asked her, examining the strange comb.

"I saw one a long time ago, baby," Sarah said, speaking in a faraway voice, mesmerized by her own hair. "I was just a young li'l gal, runnin' after this Cajun witch lady to see if she could save my parents from yellow fever. An' this witch lady had a colored gal jus' settin' between her legs, an' Mama Nadine was runnin' a hot comb through her head. I 'member seeing all the steam an' smoke rise up, an' I thought she was doing magic. So it stayed in my mind, but I hadn't really thought nothin' of it since that time. Seems almost like it was a dream.

"But last week I saw a comb that looked just like it, a comb with metal teeth, that one right in your hand. See, this one lady I wash for is from France, an' this iron comb was jus' sittin' on her table. The lady's name is Mrs. Bettencourt, but white folks from France ain't like the ones here, Lelia, an' she told me I could call her by her Christian name, which she says is Gabrielle. She said she used it to curl her hair. An' I asked her where she got that comb from, 'cause I wanted to find one. She gave it to me! She laughed an' said, 'I'll have my brother send me another one from Paris,' an' she put it right in my hand!"

Lelia's voice trembled with excitement. "Mama . . . you think your whole head would look like this part here if I oil it up and run this comb through?"

Sarah's heart leaped to hear the words spoken aloud. Her thoughts were spinning so fast in her head that she could barely catch one. "That's what I'm sure enough thinkin', Lelia. It works better than a fork, don't it?"

"Mama, do me first!" Lela shrieked, grabbing Sarah by both shoulders. "Please?"

What Sarah saw in her daughter's eyes—amazement, gratitude, even a little desperation—nearly took her breath away. *Lord have mercy*, she thought. *Look how this child is actin'! There ain't no money in the world she wouldn't pay me to put this comb in her hair.*

And Sarah felt her toes curling, as if to anchor herself from floating away.

"Lelia? What in the world you doin' standin' out in this cold—" Sadie began, then she gasped as she opened her door wider and saw Lelia standing in the lamplight from her house. "Oh, my . . ."

Lelia clutched her side from laughing so hard. "Mama, come see her face!"

Sure enough, Sadie was staring at Lelia wide-eyed, her mouth dragging to her chin. Her eyes were riveted to Lelia's hair.

After more than two hours, Sarah had finally finished combing through Lelia's hair with the hot steel comb. She'd accidentally burned the top of her daughter's earlobe (not once, but twice) and probably a spot or two on her scalp, but after her initial painful exclamations, Lelia hadn't complained. She'd never once let go of the looking glass, so she'd watched every moment of her mother's progress, seeing her hair emerge sizzling from the comb, lengthened and glistening, falling against her neck. After some impromptu barbering with the household scissors to even up a few places, Sarah had styled Lelia's hair so that it had a bang in front and hung midway to her shoulders, jet black and as close to straight as it had ever been.

Sarah barely noticed the frigid air that turned her breath to fog while she waited for Sadie's reaction. Lelia couldn't contain her giggles, posing her head from one side to the other, dramatically tossing her hair back with her hand.

Tentatively, Sadie reached up to touch the end of Lelia's hair. "Your hair grower did *this?*"

"No, this is different," Sarah told her. "I jus' put on some rod wax to grease it. Then I combed it out with a hot steel comb, an' jus' *look* at it. It's all pressed out! That hair won't give her *no* trouble brushin' through. An' she could plait it, or pin it up. . . ."

"Sarah, you're gonna put Poro to shame!" Sadie said, clasping her hands together tightly. "Ooh, Lord, where'd my coat go? We have to go show Rosetta, too. She'll faint dead away!"

"I almost don't believe it my own self," Sarah said. Her cheeks were nearly numb from the cold, but she still felt them flushing. It was the day before her birthday, three days before Christmas, and it seemed that the world had just laid itself at her feet.

Walking quickly toward Rosetta's house three blocks away, the group was like a miniature parade in the darkened street, with Lelia in the lead. Their chatter bounced off the houses they passed, lighting them up in their excitement. A wagon driver with a horse draped in blankets ambled past them on the cobblestone street, slowing as he passed them. "Merry Christmas, ladies!" he called, and they answered him in a heartfelt chorus.

It felt like a Merry Christmas, all right.

"First chance I get, I'ma quit Poro," Sarah said, breathing harder from walking so fast.

"Oh, girl, *yes*. You're through with that. Then we got to mix some more grower!"

"That's right. An' I'll start tellin' folks 'bout what that comb can do," Sarah said.

"*No*, Mama, not just *telling*," Lelia said. "Show them! Do their heads like mine."

"That's right, Sarah. And I'm next. I'm comin' first thing in the morning, so you better fix an extra plate at breakfast! I don't care how much Rosetta begs, she can't go before me."

"Mama, do you know how much money you'll make?" Lelia said, nearly shouting the words. Her voice lingered in the night air like a bird coasting on the chilled wind above them. "You could buy a motorcar!"

"What would your mama want with one of those broke-down, horse-scarin' machines?" Sadie dismissed her. "You can't hardly drive 'em through a mud puddle. What she *needs* to buy is a house, and stop paying all that rent."

Listening to Lelia and Sadie arguing about her imaginary riches, Sarah laughed, nearly slipping on a black patch of ice as she tried to walk faster to keep up with them. A horseless carriage! A house! After the burglary, she could hardly get by week to week. Even now, she was wearing a fraying old coat because she'd decided she couldn't afford to buy a new one this winter. And it was well and good to think about making more hair formula, but the sulfur and petrolatum cost *money*, not to mention her other ingredients. The more time she worked on her hair formula, the less time she would have for washing. And she would definitely need more than one steel comb, if she was going to teach Sadie how to do demonstrations on potential customers. Hell, she'd want to teach Rosetta, too. . . .

Sarah's mind was in full roar. Without realizing it, she'd stopped listening to the conversation around her, forgetting where she was going and why, not noticing how numb her toes felt as her shoes sank into the crushed, icy snow on the sidewalk.

Sarah Breedlove McWilliams was far away, already making bigger plans.

Chapter Seventeen

Sarah knew that the spring church-school picnic would be an affair to remember as soon as she woke up and saw the sunlight streaming through her window, bathing the blooming branches of her white hickory tree. It was the first picnic of the year—signaling the start of a string of summertime picnics and socials that were Sarah's only real leisure.

But this year summer picnics wouldn't mean just pleasure, no, sir. They would provide the new customers she'd need for the batches of formula she had been mixing up with Lelia, Sadie, and Rosetta. Winter had been slow, but spring would be different. She now had twenty customers who regularly used her hair formula, not even counting Sadie and Rosetta; all of them came with tin cups to scoop out their portion of the remedy from the washtub she mixed it in, and more than half of them also got their hair pressed with the comb in Sarah's kitchen whenever Sarah's schedule could allow it. So far Sarah was the only one who could press customers' heads; Rosetta had pressed Sarah's head only once, and she'd burned her so badly with that comb Sarah couldn't bring herself to let her friend practice on her again.

Because she had so many more hair customers, Sarah had been able to afford to let most of her washing customers go. She washed only two days a week, and her weekends were finally her own. But this was only the beginning, Sarah knew. She wasn't making *more* money than she'd made before, just the *same* money. She needed more customers. She wanted to be like Annie T. Malone, who was probably making more money with Poro than she could count.

Sarah fixed Quaker Oats from a box for breakfast, quickly finished her morning chores, then dressed herself in a long skirt and a clean white shirtwaist with long puffed sleeves she'd starched especially for today. Once she was ready, Sarah tentatively knocked on Lela's door. When she didn't hear a response, she knocked again. "Lela, you comin' to the picnic?"

A groan emerged from Lela's closed door, but nothing else. All the girl did on the weekends was sleep! Sarah feared Lelia was growing up to be too much like Etta for her own good. It was ten o'clock exactly. What decent woman stayed in bed all day?

"I'm goin' on by myself, then." She sighed, resigned. Only a mumble came in response.

Quickly Sarah brushed through her hair, which now grew more than halfway to her shoulders when it was treated with the comb. Papa had always claimed he had some Indian blood in him, and now that seemed apparent to Sarah. Or maybe it was all the African in her, and in another life she might have had long braids running down her back; after all, her hair was still full and textured, not limp and flat like an Indian's or like most white women's hair. And she didn't want it to look like anyone else's hair, either. Sarah liked what she had. Her hair had been breaking off most of her life, so she'd never been able to appreciate it properly. Until now.

And she wasn't alone, she thought as she pinned up her hair so she could put on her flat white spring hat, which was adorned with artificial flowers. There were hundreds, probably thousands of black women just like her who had no idea how much their hair could offer them, who wore kerchiefs all day long and barely let their hair even peek out.

Well, not anymore, Sarah told herself. She was never going to wear a kerchief again. And if she had her way, other colored women would be taking theirs off for good, too.

Today, as was the custom at many picnics, the morning was reserved for speakers. Sarah's blanket was almost smack in the center of the picnic group, so she was close enough to hear the people who stood atop a wide crate beside the old oak tree to address them, a light spring breeze carrying their voices while bicyclists sped past them on the park's twisting paths. The messages were often repetitive, but Sarah enjoyed the spirit of uplift at picnics nearly as much as when she'd heard Booker T. Washington and Margaret Murray Washington. Everything the speakers said bolstered ideas she already held dear, just like a good sermon, and every once in a while she even learned something new.

Work hard. Save your money. Avoid the sins of alcohol and tobacco. She'd heard the messages many times before, and lived by most of them as well as she could.

As she picked through her basket to find some corn bread to nibble on, an introduction caught her ear: ". . . Here to talk about the wonders of the advertising age, visiting us all the way from Denver, Colorado, Mr. Charles Walker . . ."

"Good-ness *gracious*," Sadie breathed, a voice Sarah knew well: It meant a handsome man was in her sight. Sadie would never openly admire a man with anyone except Sarah, but as Sadie had told her many times, she was married, not blind. "Will you look here?"

Sarah didn't need any prompting. When she looked up, her first glimpse of the grinning man shaking the hand of the deacon who introduced him was enough to make her forget the advertising notion that had originally caught her attention, at least for a moment. Mr. Charles Walker of Denver, Colorado, was a honey-complexioned man wearing a stylish gray mohair suit and vest, a crimson bow tie, and a finely braided flat white straw hat with a crimson band. His gold watch chain dangled from his vest, gleaming. He gave a bow, his grin wider.

"He's a dandy, ain't he? Sure seems impressed with himself," Sadie muttered.

He's got reason to be, Sarah thought. The man was striking, with broad shoulders and a smoothly contoured jawline and chin that made his face so handsome it would have been pretty if not for his well-groomed mustache. His curly hair was dark, with reddish gleams in the sunlight. Sarah guessed he had likely spent more time fussing over himself to get dressed that morning than she had. *He prob'ly smells like honey soap,* she thought, and her face flushed warm.

"Ladies and gentlemen, boys and girls . . ." the man began, raising his voice loudly enough to carry above the squawking of the ducks at the nearby pond. "How many of y'all know we're in the middle of a revolution this very minute?" He sounded like one of the barkers from the fair.

But at least he had the audience's attention. Sarah didn't blink.

"That's right! As I speak to you today, all across the country, we are smack in the middle of an ad-ver-ti-sing revolution. Advertising is changing the way we live our lives more than any other time in this nation's whole history. And folks, I'm tellin' you, we need to be a part of it before it passes us on by. How many of y'all eat Uneeda Biscuits? Come on, now, 'fess up."

About forty hands went up. A few children cheered, recognizing the name of their favorite soda crackers. "Can't *stand* them dry, nasty things . . ." Sadie muttered to Sarah.

"I only see a few hands up, but I know more of you have at least *tried* 'em, too!" Mr. Walker said, assessing the group. Sarah cast Sadie a look, and they both laughed. "Now, what's so special about Uneeda Biscuits? They usin' some new kind of flour? They taste any different than any other kind of soda cracker? I ain't tried 'em all myself, but I wager they don't. So how come all you folks are eating 'em? I'll tell you why: Because you see the posters at the train depot. Because they got Uneeda salesmen everywhere you look. Even your dang shopkeeper is wearing Uneeda Biscuits cuff links, ain't he?" He was speaking so fast, he was nearly breathless.

Sarah, joining the audience, murmured in agreement. He was right! She'd never bought any Uneeda Biscuits, but she'd bought Quaker Oats because she'd seen the ads on billboards and painted on brick walls on the buildings downtown. Mr. Walker went on: "Now, listen to this here: That company spent a million dollars—and lemme say it again, *a million dollars*—on advertising alone. Know why?"

" 'Cause they crazy!" a man shouted, and the audience laughed.

"Naw, sir, they ain't crazy," Mr. Walker said, still grinning goodnaturedly. "No more crazy than Sears Roebuck. Or Heinz 57 Varieties. Or Egg-O-See Cereal. Those companies all know advertising *works*. Now, how many of y'all got some kind of business of your own? I ain't even talkin' about a big one—whether you're making brooms, selling sweetpotato pies, or if you've got your own barbershop or mortuary, how many of y'all out there are in some kind of business tryin' to make some money?"

Quickly, Sarah raised her hand high, rising to her knees. Several others raised their hands, too, but Sarah was almost certain she had caught Mr. Walker's eye. When he spoke, he seemed to be looking directly at her. "That's good! Lots of folks in business! Now, how many of y'all with these businesses ever done any advertising in a colored newspaper?"

Sarah lowered her hand, glancing around to look at the others. Only two or three hands remained high; and all of those raised, Sarah noticed, belonged to folks rich enough to afford it.

Mr. Walker shook his head, making a clucking sound. "Good people, businessmen, I am *begging* you . . . you need to ad-ver-tise. Reverend, I hope you won't mind me saying it, but Jesus Christ himself could come give a speech at the lecture hall, and every seat in there would be empty unless somebody told folks the blessed son of God was coming today. Better be up on a poster somewhere, or better be a big ol' ad in the *St. Louis Palladium*, or the *Argus*, or *somewhere*. Now, ain't that right?"

The audience laughed. As Charles Walker spoke, Sarah felt her heart pounding. He had the same faith in his message a preacher would have in God's word, and his faith radiated from his face. If she did nothing else today, she decided, she had to talk to Charles Walker.

"Whew! That man could sell milk to a cow," Sadie said. "He's talkin' sense, though."

"I know he is."

It was more than *what* he said, Sarah realized as she listened to him and watched his eyes move from face to face; it was the *way* he said it. His voice was lulling, entertaining, and persuasive, all at once. He sounded as smart as a university graduate, yet as folksy as anyone she might meet on the street. Even Reverend Simms was smiling as he listened, despite Mr. Walker's off-color remark about Jesus at the lecture hall. The man was up there weaving magic.

And Sarah wasn't the only one who noticed.

The instant Charles Walker bowed to signal the end of his speech, half a dozen men walked up to seek him out, shaking his hand and patting his back. A few young women also scurried to the edge of the huddle, listening to the men's banter with interest; they were high-yellow women dressed in their nicest spring dresses, and Sarah was sure they wanted to meet Mr. Walker for reasons other than business. Whether or not Mr. Walker was married, those kind of ladies had a way of making men forget everything else on their minds, Sarah thought.

"You go on and eat, Sadie," Sarah said, picking up the long, thin box of samples she'd brought in an assortment of rusting tin cups. "I'ma go see if I can't talk to Mr. Walker."

"Shoot, girl, no tellin' how long he'll be tied up. You should eat first. That's what folks do at picnics, you know."

Sarah sighed, pursing her lips. Mr. Walker had been the last scheduled speaker, so the rest of the picnickers were busily unwrapping their lunches, laughing and socializing. At the other end of the park, Sarah noticed, some men and women from their group were setting up a game of croquet. She'd never played croquet in her life, or lawn tennis, either. And she could count on one hand the times she'd played whist with her friends in the past year. Watching them, Sarah wondered for a moment why she couldn't just eat and play like everyone else. Why didn't she ever sit still and catch her breath? Lela had asked her that question many times, and she didn't know the answer. There were always so many other things to think about, so many things to do.

"You know me better than that, Sadie," Sarah told her friend.

The men surrounding Mr. Walker were rattling excitedly while the women clustered behind them in silence. ". . . been advertising for ten years, Mr. Walker, and you ain't lyin' . . ."

". . . Now, which paper did you say you work for in Denver? I have an enterprise . . ."

Sarah waited patiently as long as she could, then she slowly began to nudge her way past the ladies. She heard one of the women snort behind her, but she didn't have time to address that kind of foolishness. Sarah was standing no more than two feet from him now, so close she could see the slightly discolored razor bumps on his neck and smell the freshness of his clothes. Streaks of gray hair in his sideburns gave him a distinguished air, but he didn't look like he had reached forty. *He's probably 'bout thirty-seven, the same age as me, then*, Sarah thought.

Finally the men stopped talking for a moment to share a laugh.

Sarah spoke up quickly. "Mr. Walker," she said, extending her hand to shake the way a man would. "My name is Sarah McWilliams, and I have a business, too. I sell a hair formula I make in my own . . ."

"Is that right? Best of luck, madam!" Mr. Walker said, squeezing her hand warmly with both of his, but Sarah's spirits fell when she realized how empty his grin was. His copper-colored eyes had passed across her so quickly, she wondered if he had seen her at all. He was once again gazing up at one of the gentlemen, swallowed in conversation.

Sarah glanced back, annoyed, when one of the women tittered behind her. "It's not easy to get C.J.'s attention," the woman said with a strained smile, cooling herself with a lacy fan. "And harder still to keep it."

Sarah recognized the woman from occasional appearances at church, usually at Easter and Christmastime, but she couldn't recall her name. She was tall and regal, always carrying herself with an air of superiority. She was almost fair enough to pass for white, and Sadie had told Sarah the woman somehow managed to remind folks of that as often as possible. And she'd called the man C.J. Obviously she was staking her claim. Sarah felt embarrassment glowing in her cheeks. Did this woman think she'd come all the way up here to throw herself after some strange man at a Sunday-school picnic?

"Oh, wait! I know you, Mrs. McWilliams!" the woman said, her eyes lighting with excitement that did not strike Sarah as sincere. "Don't you take in washing?" She'd said it just loudly enough that Sarah knew the woman was purposely trying to humiliate her.

"All my life, an' I saved enough to send my daughter to college," Sarah said brusquely, a tremor of pride and anger in her voice. She clutched her box of samples closer to her side. "I also have my own business, miss. I mix a hair formula."

The women shared condescending smiles between them that filled Sarah with rage. Spoiled, ignorant heifers! If she weren't within hearing distance of the minister and the deacons, Sarah would give them a tongue-lashing that would make them go pale. Sarah's jaw locked tight, but there was nothing for her to do except turn around and walk back to the picnic blanket where Sadie was waiting. But she could not. And she wasn't going to stand here all afternoon hoping to steal the attention of Charles Walker, either. Suddenly Sarah realized she had another plan altogether, and the thought of it made her heart gallop.

"Excuse me, ladies," Sarah said, forcing a smile, and she began walking toward the crate beneath the oak tree, the speaker's stump where Charles Walker had given his address.

Sarah, what in the world are you about to do? she thought desperately, even as she lifted her skirt to climb atop the two-foot crate. Then she surveyed the picnic area from her perch. She was standing at the focal point of attention, and it was too late to change her mind. Sarah felt a thin film of perspiration prickle across her face, arms, and chest. Her heart flew, and even her knees couldn't keep steady. *Girl, you've finally lost your damn mind. What's come over you?*

"Afternoon, everyone," Sarah called out, but her voice sounded fragile. There was no change in the loud murmur of conversation at the picnic, although the minister cast her a puzzled look. And Sarah couldn't quite make out all the features of Sadie's face, but she knew her friend must be shocked to see her standing there. She was a hair away from abandoning her wild notion altogether when she remembered the way Charles Walker had made his voice rise.

"Ladies and gentlemen! I know y'all are eating your fried chicken and biscuits, but I need your ear for just one minute!"

Slowly, very slowly, the conversation began to fade. Soon only a few families in the back were talking, and someone's baby was wailing as if to raise the dead. Sarah decided this was as much quiet as she was likely to get. "Most of y'all here know me, but for those of you who don't, my name is Sarah McWilliams. I'm—"

"Speak up, Sister McWilliams!" a man bellowed from the back.

Sarah paused, momentarily flustered, but then she went on. "This better?" she cried. She was straining so hard, it nearly hurt her throat, but she forgot that as soon as she heard the smattering of applause. Sarah heaved in a deep breath, wondering what she was planning to say now. But the words came to her mouth as if they didn't need her help.

"Well, now! I don't mind sayin' I sure am nervous standin' up here like this, y'all. So if I tumble down from here, you'll know my knees gave out!"

Laughter. What a beautiful sound! Sarah's throat, which had been dry from nervousness, regained some moisture. "Now we just heard Mr. Charles Walker give that wonderful talk on advertising, an' I agree with every word he said." Sarah knew the savvy man from Denver must be watching her, but she couldn't muster the nerve to glance his way. "An' the best advertising I know is what we call the grapevine. That's what got us by 'fore most of us could even read a newspaper, so that's what I'm gonna use today. But instead of goin' from blanket to blanket like I was plannin', I saw this empty stump up here an' thought maybe it was my turn to make a speech. I feel I must tell you about a hair preparation that has been no less than a miracle to me, an' it happens to be one I make in my own kitchen."

There were more chuckles. Again remembering the cue from Charles Walker, Sarah tried to find the eyes of as many ladies as she could, speaking to them directly. "I know if somebody'd said to me a few years ago they had a formula that could grow hair, well, you would've had to try to beat me off with a stick. Y'all who know me, I ain't shamed to say, I had so much botheration 'til it seemed like half the hair was about to fall out my head. Well, those days are long gone for me, and some of you may think it's 'cause I've been using a product called Poro."

A few women, probably Poro users themselves, murmured.

"Well, I ain't gon' say nothing against Poro or Annie T. Malone, since some of y'all know her, and she is a fine member of this community. But I will say that God was good enough to give me the knowledge to make up my own formula, an' I've been using it almost eight months now. I can talk about it 'til I run out of breath, but I always say the best way to make a point is to *show* it. So that's what I'ma do. . . ."

With that, her fingers trembling slightly, Sarah laid her box of hair formula at her feet. Then she reached up behind her head to unpin her hat. That done, she pulled the pins out of her hair one at a time, until clumps of it began to fall loose. No doubt, she thought, the minister might not approve of *this*, a woman loosening her hair at a church picnic! But Sarah only shook her head to further free her hair, using her hands to try to flatten it more neatly.

This time she did glance at Charles Walker, and he was gazing right back. For an instant Sarah was struck by the boldness of what she was doing, and she felt her heart trip again.

"Mr. Walker, I guess this is another kind of advertising," she said, and there was more laughter. He smiled at her. "Now I hope y'all don't think I'm bein' too immodest. But the thing is, you really have to see it or you wouldn't believe I was tellin' the truth. My hair grower has given me this hair in a few months' time. And I have another treatment with a comb to give it this length for weeks. I don't use lard, and I don't wrap my hair, neither. As you can see, it's growing to my neck. Now, I have some of my grower for sale here today, but I know there are those of y'all who still won't believe it. Reverend, like you told us at church last week, even some of Jesus' disciples who saw his miracles still had doubts. So for those folks, I say come right by my house any evenin' this week, or even after the picnic today, an' I will give you the same comb treatment—for free."

There were a couple of audible gasps from women, then warm applause.

"An' after I do it once, ladies, you'll be callin' after me all hours to get it done again. You'll never be satisfied to have your hair like it was before."

"It's true! She been combin' mine!" one of Sarah's customers called out, an older woman named Claire Newcomb. Sarah saw her waving a white handkerchief above her head.

Sarah pointed. "That's right. Now, Sister Claire, you go on and stand up an' let the folks see," she said, motioning with growing confidence. Claire had an impressive head of hair for someone in her sixties, and she obligingly pulled off her hat so the picnickers could see how she'd swept her hair into a beautiful style. "I can do the same for any of y'all," Sarah went on. "An' with so many folks out there claimin' they got a miracle cure, I thought I'd better let you know there's a miracle in your own house, so to speak. It's at a price everybody here can afford—and if it don't do what I'm sayin', well, I'll give your money right back."

When Sarah finished speaking, three women were already waiting for her to ask to buy a sample of hair formula, and all of them asked where she lived so they could come for a combing demonstration. Even as she spoke to them, Sarah noticed more women standing up, gathering up their skirts to make their way over to talk to her.

She didn't have a free moment to think about Mr. Charles Walker the entire afternoon.

By evening, Sarah's kitchen was as bustling as a barbershop. While Sadie, Rosetta, and Lelia mixed formula and prepared ingredients in jars and bowls throughout the kitchen, Sarah had one customer sitting in a chair in front of her while two others waited in chairs against the wall. The kitchen smelled of smoke from the hot comb, forcing all of them to cough occasionally. Sarah's face was knit in concentration as she tried to comb her customer's hair without burning her scalp, and her hand was already slightly cramped. The process wasn't easy; when she pulled the comb off the stove, she had to test it against a paper napkin to make sure the napkin wouldn't burn. If the comb wouldn't burn paper, she'd learned, it wouldn't burn the hair.

Sarah had sold all of her samples at the picnic, and she had at least two dozen orders to fill by the time she went to church tomorrow morning. Almost every woman at the picnic had wanted to either try her grower or send some to someone they knew, and Sarah had promised to have it ready. She'd learned from her experience selling Poro that customers easily forgot their fervor and were quick to change their minds. She only prayed that she and her friends would be able to collect enough old mason jars, tin cups, and tin cans to deliver that many orders on such short notice. Usually she was lucky to get two or three new customers in a month. She'd never expected to generate such excitement at one gathering!

Something shattered on the floor. "Ooh—damn, damn, *damn*," Lelia's voice cried. "I dropped this damn— Oh, 'scuse me, y'all."

The women chuckled, but Sarah's temples flexed with anger. "Lela, hush. I can't understand why you started cursin' like a drunkard. An' if you dropped some o' that mix, you best scoop it up in something else. I don't have it to waste."

"*Damn* isn't real cursing, Mama," Lelia said. When had this girl gotten so sassy, and in the presence of guests?

"Girl, you better find somethin' to fix up that mess, and hush your mouth 'fore I hush it for you," Sarah said. At that, Lelia sighed and began to search frantically for something to salvage the ingredients she'd spilled on the floor.

"That sho' was cussin' in my day, 'specially for ladies," Rosetta said, stirring the rod wax in her bowl. "Now you got women sittin' in saloons without no corsets drinkin' whiskey, smokin' cigarettes, an' got they legs all up so's they petticoat's showin'.''

The women shook their heads and murmured with disgust, including the woman under Sarah's comb, who nearly got burned when her head moved. Her hair was coarse, so the comb needed to be *hot*. Sarah patted her shoulder to remind her to sit still.

"Some of 'em act worse than men, you ask me," Sarah said, remembering the woman who'd behaved so rudely to her earlier that day. "Spiteful! I thought I'd have to slap one o' them heifers at the picnic. Most of y'all know I got folks dear to me who's yellow as the day is long, but this high-yallow gal today was actin' like I was out to steal her man. I should've told her, I ain't got no more use for some dandy high-tone man than . . ."

But Sarah never finished her thought because the breath had been stolen from her throat. Suddenly her imagination was playing the strangest trick on her: She was sure Charles Walker himself was standing in her kitchen entryway, wearing the same clothes he'd worn at the picnic, with his hat pressed against his belly. She blinked fast, trying to clear away his image.

But when Rosetta and Lelia both gasped, she knew it was more than a trick of her eye.

Rosetta, who had never before seen him, held up her bowl as if she planned to throw it at him. "What in—"

Mr. Walker looked sheepish, backing up a step. "Oh, ladies, I'm so sorry. The front door is open, and I heard voices back here. Didn't nobody hear me calling?"

A thick silence fell over the women in the room. Lelia's eyes were as big as saucers, and she quickly wiped her hands on her apron as she stared. Sarah's heart seemed to have lodged itself behind her tonsils. Mr. Walker's presence felt foreign, somehow deeply personal. When was the last time she'd had a man in her kitchen? She couldn't even remember.

Despite a parched throat, Sarah broke the silence. "Can I help you . . . Mr. Walker?"

Mr. Walker nodded greetings to each woman in the room before stepping forward again, his hat still in his hand. "I didn't mean to walk back an' surprise y'all lovely ladies. I was jus' wondering where a newspaperman from Denver might leave his calling card for the proprietor of this here hair business. I heard so many good things at the picnic, my curiosity got the best of me, so I decided to come see this miracle cure for myself."

Nearly too late, Sarah realized she had left her comb in her customer's hair longer than she should have. Quickly she jerked the smoking comb away, and it clattered to the stove.

Sarah's mind had been wiped empty of her thoughts, a state that shocked her nearly as much as Mr. Walker's unexpected appearance. What was wrong with her? She needed to tell this man she was busy, that he had his nerve walking back here in the company of women he wasn't properly acquainted with, and he needed to learn some manners.

Instead she heard herself speaking in her most polite tones. "Well, Mr. Walker . . . you might find some room for a calling card on that table. Lela, clear up that mess for Mr. Walker."

Lelia looked at Sarah with obvious surprise, then she exchanged a glance with Sadie, who was smiling knowingly. Finally, with her lips tight, Lelia moved aside some bowls and mixing spoons to make a clear space at the edge of the kitchen table. For a moment, none of the other women spoke or moved, as if Mr. Walker's presence had mesmerized them.

"Who is *this?*" Rosetta finally asked pointedly, breaking the silence.

"Rosetta, this is Mr. Charles Walker from Denver," Sarah said. "He's . . ." Then she faltered. She couldn't even begin to explain why he was there, since she didn't know herself.

"Madam," Mr. Walker said, moving forward to shake Rosetta's hand. "I'm sorry to intrude. I'm a newspaperman—I sell advertisements in Denver—and Mrs. McWilliams said some things today I couldn't get out of my head. I have a great interest in new businesses, you see, ventures an' such. We didn't have an opportunity to speak earlier. I was hopin' she could tell me what time might suit her."

You missed your opportunity, Sarah thought, nearly smiling. But she was still as impressed by Mr. Walker's eloquence as she had been at the picnic. He could put words together, all right! Glancing at the other women, Sarah saw that they were impressed, too. Even Lelia was gazing at Mr. Walker as if he were a prized discovery, trying to be subtle as she straightened her apron and patted down her hair.

But Mr. Walker didn't look Lelia's way. He was gazing dead-on at Sarah. "Madam, I fear you're busy," he said. "I do believe I've picked a bad time."

Madam! He'd used the word often, and Sarah liked his formal manner of address, which was so unusual to her ear. Her chest swelled.

"Well . . . you see I'm fixin' hair right now. . . . I don't know how these ladies would feel . . ."

"He can stay!" Sadie said, cutting her off. "Why not? Right, ladies?"

The other women agreed.

So, for the better part of an hour, Charles Walker stayed in Sarah's kitchen, refusing to accept food or drink, simply studying the mixing being done at the table, then strolling behind Sarah to watch the work she was doing with the hot comb. Occasionally, he asked questions—*How long does this procedure take? How long does the effect of the hot comb last? How long have you been doing this? How do you deliver your formula after it's mixed?*— but for the most part he studied them in silence.

And soon the women began talking again, nearly forgetting he was there.

Finally, standing out of her sight behind her, Mr. Walker spoke to Sarah in a low, private tone. "I need to take the Tuesday train. I really hope we'll have a few moments to talk before I leave for Denver, Mrs. McWilliams," he said, then added even more softly, "That is, if Mr. Mc-Williams won't mind."

Again, Sarah's heart danced. It was clear to her by now that Mr. Walker's only purpose in being here was probably to try to sell her an ad in his newspaper—what else would a man like him want with her?—but she couldn't control her body's excitement at the mere sound of his voice, almost as though he were touching her instead of only speaking. The blood in her veins was racing with anticipation. Even her nose was savoring his so-close scent; he didn't smell like honey soap the way she'd imagined, but his skin and clothes definitely smelled somehow sweet and masculine all at once. Lord have mercy! Sarah cursed at herself, trying to keep calm. *Remember, Sarah, he could jus' be tryin' to charm his way into stealin' your formula. What's he askin' all these questions for?* That thought helped Sarah snap back into herself again.

"Mayhap we can make an appointment Monday evening, Mr. Walker," she said primly. "And I'm a widow, sir, so it's been seventeen years since Mr. McWilliams would care 'bout my business meetings one way or the other."

Then she dared one glance around to look at Charles Walker, and the first thing she saw was his perfect, wonderful grin.

Chapter Eighteen

"I just don't like him, Mama. You saw the way he came in here all high and mighty!" Lelia said, frustrated, as she watched Sarah search her wardrobe for a dress to wear to supper with Mr. Charles Walker. He hadn't appeared at church as Sarah had hoped he would, but he'd slipped a note under her front door Sunday night, promising to pick her up at six o'clock Monday; he'd included the address of a nearby hotel and even a three-digit telephone number, which was useless to Sarah, since she did not know anyone with a telephone. Unsightly poles had been erected throughout her neighborhood like dead upright trees strung together, but most of her friends had neither telephones nor electricity. Electricity cost too much to wire throughout the house, and telephones just seemed like a needless bother.

Still, this one time, Sarah would have liked to telephone Mr. Walker to tell him she would be ready to meet him at six. It would have been nice to hear his voice, which had been fluttering through her mind all weekend.

Lelia scowled. "Mama, I've met pretty-talking men like him, and believe me, most of them aren't worth the clothes on their backs."

There was something too knowing, too wise, about Lelia's tone that made Sarah gaze back at her daughter suddenly, searching her face. Lelia's eyes held steady, and Sarah was almost certain she could see things written in her daughter's smoky eyes that she did not like at all.

Lelia sighed, searching for her words, then she went on, not blinking: "You've barely cracked a smile to a man in all the time I can remember, and you're so busy thinking about hair formula, I hate to think how long it's been since you've felt a man's hands and lips. . . ."

Shocked by Lelia's candor, Sarah whirled to face her. "That's none of your—"

"Mama, are you going to listen to sense for a minute? Try to forget I'm your daughter and let me talk to you like a grown woman."

Lelia's eyes looked weary in a way they should not, Sarah realized, as if her daughter had already been around the world and back. What had made them look that way? "Don't you get big with no child, actin' like a fool," Sarah said between gritted teeth.

Lelia shrugged. "Oh, I ain't having no babies, Mama. Don't worry about *that*."

The way she'd said that, Sarah knew there was something else behind the words, an unspoken invitation for Sarah to ask her more. But Lelia was likely to say anything at all, and Sarah realized her heart did not want to know her daughter's secrets. A woman's secrets were her own, and Lelia was a woman now whether Sarah liked it or not.

"So let me tell you what I think about this Charles Walker," Lelia went on, uninvited. "I can tell just by looking at him he's got a woman in every city he sets foot in. Men like that don't marry, 'cause they like the bachelor's life. They talk like gentlemen and dress like gentlemen, but they don't act like gentlemen."

Sarah felt her face turning dark. "Lelia, you act like we courtin'! The man asked me to supper to talk 'bout business."

Lelia put her hand on her hip, gazing down at Sarah as though she had never heard anything so silly. "Why would a man all the way from Denver care about what we're mixing in your little kitchen, Mama? You don't have to go to supper to talk about that. You can talk on the porch."

Maybe he believes in me, Sarah thought stubbornly, but she didn't say the words aloud. Lelia was right; Charles Walker had no reason to believe in her the way Lelia, Sadie, and Rosetta did. He didn't know her. He had no idea where she'd come from or what she'd been through. But what did he want with her, then?

"Just don't forget yourself, Mama," Lelia said, her tone softening. She wrapped her arms around Sarah in a hug. "There's some men who leave heartbreak behind them."

"Did someone do that to you, Lelia?" Sarah asked her, still afraid to know.

Lelia shrugged. "Maybe once, but that's all over for me," she breathed close to Sarah's ear. "In fact, Mama, I have something to tell you. . . ." Sarah felt her insides clench as tight as a fist, bracing for terrible news while Lelia put her at arm's length so she could gaze down into her eyes. "With my friends, I've been using a new name I made up for myself. I didn't tell you because I was afraid you'd think it was an insult to you and Daddy."

"A new name?" Sarah said, confused.

"It's like Lelia, but it's different," she said. "It's A'Lelia. I put an 'A' in front. I'll write it down for you so you can see how I like it. But don't get mad, Mama. Please?"

Sarah's heart leaped with relief. Compared to the unthinkable events she'd been afraid of, Lelia's news was so mild that Sarah almost smiled.

A'Lelia. The new name was close to Lelia's birth name, yet it was more suited to the tall, mysterious woman that Lelia had become. Sarah was honestly impressed that her daughter had enough creativity and confidence to want to choose her own name—just like Mrs. Brown, when she'd begun calling herself *America*—but it also saddened her. Her little girl was gone. The woman she'd become was fascinating company, changing so quickly and saying anything that popped into her mind, but Sarah was sure as hell going to miss her child.

"A'Lelia," Sarah said, trying the name on with her mouth. Her eyes smarted.

"Isn't it pretty, Mama?"

This time Sarah did manage to smile. Lelia sounded so eager, so pleased, and Sarah didn't want to ruin her joy. "It's pretty, all right," she said, meaning it. "I just hope you ain't expectin' me to remember to call you by that. You'll always be Lelia to me."

Lelia shook her head, smiling with gratitude. "I'm just happy you're not mad," she said, and hugged her again. "I'm miserable when you get mad at me."

But Sarah already knew that. For all Lelia's faults, she really did try hard to please her. She always had, from the time she'd stayed up late studying as a child to the way she still spent so many long hours helping Sarah experiment with her hair formula long after Sadie and Rosetta had gone home. Lelia had subjected herself to so many hair treatments, it was a wonder the poor girl's hair hadn't fallen out. And Sarah couldn't think of one time her daughter had complained.

"I know, baby," Sarah said, squeezing Lelia as she kissed her long neck. "Now leave me be, child. I've still got to get dressed for supper."

Lelia scowled. "You didn't hear a word I said just now, did you, Mama?"

"Oh, Lelia, stop. You don't got to worry 'bout me like I'm a schoolgirl. I've been a long, long way from that just about my whole life."

But in a corner of her soul where she could be honest with herself, Sarah wondered if she was only trying to fool them both.

A two-passenger black buggy arrived in front of Sarah's house at six o'clock, and the sight of it froze Sarah in her doorway. The stylish buggy looked nearly new, its paint gleaming, and it was canopied with a buffed black leather top. Two pretty lamps hung from its sides, and the seat was cushioned with leather. Even the steel spokes of the tires glistened. A quality buggy like this one might have cost two hundred dollars or more, Sarah thought. Mr. Walker sure had borrowed a handsome vehicle!

Mr. Walker reined the spotted white horse to a stop, grinning at her from where he sat on the shaded, cushioned seat. He pulled the hand brake in place, then leaped down. "Evenin', Mrs. McWilliams," he said, half bowing as he tipped his flat white hat.

"Evenin', sir," Sarah answered stiffly. Lelia was right; she hadn't courted in her whole life, not really, and suddenly she felt like a visitor to a strange land where she didn't know the first thing about the customs. *We jus' goin' to supper to talk about business,* Sarah told herself, repeating the reminder several times so she could gather the nerve to face Mr. Walker. "I may be back late, Lelia," Sarah told her daughter, and closed the door behind her before Lelia could mutter anything she might not want Mr. Walker to hear.

"Hope you like ragtime, Mrs. McWilliams, 'cause I've got a treat in store," Mr. Walker said, taking her hand to help her climb into the buggy, which sank slightly beneath her weight. The horse huffed and shifted its hooves on the cobblestones, but the buggy didn't move.

Sarah forced herself to ignore the soft warmth of Mr. Walker's hand around hers. It was easy to tell he was a man who worked behind a desk instead of a plow. Suddenly she felt self-conscious as she realized her own hand might not feel nearly as soft to him. "I thought we was goin' to supper, Mr. Walker."

"Well, I don't know 'bout you," Mr. Walker said, walking around the buggy to take his own seat, "but to my experience, a little good music helps me digest my food better."

With a snap of the reins, Mr. Walker began the thirty-minute drive through St. Louis's major thoroughfares, where he had to patiently wait his turn behind stopped streetcars, slow down for pedestrians darting across the street with packages or baskets of fruit, and take his place behind the other carriages, surreys, and automobiles that shared the road with them. The ride was smooth on the freshly paved road, and Sarah enjoyed the brisk pace of their journey as the early evening breeze kissed her face. Electric signs lit up brightly all around them in the waning daylight, proclaiming banks, markets, and casinos. Sarah was usually in such a hurry to finish tasks and chores, she realized, that she almost never visited the city at night to appreciate its liveliness, even when she rode the streetcars. A leisurely carriage ride was an entirely different experience! All she had to do was sit back against her soft seat, her feet nestled atop the carpeting, and watch people and buildings fly past her. She didn't have to worry about sore feet, strangers' leers, or unexpected heaps of horse manure in her path. In Mr. Walker's buggy, she felt as though she didn't have to worry about a thing.

He took her to a Market Street supper club called the Rosebud Bar, which had lightbulbs flashing in the window to proclaim that it was open all night. Before Sarah would climb out of the carriage, she ventured glances up and down the street to try to guess the character of this neighborhood. There were no children or families in sight, mostly men in business attire and a few women whose manner of dress, frankly, reminded her of Etta's.

"What's wrong?" Mr. Walker asked, waiting for her with his hand held out.

"You sure this is a proper place for a lady, Mr. Walker?"

"Well, it is in my book," Mr. Walker said, shrugging. "I'd be lying if I said there wasn't smoking, dancing, and drinking inside, but there's no danger to a lady with an escort. Course, there's some ladies who think there ain't no proper place for them except a church sanctuary or their husband's kitchen. But you don't strike me as that sort, Mrs. McWilliams."

Mr. Walker's response hadn't done much to relieve Sarah's doubts, but she also burned with curiosity. She had never been to a supper club like this one, even though she'd heard so much about the performances of singers, musicians, and dancers in the newspaper. Besides, Mr. Walker was right; she had an escort, and that made all the difference.

"Seems like a funny place to do business," Sarah said as she took his hand.

"I do business in all sorts of funny places," Mr. Walker said, his oddly colored eyes flitting away. He left it at that, and Sarah was glad. She felt Lelia's warnings trying to surface in her mind, but she ignored them. She was going to have supper with the man, that was all, and she didn't expect anything else. For once, she was going to have a good time! Didn't she deserve it?

Inside, the large bar was a world of its own, crowded with men engaged in boisterous conversation, sitting at spare tables facing a piano player on a small stage. The broad-backed musician was playing the keys furiously, filling the room with quick-paced melodies. But C.J. took her to an adjoining room that was much quieter, decorated in gaily colored wall coverings that looked like linked roses. There were at least three dozen candlelit tables fanned across the floor, and Mr. Walker navigated his way through the room just as he had on the road.

"C.J. Walker!" a long-haired octoroon woman in a red dress squealed from a table, and Mr. Walker laughed with recognition, leaning over to kiss the back of her hand. Sarah felt a twinge and forced herself to look away.

"Hey, hey, Scotty," Mr. Walker said, stopping at the next table to shake the hand of a modest-looking young man sitting alone with papers spread across his table. Looking at the papers more closely, Sarah noticed that they were filled with the same squiggles and symbols from her church hymn books; the man was writing music. "What you doin' in this barrelhouse?"

"I promised Tom Turpin I'd pay a visit. Better not let him hear those aspersions, C.J."

"Oh, hey, I'm just makin' a little joke, now. Tom knows I love this place, or I wouldn't have helped him with his ads in the *Palladium*. Scott, meet Sarah McWilliams. Mrs. McWilliams, this is Scott Joplin."

The man, who was dark-skinned with closely cropped hair, kissed Sarah's hand and gave her a gracious smile. There was something absurdly familiar about his name, she thought in an instant of excited recognition, but she just couldn't quite . . .

"Tom started it with *Harlem Rag*, but when you came out with that *Maple Leaf Rag*, boy, ragtime took over the whole world," Mr. Walker congratulated him, and then Sarah remembered why she knew Scott Joplin's name. She had heard about his music, of course!

"Taking over the world isn't always the blessing you'd think," Mr. Joplin said with a touch of weariness. "Pleasure to meet you, Mrs. McWilliams. You two have a good night." He lowered his head and went back to work, writing his markings with impossible speed, and Sarah noticed a nearly haunted expression on the young man's face.

"Some folks don't know a good thing when they got it," C.J. muttered to Sarah, and he guided her to the empty table where their escort was waiting. "They're sayin' he's hell-bent on writing opera. Ain't that something? A nigger tryin' to write opera. Can't be satisfied."

By the time she sat down, Sarah felt nearly dizzy. "Where do you know him from?" she asked, already imagining how surprised and jealous Lelia would be when she told her she'd met the King of Ragtime.

"You meet lots of folks when you travel like I do."

Oh, I'm sure you do, all right, Sarah thought, remembering the woman in the red dress, but she vowed to control her reservations. By the time she'd put in her order for prime rib of beef and begun sipping a glass of red wine (C.J. had reminded her that even Jesus turned water to wine), Sarah felt at ease in the lively supper club. She tapped her foot under the table to the muffled sounds floating through the wall.

"What do you want with me, Mr. Walker?" Sarah blurted, bolstered by the wine.

Mr. Walker's eyes widened with surprise as he sipped from his whiskey glass, then he laughed, nearly spilling his drink. "What do I want . . . ?"

"That's right. Why did you follow me from the picnic to my kitchen, and why are we sittin' here tonight? It ain't like you couldn't find no other lady to put on your arm."

Slowly Mr. Walker's smile faded and she saw earnestness creep into his eyes. "Well, all right, then. But first off, I wish you would call me C.J."

Sarah considered that, then shook her head. "I only call friends by their Christian names, and we ain't friends, Mr. Walker."

Mr. Walker chuckled. "There it is again! Mrs. McWilliams, you're 'bout one of the most direct women I ever did meet, besides my own mama. That's why you sold so much of your hair product at the picnic, you know, and that's why you're gonna sell a whole lot more."

At that, Sarah relaxed. She'd been right! Mr. Walker *did* want to talk business with her. She felt both vindication and a flash of disappointment, though her disappointment soon gave way to relief. She might not know much about courting, but she *did* know about selling her formula.

"I'm listenin'," Sarah said.

Mr. Walker folded his hands in front of him and leaned forward, his eyes boring into her. "Mrs. McWilliams, I've been in advertising a long time, and I'll tell you what I know: You can shout what you're selling from the rooftops, but in the end it won't do you no good if what you're selling ain't worth a damn. So when I see somebody who's selling something worth a damn, it gets my blood to boiling. Now, when you got up in front of all those folks at the picnic and let down your hair and said you had a miracle cure, you made me want to believe you. You have what's called the gift of persuasion. And when I went to your kitchen and saw what you were doing with that comb, I *knew* you had somethin' worth selling."

Sarah was pleased, but she tried to hold her face steady. Mr. Walker was probably about to try to ask her for something, and she couldn't let his flattery blur her common sense. He had the gift of persuasion, too. "So what do *you* want?" Sarah asked him.

This time Mr. Walker didn't blink. "I want to tell you the truth, that's all. Most folks don't want to hear it, but in my heart I think you do. Do you want the truth, Mrs. McWilliams?"

Sarah was confused, but she nodded.

Mr. Walker began. "What I saw in your kitchen was a mess, so help me, like a Mississippi rib joint on a Friday night. Nothing but clutter every which way, so much smoke I could barely breathe, and y'all scooping that hair formula into cups and cans like it was bacon grease. I've seen all kinds of ways to run a business, Mrs. McWilliams, but that ain't no kinda way."

Sarah's mouth fell open, and she felt her body stiffen so rigid that it hurt. Her tear ducts smarted, but she wouldn't allow any tears to come.

"This is St. Louis, Mrs. McWilliams, and St. Louis belongs to Annie Malone and Poro. Everyone in this town knows her product. It's bull-headed to try to compete with her in the first place, but what you're doing ain't no kind of competition at all."

"You done yet?" Sarah whispered, her voice raking her throat.

"You asked for the truth." Mr. Walker's face didn't soften.

"Just 'cause you're payin' a few dimes for my supper don't mean I expect you to insult me to my face. You don't know how hard I been workin'—"

"Mrs. McWilliams, folks who can't hear the truth won't succeed. That's a fact."

Before she even realized what she was about to do, Sarah's hand flew out and lashed across Mr. Walker's cheek. She didn't hit him hard, but she was shocked she had hit him at all. It had just suddenly felt as if Mr. Walker were ridiculing her child, her flesh and blood. Sarah's anger gave way to mortification, and she crumpled back against her chair. "Oh, my—"

Mr. Walker hardly blinked. Very slowly, he raised his fingertips to his cheek to feel the sting, then his lips rose into a small, sad smile. "Well, I'm glad that's over with. Now maybe the air is cleared up and we can finish our talk."

"Mr. Walker, I ain't n-never—"

"Oh, that's all right. I have a knack for bringing out the violent tendencies in ladies. My mama used to blame my mouth on my daddy's side. I guess the thing is, Mrs. McWilliams, it's up to you whether you want to see my face again, but I don't want you to forget what I had to say."

"You can bet on that," Sarah said softly, steely-eyed. "You may know a heap about advertising, but you ain't learned nothin' about makin' friends."

The waiter brought their food on steaming plates, and they ate hurriedly in a strained silence. Sarah had never had prime rib and she'd been looking forward to her meal, but she barely noticed the taste of her juicy meat. She felt as if her spirits were on the floor. Now the cheerful music sounded irritating instead of pleasant.

Finally Mr. Walker sighed. "The only point I was tryin' to make is that you need some changes, or you'll never get out of your kitchen. Advertising can't fix everything."

"Thank you for the advice," Sarah said stiffly, barely concealing her sarcasm. "And thank you for the meal. If you don't mind, I'd like to go—"

"You *do* have a miracle cure, Mrs. McWilliams," Mr. Walker said, his voice suddenly passionate, nearly pleading. "I don't know what your hair grower can do, but I do know what that comb can do. My sister would love it. My mama would love it. And so would every lady I know. If you listen to what I'm sayin', you can have everything you want. And I'd hate to see you walk away from that just 'cause you got your feelings hurt. In business, you need skin like leather. If what I said came out wrong, I'm sorry. But if you do this right, and you go to the right town to start, you could be as big as Poro. I promise you that."

In that instant, Sarah suddenly realized that Charles Walker was being as sincere as he knew how. Somehow, just as she'd told Lelia before she'd left home, this man believed in her.

"You're sayin' . . . I should leave St. Louis?"

"Even David needed a rock to slay Goliath. You don't even got a rock yet, Mrs. McWilliams. You need to start somewhere you can have a chance."

Sarah played with that notion. Where would she go? Back to Vicksburg? No, sir. That would be going backward, as far as she was concerned. But she couldn't stomach the idea of going somewhere she didn't know *anyone*. Then the thought came to her like a bullet: Her sister-in-law and nieces lived in Denver. Alex's widow was always writing about what a hard time she was having, and she needed help. Sarah could help Alex's family, and they could help her.

"I don't know what your brain is saying to you, Mrs. McWilliams, but I like the way I see it workin'," Mr. Walker said, his lovely smile returning.

Sarah couldn't help smiling back at him.

Once Sarah and C.J. Walker left the supper club, he drove the buggy aimlessly through the city streets as the two of them talked back and forth. He told her about his travels, his work, and his brushes with danger with whites in small Southern towns. He had educated himself, he said, and he'd been determined not to destroy his lungs mining coal the way his father had. She told him about her childhood, and how Moses had died. Then she told him about her hair problems, and how she'd struggled so hard to find a cure until she decided she needed to make one herself. They spoke in low tones, and Sarah couldn't believe how natural it felt to talk to him. She'd heard people claim they'd met people they felt they'd known a long time, but she'd never experienced it herself until tonight. Sometimes he seemed to know what she was going to say before she even opened her mouth.

"When I first started mixing a hair cure, most folks I knew thought—"

"—You were plumb out your mind. Thought you were wasting precious time," Mr. Walker finished, nodding as the horse clopped along the silent, moonlit street of well-kept homes. A few lights burned dimly from the windows, although it was so late that most families had retired for the night. "I know all about that."

"Even my own sister," Sarah said. "But we never did think the same way. Lou's always been ready to settle for what life would give her. But not me. I figgered if other folks could do it, why not me? An' maybe I could even do it better."

He laughed. "Oh, yeah. That sounds like me, all right. And there's always some fool who can't wait to tear you down for tryin', like those ol' Toms who used to run back and report every little thing to Massa."

He sounded so much like Moses! Sarah looked at this man who, suddenly, seemed to have been heaven-sent. His face was so smooth, and his lips were an unusual rosy pink beneath his trim mustache. Sitting beside him in the buggy, she could feel him breathing next to her, and his scent surrounded her. She couldn't utter the words on her mind, so she said instead, "If you know so much about selling a business, Mr. Walker, how come you ain't never had your own?"

"You got to have something to sell first," he said. "I get excited when I see somethin' I know folks will want. But *making* somethin' folks want, well . . . that's another story."

"If you had yourself a partner makin' somethin' you got excited about, I suppose that would be your dream come true, huh?" Sarah said, thinking aloud.

"Oh, yes, ma'am. I've thought about it many times, and I've tried it, too. But it takes more than the right product to make a partner, Mrs. McWilliams, believe me. Much more."

When the buggy finally pulled in front of Sarah's sleeping street, she was amazed to realize that the sky was turning gray and pink at the edges, already betraying the oncoming daylight. She and Mr. Walker had stayed out nearly all night! She felt tired, but she also wished it weren't time for the evening to end. There was so much more to say.

And Mr. Walker had told her he was leaving for Denver on the Tuesday train. What if she truly never saw him again? Her fanciful thoughts about moving to Denver to be close to her nieces and sister-in-law seemed like a very far-fetched notion as she gazed at the comfortable house she had lived in all these years, and at the street where she was known and well liked. She'd never lived in any one place so long, and she liked the security of having a home. But she also felt swamped by a sudden sadness that nearly panicked her.

"Well, Mrs. McWilliams, you'll be ready to start buyin' some advertising soon if you remember those things I told you," he said. "Even the things you didn't like."

"Oh, I'll remember."

The buggy was stopped, but neither of them moved. Sarah's heart was thundering in her breast. She thought of the beautiful high-yellow woman at the church picnic, and the octoroon in the red dress at the supper club. Were those women truly what Charles Walker wanted? Had he ever stayed up all night long talking to either of them?

Of course not, she realized. He'd probably done that with no one but her.

"C.J. . . . ?" she began, and his eyes brightened at the sound of his nickname. Then, letting her mind and doubts shut down, Sarah leaned over and pressed her lips to his. He was surprised, and his lips felt firm and guarded against hers at first, but then he yielded. He suddenly pulled her closer to him, tasting her with his broad tongue, and she met his with hers. A fire seemed to roar between them, and Sarah kissed him as she'd kissed no man since Moses. She held his head with her hands, pressing her fingers into his hair as their mouths played. Her body craved the warmth of his, and she didn't even take offense when his hand brushed across her bodice. Her breasts sang beneath the promise of his touch.

Then, quickly, C.J. drew back. He was breathing hard, nearly panting, and his eyes were slitted. "I . . ." His mouth froze for an instant, and he paused before finishing. ". . . I think this is where we say good night, Mrs. McWilliams."

Sarah's heart tripped and sank. No, she was not what he wanted, she realized. His true intention had really been to take her to supper to talk about business, just as she'd told Lelia, and that was all. That thought woke up a disappointment in Sarah so keen that a bad taste flooded her mouth. She was embarrassed, but she wasn't sorry for the kiss. He might not know what to make of her boldness, but it was better to share one kiss with a dashing man like Mr. C.J. Walker than to go through life always wishing she'd dared, she thought.

Still, in the instant she'd kissed him, she'd felt *so* sure. . . .

"I will think on what you said, Mr. Walker," she said, matching his more formal address as she allowed C.J. to assist her from the buggy. "Matter of fact, I have kin in Denver. I'm thinkin' that might make a good new home for me and my hair cure."

C.J.'s face went slack with surprise. Satisfied with his silent reaction, Sarah turned and began to walk toward her front door at a languid pace. She didn't turn around to wave back at him even when she reached her porch and let herself safely inside her door.

Sarah knew C.J. Walker was watching her the entire way.

Madam

Love builds. . . .

—MARY MCLEOD BETHUNE

Only the black woman can say, "When and where I
enter, . . . then and there the whole race enters with me."

—ANNA JULIA COOPER

*T*he Long woman was in her library, Sarah was told.

Sure enough, Sarah found Lillie Long beneath a lamp in one of the gold-trimmed, upholstered Italian-style library chairs, engrossed in one of the crisp new volumes, six hundred in all, that lined the library walls. Snow flurried outside of the large window behind her guest, but the house was warm. Sarah had contacted Anna Burney Long because she needed an affidavit proving her birthplace so she could get a passport for her planned trip to France with Lelia this summer; and it had been Sarah's idea to have her daughter bring it to her in person. I have a brand-new home, Sarah had said in her invitation. Let her visit awhile.

Miss Long looked up, startled. "Madam Walker!" she said, closing the book. "They told me you would be resting today." She began to rise to her feet.

"No, please don't stand," Sarah said. "I'll sit beside you. I'm so glad you could come."

Miss Long's cheeks were flushed bright red. Sarah had not seen her in nearly three years, since her visit to Delta, but if anything Miss Long looked more vital, and her hair was pinned attractively. Sarah could see traces of Missus Anna in her daughter's eyes. She seemed like a smart girl, and it was a shame she had never married, Sarah thought. I guess marriage just ain't for everyone these days, she thought. Lelia had been too long without a husband, too.

Miss Long's eyes sparkled. "Madam . . . in Delta, you told me and Mama you had a town house. Why, when your driver met me at the train station and drove me up that long driveway . . . I expect I could have fainted dead away. Those columns, and the marble! This house is . . . a palace. I feel like I need a camera or I couldn't even describe it to Mama."

"Yes," Sarah said, smiling. "I gave the town house in Harlem to my daughter. I live here now. Real country life, ain't it? It's too bad it's winter and you can't see the garden and swimming pool. You would have liked a swim."

"Oh, but I love to read, so I like the library fine. And that music room done up in gold! I tell you, Madam Walker, I don't think I've ever seen a gold-leaf grand piano in my entire life, and I think I never will again."

Sarah nodded, examining her library. Here her tutoring had truly paid off, because Sarah had selected many of the books herself, not only for their literary value, but for their preciousness. The fine leather bindings on her bookshelves housed the works of Twain, Longfellow, Hawthorne, Cooper, Lady Jackson, Dickens, Balzac, and, of course, Shakespeare. She'd also collected complete works she would like to read when she had more time: Rousseau, Casanova, Rabelais, and Plato, among others. And her beautiful opera books! Her expensive opera volume collection, with an introduction by Verdi himself, had cost $15,000; the fine books had morocco bindings and hand-painted plates. Then there were her Bible volumes. The Bible Lou had given Sarah in Vicksburg had a permanent home on her bedroom table upstairs, but the library had been furnished with fourteen Bible volumes specially bound in covers that were half wood and half pigskin, with pages she'd been told would never perish.

These books would outlive her, she mused, before pushing the thought away.

The villa wasn't perfect, not at all; somehow the architect had neglected to put any drawers in the kitchen, and the garage that housed her four automobiles was leaky. But all in all, she was proud of Villa Lewaro, and she knew her parents would be proud of it, too.

This home belonged to all of them now.

"I don't know what I'd do with myself if I woke up every day in a house like this," Miss Long said in a dreamy voice. "One thing, I suppose I'd never leave! I might never leave this one room, in fact. I think I'd make a bed and sleep in here."

Sarah chuckled. "Guess you could at that."

"I've been thinking about what you did, starting a business, and I can't think of one other woman in the whole world who's done what you've done. Not just colored women, mind you—white women, either. The papers say you're worth a million dollars! All the well-to-do white women I've heard of inherited their money or got it through marriage. How do you account for it, Madam Walker?"

"Oh, I had help, child," Sarah said. "Like my brother Alex used to say, if you see a turtle a-sittin' on top of a fence post, you know he didn't get up there by himself. Believe me . . . I had help."

Chapter Nineteen

JULY 1905
DENVER, COLORADO

U ntil the day Sarah boarded a train at Union Station in St. Louis and traveled nine hundred and thirty miles to a train station of the same name in the mountainside city of Denver, Colorado, she hardly believed she was really going to leave. Neither did anyone else she knew, Lelia most of all. *You're going to give up everything in your life to chase after some man?* Lelia had asked, as if their roles as mother and daughter were reversed.

Lelia was right about one thing: it would be foolish to leave St. Louis because of C.J. Walker, and she knew it. His only communication with her since he'd left had been a maddeningly polite answer to her letter thanking him for his advice. In his note, he hadn't asked whether she was moving to Denver, and she guessed he might not care if she did. But while the other reasons to go were few, they were compelling: *Poro. Family. Make a change.* Of all those reasons, the one that gave her the most resolve was the last.

Even before C.J. Walker said a word to her about leaving St. Louis, Sarah had begun to wonder herself if it wasn't time to move on. She'd lived in the city as a washerwoman for so long, it was hard for anyone to imagine her as anything else. Now she was nearly thirty-eight years old, and maybe moving to Denver *would* give her and her business a boost. It was impossible to explain to Sadie, Rosetta, and even Lelia, but Sarah finally decided to leave.

"Oh, Mama, please don't make me go, too," Lelia had begged when she realized Sarah had made her decision. "Hazel's family has room enough for me to move in, and I'll find work. I don't have to go start my whole life over again in a place I don't know."

Fine, Sarah had told her, although she was hurt because she longed for her daughter's support. So far, in all these years, Lelia had been the only one who listened to Sarah's ideas with barely a blink, encouraging her at every step. Now she'd lost that, too. At least for now.

By the time Sarah had paid her expenses and train fare, she was alarmed that she had only a paltry $1.50 left in her handbag. And, just as before, she owned very little of real value to her: the Bible from Lou, her framed photograph of her father, Lelia's high-school diploma, her letters, and the precious steel comb. But that was all she needed, she figured. Everything she knew about making her hair formula was safely tucked in her memory and a few scribbled notes, and that was the easiest of all to take with her wherever she went.

The day before she left St. Louis, C.J.'s polite response to her second letter finally arrived, answering her questions about potential employment. She'd told him she would prefer cooking jobs to washing—if she never saw another washtub in her life, it would be too soon to suit her—so he sent her a newspaper page with ads for people searching for cooks. He'd circled one ad in particular, from a man named E.L. Scholtz, scribbling in the margin that Mr. Scholtz was one of the leading businessmen in Denver, and C.J. would put in a good word for her. *He has a pharmacy*, C.J. had written, which made Sarah's spirits rise. A pharmacy! Who better to work for than someone who was familiar with chemicals?

Sarah took that as a sign from God that she had done the right thing. C.J. still hadn't mentioned that he would be happy to see her, but at least he was being helpful. Maybe that was all he'd been brought into her life to do, she thought. She vowed not to raise her hopes about how much she would be seeing of C.J. Walker.

Union Station in St. Louis was a monstrous stone structure modeled after a French château, humming with activity. Walking through the belly of the station in search of her train with a suitcase that felt more impossibly heavy with each step, Sarah spotted a porter in a white coat curled in a corner with his eyes focused on a book in his lap. He looked so studious that the sight of him transfixed her. *Here's someone like me*, she thought.

The porter looked like he was Lelia's age, with a handsome face and rich brown-red skin. Sarah walked to the boy, who looked up, startled, when her shadow blocked the light he'd been reading by. He slammed his book shut. "M-my shift doesn't start for an hour, ma'am—" he began, but Sarah's wide smile told him she hadn't come over to scold him for laziness.

She asked him what he was reading, and he said it was a book for college. He had the summer off, but he said he was a student at Walden University in Nashville. "I'm working to save money for schooling. I'm going to be a lawyer, ma'am." He gave her a sheepish smile.

"Well, ain't that somethin'!" Sarah said. Despite his proper way of speaking, she thought she recognized the boy's accent. "Where's your family from?"

"Mississippi," he said. "I was born in Grenada, and my parents raised sixteen children down there. Do you know where that is?"

"Yes, I sure do. I thought I heard some Mississippi in you. I grew up in Vicksburg," Sarah said, her warmth for the boy growing. "What's your name?"

"Freeman, ma'am. Freeman Ransom."

"Well, I'm gonna remember that name, Freeman Ransom. I'll keep my eye on you. My name is Sarah McWilliams, and I'm on my way to Denver to start my own hair-growing business. Folks in business need lawyers, don't they?"

"Yes, ma'am," the boy said, his face lighting up with a grin. Then he leaped to his feet and offered to carry Sarah's suitcase for her. She'd need to hurry to catch the train to Denver, he told her, and he didn't want her to be late. Walking behind the eager college boy as he led her through the train station's bustle, Sarah marveled at the truth of the words she'd just spoken to him. She *was* going to Denver, she thought in disbelief, and she *was* going to start a business. Maybe she could do as well as C.J. had said, or maybe she'd always be a cook. And maybe this Freeman Ransom would be a lawyer one day, or maybe he'd spend the rest of his days working as a porter on the trains.

But that didn't even matter now, she realized. They were a bold pair, the two of them, and the only thing that mattered now was holding tight to their dreams.

Alex had left his family a modest but modern house that had an indoor flush closet instead of an outhouse, more than Sarah had enjoyed in St. Louis. He'd made enough as a hotel porter to buy a home and support his family, and his widow's only job, until now, had been to raise their children. But as pleasant as the tastefully furnished house was, the only place Sarah could make a pallet to sleep was in a parlor where she had no door for privacy, just like when she'd been at Mr. William Powell's house in Vicksburg. Her sister-in-law and four nieces had welcomed her, but Sarah knew the sooner she got a job, the better. She needed a place of her own.

Denver fascinated Sarah from the moment she arrived. She'd nearly expected to find only an overgrown frontier town, but the city was large and modern, with expensive buildings that looked so stately that she wondered if they were meant to rival the nearby Rocky Mountains. The streets seemed cleaner than they had been in St. Louis, and there was none of the hazy, smoky air from factories. The summer sun was hot, but the heat seemed to have no moisture at all, and it warmed her skin without making her perspire. Sarah definitely felt the difference in the atmosphere when she walked along the city's streets, because even though the air tasted cleaner, she had a little trouble catching her breath at first.

Touring through Denver on the "Seeing Denver" streetcar, Sarah learned that Denver considered itself *The City Beautiful*, and for good reason—she was sure there must be poor folks somewhere, but they were safely hidden away, because every neighborhood she saw looked well kept. When the nearly block-long Tabor Grand Opera House appeared before Sarah with its regal pinnacles and handsomely designed exterior, a smile came to her lips. And right across the street, she saw a name she recognized that made her smile grow even wider: Scholtz Drug Company. Just like C.J. had said!

Sarah rose early the next morning and went to the Breedloves' kitchen, determined that this was the day she would win a job with Mr. E.L. Scholtz. The Scholtz ad instructed applicants to reply by telephone or mail, but Sarah wanted to stand out from the others, and she figured the best way to get a cooking job was by *cooking*. The prime rib of beef she'd had with C.J. at the Rosebud Bar had been good, so she re-created the recipe as best she could from her memories of the spices she'd tasted: garlic, onion, and black pepper. Soon, as she cooked, every corner of the house smelled like prime rib.

With the prime rib meal wrapped up in a basket to keep it warm and her niece Anjetta on her heels, Sarah set out for the Scholtz Drug Company at the corner of Sixteenth and Curtis streets in downtown Denver. With any luck, she could arrive in time to entice Mr. Scholtz to eat her meal for lunch.

"Aunt Sarah, Daddy never told us you were crazy. This here is the biggest drugstore in the West, and Mr. Scholtz is a important man. You can't just march in there and hand him a plate of food like you're his mama," Anjetta said, hesitating outside of the large two-story brick structure that hugged the block in a V shape. Anjetta was slightly younger than Lelia, and much more petite. Sarah could see traces of Alex's face in her niece's nearly masculine jawline and closely set eyes, and she could hear Lou and Lelia in her sassy mouth.

"Why not?" Sarah challenged her.

Anjetta had no answer, so they walked inside, where Sarah saw the longest soda-fountain counter she'd ever laid eyes on. Nearly two dozen customers sat eating ice cream and drinking fountain drinks at the counter that stretched the length of the narrow room. Undaunted, Sarah stood behind a man on a stool until she got the Negro counterman's attention.

"Excuse me, but where do I take lunch for Mr. E.L. Scholtz?" she said.

That tactic, repeated three times with three different employees, took Sarah through the maze of a building, which included a large pharmacy with endless rows of remedies stacked high; again, she'd never seen a bigger one. One day, she thought, she would have a neat and efficient place to sell her products, too.

Their last stop was at the desk of Mr. Scholtz's secretary outside his closed door. "Mr. Scholtz's lunch is here," Sarah announced. The young blond-haired woman looked up at Sarah, her fountain pen frozen in mid-stroke. From her face, Sarah knew she had no idea why she was there, but she looked nervous, as if she was supposed to.

"Er . . . well, if you'll just set it on my desk, I'll take it—"

"I'd like to deliver it to him myself, if that's all right," Sarah said in her best official tone. "He's run an ad for a new cook, and I intend to be that cook."

Then the wooden office door was flung open. Sarah felt Anjetta take a step back, but Sarah only gazed steadily toward the emerging man with her best ready smile. E.L. Scholtz was a ruddy-faced man with graying hair and a slightly portly build, wearing a finely tailored pin-striped suit and vest. Something in his face told Sarah he deserved her respect, but she knew she should not be intimidated by him. "Mr. Scholtz, I hope you're hungry. I've brought you prime rib for lunch," Sarah told him quickly. "My name is Sarah McWilliams, and—"

"Oh, no, Sarah," the young woman cut her off. "You can't apply here."

"I wondered why the most glorious smell was wafting beneath my door . . ." Mr. Scholtz said pleasantly, hooking his thumbs on his pants pockets. His words landed heavily, with a nearly buried accent Sarah thought might be German. He gazed at Sarah from under his bushy eyebrows, then his eyes rested on the covered basket Sarah held in front of her. "There's no harm, Lilly. If this tastes as good as it smells, I could hardly do better. What will it cost me?"

"Not a penny. My address is in this basket, sir," Sarah said. "If you like the rest of what's in here, all you have to do is write, and you've got yourself a new cook."

E.L. Scholtz's eyes virtually gleamed, and Sarah knew right then she had a job. She'd never won a job more easily.

Two weeks later she also had a place to live. The attic she'd rented was drafty, with rough walls and grimy windows, but she decided it was a good place to make a start. It was only a ten-minute walk from Alex's house, and a twenty-minute streetcar ride from Mr. Scholtz's lavish colonial-style house, where she worked each weekday in his kitchen to prepare his meals. Cooking entailed long hours and was its own form of drudgery, but Sarah appreciated the creativity she had in the kitchen, testing new recipes on her cheerful new employer. And her evenings were her own, so she ate supper with her relatives. Afterward, she used Alex's kitchen to prepare the ingredients she could afford for her first new batches of hair formula with her nieces. Soon she would be ready to sell it door-to-door.

Sarah kept busy, taking little time for reflection and dulling her emotions so she would not feel any doubts or fears about her move to Denver, or miss her friends too much. Often she gazed at the dramatic mountains beyond the city and inhaled the dry, crisp air and felt the distinct sense that she must be dreaming. She was startled to realize one day that she had already been in the new city more than a month. In all that time, she had hoped C.J. would ask after her at the Breedloves' home, but there were never any messages from him. He had never responded to the thank-you note she'd written him when she first arrived, and she wasn't about to start running after him like a love-struck girl.

Despite how well her plans were coming along, Sarah remembered how close she'd felt to C.J. that night they stayed up talking, and especially their marvelous predawn kiss, and she felt pangs of sadness and disappointment. Her time with C.J. at the Rosebud Bar seemed like the last real day of her life, or else the first day of a new one. But that had been months ago.

At least that sometimey Negro could have asked if I got work or if I'm walkin' the streets, she thought. *Lelia sure was right this time. I don't know men at all, and I prob'ly don't want to.*

Sarah was picking through fresh celery stalks at a street-side fruit and vegetable stand on her way home from church one Sunday afternoon when her eyes happened to glance eastward, and she noticed an unmistakable gait, a hitching step she'd seen before: C.J. was walking toward her from the other side of the street with a woman on his arm, fully engaged in conversation. As always, his manner of dress was colorful and handsome, and his flat white summer hat was skewed stylishly to one side. The sight of him momentarily clogged Sarah's breath. She had forgotten what a striking man he was.

In that instant, he saw her, too. Sarah felt a current trip up her spine.

C.J. stopped in his tracks, as startled as she was. He patted the hand of his pretty young escort, saying something close to her ear. Then he left her standing where she was, and scurried out in front of the traffic of horse buggies and wagons to go to Sarah. He was grinning.

"Sarah!" he greeted her when he reached her, and he kissed her hand.

"You shouldn't look so s'prised to see me. You knew I'd moved to town," Sarah said.

A shadow of some kind passed across C.J.'s face, but his grin didn't falter. "Yes, I knew it, all right. But it's one thing to know it and another to see it with my own eyes."

Sarah ventured a quick glance at the woman he'd left across the street; she was thin and lovely, and her arms were folded across her chest with good-natured patience while she waited. Apparently interruptions were not new to her. "I didn't mean to disturb your afternoon plans," Sarah said as pleasantly as she could.

"Yeah . . . well . . ." C.J. shrugged, but didn't elaborate. That was probably for the best, Sarah thought, since it was none of her business. "Listen, Sarah, you sure don't waste time when you set your mind to something, do you?"

"Time goes by too fast at my age to waste it. There's a lot I aim to do."

"That there is, I'm sure," C.J. said, taking off his hat. He sighed, lowering his voice slightly so he would not be overheard by anyone nearby. "The truth is . . . I've been meaning to call on you. But I worried that . . . well . . . certain *indiscretions* of mine that could be blamed on whiskey and a moonlit night, you see, might stand in the way of a . . . friendship." She had never heard him fumble so much with his words, but his coppery eyes shone with sincerity.

Sarah forced herself to smile, glancing again at his waiting escort. "Well, at least I'm glad to hear you call me Sarah," she said. "Since that's what friends do."

C.J. looked relieved by her response. "Of course they do! I've just learned the hard way, Sarah, that when it comes to certain matters of business and such, it's more than a trifle easier to stick to business all the way through."

Sarah nodded. "Oh, I imagine so, C.J."

"But lemme hear your plans, if you have time in the next week. I can help you get started out here. Colored folks in Denver can be mighty standoffish and stick to their own circles, but they make good wages, and your product will warm them up to you, believe me." Sarah had noticed the standoffishness in Denver already, the way better-off people she spoke to at church instantly lost interest in her when she mentioned that she was a cook, no matter how careful she was with her grammar and diction. She needed C.J.'s help, and he wouldn't offer guidance if he felt uneasy in her presence. If friendship was all they were destined for, then so be it.

"I'd like that, C.J. I'm at the Breedloves' most every evening. Come for supper."

C.J.'s grin widened. "Well, all right, then," he said. His gaze lingered on her eyes. "I tell you, it sure is good to see you again. I really did enjoy that talk we had."

But before Sarah could even answer him, his eyes had darted quickly away.

Chapter Twenty

C.J. Walker quickly became a fixture in the Breedloves' home, dropping by three or four nights a week to have supper with them—charming the table with his jokes and stories about his travels—and then staying up talking with Sarah in the parlor until late. Sarah eagerly awaited those evenings, taking special care with her appearance, and the sessions took on a magical quality even though they never discussed anything except business. Still, Sarah imagined that she and C.J. were like two fireflies meeting in the night, lighting each other in their excited glow. There was nothing the least businesslike about C.J.'s heavy gaze when he talked to her; he offered her ideas the way a lover would offer promises.

"See, Sarah, first off you need a *strategy*, or else your business won't grow the way you want," he told her one night, nearly breathless. First, he said, she needed to have a system so she could have plenty of formula on hand when the time came. Next, she needed to introduce herself around town and build excitement. And lastly, he said, he needed to design ads for her so people could order her hair grower through the mail.

With a few extra dollars from C.J., Sarah paid a steelworker to design a comb for her that was *exactly* what she wanted; the teeth were much closer together than the comb the French woman had given her, and they turned slightly *away* from the scalp because experience had taught her that it would be easier to manage that way. If she was happy with the comb, C.J. told her, she would one day need to order dozens of them, even hundreds. It was very important for her pressing comb to be of her own design, he'd said, because that would help protect her against people who would try to imitate her once she was better known.

"And believe me, my dear, they'll imitate," C.J. said, reclining in the broad parlor chair where Alex had once sat. Like all of the Breedloves' furniture, the parlor chairs were simple but tasteful in a way Sarah had never had time to strive for in her own furniture in St. Louis. She never had extra money for furniture that wasn't absolutely essential. The crimson-colored seat cushions were badly faded, indicating that Mrs. Breedlove had probably bought her family's parlor suite secondhand at a reduced price. "But first, we gotta bring in the customers, Sarah."

"In St. Louis," Sarah said, "I never got so much fuss as one time when I combed out a lady's hair on her front porch. Folks came and carried on 'til you'd think it was a circus act."

"That's right!" C.J. said. "That's what you need to do here. Do your demonstrations in public places as much as you can. Have chairs so folks passing can take a seat an' even drink a cup of coffee while they watch. We want to get to the point where folks pass by and say, 'Oh, look, there's Sarah McWilliams! She's that lady who grows hair!' And that brings me to the ads. . . . Sarah, you told me how your hair was falling out. Do you have any photographs showing the way you used to look before?"

Surprised, Sarah paused. "Well . . . I might have one hid somewhere. . . ."

"See, here's what I'm thinking: You know why you were so big at that church picnic in St. Louis when you let your hair down? 'Cause those folks *knew* you when you were having those troubles. They could see the difference and say, 'Damn, I gotta have some o' *that.*' So if we put a photograph in the newspaper showing the way you used to look—"

Sarah shook her head firmly. She'd taken such care with her thick hair, which grew to her shoulders when it was combed out and pressed, and now he expected her to show the whole city what she'd looked like in the midst of her misery. She wouldn't even want C.J. to see how she'd looked then! A cruel, careless voice seeped into her memory: *Ain't nobody here but that baldhead washerwoman.*

"I'd be so ashamed, C.J."

"Yes, Sarah, but right next to it we'll put a photograph showing how you look *now.* You don't think it would sell hair grower if everyone could see the difference just like in St. Louis?"

Sarah's heart surged. He was right! If people saw the way she looked now and compared her hair to the patchy, tangled mess in a photograph Etta had talked her into taking a long way back, they would *have* to believe her hair grower worked. She was the proof!

C.J. grinned at her, seeing her mind at work. "Now you got it! See what I'm talkin' 'bout? There ain't nothin' to be 'shamed of if it sells your product. That's the first rule. Next, you need a name for it."

"Wonderful Hair Grower!" Sarah said quickly. She'd been thinking about that for some time, and she liked the sound of it.

C.J. considered it, pursing his lips with a nod. "That sounds good. Folks will remember it. But you know what? I say it needs to be more personal, more about *you.* It's your face we're selling in the ads, remember, and you're the one who'll be doing demonstrations."

Anjetta, who had been knitting quietly in a corner as she listened, startled Sarah when she spoke suddenly: "Aunt Sarah's Wonderful Hair Grower," Anjetta piped up. "Like that lady Aunt Jemima who has that flapjack batter!"

Sarah made a face, shaking her head. Anjetta wasn't old enough to have been called "Auntie" by whites, so she wouldn't understand how insulting that sounded to Sarah's ears. "I'm sorry, sweetheart, but I ain't tryin' to be nobody's aunt but yours," she said. "No, thank you."

"Madam Sarah's Hair Grower?" C.J. suggested.

Sarah wasn't sure. She liked the sound of *Madam*, all right, because it reminded her of Madam Mary McLeod Bethune, who had started the school for colored girls in Florida last year. The word definitely had an air of dignity, and she'd played with it herself. But somehow . . .

Sarah sighed. "Madam Sarah sounds like I'm some kind of fortune-teller, don't it?"

"Well, you better think about it. Maybe we don't need the whole name when we're just starting out, but it makes a big difference if people know what to ask for."

Sarah smiled to herself. C.J. certainly used the word *we* a lot, she had noticed. He considered her a project and an investment, since he'd been kind enough to give her a few dollars to buy supplies she needed, but the word *we* had a sweet ring she hadn't heard from a man's lips in what seemed like a lifetime.

Again, C.J. was gazing at her as if he knew exactly what was in her mind, and then his gaze vanished. "I guess that's enough business for tonight," he said, standing up as if on cue. He straightened the creases in his pants. "Just think about what you want your name to be, Sarah."

"I sure will, C.J.," Sarah said, trying desperately to ignore a persistent voice in the back of her mind already playing with a name she might not mind writing on the new Wish Board she'd nailed over her bed: MADAM C.J. WALKER.

It sounded like the most perfect name in the world.

"Get in the wagon, ladies! We're goin' to church."

C.J.'s arrivals were rarely announced and somehow always unexpected. Some days he wanted to take her for long walks, and sometimes he hurried her to social events to show her off like a prize. This time he pulled up in front of the Breedloves' house with a horse-drawn wagon with seating for six. The wooden wagon was much older than the buggy he'd appeared in when he first picked Sarah up in St. Louis, and Sarah guessed he must have borrowed the buggy from a friend with more means.

C.J. was dressed in a sober black suit and tie and a black derby, looking like a preacher himself. She almost didn't recognize him.

"Since when do you go to church?" Sarah asked. The Sunday-school picnic was the closest she'd ever known C.J. Walker to come to a church. She and her nieces Anjetta, Thirsapen, Mattie, and Gladis had gathered on the porch, ready to begin their walk to services. "You goin' to Shorter Chapel AME? That's where I belong."

"Not today you don't. We're goin' across town to Shiloh Baptist. Come on, or we'll be walkin' in late," C.J. said.

Her nieces gave her questioning looks—and Anjetta complained loudly that she'd been looking forward to seeing a young man at Shorter—but Sarah convinced them to climb into C.J.'s wagon. "Hold on, ladies," C.J. warned them, then, with a high snap of his horsewhip, his two horses seemed to nearly gallop down the street. Thirsapen, younger than Anjetta and more excitable, let out a startled yell as their seats jounced across the cobblestones.

"I still don't know what we're doin' here, C.J.," Sarah hissed after they'd arrived at the distant church, their hair slightly mussed and their hats askew from the ride. Groups of strangers filed into the brick structure, gazing at them with curiosity.

"You'll know soon, my dear," C.J. said, patting her hand the way he always did to assure her that he knew what he was doing. So far he always *had* known, so Sarah held her tongue.

Once they were seated and C.J.'s hat was off, he looked uncharacteristically reflective, his head turned upward toward the pulpit with rapt interest. Occasionally he even closed his eyes and nodded. What had happened to him? Sarah wondered. Had he found Jesus overnight?

She got her answer when a deacon mentioned C.J.'s name soon after the service began.

"Of course, many of us know Brother Walker from his doings around town," the deacon said, "and he has asked to speak a few words to us."

Slowly, soberly, C.J. brought himself to his feet. His hands were folded in front of him, and he hung his head slightly as the members of the church whispered to themselves and rustled in their seats to turn around and face him where he stood at the center of the church. Apparently his presence was a surprise.

"Thank you for letting me speak today, Deacon, good Reverend—church family." C.J. drew a long, choppy breath, and Sarah wondered for an instant if his eyes were misting with tears. "Like a wanderer who has been abroad and lost his way, I have been much too far from home."

There was a gentle chorus of *amens*.

C.J. bit his lip, then he went on. "Some of y'all may know how far my travels have taken me from time to time, and Satan loves a man on the road, good folks. Every sin you can think of is waiting for any man right outside the train depot. But I'm so happy to come before you today to let you know that while I have fallen to too many temptations Satan has put in my path, I never lost sight of my way in the fog, and at long last I have come back home. Praise God."

This time, the *amens* were rousing and heartfelt. A few people even applauded, including Sarah, who was gazing at C.J. in awe. She was accustomed to his eloquence by now, especially when he spoke before groups, but she had never been allowed to glimpse so deeply into his heart. She still had a lot to learn about him, but why hadn't she known . . . ?

"We all came to hear God's word and a song this mornin', an' I know you've all got your fine Sunday suppers waiting back at home, so I don't want to keep you . . ." C.J. said.

"Take your time, son," encouraged an old man from their pew.

"My heart is full today," C.J. went on in a singsong voice, "and I just wanted to share my joy. Because God has *blessed* me. I mean, He has truly blessed me. He blesses me from the time I open my eyes in the mornin' 'til I close 'em again at night. Any of y'all feel blessed today?"

The congregation answered as one, the applause louder this time. The organist even played a flourish from the pulpit, giving his words more strength. Sarah's heart danced. By now, she felt so awestruck that a small doubt began forming in her mind. Was he being sincere?

"But family, I *know* I am blessed today because God has brought a special person into my presence, and it would be a genuine sin not to share my bounty with all of you. A woman has moved all the way from St. Louis, Missouri, to join us in Denver, and I believe God helped me find the right words to convince her to come to us. Family, this woman has a hair preparation that God whispered to her in a divine dream—a preparation that *grows* hair—and she has made a new home here so that *all* colored women right here in Denver can have the beautiful hair God intended. If I can just ask her to stand . . ."

Sarah's heartbeat, which had begun racing as soon as C.J. uttered the words *woman* and *St. Louis*, was now so loud in her ears that she couldn't hear anything else. C.J.'s mouth was still moving, but she couldn't make out what he was saying. She felt weak, grasping at the smooth wooden pew in front of her so she wouldn't sway in her seat. What was he doing?

C.J. pulled gently on her arm, bringing her to her feet. "That's right . . . Here she is in person at our congregation today . . . the divinely touched Madam Sarah McWilliams!"

If Sarah could have picked one moment in her life to suddenly disappear from sight, even if it meant dropping dead on the floor, it would have been right then. Her nieces stared at her in a row of four wide-eyed faces. Sarah practically had to lean on C.J. for support as she stood up in the crowded church. The only reason he'd stood up at all was to pretend to repent so he could advertise her hair product right in the middle of services! And he'd told an outright lie, at that. Why had he said her formula had come to her in a divine dream?

He's goin' to hell for sure, and he's about to take me down there with him, she thought.

Sarah was mortified, angry, shocked. But all she could do was smile and nod at the worshipers, who were applauding for her with glowing, smiling faces.

"I thank Jesus for giving Madam Sarah McWilliams her divine knowledge, and I know you all will, too. Good morning, y'all, and God bless," C.J. finished with a small wave, and sat down.

Sarah had collapsed back to her seat as soon as he released her arm, her heart still pounding. Unable to contain her anger, she stamped on C.J.'s foot. His muffled cry was drowned out as the choir stood and began to sing.

"What's wrong with you, woman?" he whispered in her ear.

"What's wrong with *me*? Why'd you stand up tellin' those lies? You know good and damn well I didn't have no dream—"

"Shhhhh," C.J. cautioned her, patting her hand before she drew it quickly away. "What you expect me to say, you're a washerwoman who cooked it up on your kitchen stove? Trust me, I know how to get folks' attention. Now, hush."

Trust me. No she wouldn't either, Sarah thought. This would be the last time she'd jump blindly into C.J. Walker's wagon and let him drag her across town. She was grateful for his help, but she wasn't going to be humiliated again. And in God's house! Sarah seethed through the service, gripping her hymnal tightly. She couldn't wait for the service to end, because she was ready to finish telling C.J. exactly what she thought of his fast-talking, truth-bending ways.

But she didn't have the chance. After the service was over, Sarah was penned in by a dozen women complimenting her hair and asking about her divine formula. When Sarah caught C.J.'s eye, she saw him standing at the end of the pew with her nieces, smirking. He winked.

"Madam McWilliams, could you tell me about your dream?" asked a beautiful brown-skinned young woman with dimpled cheeks. The hair visible to Sarah beneath the woman's hat looked coarse and dry, exactly the way Sarah's had once looked, and Sarah knew she could work wonders for this woman with her hair grower and pressing comb. If she had the chance.

"Why don't you let me show you instead?" Sarah said.

Sarah traveled to a new church with C.J. on Sundays as often as she could; each week, as his testimony sounded more and more repentant, the crowds around Sarah grew. Soon she had to keep an appointment book for all the ladies who wanted her to press their hair, and she and her nieces had to work diligently in the kitchen to keep up with the orders for her Wonderful Hair Grower. Most of her new churchgoing customers confessed they'd been intrigued not only because of Sarah's lovely hair, but because the formula had come to her in a dream.

Remembering her long-ago dream about the African man who gave her a black rose, Sarah began to wonder if there was any chance she might have really dreamed her formula, just like C.J. said. She'd woken up from a dead sleep when she got the idea to use sulfur, hadn't she? She often got her best ideas when she was trying to sleep, or when she first woke up in the mornings. Maybe the sulfur had been part of a dream, too.

The longer Sarah heard herself repeating the story about God's whispers in her ear, the more she believed it herself.

Chapter Twenty-one

As she slapped a cooling carrot cake with the last of her homemade cream-cheese icing, Sarah saw a shadow stretch across the table in the bright light from the electric lamps in the Scholtzes' roomy kitchen. Sarah's mind had been firing off lists of things she needed to do when she finished her hair appointment immediately after work, but she brought her full attention back to the cake when she realized someone was watching her. She was being too sloppy. She was so tired, she'd hardly been able to keep her eyes open while she waited for the cake to finish baking in the gas-powered oven.

"What's this? Cake again?" Mr. Scholtz's voice grumbled from behind her. "I'm convinced of it now, Sarah: You're on a mission to make me outgrow my entire suit of clothes." Then he laughed ruefully and sat down at the kitchen table near Sarah, opening his *Denver Post*.

"I guess you've found me out at last, Mr. Scholtz."

He ruffled the newspaper page as he read. "This Albert Einstein and his Theory of Relativity . . . the more I hear about it, the less I know what to make of it," Mr. Scholtz said. "The man's either a genius or a fool, and I'm not qualified to say which. What's the use of it? But I suppose it's all progress, like the Curies, or the Wright brothers and their flying machines."

"You wouldn't get me up in one o' them heavier-than-air planes," Sarah said.

"Yes, it's hardly natural, men flying in the air," Mr. Scholtz said, and went on reading. "Ah . . . now, look at all this talk about immigration! You know what, Sarah? I don't give a hoot if there *were* more than a million immigrants to this country last year, or how many more are coming. Don't we all come here from immigrants?"

"In a way of speakin'," Sarah said, although she would have liked to point out that Negro slaves could hardly be called immigrants. "Wasn't anybody here at first but the Indians."

"Exactly! So why shouldn't new immigrants have the same chances our parents did? This is a big country, with room enough for everyone. One thing's certain, without immigrant labor, big business would . . ." He stopped and sighed. "Ah, well, that's just business talk. I won't bore you with that, Sarah."

Mr. Scholtz spent long hours with his brother at their pharmacy and often came home too late to eat dinner with the rest of his family, so Sarah saw him only rarely. But every so often, whenever he did speak to her, she was grateful that he didn't lord himself over her the way some of her other employers had, both white and colored. It was as though Mr. Scholtz did not see skin color, like the French woman in St. Louis who had given her the steel comb.

"I like to know what's goin' on in the world, Mr. Scholtz," Sarah said.

Mr. Scholtz gazed at her over the top of his reading spectacles. "You're not fooling anyone, I hope you know. Least of all me." His voice, this time, was more somber. "You're no cook, Sarah McWilliams. That's for certain."

"Sir . . . ?" Sarah said, troubled.

Mr. Scholtz waved his hand. "Don't worry, I've no complaints. But what I said is true just the same. You're no cook. Now tell me the truth. Who are you really?"

Relief floated inside Sarah's chest. Sarah knew from experience that, in time, long-term domestics often became woven inside the families of their employers, but their own personal lives were considered irrelevant, as if they existed only to serve the people they worked for. Their own families, their church involvement, and their troubles were a secret life, and whites seemed to like that just fine. Sarah had worked for people for years who knew no more about her than the Man in the Moon. Mr. Scholtz seemed to want to know more.

"I'm a businesswoman, Mr. Scholtz," Sarah said. She'd been waiting for the right time to talk to the respected pharmacist about her hair formula, and maybe she'd found it at last.

Mr. Scholtz's eyes glimmered with what might have been amusement. "A businesswoman, eh? An entrepreneur? What kind of business would you be in?"

"I make a hair formula for colored women that grows hair. I've used it on myself, an' now me an' my partner's gonna expand to a mail-order business. We're buildin' up our customer base here in Denver, trying to get more exposure and recognition." Sarah's business class in St. Louis, along with C.J.'s coaching in business terms, flowed easily from her lips by now. "Until that happens, I'm a cook. Supplies cost money, you see, so I need the income."

Mr. Scholtz couldn't hide his surprise. His lips were pinched into an O, and he stared at Sarah as if he had never seen her before. *He prob'ly ain't heard no colored woman talk to him like that,* Sarah thought. *Maybe no woman at all.*

Slowly the pharmacist took off his spectacles and rested them on the table. Then he ran his fingers through his tufts of graying hair. She wondered when he had started out, and how long it had taken him to build his company. She would ask him one day soon, she knew. She had a chance to learn about business from someone who might be one of the most successful entrepreneurs she would ever meet. "This invention . . . how did you—" Mr. Scholtz began.

"I dreamed some of it. The rest was trial and error."

"And the formula . . . do you mind if I ask . . . ?"

Here, Sarah paused. She hadn't discussed her secret ingredient with even C.J., and he had never pressured her to tell him. Should she trust this stranger? *He's a chemist, girl! He can show you how to make it even better,* a voice inside her trilled. Then a glummer voice spoke up: *Yeah, or else he could steal it.*

Mr. Scholtz noticed her hesitation. "You don't have to say. I only thought I might . . ."

"Sulfur," Sarah said, after taking a deep breath. "There's other ingredients, too, but I think the one that works best is sulfur." Her heart was pounding, and suddenly her fingers didn't feel quite steady. Would a man of science think she was a fraud?

Mr. Scholtz gazed at her, blinking. "That's good, Sarah," he said, sitting up straight in his chair. The surprise had left his face, giving way to admiration. "Of course! Yes, with the poor nutrition and unhealthy scalps, sulfur could very well make the scalp healthier, encourage the hair to grow. I dispense sulfur soap for skin problems, and the powder is wonderful for injuries. And you sell this to grow hair! What else do you sell?"

So Sarah told him about her pressing comb and the lighter oil she was developing, made with petrolatum, to help the comb make hair less kinky. He listened with great interest, his palm flattened against his cheek as he sat with his elbow on the table. Occasionally, he nodded his head and said *yes, yes,* encouraging her thoughts, and sometimes his brow was furrowed in silence. Suddenly Sarah felt the strangest sense that she was no longer talking to her employer, but to a peer. The feeling came so unexpectedly, it made her temples throb.

"Those ads with the two photographs—wonderful! When you begin publishing them, they'll bring in sales full chisel," he said. "At the outset, you'll have to spend more money than you're making so your product and manufacturing line will be in place. If you don't, you'll have disappointed customers warning people away. You always want your customers to come for more. Repeat business is the key."

"Yes, that's what C.J.—" Sarah stopped herself, deciding that

C.J. Walker's nickname didn't sound professional enough to use with Mr. Scholtz. "That's what my partner says."

"What about shampoo, Sarah? Everyone washes their hair. You should have a special shampoo with carefully selected ingredients, and tell your customers it'll make the hair grower work better. They shouldn't want to buy one without the other. Increased sales, you see?"

Sarah felt a jolt of adrenaline that made her toes tingle, the way she felt when she was exchanging ideas with C.J. and when her mind was racing late at night. "That's true! And maybe . . . a skin cream, too. I should have a whole shelf of products from Madam Sarah."

At that, Mr. Scholtz began to chuckle. His chuckle soon turned to a full-fledged laugh. "Sarah, I must tell you . . ." he said, shaking his head when he'd found his voice. "When I asked you who you really were a moment ago, I expected to hear 'I'm a mother, I'm a wife, I'm an elder in my church. I sing, I sew, I nurse my aging parents.' I didn't expect this Madam Sarah and her whole shelf of products!"

"That's all right, Mr. Scholtz," Sarah said, smiling. "Nobody else is expecting it neither."

Mr. Scholtz folded his newspaper under his arm and stood up. "Well, I'd be a fool to encourage you, wouldn't I? I'll lose my cook! My wife isn't happy when she's exiled to the kitchen even for a day, and I'll confess I'm not too keen on it myself."

"Now, I can't lie 'bout that, Mr. Scholtz," Sarah said. "I got a hair appointment waitin' for me when I get home tonight. Before too much longer, I'll have to leave this job or else faint." Maybe it was a foolish thing to say, but Sarah said it anyway. He deserved the truth.

Mr. Scholtz considered that, then blew air from his lips in a silent whistle. He began to walk away. "As for your hair grower, I'm sure you know which oils you should use . . . ? Coconut, almond, rosemary, olive . . . " he said, as though he were speaking to himself. He paused, glancing over his shoulder at Sarah's face. "Don't you?"

"Coconut and . . . olive oil?" Sarah said, intrigued.

Mr. Scholtz once again made his way toward the doorway, his voice still sounding distant and distracted. "And if I were going to sell a shampoo, I wonder what ingredients I'd use besides glycerine, of course. And henna. Yes, I think henna would work nicely. But I'll want to give that some thought. . . ." He was still talking, but his voice faded as he walked away.

"Mr. Scholtz!" Sarah called, following him. The halfway-iced carrot cake on the table was nowhere on her mind. "What's that you said?"

"I said I wouldn't quit my cook's job quite yet if I were you," Mr. Scholtz called back, giving her a coy glance. "There are some circumstances, I think, where a little patience can be very valuable. It gives a busy man time to think about all sorts of possibilities."

Sarah put her hands on her hips. That sounded like blackmail to her, all right, but it might be worth the trade. A little more cooking for a few good ideas? Why not? She needed the money anyway, at least for now, and he clearly wasn't eager to have his wife in the kitchen.

"So, Mr. Scholtz . . . You think that busy man would think better with a can of hair formula he could study?" she said. "I can bring one tomorrow."

"Oh, I think he just might, Madam Sarah," Mr. Scholtz said. With that, he vanished through the doorway, and she could hear him chortling as he walked down the hall.

"Well, you're in a mood," C.J. complained as they walked down the rainy street underneath his broad black umbrella. It was late; they had just left a formal meeting at a colored lodge, where Sarah had addressed more than a hundred women, telling her familiar story about her hair grower and her divine dream. She'd sold out of all the jars they brought with them, and her appointment book was so full that she'd had to tell some of the ladies they would have to wait at least two weeks to have their hair pressed. "It went well tonight, Sarah."

Sarah hadn't spoken a word to C.J. since they'd left the meeting hall. C.J. had advised her to buy at least one new dress, since he said it wasn't becoming to wear the same clothes to every occasion, although Sarah hated to sacrifice to buy clothes when the two good dresses she had were perfectly neat. Still, she'd gone out the day before and bought a beautiful royal blue velvet dress decorated with rows of gold braid, one that even made her waist look slim because of the cut of the jacket. Her nieces had fawned over her, telling her they'd never seen her look so lovely, but when C.J. picked her up at the door, he hadn't remarked on the dress. He'd only puffed his apologies about being late and rattled off things she should re- member to say and do.

Whose hands to shake. Whose eyes to catch. Which people to avoid. All night long, she felt as if he'd led her around like a trained pony.

"I need to eat," Sarah finally said. "Why don't hinkty Negroes ever serve any real food? Those little wafers and whatnot just make me hungry. They act like they're ashamed of fried chicken and pig meat."

"Well, Jake's is close, and they'll have food this late. But it's a bar. . . ."

"Fine by me, C.J. I just need food."

With a small, frustrated sigh, C.J. gently steered her around the corner. Sarah knew he was dying to crow about how well the hair grower had sold, but she wasn't in the mood. She and C.J. had visited meetings to talk about the Wonderful Hair Grower almost every night this week, thanks to C.J.'s knowledge of local social circles, and he grated on her nerves more each night. If he asked her, she wouldn't even know how to explain *why*. Even his smile annoyed her. Now, as they walked, she was very conscious of how close they were as they both sought refuge under his umbrella from the pelting droplets. He had a protective arm around her, and her breast was crushed against his side. His lady friend would feel scandalized if she saw them now, she thought. Sarah had seen them together at a nickelodeon two weeks before, and the sight of them together had made her stomach go sour.

Jake's, which was near Union Depot, was crowded with men in varying degrees of dress; some, like Sarah and C.J., looked like they had just finished a night on the town in their crisp suits and hats, and others were wearing grimy overalls, as if they'd just gotten off work at the train station. Their laughter, arguing, and good-natured jostling in the smoky bar were loud to Sarah's ears, so boisterous compared to the prim event they had just attended. A piano player hidden behind the crowd was playing *Maple Leaf Rag*, which made Sarah remember how she'd met Scott Joplin the first night C.J. took her out to supper. Then she remembered the feel of C.J.'s moist lips and tongue against hers, and her stomach squirmed.

The scent of C.J.'s perfumed shaving soap floated to her nostrils as he leaned close to her to be heard over the din. "There's a table in back," he said, pointing.

As they walked through the crowd, Sarah noticed an intense pair of eyes upon her. The eyes belonged to a dapper man in a brown jacket who was grinning wide. "C.J. Walker? Where you been, Redbone?" the man said, although his eyes were planted on Sarah. She turned quickly away as the two men greeted each other.

"Been busy, Len."

"So where's Paulette, boy? I thought"—the man spoke into C.J.'s ear, obviously believing Sarah would not hear him, but her honed ears picked up his words—"I thought you said you didn't deal in no coal, C.J. What you doin' with some lovely brown sugar like *that*?"

Sarah saw C.J.'s face turn dark. "Neigho, pops, don't be puttin' no words in my mouth. You watch yourself in front of this lady. This is Madam Sarah, and she's about to be famous in Denver. We're doin' some business together."

"Oh, is that what you're callin' it now?" The man slapped C.J. on the back, laughing.

The man's laughter followed them to their table, and C.J.'s face was rigid with irritation long after they were seated. He apologized to Sarah, muttering that he should have known better than to bring her to Jake's. "A lady like you deserves to dine in a place more proper," C.J. said, nearly mumbling, his face buried in his menu. "A dress that pretty will catch unwanted attention."

So he had finally noticed her dress! It was easier to grab an eel out of the water than to get a compliment from C.J., Sarah decided. "So you like it?" she said. She hated to sound so eager, but couldn't help it. When she was around C.J., all sorts of strange voices flew from her.

C.J. glanced at the thin gold-colored braids strung across her bosom, then he looked back at her eyes. "I'm a fool for certain, but I assure you I ain't blind, Sarah. Of course I like it."

"Well, I didn't know," Sarah said softly. "I guess I need to hear the words."

C.J. sighed, squirming. He looked over both of his shoulders in search of someone to take their food order, and Sarah figured he wouldn't mind ordering a drink, either. When he didn't see any employees, C.J. turned back to Sarah, twisting the dinner napkin in front of him. "I think I know why you've been so fit to be tied tonight," C.J. said.

Sarah's heart pounded. Instead of answering, she waited for him to go on.

"You're a lady in a new town, you're meeting a lot of new people, including a few gentlemen, and you'd like to have more of a social life. You don't want to spend every waking hour thinking about business. I understand that." He paused, but he didn't look up at her for a response. "I know it's hard, Sarah, but you're not the only one it's hard on. This is just one of those sacrifices folks have to make when they want to rise above the rest. You know, I don't . . . I don't have much time for a social life either."

Sarah lowered her gaze, leveling it at him. "You seem to do fine."

"Well, it's not like you think, not no more. How do you expect any young lady would feel if a man wanted to spend two, three, and four nights a week with someone else? Let's just say we've both had to make sacrifices."

Again, Sarah didn't answer, although her thoughts were at a boil. Did that mean he'd parted ways with his lady friend? Why couldn't he just say so and go ahead and profess his feelings for her? Either C.J. plain didn't feel the special attraction between them, or he thought she was fool enough to believe it wasn't there simply because he refused to ever acknowledge it. Neither scenario suited Sarah.

C.J. cleared his throat. "It works out best this way, you know," he said in a low voice, staring at the table. "This way we keep business at the top of our minds."

The music and all the other voices in the room seemed to vanish, until Sarah thought she could hear their heartbeats mingling. "Must be nice to be able to bridle your mind like that," Sarah whispered. "Wish I could."

At last his eyes found hers, and she saw sadness there. "I do the best I know how," he said, his eyes glassy. "What do you want me to say, Sarah? That I'm like a thief stealing stares every time you turn your back to me? That I have to wipe my palms dry like a boy in short pants after I help you step down from the wagon? Or should I tell you how I couldn't hardly muster a single sensible thought in my head when I first saw you in that dress tonight?"

Sarah's heart flipped in her breast, and she didn't even realize she was holding her breath. She'd heard C.J. say those words to her countless times in her imagination, but her daydreams hadn't prepared her for the spell of his professions to her ears.

Slowly, as if answering her thoughts, C.J. shook his head. "I could say those things, Sarah, and we both know they'd be gospel truth instead of just a few pretty phrases. But there's no point to it. I'm old enough to know where I'm weak and where I'm strong. God as my witness, Sarah, I fail every time when it comes to the art of love, but I can sell a business better than anything or anyone. If you were me, which would you choose?"

"I don't see where it has to be a choice," Sarah said.

"Oh, yes, it is, Sarah. You might as well pour red ink and black ink in the same inkwell. The color you get ain't red no more, and it ain't black no more. And once it's done, there's no changing that ink back to what it was."

So, there it was, plain as day. He loved her, but his head would overrule his heart. If that was true, Sarah thought, it would have been better if she'd never met Charles Joseph Walker. She'd been living her life just fine without the faintest notion that her heart had always been wide awake inside her, just waiting for him.

"Well . . ." Slowly, painfully, Sarah exhaled. "I guess I'm not as good a master over my mind or any other part of me. I want what I want, C.J. Maybe when you've lost as much as me, you don't take happy for granted. You scrape and hoard every piece of happy that comes your way. And if I have to go on tryin' to convince my heart it's not supposed to feel happy when you come to call, then . . . it's near impossible for me to sell a damn thing."

Reaching across the table, C.J. patted Sarah's wrist in his usual gesture of assurance. Then, after a hesitation, his hand simply rested on top of hers, warm and heavy. The spot where they touched seemed to kindle the entire length of her arm. C.J. left his hand on hers until Sarah felt tears pricking her eyes, then he moved it away. "Let's get you some food," he said.

Sarah's appetite was gone, but she managed to pick at a plate of chicken and dumplings. She felt a new appreciation for the laughter, noise, and music inside the bar because she wasn't looking forward to returning to her lonely rooming house. She might have to sell Madam Sarah's Wonderful Hair Grower by herself, then. Maybe she couldn't do it as fast or as well on her own, but she knew she could do it. She'd started before she met C.J., and she could go on without him. She couldn't spend the rest of her days hoping C.J. Walker might change his mind, not if waiting brought this kind of pain.

"Excuse me, madam," a gravelly voice said beside her, and she looked up to see the man in the brown jacket who had spoken to C.J. earlier. He held his derby in his hand, and there was no playfulness in his face this time. "I've been thinkin' it over, and I hope you didn't take offense at the way I was cuttin' the fool with my friend C.J. before. I take it *madam* means you're a married woman, and I didn't mean no disrespect to you or your husband."

"I'm a widow, sir," Sarah told him. She held out her wrist to him, and he kissed it, though his eyes never left her face. At the word *widow*, he brightened. "No offense taken."

"All right, Len, much appreciated," C.J. muttered. "Now move on. We're at a meeting."

The man ignored him, addressing Sarah directly. "My name is Leonard Styles, madam, and I hope you won't take this wrong neither, but that piano kid sure is playin' his heart out, an' when my feet hear music, they like to dance—"

"Nigger, you must be crazy," C.J. interrupted him, angry.

Politely, Mr. Styles took a step back. "C.J., unless I was mistaken, I'm talkin' to this here elegant lady. She looks to me like she has the vocabulary to answer for herself."

Despite her sad mood, Sarah felt herself smiling. The thought of getting up to dance in a bar full of strange men, and in this dress! Lelia would think she had lost the last bit of her reason. But she was a stranger here, wasn't she? What difference would it make? The music *did* sound lively. *Besides, just once I'd like to have a good dance without worryin' 'bout kickin' up a dust.*

"So what you say, Madam Sarah? One dance?"

Cautiously, Sarah glanced at C.J. His eyes pierced her, but he waved her away glumly. "Do what you want," he said.

So she did. With the entire bar watching, Sarah walked alongside Leonard Styles to a small dance floor where one other very young couple was following the syncopated beat of the music with shimmying dance steps. Sarah was nervous, but she also felt invigorated, as if she were about to set something inside her free. To hell with what other folks might think!

"I'm not such a good dancer," Sarah admitted as Mr. Styles clasped both her hands.

"Well, it so happens I'm a very good teacher," he said, smiling.

Rocking her arms gently back and forth, he helped Sarah hear the music's bouncy rhythm, until her ears picked up the beat naturally. Then, following his lead, she began to shift her weight from side to side, then backward and forward. They danced arm's length apart, never close enough that Sarah felt compromised. She glanced over her shoulder at C.J.'s table, and she saw him sprawled in his chair, holding his whiskey glass close to his face, watching them. Other men were watching her, too; some with their lips curled in distaste, others with mischievous grins.

"Don't you worry none about C.J., Madam Sarah. That old hound don't bark."

Sarah laughed, slightly breathless from the dancing. The faster the teenage pianist played, the faster their feet moved. Mr. Styles began to show off for her, improvising quick-shuffling steps and twirling her around. Sarah felt the cloud over her spirits lifting as she forgot all about yesterday and tomorrow, feeling rooted in the music and her first bar dance.

The next time she looked toward their table, however, C.J. was gone.

Just that quickly, Sarah's cloud was back, and the room seemed to grow dark. Sarah lost her rhythm, nearly stumbling into Mr. Styles. She felt sick to her stomach. What had she done?

Then, magically, C.J.'s voice was impossibly near. "Excuse me, Len," his voice said from behind her, "but I need to cut in with this lovely lady of mine."

Sarah felt slightly dizzy and winded, so the sight of C.J. was dreamlike. There was something in his face she had not seen since her first night with him. He gave her an open, welcome smile, and she glided into his open arms. C.J. pulled her much closer to him than Mr. Styles had dared, until they were nearly touching. He slid back and forth to his own slow rhythm, as if he couldn't hear the faster-paced music, and she followed his movement, swaying.

"You're gonna be a handful to the man who loves you, ain't you, Sarah Breedlove McWilliams?" C.J. said. Their eyes locked.

Sarah nodded, her heart roaring. "I hope that's what you want, C.J."

"Guess it must be, or I'd know how to leave well enough alone. You sure you've got any use for a dandy, high-tone man like me?"

Sarah hadn't realized, until now, that C.J. had overheard the remarks she'd made about him to Lelia, Sadie, and Rosetta when he visited her kitchen in St. Louis, on the day she first met him. Embarrassed, she laughed. Then her eyes settled back into the sunlight in C.J.'s gaze.

"Oh, yes, C.J.," she said. "I've never been more sure in all my days."

Chapter Twenty-two

Sarah had never felt so special as she did the day she married C.J. Walker, and she could hardly imagine that there might be a day she would feel so special again.

From the time their engagement was first announced in the newspaper— the only time *any* of her doings had been announced publicly—Sarah had found herself doted upon and congratulated. A kindly couple from church, B.F. and Delilah Givens, insisted that they host the ceremony at their home. A young chambermaid and dressmaker who used Sarah's hair grower, Lizette, begged for a chance to sew her a bridal dress, promising to replicate a design in the *Elite Fashions* catalog at a price Sarah could afford. The Scholtz family delivered a beautiful sterling silver tea set to the Breedloves' as a wedding gift, and it shone so brightly that Sarah nearly screamed when she unwrapped the gift box.

Then the letters began arriving. Sadie and Lelia had both written to say that they were going to come. Sarah was glad, but she felt a twinge of guilt because the trip would pose such a sacrifice to them. If she'd had the money, she would have gladly paid their fares from St. Louis herself, but she could not. Her Hair Grower was selling better than it ever had, but she was also spending more money on ingredients and the ointment jars C.J. had insisted she should use to package it. Guilt or no guilt, though, Sarah savored the words Lelia had written her, and she read her letter over and over after she received it: *Mama, nothing in the world could keep me away.*

But the biggest surprise of all had come two days before the wedding, when Anjetta told Sarah that someone was waiting for her on the Breedloves' front porch. There, a portly woman bundled in two mismatched overcoats and a scarf stood in the frigid air, a suitcase in her hand.

" 'Bout *time* you got yo'self a new man, Sarah! I'd 'bout given you up."

Sarah almost didn't recognize her. At the mature age of forty-three, the woman had gained at least forty pounds, which had rounded the shape of her face, and her hair was streaked with lines of gray at her forehead. But her eyes hadn't changed, and neither had her voice. When Sarah saw her, she shrieked. They hugged each other so hard they looked like they were wrestling, nearly toppling off the Breedloves' porch.

It was Lou! Alternately laughing and crying, the sisters hugged without making a coherent sentence. Nearly twenty years had passed since they had seen each other last, and Sarah felt time melting away as she sank into her older sister's breast. She and Lou had started out together with only each other to rely on, and they'd been struggling far apart in all the years since. How could they put that feeling into words? Finally Sarah's confusion broke through her wordlessness. She didn't think Lou had left Mississippi once in all her life, and since her divorce from Mr. William Powell, Sarah couldn't imagine how Lou could have afforded the train fare.

"But Lou . . . how did you . . . I mean, who . . . ?"

Then, finally, Sarah noticed C.J. standing on the sidewalk beside his wagon. He was watching them with satisfaction, his arms folded across his chest. He winked. C.J. must have brought Lou to surprise her! If Sarah hadn't already been betrothed to marry C.J. Walker in forty-eight hours, she would have fallen in love with him on sight.

So, on her wedding day, draped in the lovely dress of brocaded satin and lace sewn for her by her neighbor, Sarah realized that she was standing in a room filled with her closest friends and family, all of the people she loved, for the first time in her adult life. Lelia was there, tall and smiling; Sadie beamed at her with glistening eyes, hardly able to keep from squirming with excitement; Lou gazed at her with a combination of pride and what was no doubt envy (she knew Lou, after all); and her neatly dressed nieces and sister-in-law were there as well. There were only a dozen people in the Givenses' bookshelf-lined parlor, but Sarah felt as if she were back in the Great Hall at the World's Fair.

Then there was C.J.

C.J. had spoken to her in the gentlest tones since the night he'd admitted his love for her, keeping his eyes intensely upon her when they were together, and today his face was filled with utter softness as he watched Sarah walk toward him in her floor-length wedding dress. He had shed all reserve, all restraint. So much love burned in his eyes that Sarah wondered how he had managed to keep it a mystery for so long. She could wrap herself up in those eyes.

Reverend Dyett, an elderly colored man, asked her questions she felt need not be asked, that she believed must be apparent in her face: "Do you, Sarah Breedlove McWilliams, take this child of God, Charles Joseph Walker, as your lawful-wed husband? In sickness and health, for better or worse, forsaking all others? To love, honor, and obey as long as you both shall live?"

"Yes." Sarah's voice was a breath. She heard the fireplace crackling behind them.

Next, it was C.J.'s turn. His face held a beatific smile as he nodded slowly to the pastor's words. He seemed to repeat the vows in his mind while the pastor spoke, studying them. "Yes, Reverend, I do," C.J. answered in a firm, clear voice. His eyes shimmered, unblinking.

The pastor smiled. "Well, I do now pronounce you man and wife."

Man and wife. Mr. and Mrs. C.J. Walker, Sarah thought, virtually disbelieving. Then Sarah corrected herself: *No . . . it's Madam C.J. Walker.*

She would keep that name for the rest of her life.

Sarah saw C.J. Walker's house for the first time on their wedding night. As the hired carriage driver took them toward C.J.'s unfamiliar street, Sarah remembered her nervousness when she'd married Moses, and felt the first genuine stab of sorrow she'd experienced over Moses in a long time. What a day she'd just had! A wedding ceremony, and then a wonderful dinner of Cornish hens with her family, friends, and new husband. Sarah never questioned for a moment that Moses was watching over her, and that he was happy with her new union, but she was sorry her happiness today had been at the cost of a man who had been so good to her.

"We're here, Madam Walker," C.J. said, gently nibbling her earlobe. His warm breath in her ear traveled up and down her frame, and she clasped his hand tight.

C.J.'s bungalow-style house was compact, almost identical in size to the one she'd left behind in St. Louis, but she noticed some differences right away. First, he had electricity—he flipped a light switch on his parlor wall, and the whole room was brightened by a lamp on the ceiling above. And although there was a drabness to the room she'd imagined might be typical of a bachelor, C.J. had indulged himself with a few niceties she had never been able to afford because she'd always saved her money so religiously. A large crimson rug covered nearly the entire wooden parlor floor, he had floor-length draperies, there were stylish lamps on his tables, and he even had a framed painting of a mountain landscape on his wall. He could definitely use a woman's touch in terms of the cleaning, she noted when she saw the film of dust covering his table legs, but he had done well for himself. It was a far cry from the bare little home Moses had offered her on their wedding night.

Still, though, C.J. sounded apologetic. "One day soon," he said, "we'll have the grandest house on this street. In the whole neighborhood."

His attached bathroom, as far as Sarah was concerned, was an utter luxury. As she dressed herself in the special white muslin gown she'd bought for their wedding night, Sarah enjoyed the washbasin where she could easily wash her face from the faucets of running water. And she looked forward to reclining in his porcelain claw-foot bathtub, which was a delightful improvement over the cramped, uncomfortable tin tubs that had served her for bathing until now. And a flush toilet! No snakes, no lingering odors, no journey outside into the cold air just to do her business. All she had to do was sit and flush when she was done!

So this is how the middle-class folks live, she thought.

Her hair was brushed down, and the jet-black strands fanned across her neck and shoulders. For an instant, gazing at herself in the lacy collar of her elegant nightgown in the looking glass over C.J.'s washbasin, Sarah felt as if she'd stepped into someone else's life. How had all of this happened so fast? Only yesterday, it seemed, she couldn't get her hair to grow at all, and she'd had no real expectation that a man's hands would touch her body again. Now, she was a new bride on her wedding night.

"My, my, my . . ."

When Sarah stepped into the doorway of C.J.'s dimly lighted bedroom, his voice was so low it was nearly a growl. C.J. was still clothed except for his shoes, but he was already lying back on his iron four-poster bed, his arms folded behind his head as he propped himself up against the rails of the headboard. Candlelight glowed against his wall coverings, but she could barely see the features on C.J.'s face, except his wide smile.

Sarah clenched her fingers tight, hearing the earthy desire in C.J.'s voice. She knew that desire, too. There was a gentle rustling from C.J.'s window as snowflakes landed against the pane. She was warm in her gown, but her body felt rigid from eager waiting.

"Tell you what, Sarah Walker . . ." C.J. said. "I knew I was in trouble with you from the first time we sat down to supper."

"When I hit you?" Sarah asked, teasing gently.

C.J. laughed. "Naw, girl, it wasn't that. I figger I had that coming. What I mean is, you're the kind of woman a fellow figures he has to either marry or forget about. I didn't think I was ready to be nobody's husband, but I sure as hell didn't know how I could forget you either. You're a woman no man could forget if he lived to the next century."

His voice warmed her just like a roaring fireplace.

"Know what I think?" she said, taking a step toward him. "I think sometimes folks meet, and it's set from the start they should be together. There's nothing they can do to change it."

Grinning, C.J. sat up and swung his legs over the side of the bed. "Close your eyes, Sarah. I've got somethin' for you."

"But you've already done so much, C.J., bringin' Lou out here and—"

"*Shhhhh*," C.J. said. "No back talk, woman."

Bowing her head slightly, Sarah closed her eyes as she'd been asked.

She heard C.J. open a drawer, then his feet padded closer to her. She knew he was standing in front of her because she could smell his clean scent.

"Okay. You can look now," he said.

Sarah opened her eyes, and she looked down at C.J.'s hands. He was holding a small figurine of shiny porcelain, a replica of a single flower in a vase. As he raised it closer to her, she could see that the petrified flower was a dark, open-budded rose. Its leaves, thorns, and petals were as lifelike as any real flower, if smaller.

"C.J. . . ." she whispered, struck by its simple beauty.

"Now, they didn't have it exactly like I wanted it, so I had to have it painted special. I remember you told me 'bout that dream you had one time . . . you know, with the African man. . . ." At that, Sarah nearly gasped. The rose was not just dark, she realized; it was *black*. It shone up at her like a boundless night sky. "I figgered since I'm your man now, then I must be the one in your dream. And if he gave you a black rose, then I should, too."

Sarah couldn't speak. C.J. stroked the side of her face with his warm, soft palm. "Yeah . . ." he said, nodding as if he liked the sound of it. "I'm the man in your dream, and you're the black rose. My black rose."

At that, Sarah pulled C.J.'s head closer to hers and raised herself to her toes so she could kiss his mouth. This time there was none of the hesitation of the first night when their lips and tongues met; C.J. hugged her close to him as they kissed, and he rubbed his torso against her so she could feel the solidness of his waiting manhood. Sarah's body seemed to seep through the fabric of her gown, cleaving itself to him. C.J. made small moaning noises, his hand roving across her backside, fumbling for the ties at the back of her gown. Sadie had told Sarah once that she'd never undressed in front of her husband in all the years they'd been married, except under their bedsheets when her husband was seized by the mood, but Sarah realized suddenly that she wanted to shed her gown and stand in front of C.J. Walker in all of her bold, womanly nakedness. So he could see every brown curve and inch of her.

Suddenly C.J. pulled his mouth away from hers, breathing slightly harder as he gazed at her with heavy-lidded eyes. "You ain't tired, are you, Sarah? I remember you sayin' how you've got to get up early tomorrow for that demonstration over at—"

"Well, then," Sarah interrupted him, wrapping her arms around his midsection to anchor their hungry bodies together, "I guess we better get to bed, then, huh? It's time for something else right now."

C.J. grinned, pleased, and he swallowed her with his mouth once again.

Chapter Twenty-three

"A colored man owned this?" Lelia asked with surprise, trailing behind Sarah and C.J. into the gaily decorated ballroom of the lovely hotel in the heart of Denver's business district. Tired of her independence, Lelia had moved to Denver to live with Sarah and her new husband and help with their growing business. Sparkling chandeliers hung from the ceiling, casting bright light down onto the revelers on the slickly polished ballroom floor below. The Summertime Grand Ball at the Inter-Ocean Hotel was being billed as one of the biggest colored affairs of the season, and C.J. had secured his family's invitation through Mr. Joseph D.D. Rivers, who owned *The Colorado Statesman* and knew C.J. from his advertising work.

"Yep, this hotel belonged to a man name of Barney Ford," C.J. answered Lelia, steering them through the room. "He died four years back, but he had a little piece of everything in this town at one time or t'other. Way I hear it, colored men in Denver owe their vote to him and two other fellows, Henry Oscar Wagoner and Edward Sanderlein. They put up a fight."

"What about colored women?" Lelia said defiantly. "I don't see why we can't vote, too."

C.J. shrugged. "Tell you what, Lelia, the way some of you ladies hagride your men to get 'em to the polls to vote this way or that, it's the ladies' votes that really count." Then he laughed in a way Sarah knew would annoy Lelia, who didn't need much provocation. Lelia had confided to Sarah that she thought C.J. was crass and conceited. Sarah thought C.J.'s sense of humor could be low sometimes, but she didn't see him the same way. C.J. just knew a lot, and he liked to share what he knew.

"Call me A'Lelia, please," Lelia told C.J. impatiently. She tolerated Sarah calling her *Lelia*, but not C.J. She was determined her new chosen name would stick.

"Sorry, Miss A'Lelia. Slipped my mind."

"Women will vote soon enough," Sarah said. " 'Fore long, there won't be a single thing men can do that women can't. Just wait 'til we start proving ourselves in business, too. Now, C.J., tell me which of these folks I need to meet."

Sarah felt intimidated in the ballroom full of nattily dressed colored folk, many of whom looked like mulattoes and quadroons, but she didn't want it to show. She was wearing her richly colored blue dress with the golden braid—still the nicest dress she owned, aside from her wedding dress—but it was obvious that many of the other women had spent fortunes on their summer costumes, and most of the men sported tuxedos and tails. C.J. looked dapper as usual, but tonight even he was outclassed. And Lelia's modern-style suit was lovely on her, but it was plain compared to the intricate layers of fine fabrics draped on the women around them. Did these Negroes buy their clothes in France? *Seems like we never look quite right*, Sarah thought.

But no matter. Part of C.J.'s plan was to create her mystique as Madam C.J. Walker, and she was here to meet people, so that was what she would do. "Over at that table by the stage, that's Dr. P.E. Spratlin, who's very high up in politics," C.J. said, gesturing subtly across the room with a jerk of his chin. "There's, uhm . . . the Hackleys beside them. Edwin Hackley is an attorney." No matter what the event, if C.J. didn't personally know most of the people in a room, he could at least name them. That was a talent Sarah wanted to learn for herself, she decided.

A string quintet was seated on the stage, the Negro members sitting poised and ready with their violins on their chins and shoulders, and one had a towering string instrument between his knees that Sarah didn't recognize; when the white-gloved conductor moved his baton, the musicians began to play a lively waltz. Their bows moved in unison, filling the room with a sweet, delicate music that delighted Sarah's ear. Could Moses have played well enough to join a musical group like this if he'd ever had the chance?

"Ah, that's the new *Vienna Blood* waltz Strauss wrote right before he died," Sarah overheard a man behind her say. "I heard it performed in New York. You need a full orchestra to do it justice."

"It still doesn't measure up to *Blue Danube*. That was his heyday," another voice added.

Sarah had to restrain herself from whipping her head around to see who was speaking. Who were these men criticizing the beautiful music? And how often had they heard it, that they could know a piece as soon as they heard the first strains? She felt lucky that the music sounded fresh and wonderful to her unlearned ear, but she wondered how much more music was as foreign to her as the piece the musicians were playing now.

"There's another attorney, John Stuart . . ." C.J. was saying, but Sarah's thoughts had become lost in the music. She gazed out at the dance floor, where a dozen couples had begun to dance the waltz, twirling in regimented steps as if they had practiced for hours on end. The women's skirts flared around their ankles as they whirled. They looked so elegant, Sarah was transfixed. *They have their own world*, Sarah thought. But for one night, at least, this was her world, too.

Sarah walked in careful, dainty steps, imitating the other women around her, and she was painfully careful with her diction and grammar, speaking in short sentences. Soon, after Lelia discovered a young woman her own age and C.J. wandered off in search of refreshments, Sarah found herself surrounded by a group of women who seemed genuinely glad to meet her. They asked her how long she had lived in Denver, whether she planned to stay, and how she liked the city. For the first time all night, Sarah felt at ease.

"Do you have a taste for literature, Madam Walker?" one of the women said brightly. She was very fair, her hair closer to red than brown, and she wore small, ladylike spectacles. "We're all members of the Eureka Literary Club. You and your husband should join!"

Sarah felt the nervousness creeping back into her stomach. She'd never seen C.J. read anything except business books, and reading was still such a struggle for her that it had taken her months to fight through the text of Booker T. Washington's *Up from Slavery*. She read newspapers, letters, and Bible verses, but whole books were still too much of a challenge for her.

"I thought *Up from Slavery* was one of the great works of our time," Sarah said with more confidence than she felt, and she was gratified when the women echoed her feelings.

"Oh, yes, of course we've read that," the redheaded woman said. "Have you read *The Souls of Black Folk* by W.E.B. Du Bois?"

Another woman joined in. "Oh, don't you just love Paul Laurence Dunbar's poems! His death in February was so sad . . . such a young man . . ."

"Do you admire Anna Julia Cooper, Madam Walker?"

The women were speaking quickly, and all Sarah could do was nod her head as they penned her in with their eager questions, their love of books burning in their eyes. How could she admit she had read none of these other writers, that she had so little schooling?

"But you shouldn't think we read only Negro writers, Madam Walker. You've read *Jane Eyre*, of course?" The question came from a woman slightly younger than Sarah who seemed to be disguising a Deep South country accent; despite her elegant royal blue silk dress, Sarah didn't think this woman had been born to manners any more than she had. And the woman's gaze was not entirely kind. The other women had fallen silent, their eyes on Sarah as they waited for her answer. This group was ready to accept her, if only she could say the right things!

"Oh, yes. Jane Eyre is a very fine author," Sarah answered, nodding, but she knew instantly that she'd made a mistake. The women's faces turned from expectant to puzzled, and they glanced away one by one, embarrassed for her. The young woman who'd posed the question could barely conceal her smile.

Finally, gently, the redheaded woman spoke. "*Jane Eyre* is a novel, Madam Walker. The author is Charlotte Brontë."

Hot blood rushed to Sarah's face, but she struggled to keep her composure. "My mistake," she murmured. "I guess y'all can see I don't read as much as I'd like."

By now, the gracious smile on the lips of the woman in the blue dress looked distinctly false. "I think I remember where I've seen you now, Madam Walker," she said. "Isn't your photograph always in the newspaper ads? You sell some kind of hair grease."

"Oh, my goodness, that's right! The 'Before' and 'After' photographs," the redheaded woman said, recognizing her. "I must be blind not to have noticed. What an ad!"

"I don't use those sorts of products myself, of course," the woman in the blue dress went on. "My hair's too fine to muss with grease. But the girl who cleans for me and my husband would *love* it. If it works like you say, that is."

For the first time, Sarah wondered if this woman in blue might not have purposely tried to make *Jane Eyre* sound like an author's name, laying a trap to humiliate her. The woman had probably seen through her ignorance right away. But Sarah could see through her, too. "It's a hair grower, not grease," she said evenly. "It has science-proved ingredients, and it works like I say, or I wouldn't say it."

The woman's lips parted. "Oh, well, I didn't mean—"

"I know what you meant," Sarah told her, fixing a gaze on her that spoke her mind: *You don't fool me. You prob'bly cleaned somebody's house or took in laundry, too, one time or another, before you married yourself a rich man some way. You're one o' them folks who's ashamed to be colored, who can't feel good except by tryin' to make other folks feel bad. But don't try it on me unless you wanna be shamed in front of your friends. I can be nigger-ish, too.*

The woman's eyes dropped away, as if she'd heard every unspoken word.

Minutes later, Sarah only mumbled a thank-you when C.J. brought her a glass of iced tea at a secluded table she'd found. The ballroom felt too warm by now, the music had lost its dazzle on her, and Sarah was ready to leave. When C.J. asked her what had changed her mood, she told him about her encounter. "I ain't in the mood for no more mixing, thank you," Sarah said.

C.J. chuckled, shaking his head. "Aw, girl, come on. Where's that tough skin?"

"These kinda folks make me sick, always thinkin' they're better than somebody."

"I know what you need," C.J. said, pointing. "Look at A'Lelia."

Sarah followed C.J.'s gesture toward the ballroom floor, and she smiled instantly. Lelia was dancing a waltz with a handsome young man who, surprisingly, stood a full inch taller than her statuesque daughter. Lelia had a wide smile on her face, one of the few times Sarah had seen Lelia look happy since she came to Denver. Lelia's biggest complaint was that she didn't know anyone except her cousins, and it was hard to make friends.

"Who's that boy?"

"Can't recall his name for once, but he's a college boy. I've seen him at the Church of the Redeemer, where all the monied folks go. His father might be a new doctor come to town."

Sarah felt a strong sense of contentment as she watched her daughter dancing in the sure arms of a young man who looked accomplished and well mannered. Sarah still often feared Lelia wasn't mature enough to make a good life for herself, but what if Lelia ended up matched with a man of education and intelligence who could provide for her and their children? This young man was a far cry from the crude musician who'd been kissing and sweet-talking her behind the bushes years ago. The bushes! The mere memory of that day made Sarah shiver with distaste.

The musicians ended their waltz, and the ballroom filled with applause. Then, almost without pause, a new waltz began. Sarah recognized this piece vaguely, she thought. *Blue Danube*, she heard guests murmuring, and a steady stream of new dancers made their way toward the ballroom floor as the music grew toward a gay crescendo. *Blue Danube*. She would commit the melody to memory so she would know it if she heard it again, she vowed.

C.J. extended his arm with a half bow. "Shall we, Madam? I apologize it's a mite more proper than dancing in a barrelhouse," he teased. "I know you like it better at Jake's, out there shakin' it with no shame. Shoot, looked to me like it wasn't your first time, neither—"

"You hush, C.J. Walker, before someone hears you," Sarah hissed. But she was smiling.

As C.J. led her to the dance floor, though, Sarah had second thoughts. What did she know about waltzing? And in front of all these people? But C.J. patiently guided Sarah's arms to their proper position, clasped her hand, and began to lead her in the one-two-three step of the waltz. He danced very slowly at first, and she felt his hand pressing the small of her back, guiding her. Although she was terrified of stumbling, Sarah followed him the best she could, holding herself stiff. One-two-three, one-two-three. Soon, while C.J. nodded to the beat, they began to dance faster, drawn into the music's flow. He seemed to lift her into flight. She was waltzing!

"You're doin' so good, Sarah," C.J. said close to her ear, and at first she thought he was complimenting her dancing. "You sure do make a hulla-baloo. I've been listening to folks, and they're all talkin' about Madam C.J. Walker. You just wait and see what happens."

One-two-three, one-two-three. All the stiffness had vanished from Sarah's limbs, leaving her buoyant as C.J. guided her first one way and then the other, the room spinning around her in a dizzying blur. Sarah's body felt limber and light as she and C.J. danced amidst the wash of beautiful music beneath the grand ballroom's glistening chandeliers.

She hoped the violins would never stop, because she could dance all night.

As a hidden sparrow whistled its morning song from a telephone pole above her, Sarah paused before walking into a nondescript one-story brick building sandwiched between a small five-and-dime and a buggy repair shop a few blocks' walk from the Breedloves' house. Automobiles and commercial wagons loaded with crates rumbled past Sarah as she stood on the sidewalk and surveyed the building with the same sense of mingled aston-ishment and disappointment she'd felt since the day she first saw it.

I've got a surprise for you, Sarah, C.J. had said two months before.

It had been a surprise, all right. Only a small, hand-painted sign in the corner of the window identified the building's new occupants: WALKER MFG., it said. The sign was overshadowed by the much larger advertise-ment painted on the west wall of the building in bright red, with white script declaring COCA-COLA—"RELIEVES FATIGUE." Still, if a passerby was looking carefully enough, the Walker Company sign in the window was plain as day.

Her company finally had a home of its own.

Unfortunately, though, C.J. had been able to get the building for such a bargain only because it had been partially ravaged by a fire some months back. Although the interior had been cleaned out and repainted, the exte-rior was still an eyesore because portions were charred, streaked, and flak-ing. Besides, even the inside smelled like soot to Sarah. That was the first thing she'd noticed when C.J. proudly toured her the first day, and she no-ticed it again now.

As usual, Sarah was the first one to arrive this morning, so the room was deserted. She gave a frustrated sigh as she noticed the empty boxes strewn around the floor; she'd asked Anjetta and her sisters to put them neatly in a corner before she'd left them the day before. Their place might not be fancy, but there was no reason it shouldn't look neat. At least the long countertop had been wiped clean of spilled ingredients, she noted. They knew she wouldn't tolerate that kind of mess, and neither would C.J.

The space had served as a commercial laundry, so it was plumbed with running water and equipped with two large laundry stoves and the long countertop, which had all been spared by the fire. (If her hair business didn't work, Sarah told herself wryly, it would be only a small step to go back to washing.) There was also just enough room for a row of mismatched chairs for her customers who wanted their hair pressed, and Sarah had assembled them neatly near a stove. It wasn't a beauty salon by far, but it was better than running her business out of her kitchen.

Here, Lelia, C.J., and her nieces helped her mix the ingredients and scoop them into jars and bottles that could be mailed to their customers, who wrote from all parts of Colorado and as far east as St. Louis and Indianapolis. The ads C.J. had designed were running regularly in colored newspapers in Denver and elsewhere, and they were working. Mail orders for Madam C.J. Walker's Wonderful Hair Grower, Glossine pressing oil, and Vegetable Shampoo were trickling in more each week, waiting for them daily at the post office. Even despite their rising costs in advertising and rent, the company was still earning nearly ten dollars a week, just as C.J. had predicted. There were so many orders, in fact, that Sarah had finally told Mr. Scholtz it was time for her to quit her cooking job. He'd kept his bargain with her: In exchange for the extra time she cooked for him, he'd given her valuable advice on her hair products, especially the Wonderful Hair Grower and her all-vegetable shampoo. He'd even given her ideas for skin products she might want to add to her line later. Mr. Scholtz hadn't been happy to see her go, bless him, but he'd been very happy for the reason. *We started out small, too, Sarah*, he'd told her. *There's no grand mystery to it. You just don't give yourself a moment's rest until you have what you want.*

Well, they were a long way from what she wanted, Sarah thought, surveying the dank room that still smelled bitterly like a doused fire. But at least she'd made a start.

"Madam Sarah?"

A voice behind Sarah made her jump, since she hadn't known anyone else had come in. It was Lizette, the woman who had made Sarah's lovely wedding dress. The energetic little sprite of a woman, not even five feet tall, had also begged Sarah to teach her how to use the steel comb to treat hair; by now, besides Lelia, Lizette was Sarah's most successful student. Lizette worked as a chambermaid several days a week, sweetening her income with her dressmaking and hair-pressing. Sarah admired the young woman's drive, wishing Lelia would strike up a better friendship with her. Lizette was only a year older than Lelia, but since Lizette never had time to visit the nickelodeons or go roller-skating in Lincoln Park, Lelia thought she was a bore.

"Why are you out here so early, Lizette?" Sarah said. Sarah knew that Lizette cleaned hotel rooms in the mornings, so she didn't expect her to help her with hair customers until the afternoons, when she brought her young son in tow. The four-year-old boy, Reed, was with her now, clinging to his mother's hand as he gnawed on a half-eaten apple.

Lizette had almond-shaped eyes that reminded Sarah of Anjetta's, and they were shining brightly this morning. "Madam, I just have to give you a big ol' hug," the woman said, wrapping her arms around Sarah. She was so spirited, she nearly knocked Sarah off balance.

"What's into you, Lizette?"

"You ain't never gonna guess what I just finished doing this very minute!" Lizette's face beamed with a smile as she inhaled a deep, satisfying breath. "I walked right to that hotel that's been running me silly, and I told my boss man I wasn't going to clean nary a room in my whole life 'cept in my own house. You should've seen that man's face!"

Sarah knew Lizette was unhappy at her job, and she had confided that her boss sometimes tried to grab her and kiss her, as he'd apparently done with many of the colored women who worked for him. Lizette was afraid to tell her husband about the man's advances because she was sure her husband would try to retaliate, which would be a disaster for her family.

"I figured it out last night after church, Madam! I been pressing heads in my kitchen after I leave from here, right? Well, I been pressin' so many heads 'til I can make up for that cleaning money an' still have some left over. That job wasn't giving me nothing but botherment! When I'm pressing heads at home, I can watch my boy, too. An' I still have time to sew."

Lizette had been free to find her own hair customers as long as she used the Glossine and recommended the other Walker products to her customers. Sarah knew Lizette was making good money with hair, but how could she already be earning enough to quit her job?

"Lizette . . . are you sure, child? That's a mighty big change—"

"Madam, I even did the figures on paper. Like I done told my husband, I'm workin' for my own self now!" Lizette said, patting her breastbone with her palm.

"Mama's *own* self!" the boy repeated, mimicking his mother.

There was a pride shining from Lizette's face Sarah couldn't get out of her mind.

C.J. fell away from Sarah beneath their bedsheets, his slick chest heaving with his rapid breaths. "Lord have mercy . . ." he managed to say between pants. "Damn, I'm 'bout wore out. I thought you said you wanted to drop right to sleep, Sarah."

Sarah closed her eyes, savoring her body's thrilling to the memory of C.J.'s warm weight on top of her. She quivered, catching her breath. She saw beads of perspiration glistening on her naked chest before she covered herself. "I thought I did, too," Sarah said.

C.J. pulled her against him, and they lay in silence for a moment in their moonlit bedroom, listening to each other's slowing breaths. Sarah's appetite for C.J.'s touch shocked her. She had nearly forgotten what it was like to make love to a man, but it was also different somehow; the years seemed to have made her responses deeper, as if her passions had been steeping all these years like a pot of tea.

C.J. laughed, and to her his laugh sounded like warm honey being poured on her from head to foot. "I ain't complainin', though," C.J. said. "I better count my blessings. It's fine with me if we forget to drop right off to sleep every night of the week."

"I'm just tryin' to keep you busy so you'll forget your old habits, that's all," Sarah said, only halfway joking. She couldn't help wondering if C.J. missed the female company he'd always had in such abundance before now. She could still hardly believe he was really hers.

C.J. leaned over her, kissing her forehead, her nose, and then her lips. He met her eyes. "My only old habits are a little whiskey and a cigar now and again. If I'd expected I'd need *all* my old habits, I wouldn't have taken you for my wife. So you just put that thought to rest."

Sarah smiled. If she'd had one lingering doubt about the new plans that had been formulating themselves in her mind for the past few days, it had been the question of how her marriage might fare under the strain of long absences. She couldn't stand it if she thought C.J. would take someone else to his bed. There was no room for lies between them.

"Why so quiet?" C.J. asked, still gazing at her.

"I've got some ideas for the company, C.J., but I don't think you'll like them."

"You know I love your ideas, Sarah."

"You might not now."

Sarah was silent for a moment, and C.J. waited. Then, slowly, she began to tell him about her conversation with Lizette. As she talked in a hush, recounting how Lizette had said she was working for her *own self*, Sarah felt her heartbeat quickening. "Sure, Sarah," C.J. said when she was finished. "What you expect? That girl's been sellin' Hair Grower for us like blazes ever since you taught her how to use that comb."

Sarah bounced on the mattress beside him, her mind on fire. She'd made the mistake of drinking a Coca-Cola earlier that evening; she loved the sugary soda drink, but she knew it would keep her wide awake a good part of the night. *Relieves Fatigue* was the truth! "Well, C.J. . . . don't you see? How many women like Lizette you think are out there wishin' they could up and quit?"

"A whole lot. You included, 'til now," C.J. said.

"That's *right*." Sarah felt a surge of adrenaline, and her voice rose. "That's how I figured out what we need to be doin'. We need to be trainin' women on how to use that comb. We need to let them sell the Wonderful

Hair Grower and Glossine on their own. All the ads in the world won't do what I'm thinking about, C.J. If colored women start doing the hair themselves, they'll sell it for us just like Lizette. We'll make a profit, but at the same time we'll be givin' these women something they've never had before. We'll be givin' them *freedom.*"

"Wait, wait, wait . . ." C.J. said, shifting until he was sitting up. He sighed. "Sarah, hold up. Now, I agree with you. But you're putting the cart before the horse. You'd need to open up—"

"A school!" Sarah said. "That's right. I open a school, and then I charge a price to take the course to fix the hair. And I'd teach it right, too, not just any ol' slipshod way. When they're done, they get some kind of paper from me and they're in business."

Patiently, C.J. reached over to hold Sarah's shoulders so he could look into her eyes. "You been drinkin' that Coca-Cola again, ain't you?" he said. "I told you about that at bedtime."

"That's not it," Sarah said. "I'm just seein' something, C.J. I'm seein' how Walker Manufacturing Company is about more than selling Hair Grower. If you'd seen Lizette's face, the way she told me she was out from under that boss man's thumb . . ."

"Shoot, you don't think my mama cleaned and cooked, too? I *do* see it, Sarah. But I also see how everything has to be in time. You need to make a name for yourself first."

At that, Sarah sighed. She knew C.J. was right. But she had already decided she couldn't make a name the way she wanted to in Denver. It was fine to base the manufacturing office here, but the city didn't have enough Negroes to support her. There weren't nearly as many Negroes in Denver as she had hoped, not like there had been in St. Louis.

"C.J., remember what you said to me at the ball? How I make a hullabaloo? Well, I don't need to go around a bunch of biggity balls doin' that. I need to go out and talk to folks—you know, beat 'em out the bushes. I need to find the ladies who cook and clean and wash, folks that don't read the papers and don't dance the waltz. And I need to get it so they're either using our products or else selling them. Now, *that's* how you build up a name, C.J. When people see you in person, they remember who you are."

"You're talkin' about bein' a drummer," C.J. said. "That's not for you, Sarah. I've done it myself, and a drummer's life is no kind of life for a man, much less a woman. Livin' on trains, folks slamming doors in your face, runnin' you off with a shotgun sometimes. Come on, now. The ads are going fine. It's better to let people come to *you.*"

Sarah sighed. "Yeah, but most folks out there don't know the difference between Madam C.J. Walker and a whole bunch of other ads for hair growers, and most of 'em don't work worth a lick. Why should they try mine?"

"The ads," C.J. said, sounding slightly irritated for the first time that night. "What have I been saying? We do a better ad, and it's the advertising that brings them."

"It's not enough," Sarah said, believing it with all her heart. She and C.J. could advertise for years and never attract people the way she wanted, she thought. Besides, she would need more than ads to teach women how to use her combs.

"Look, Sarah," C.J. said, stroking her hand. "Think about what I told you 'bout Scott Joplin that first night. Remember? Look at him: He's on top of the world with ragtime, but he can't be satisfied. An' I bet if he does do some opera, he'll want somethin' else next."

"What's wrong with that? He just wants more," Sarah said. She'd expected resistance from C.J., but she still felt rising disappointment as she realized she might not be able to convince him to share her vision for what the company could be. More and more, C.J. had been making satisfied noises, settling in, when Sarah just felt herself growing more impatient.

"Folks like that can't never be happy, that's what's wrong with it," C.J. said. "You never look at what you've done, put your hands on your hips, and say with pride, 'I did it.' Shoot, Sarah, when I showed you that building I found cheap as dirt, you hardly gave me a smile."

At that, Sarah felt a twinge of guilt. C.J. had worked hard to find them an affordable rent, and she knew he'd felt hurt when she wasn't more excited. When she was silent, C.J. went on. "And I know A'Lelia and me don't always see eye to eye, but you just ask her. She would agree with me. You need to learn how to be satisfied."

Satisfied?

Suddenly C.J.'s words sounded like a betrayal. What was the point of trying to build a company at all, if she was supposed to be satisfied from the very start? What if she'd just been satisfied washing clothes? Or satisfied to go bald?

"I don't believe this is C.J. Walker talking," Sarah said. "Mister 'Advertising Re-vo-lu-tion.' Mister 'I know how to sell a business better than anyone or anything.'"

"Don't mock my words," C.J. said. She knew she'd stung him, because his voice was tight. "I *do* know how to sell a business, but I also know how to keep my senses. Woman, we just rented an office space we can barely pay for, and we've got orders to fill. We don't have the money to send you or nobody else on a sales trip. And even if we did, we don't have time. We need to be here. I don't see why you're gettin' all excitable just when things are startin' to work out right. You ever heard of bankruptcy, Sarah? That's what happens when businesses run out of money. And what you're saying sounds like bankruptcy to me, all right."

Frustrated, Sarah blinked fast. How could she make him understand?

"C.J. . . . ." she said, her tone gentler. "You know how you like me tellin' folks I got my formula from a dream? Well, I think maybe I did at that.

Maybe it's dreams that keep me awake when I try to go to sleep, when I get all these ideas and I can't stop thinkin' about them. If that's true, then maybe this idea is part of a dream, too. Some dreams come when you're asleep, and some come when you're awake. I can't explain to you how I know it, but I know it just the same: The Walker Company will never be what it can be if I don't go out and tell those ladies what I can give them. They need me, and I need them. Now, you may be right—maybe we can't afford for us both to go—but one of us has to. And that one's got to be me."

There was a long, strained silence in the room. After a while, Sarah began to wonder if C.J. might not say another word. Then, at last, his voice came in the darkness.

"You don't like to leave nobody with choices, do you, Sarah?" he said. "I could say, 'Well, fine, Sarah, but let's wait a year 'til we have more money.' Or I could say, 'No, Sarah, I think that's pure crazy talk.' But nothing I can say would matter to you. Once it's in your head, it's set, no matter what. That's not right, in my book. Not when folks are partners."

The words, spoken so plainly, sounded ugly to Sarah's ears. She opened her mouth to deny his charge, but could she, really? What *could* C.J. say that would change her mind?

"One thing could sway me," Sarah said. "If you said you'd be gone when I came back."

She'd meant to let C.J. know she cared for him so much that her feelings were more important than her ideas, no matter how much she believed in her ideas. Instead her words had come out sounding like she expected an ultimatum. And what if he gave her one? What then?

C.J. gave a sound that was a mingled sigh and chuckle, shaking his head. "That's no kinda choice, woman," he said. "Maybe you just don't know nothin' about giving choices."

"Maybe I don't, then," Sarah said quietly. "Nobody ever gave me none. You?"

C.J. wrapped his arm around Sarah, kissing her cheek. "Guess not," he said, resigned.

The two of them stayed half awake nearly all night, unable to sleep, unable to talk, with nothing left to do except wait for the morning light.

Chapter Twenty-four

My Dearest Sarah,

 I have done nothing but worry since we parted in New York. I hope this letter finds you safely with your sister in Vicksburg and I hope your journey through Mississippi goes well. As you know I did not think you should want to travel through there now when I am called away, but my opinions are no secret. You will be happy to know A'Lelia has risen to the ocasion and had the crisis well in hand by the time I returned. The orders finally went out after delay and she has printed dozens of letters of apology to our anxious customers. She has already hired more help, a woman you do not know who is very reliable for mixing and cleaning both. I hope this is the end of Anjetta's complaints!

 A'Lelia is awful good with figures, which I am glad because they vex me so. You will be very pleased with the new numbers. We have seen many orders from Oklahoma and New York already, so the visits are paying off! Our weekly orders are now at $35 and I have no doubt they will keep rising through the month. At least I hope so because we are spending it all on train tickets and boarding! Letters are coming asking when you will open the college you keep talking about. Maybe it isn't smart to make promises we cannot afford to keep? You know how your speeches cause a stir.

 That is all I will say about business. We all miss you madly, but I miss you in a more special way because we have had so little time as husband and wife. It must be true that absence makes the heart grow fonder because I can hardly think of anything except how much I wish I could be with you to keep you safe. We must finish your plans for next month so I will know where to join you again. A man's

*place is at his wife's side, my Rose. I would be lost if Fate took you
from me.*

    A'Lelia sends her love and of course you have
    All my love,
    C.J.

Sarah had read the letter in C.J.'s jagged-edged handwriting at least a
dozen times in the week since Lou picked it up for her at the post office
in Vicksburg, but she took it from her handbag, unfolded it, and read it
again in the dim twilight as the train bounced and groaned along the
tracks. The waning daylight glowing through the train's dusty windows
worried Sarah; that meant the train was running late, and she would arrive
in Meridian well after dark. The church that had invited her had promised
to send a driver to meet her at the station, but she knew that her delay
might force a change of plans. And she needed help more than ever, with
the crates of supplies that had been mailed to her in Vicksburg in the
train's cargo car. How would she fare alone in a strange Mississippi town? If
only C.J. were here with her!

A sudden blast of the whistle made Sarah's shoulders tense with nervousness. To keep her mind calm, she forced herself to concentrate on the
letter in her hands. *A man's place is at his wife's side, my Rose.* She could almost hear C.J.'s lulling voice in her imagination, and when she closed her
eyes she could remember her joyful dance with him at the ball. Things had
been going so well between them. . . . She should have listened to him this
time, she thought.

Or, at the very least, she wished she hadn't quarreled with Lou. Sarah
had planned to treat her sister to a trip through Mississippi with her, but a
week in Vicksburg with Lou had been more than enough for her, so she'd
left Lou behind. She'd forgotten how much that woman could test her
nerves! Lou was set in her ways, so slow to accept new ideas. Complete
strangers gave Sarah encouragement and praise, but her own sister usually
offered only complaints or belittlement, as if Sarah were still a child: *Why
you got us standin' out in this hot sun, Sarah? Ain't nobody interested in washin'
they heads in no vegetable soap. How come you puttin' on so many airs when
you talk now? Look to me like you jus' burnin' up folks' heads with that comb.*

Sarah was grateful Lou had allowed her to stay at her home in Vicksburg, but she'd been happy to get away. The hair demonstrations had gone
better than she'd hoped, drawing large crowds to Lou's porch, but Sarah
was almost sorry she'd gone back to Vicksburg. So few of her memories
there were good ones, and all the faces had changed, making her a stranger
there now. Even poor Miss Brown was dead and gone. And little Willie
still in prison! How could Lou's sweet little boy, who used to dance to
Moses' fiddle, have gone so wrong in so little time? And while Delta had

beckoned her from right across the river—Lou even told Sarah she'd heard that the Longs still lived in their old house, and that their childhood cabin still stood—Sarah hadn't had the heart to venture there and visit her parents' resting place. Someday, but not yet.

Feeling a stab of sadness, Sarah again sought solace in the lines of C.J.'s letter. She read his words again and again, until there was too little light to see them clearly even with the gas lamp hanging in the rear of the car casting shadows all around her.

It was getting late. Sarah opened the sterling silver watch case C.J. had given her right before they first set out on the trip in September, which was hand-engraved with the image of two roses. The face of the watch told her it was already after eight o'clock, which meant she could expect to arrive in Meridian by nine. After spending so many months on the trains, Sarah was good at guessing times and distances.

Sarah sighed. Even with the daylight gone, the colored train car was so hot that her arm ached from her constant fanning as she tried to cool herself off. During winter, the train cars had been so frigid she had to wear every piece of clothing she'd brought just to keep warm, but now it was the constant baking heat in the car that bothered Sarah. She could feel the film of damp perspiration across her face and under her clothes, especially gathering where she sat against the hard wooden bench. It was almost as if she'd wet herself.

An' I'd almost rather wet myself than visit that toilet again, she thought. Sarah was grateful for shorter journeys, because her visits to squat over the two-handled rusting tin bucket behind the curtain at the rear of the car were an adventure that too often ended in humiliation. She'd spotted her clothes with urine more than once from the constant jouncing, and she'd prefer any backwater outhouse to that bucket's foul stench. But Sarah had learned the hard way that holding in her water had bad consequences; she'd begun suffering from bladder infections when she traveled, which gave her a painful stream. One had been so bad that she let out a whimpering cry when she felt the burning between her legs. Have mercy! She'd been scared to death of the toilet for a whole week, until the diet of cranberries a woman in New York recommended finally gave her some relief. That sprawling northeastern city had almost been too marvelous to be real, especially with C.J. at her side, but the long train rides to get to and from New York had nearly blotted out her good memories.

To make it worse, no matter how many hours she spent traveling, Sarah was afraid to shut her eyes to take some rest when she was on the trains. Too many thieves. Once, early in their trip, she and C.J. had awakened from a night's fitful sleep to discover that someone had stolen a box of samples right from under their feet. Thank goodness their money had been safely tucked away, or their trip would have been finished from the start. Sarah saw families on the trains from time to time and enjoyed watching the antics of children, but the other passengers were usually men who seemed to forget she was present, smoking and telling each other bawdy stories to pass the time. Worst of all were the whites who visited the colored car occasionally to harass passengers or simply be rowdy. They were usually harmless, but Sarah could never be sure of their character. Sarah's favorite place to sit was the back corner, where she hoped to be inconspicuous.

As much money as she was spending on train fare, Sarah felt more like cargo than a passenger. The seats were rickety, without padding, the air was stale, and the colored porters in white coats she saw in armies at the train stations seemed to make little attempt to keep the colored car clean of discarded papers or food. Maybe they were just too busy with the white passengers, she thought. And the ash! Her rides usually left Sarah dusted with fine, acrid ash she tried desperately to brush from her clothes. The only time Sarah felt the least bit looked after was when she ran across the young colored porter she'd met in St. Louis, Freeman Ransom, on the western train routes; he told her about how his studies were going and sneaked her pillows to make her seat more comfortable.

A few times, Sarah had been able to catch a glimpse into the finer Pullman cars available to white travelers, and she felt angrier with each peek. The seats had fine upholstery, the floors were carpeted, and she even felt drifts of cool air when the doors drifted open. Some of the cars looked like elegant parlors, not like train cars at all. And the dining cars! Through the windows, Sarah had seen row upon row of little tables in fine white tablecloths, decorated as if they were part of an exclusive restaurant. Diners sat drinking from glasses of wine and sipping from their soupspoons, gazing peacefully at the scenery through their windows. Meanwhile, Sarah was sick to death of soda crackers, dried pork, fried chicken, and apples, the foods she always bought in grocery stores when she was hungry because they kept longer in her basket during the long, hot rides. Most restaurants along the train routes would not serve colored patrons, and now that she was back in the South, she'd learned better than to even inquire.

And the train rides won't be better for you anytime soon, either, no matter how much money you make, she reminded herself. Race, not money, separated her from the comfort afforded to the white passengers in the South. Obviously, judging from the pillows, fresh linens, and blankets Sarah saw porters loading into the more favored cars, the train company wanted to make the white customers feel special; if anything, she guessed, they must want colored passengers to feel like a nuisance, as if they were *lucky* to have their money taken from them.

Sarah hated to dwell on the differences long, or her temples throbbed with rage. She had hoped this sort of racial nonsense would have ended by the time Lelia was a grown woman, but instead it seemed to be getting worse. This was the twentieth century! And now that she was in Mississippi, some of the dignities she'd begun taking for granted in Denver—like enjoying an ice-cream drink at a soda fountain or trying on clothes in the shops—seemed like a distant fantasy. She could expect one inconvenience after another, she knew.

Lord, please let my ride be waitin' on me, Sarah thought. *They likely won't even have no place for a colored woman to sleep in this li'l ol' town.*

The train whistled again, lurching her into the night.

In Meridian, it was raining in driving sheets that clamored across the roof of the train car. Sarah must have dozed to sleep, because the rain awakened her even before the train whined to a stop, bucking her forward. Her knees banged against the hard seat in front of her, and she cursed to herself. But she was glad she'd finally arrived. She couldn't wait to climb into a bed! She was scheduled to do demonstrations at the church after the sermon tomorrow morning, and then she would take another train early Monday to Tupelo. As usual, she had little time for resting.

Sarah traveled in clothes appropriate for her work, because she had to present herself well at all times. Despite the grime she'd picked up during the long ride, she was wearing a white shirtwaist and long blue skirt, and she brushed her hair to make sure it was still presentable. She sure wouldn't sell too much Wonderful Hair Grower if she turned up with a head of wild-looking hair, would she? Sarah had misplaced her umbrella on her last train, which had been so crowded that she'd been lucky to find a seat at all, so she had only her overcoat and a scarf to protect her from the rain as she climbed off the train to collect her supplies. She carried her clothes and personal items in a bag she kept with her at all times, but she'd had to entrust her crates to the train's crew. The train depot in Meridian was tiny and uncovered, just a wooden platform alongside a web of rails, built close to the sidewalk on a dreary, sleepy-looking street. The only shelter was the small ticket office, which was dark and had apparently closed for the day. Quickly, Sarah glanced around for anyone who might be looking for her. There were two buggies waiting in the rain, but white men climbed out and walked toward other passengers with grins of recognition. No colored driver in sight. No one came toward her.

"These yours, Auntie?" the train conductor said to her, gesturing toward a crate in the baggage car. The crate was stamped WALKER MFG.

"Yessir," Sarah said. "And three more like it."

"Oh, Jesus Almighty." The conductor groaned as he and a young colored porter heaved the crates, pulling them out to the platform. "There's only two more," the conductor called to her over his shoulder.

"Well, are you sure you looked—"

"I looked as much as I aim to," the conductor said, dropping the third crate unceremoniously to the ground. "This train's runnin' late, an' I don't have all night to be searchin' after a darkie lady's box of God-knows-what."

What was in the missing crate? Combs? Pomade? Something she would sorely miss, she knew. Quickly, Sarah began to rummage through her handbag to see if she could find a little extra money to entice him. "Sir, please, if you just look real good back there, I'll give you—"

"Auntie, you ain't got nothin' I want. Come on, boy," the conductor said, waving to the porter as he slammed the cargo door closed. The young porter looked at Sarah apologetically.

Don't get riled, Sarah, she told herself. *That crate's the least of your problems tonight.*

As the train chugged away and the buggies drove off with their claimed passengers, Sarah realized she was standing alone at a train depot without the first idea of what to do. She had a telephone number for the Reverend Jacob Pearson, who had invited her to the church, but as she glanced up and down the rain-drenched streets, she didn't see anywhere she could find a telephone exchange. The only buildings on this street, which were also dark and no doubt locked up, were a feed store, a grocer, a lumberyard, and a farming supply store. No homes in sight. And even if there *were* homes, what chance did she have of finding someone willing to direct her?

Sarah barely noticed that she was getting drenched in the relentless rain. With low spirits, she began gathering her crates together, making a stack. There was nothing to do but wait. She just hoped the driver would come soon. Sarah was frustrated, angry, and lonesome, but she didn't actually begin to feel *worried* until she heard the echo of glass breaking somewhere many yards down the street, followed by the low laughter of two or three young men. Her heartbeat began to quicken. Were they colored? She prayed so, but something in their tones and cadences told her that the approaching men were white. And they were probably drinking spirits, she thought.

Sarah saw three men appear from the darkness twenty-five yards from her, walking lazily as they enjoyed each other's company. Maybe they'd pay her no mind, she thought. She longed to ask them to direct her to Reverend Pearson, but that would be downright foolish, she knew. The less a colored woman had to do with a pack of liquored-up white men, the better.

As the men's laughter and voices grew louder, Sarah felt her heart tremble.

Suddenly one man hushed the others in a slur. "*Shhhhh.* We got a *lady* standin' there."

"Shit, that ain't no lady, that's a goddamn nigger!" one of them shouted, and they stumbled into each other as they laughed. The men wrestled each other to the muddy ground, all three of them rolling around in the muck like schoolchildren, whooping. To Sarah, those whoops were a bloodcurdling sound. *Leave here, Sarah,* a voice inside her urged. *Leave here right now.*

But even as Sarah contemplated slipping into hiding while the men wrestled each other, she gazed with disdain at her stack of crates. The crates were conspicuous, and the men would probably either steal or destroy them. If she lost her remaining supplies, it might take weeks to receive new ones, and she couldn't do any demonstrations or make sales without them. Her common sense told her she needed to leave, but she could not. She couldn't abandon her crates.

"Hey, what you doin' out here on this street?" one of the men called to her. "You sellin' some o' that coon snatch?" Sarah's ears burned from the vulgarity, and the men laughed again.

Don't even look their way, Sarah. Just ignore them.

She should have vanished while she had the chance, she thought. If she tried to run now, instinct alone would entice them to chase her. She might outrun one of them, but not all three.

"Hey, Auntie Jane, you ain't heard what we asked you?"

They were still ten yards away from her, but they had fanned out, forming a loose half circle. Their faces were mud-spattered and their shoulders were broad, but Sarah could tell they were very young men. Twenty-one, maybe, and a wiry one looked younger than that.

"Y'all boys git on," Sarah said, surprising herself with the authority in her voice. She could hear a slight shaking beneath her words, but she doubted they could. "Ain't nobody botherin' you. Your mamas wouldn't cotton to y'all out here makin' this ruckus." She'd lapsed back into her country-bred way of speaking, because she knew there was no surer way to rile poor white folks than to sound too superior.

The boys glanced at each other, as if each of them hoped to find a hint of what to do. Finally the biggest one spit out a wad of chewing tobacco, staring at Sarah askance. His fingers were twitching. "You tryin' to boss us, darkie?" he said. It was a challenge.

"No, sir," Sarah said, forcing herself to look away from his eyes as a sign of respect. "All I'm sayin' is, I know your mamas is fine women who raised y'all better'n to be messin' after a nigger woman like me." Even while she spoke, Sarah wished she had the strength to knock all three of these little fools flat on their backsides. If they did try to grab her and take liberties, she thought angrily, they'd wear scars to remind them of it the rest of their lives. Without realizing it, Sarah had clenched her fists tight.

Again, there was an uncomfortable silence between the boys.

Sarah, taking a chance, opened her mouth again. "Now, if y'all would be so kind, I need somebody to tell me how I can find Reverend Pearson?"

The men looked startled. Then the youngest man's eyes drifted behind her, and she saw his expression shift. "Here he comes now," he said, raising his hand to point.

Cautiously, Sarah turned around to follow his finger. Sure enough, at the end of the road a buggy was in sight, drawing closer. The driver was a tall colored man in a black coat and hat. Only after Sarah saw him did she realize that she could hear the welcome sound of his horse's clopping on the road, the splashing of wheels in the mud. The driver snapped the whip, and the buggy's approach quickened. Before Sarah could turn back to the boys again, she heard them walking away, jostling each other. "I was sure ready to take me some of that snatch," one of them said, and Sarah felt fingers of ice crawl against the back of her neck.

Seeing the boys walking away, Sarah felt her heart unwrap itself in her chest, and she could breathe again. Her knees went weak, and she balanced herself against the crates. *Thank you, Jesus.* She'd never been happier to see a preacher in her life.

Reverend Pearson was a dark man wearing rain-spotted spectacles, with generous splotches of gray in his hair and mustache. Was she all right? Had those men been bothering her? He apologized profusely for the delay, blaming an unreliable youth who waited nearly an hour for her train before leaving his post. By the time the minister heard she no longer had a ride, his only alternative was to pick her up himself. He had a towel in the buggy so she could wipe her face dry, and he loaded her crates and bag safely beside her.

But just as Sarah was beginning to feel good again, the minister's voice turned more solemn as he leaned in through the door before returning to his driver's berth. "Madam Walker, I don't know how best to say this, so I'd better just come out with it direct. I'm 'fraid you've made this here trip to Meridian for nothing."

Sarah couldn't make a response. She was sure she'd heard the man wrong.

The minister sighed. "Now, some church ladies heard 'bout you from folks down in Vicksburg, an' they thought we could bring you in. But it's caused a fuss, you see. The thing is, my wife and some others . . . well, they don't look kind on folks tryin' to make their hair straight."

"I don't straighten hair, sir, I—"

"Say it how you want, Madam, but folks is callin' them combs you got straightenin' combs, and you an' me both know what sells 'em is ladies thinkin' they can get straight hair. So a bunch of folks had a meetin' at the church last night, an' they voted not to let you do no demonstrations after service tomorrow. Mayhap you can find another place, but—"

"I have a train on Monday!" Sarah said. She didn't dare cuss out a minister, but that was exactly what she felt like doing. How dare this church invite her and then turn her away! "You knew I was comin', Reverend. Least you could've done is wait to have that meetin' an' give me a chance to say my piece—"

The minister's eyes looked sad. "Madam, I sure am sorry, but it's all been decided. I wish I'd never said you should come all this way. I'ma see to it we pay your room and board while you're in Meridian—we're goin' to the boardin'house now, an' it's a right nice place, best breakfast biscuits in this whole town—but we got too many ladies thinkin' it's a sin to mess with the hair God gave 'em. An' I guess I figger they got a point. I'm sorry."

From his voice, at the edge of politeness, Sarah knew that was the end of it.

In the solitude of the buggy while the minister drove her toward the boardinghouse, Sarah felt tears creeping from the corners of her eyes for the first time all day. She could tell she was damp through and through from the rain, she was sore from sitting on the train's hard bench for so long, she'd lost one of her precious crates, and she'd very nearly been raped. And for what?

Thunder growled above her, and she saw the sky outside flash with streaks of lightning. What was C.J. doing tonight? Was he keeping his vow to be true to her, or was he seeking a woman's comfort elsewhere? Was Lelia at a nickelodeon laughing at the moving pictures? In that instant, Sarah missed them both so much that her sight blurred. The company was making thirty-five dollars a week, plenty to live on and more money than she'd ever hoped for, and she was still out here living between trains and boardinghouses. C.J. was right. This was no life!

"You're a fool, Sarah Breedlove Walker," she whispered. "A damn fool."

Maybe it was time to go home, she thought.

It was nearly ten o'clock when Sarah was deposited at a neat, two-story brick boardinghouse on a dark residential street. She could hear the fussing and clucking of a neighbor's chickens as she climbed out of the buggy and the minister hurriedly took her crates inside. While the smiling, elderly proprietor in a kitchen apron looked on, Reverend Pearson apologized again and put an envelope in Sarah's hand. "For your trouble," he said.

Sarah used her last bit of that day's civility to smile sourly at him instead of snapping that he didn't *have* enough money to pay for her troubles today. She'd go to her room, close her door, and get to sleep. At least she'd have a bed tonight, she thought. *And those goddamn biscuits better be good in the morning, too. . . .*

"You poor child, you're all soaked," the proprietor said, taking off Sarah's coat. "I better sit you in front of the stove before you catch your death out here. You want some coffee?"

The woman looked to be in her sixties, slightly bent over, but she had one of the most cheerful faces Sarah had ever seen. The woman's kind face helped improve Sarah's mood. "Yes, ma'am, some coffee would suit me fine," Sarah said.

Everything happens for a reason, Sarah reminded herself. Maybe she'd been stuck in this town because she needed to rest. C.J. was always telling her she pushed herself too hard, and Sarah knew he was right. Was it really so awful to have a day off?

The old woman's eyes glittered as she led Sarah down a hallway, toward a swinging door Sarah guessed led to the kitchen. She spoke in a hush. "Madam Walker, I know you're bushed, and I hate to ask you for anything as late as it is . . . but you know how word gets out in a small town. We've got some ladies so upset 'bout that ruckus with the church, an' they heard you'd be stayin' here tonight. . . . You see, they were afraid they wouldn't have a chance to see you. . . . I hope you don't mind, but you don't know what it would mean to them. . . ."

When the kitchen door swung upon, Sarah's heart caught in her throat. There were more than thirty women crowded inside the large kitchen, waiting for her with eager faces in the light from kerosene lamps. Most of them were standing because there weren't enough chairs, and their clothes and hair were damp from the rain, clinging limply to their skin. A stout woman missing one of her front teeth gave Sarah a broad grin, and a girl who looked only fourteen clasped her hands in front of her face with excitement as soon as Sarah was in sight. They looked like a classroom full of students waiting for their revered teacher to arrive.

And they were waiting for *her*, Sarah thought with disbelief.

"Evenin', Madam Walker . . ." the women mumbled shyly in waves, standing erect.

The proprietor stroked Sarah's arm gently. "You think you might feel up to one little demonstration tonight, Madam? We've heard so much about your comb, an' we sure are hopin' us citizens of Meridian can use that Wonderful Hair Grower, too. Is it too much trouble?"

Sarah shook her head. Gazing at the eager faces of the women who had come out to see her so late on a dreadful night, she sucked in a deep breath that sounded almost like a sob. Her long journey had been worth the sacrifices, after all.

Chapter Twenty-five

"First, the hair must be clean. You shouldn't want to treat dirty hair any more than you'd want to set your food upon dirty dishes." Lelia's voice rang through the small classroom as she instructed from memory, standing with her back straight and her hands clasped behind her. She was wearing a white instructional dress that made her look as crisp as a scientist. The sun shone brightly through the large windows, spilling across the room's neatly polished floor. A Walker employee sat in a salon chair near the classroom's sink, draped with plastic across her shoulders so she would not get wet.

Ten women, all of them new students from Pennsylvania, West Virginia, and Virginia, sat in chairs before Lelia, their faces upturned in rapt attention or scribbling notes as they listened. They were washerwomen, cooks, clerks, and cleaners, and they had come to change their lives.

"Many of your customers, to save money, will try to tell you they've washed their hair at home," Lelia went on. "Even so, you should wash their hair yourself to make sure the cleaning is thorough. You do not want anyone to complain to you that they're dissatisfied with the Walker method because their hair was not washed properly beforehand."

Sarah, standing unnoticed in the open doorway, stared at her daughter with a momentary sense of wonder and pride. Look at this girl! A year ago, with help from Lelia and C.J., Sarah had found a large brownstone in Pittsburgh where she could live in comfort and set up Walker Manufacturing, a small beauty salon, and two classrooms for the school she had been envisioning for so long. Lelia College. What could be more fitting? A few short years ago, with her savings stolen from her, Sarah had not been able to afford to send her only child to college the way she'd sacrificed so many years to do. But now Walker Manufacturing was making so much profit that, at long last, Lelia had a beauty school bearing her name. Even a year later,

Sarah felt a wave of gratification every time she stood in one of the classrooms or gazed at the neatly painted sign in the window of the street entrance: LELIA COLLEGE.

And Lelia had blossomed so much, Sarah thought. Her conservative dress showed off her ample figure, and she spoke as if she'd been addressing groups her entire life. At twenty-four, had Lelia finally grown up? Watching her daughter command a classroom, Sarah thought so.

"You will want to clear the head of dandruff," Lelia went on. "If you're scared of dandruff, ladies, then you need to reconsider your decision to be a Walker hair culturist. There is no escape from it. You might as well be a surgeon who faints at the sight of blood."

The women in the class laughed, and Sarah nearly laughed with them. She didn't like the way Lelia often parted from the guidelines they had devised so carefully for the Walker course, but she couldn't help admiring her daughter's sense of humor. Lelia had her own ways, no doubt about it. Friends and neighbors had been pointing out Lelia's charm ever since they moved to Pittsburgh, telling Sarah how lucky she was to have such a fine daughter, and Sarah had to agree.

But not all moments, Lord knows. The memory of their argument that morning washed over Sarah, stealing her smile. They'd done nothing but argue these past few months, it seemed. Sarah hadn't even been able to sit back and enjoy smoothing the wrinkles out of the Pittsburgh manufacturing office and Lelia College for half a minute, it seemed, before the arguments had begun. Finally, after days of screaming and days of silence, Sarah had resigned herself to giving up. Lelia had proven herself very responsible in the past two years, more than ever. Because of her high-school training, Lelia had been instrumental in helping Sarah establish the school; and she'd just returned from Bluefield, West Virginia, after spending nearly a year recruiting Walker agents and students for the school. She'd done everything Sarah had asked of her, and even a few things she hadn't. So no matter how rash or silly Lelia's latest decision seemed, Sarah had no choice but to trust her daughter.

Why was such a small thing so hard for a mother?

After asking her students to stand and gather around her, Lelia stood over the woman in the demonstration chair and carefully began to part her hair with a plastic comb. "You part the hair in the center. Then you'll want to lift the dandruff with the comb using a rotary motion, like this, with the comb almost flat against the scalp. Don't jab at the scalp with the teeth of the comb, or you may scratch it and cause an infection. You'll continue like this, parting the hair off into small sections. . . ."

For a brief instant, Lelia looked up and saw her mother watching her. Sarah recognized the usual nervousness that crept over her daughter's face when she was being supervised—*Mama, why do you have to stand over me like you expect me to set somebody on fire?* she often asked—but then her expression hardened, becoming defiant. Lelia continued her instruction, her voice clear and knowledgeable, not missing a beat.

Sarah had never had a home like the one she and C.J. bought at 2518 Wylie Avenue in Pittsburgh, and often as she walked inside she scarcely remembered it was hers.

As soon as Sarah visited Pittsburgh for the first time as part of her sales tour, she knew Wylie Avenue was the place she wanted to be. It reminded her of Papin Street in St. Louis, teeming with Negroes who wanted to make good homes and open their own businesses. Some sections of Wylie were less than desirable, but by the time Sarah arrived in 1908, Wylie already had colored barbershops, two colored grocery stores, two confectionary stores, and a shoe store. She'd also heard about other Negro businesspeople in Pittsburgh who owned a stationery and bookstore, a photography gallery, a loan company, a real estate company, and an insurance company. There were even a few doctors and lawyers.

What had really made her decision was the large two-story brownstone on Wylie that had caused the back of her neck to tingle when she saw it standing on the corner, as if it had been waiting for her. She would live upstairs, she decided, and remodel the downstairs for the business and college. Aside from a few scant pieces of furniture they shipped from C.J.'s house in Denver, the new six-room house upstairs represented a new beginning for both of them. Because they were so busy and had little time to visit local furniture stores, they furnished it almost entirely during late-night huddles over the Bloomingdale's and Sears, Roebuck & Co. mail-order catalogs. The process, to Sarah, had been like she imagined Christmas must feel to children whose parents could afford to pamper them; she studied page after page of furnishings and decorations, giddy with delight, and pointed out one luxurious-looking item after another. *Can we afford this?* she asked C.J. time after time, and he said of course they could. But she knew that, didn't she? They could afford almost anything.

The Walker Company was making four hundred dollars a month—what some people made in a year—and all signs told Sarah their profits would continue to grow. There were steady orders for Wonderful Hair Grower and Glossine from every region Sarah had visited on her exhaustive eighteen-month tour, Lelia College was turning out dozens of culturists who paid twenty-five dollars for the course and then returned to their homes and recruited even more Walker customers for their kitchen beauty parlors, and her steel "straightening" comb, as customers insisted on calling it, captured the imagination of almost every colored woman who saw what it could do.

Sometimes, with the mail-order catalogs spread out on her bed, Sarah felt pangs of guilt. Why should she have so much when so many other colored people had so little? Pittsburgh attracted hordes of poor Southern blacks who overcrowded houses and even slept in alleyways, hoping to find jobs in the steel mills but often falling to the easier temptations of bootlegging, selling cocaine, or prostitution. The poverty here seemed even more dire to Sarah because the city's industry made it so *ugly*; it was smoky, with its landscapes marred by towering converters, furnaces, and ovens, making the Allegheny and Monongahela riverfronts anything but scenic. Pittsburgh residents were boastful about how visible their industry was, but Sarah couldn't help comparing the city to the airiness she'd just left behind in Denver. Pittsburgh, it seemed to her, made some of its residents rich and choked others in its smoke.

So far she was one of the lucky ones, but how long could she count on that? She'd been in the habit of hoarding her money for so long that her stomach felt tense even when she ordered tiny items she wanted but didn't really *need*. When she asked C.J. *Can we afford this?*, sometimes she felt as if she were really asking *Do I deserve this?*

And C.J. knew it, too. Her questions seemed to aggravate him. "As hard as you work?" he'd told her more than once. "Woman, what's wrong with you? I know you ain't hardly ever home, but you might as well enjoy what home you've got. Don't you read those letters you get from those Lelia College graduates? You're not just makin' money off those women, Sarah, you're doin' exactly what you said you wanted—you're givin' them freedom. And if givin' people freedom makes you rich, then so be it."

C.J. did not have the same qualms about spending Walker Company money. His collection of suits had been growing steadily since they lived in Denver, and he had two wardrobes filled with fashionable clothes and shiny pairs of shoes. C.J. had a taste for New York–style fashions, and he was often one of the first colored men on the streets to wear a new cut of suit, a new width of necktie, or an outrageous new shade of color. *Anyone can see C.J. Walker coming a mile away*, Lelia had complained once.

Sarah, too, had bought herself clothes. She had more than a dozen dresses by now, from very formal to merely tasteful, and most of them were tailor-made to fit her wide hips better than the narrow-waisted clothes in the shops. But, unlike C.J., she bought almost all of her clothes with business in mind. How would she look at church? How would she look at a local meeting of the National Council of Negro Women? How would she look at a banquet? Lelia had tried to urge Sarah to buy clothes *for fun*, but Sarah couldn't imagine when she would have time to wear anything frivolous that wasn't suitable for her meetings, demonstrations, or travels.

While their taste in clothes didn't match, Sarah and C.J. shared a taste for furnishings. For the first time in her life, Sarah lived somewhere she was proud to show off to company. Their fully carpeted parlor was suited with a brand-new matching satin brocatelle settee and parlor chairs, their curtains were black Chantilly lace, and their walls were covered with paintings of peaceful wooded and mountain landscapes. They even had a separate room they'd designated as an office and library, brimming with bookshelves and rows of books Sarah hoped to someday learn to read: the entire Encyclopedia Britannica, a Webster's unabridged dictionary, and books by authors like Mark Twain, the Brontë sisters, Alexandre Dumas, William Shakespeare, and W.E.B. Du Bois.

They also had their toys.

C.J.'s most prized purchase was his pearl-handled, .22-caliber derringer, which he kept polished to a high gleam in his office desk drawer. They also collected fine ornamental clocks, china pieces, and a Magic Lantern to show her photographic slides. But the item Sarah cherished above everything else in her house was her thirty-dollar Columbia gramophone, which had a lovely oak cabinet and a brass horn. The glorious talking machine played wax cylinder-shaped records with a turn of the crank, filling the parlor with *music*. Sarah bought almost every wax cylinder recording she could find, even minstrel songs recorded by whites that riled her with references to *pickaninnies* and *darkies*, because she loved having music in her home.

Sarah longed to hear recordings by colored performers, but since she couldn't find any, she and C.J. sat in their parlor in the evenings listening to two-minute recordings by the Edison Symphony Orchestra, the Edison Military Band, the Columbia Quartette, and lovely solos by Ada Jones and Frank C. Stanley. C.J. couldn't hear enough of the popular Edward Meeker song *Take Me Out to the Ballgame*, and they both enjoyed the comic song *I'm Afraid to Come Home in the Dark* by Billy Murray. Best of all, Sarah had found a recording of the waltz *On the Beautiful Blue Danube* by Johann Strauss II. Every time she played it, her dance with C.J. in the ballroom seemed to come back to life. Not long ago she hadn't known it, and now she had her own copy.

Life was so full of blessings! Her only true heartache now, Sarah realized, was Lelia. If only her daughter weren't so impulsive . . .

"There's no sense in a girl like Lelia gettin' engaged to a boy like that," Sarah said, shaking her head as she tied the bow at the collar of her shirtwaist, gazing at herself in their bedroom's full-length mirror. "What can he give her? He works in a hotel."

"Your brother worked in a hotel," C.J. reminded her. He was standing behind her, admiring his new Italian-style smoking jacket in the reflection. He wore his smoking jackets when he enjoyed one of his Havana cigars in the parlor. "Anyhow, I thought she said he's the telephone operator over at the Fort Smith Hotel. It ain't like he's cleaning toilets."

"C.J., you know what I'm talkin' about. We're gettin' to a place now where she can meet anybody she wants. She could be the most prized young colored lady in Pittsburgh, an' she's set on marryin' that sawed-off little pup."

C.J. winced. "Woman, you've sure got an evil mouth when you want to."

"Well, ain't he, though? The boy ain't even five-foot-ten, with Lelia standin' over him like some kind of giant. An' she keeps talkin' 'bout his *music*, how their lives will be so good when he gets more work playing. You know what kind of life musicians lead. I know you're friends with plenty of 'em, C.J., but they're not the steady sort you would want your own daughter to marry, and you know it."

C.J. dropped his hands to her shoulders and squeezed hard. "This ain't your battle to fight, Sarah. A'Lelia's grown, and she's made her mind up. You don't have to ask where she gets her stubbornness from, so leave it alone."

Sarah made a face. "I don't know what kind of young man would even think about marrying a young lady without asking us for her hand first. Even croppers with nothing but a shack to their names got manners enough to know that. I bet he was seein' her when she was down in Bluefield, sneakin' down there like she's trash. He's a coward, you ask me. He should've come to us himself. Instead, Lelia comes tellin' me like it's all decided."

"It *is* decided," C.J. said, his voice firm. "You still don't understand, do you, Sarah?"

"Understand what?"

In the reflection, his eyes met hers, and they suddenly looked hard as steel. "You don't have the say-so over everything. You best figure that out."

Sarah's lips tightened with irritation, but she didn't say anything. He would have the last word, then. This was an old argument between them they could choose to uncork at any time, but Sarah wasn't up to it tonight. It was bad enough she would have to spend an evening socializing with the family of Lelia's fiancé; she didn't want to add strife with C.J. to her burdens.

C.J. had been more opposed to the move to Pittsburgh than he'd been to her long sales trip. In fact, it had taken him so long to sell his house and join her that some folks had begun whispering they were separated. She'd almost begun wondering if she still had a husband herself! Well, couldn't he see now that both decisions had been smart? Pittsburgh had about 25,000 Negroes, five times the number in Denver, and business had flourished since their move. She just saw some things faster than he did, that was all.

"What's the harm in marryin' a musician, Sarah?" C.J. said after a long pause.

Sarah knew full well C.J. was trying to provoke her, but it still worked. "Musicians are never home. You know how they stay on the road. When would he see her? Most of 'em I've met, all they really care about is their mu—" Then she stopped, and she felt her face tingling with anger. As much as she wanted to avoid an argument, Sarah couldn't keep silent: "Charles Walker, if you've got somethin' to say to me, just say it. Don't run me 'round the barn an' back."

C.J. shrugged, his eyebrows raised innocently. "What do you think I'm tryin' to say, Sarah?" His tone was nearly mocking, and it infuriated her.

After giving him a glare in the mirror, Sarah pushed past C.J. to find the matching jacket to her skirt, which she had laid across the bed. The one curse to love, she told herself, was that loved ones could make you madder than anyone else. C.J., with his gentle sarcasm and probing, could set her off with merely a look.

"Don't try to tell me you don't care 'bout this company the same as me," she said, her voice trembling. "Don't tell me you don't like that new jacket an' those new shoes. Oh, an' how 'bout that pretty buggy you just ran out and bought, and that black mare—"

"You're right, Sarah," he said, leaning over to kiss the back of her neck. His lips felt dry against her skin. "I'm yours. You've got me."

But Sarah did not feel comforted.

The Robinsons were a middle-class family who lived in a suburb on the east end of Pittsburgh, and their pleasantly modest home was decorated with glowing green lamps for the dinner celebrating their son's engagement. Sarah, Lelia, and C.J. had barely spoken throughout the long drive in the buggy, so the festive piano music they could hear through the open window as they pulled up to the curb did not match the family's mood.

"That's Johnny on the piano," Lelia said, a tinge of excitement in her voice Sarah longed to share with her, but Sarah didn't answer. *What's the harm in marryin' a musician, Sarah?* C.J.'s words still irked her. She knew perfectly well what he'd meant: Lelia's life married to a musician wouldn't be the least bit different than C.J.'s life married to her. Was that the way he really felt? Sarah's face was solemn as she wrapped herself in her stole and climbed out of the buggy.

Inside, they found a house full of warmth and smiles. The Robinsons had invited some friends to the occasion, so there were two other couples present. As handbags, wraps, and hats were taken out of the room, there was a round of introductions. Edith and Joseph Robinson were the boy's parents, and they greeted Sarah and C.J. with cordial handshakes, even if their faces didn't look any more pleased than Sarah's. Next, Sarah met Dr. and Mrs. Joseph Ward, a pleasant couple who were visiting the Robinsons from Indianapolis. The third couple, slightly older than the rest, were Mr. and Mrs. Reginald Parks, longtime Pittsburgh residents—known as "OPs," or "Old Pittsburghers," part of the city's colored elite—who had known the Robinsons for years. Joseph Robinson and Reginald Parks were both clerks in city government, Sarah was told, rare positions for Negroes.

Finally Sarah met John R. Robinson, the boy Lelia was planning to marry. He was Lelia's age, nearly handsome, with brown skin, clean teeth, and a slight build. She had seen him once before, when Lelia pointed him out at church. Now, as before, Sarah could find nothing remarkable about him. "Pleasure to meet you, Madam Walker," the boy said. "You, too, sir."

Despite her best efforts, Sarah couldn't even force a smile. As John Robinson stood alongside Lelia, the only thing that struck Sarah about this boy was how much shorter he was than Lelia. Sarah was about to ask how tall he was when his mother tugged gently at her arm.

"John was playing some Chopin for us a moment ago," his mother said, her pride apparent in her voice. "He prefers rags, like all the young people, but we raised him to be well rounded."

You didn't raise him to know the proper way to ask for a young lady's hand, and you sure didn't raise him tall, Sarah thought, annoyed. Sarah didn't know any Chopin, and since she wasn't in the mood to try to impress anyone, she only nodded politely.

"What sort of piano do you prefer, Madam Walker?" Mrs. Robinson asked.

Sarah gave her a level, disinterested stare. "We don't have a piano."

Mrs. Robinson looked surprised, an expression that clearly said *But I thought* everyone *had a piano,* but she didn't answer. When she excused herself to look after the caterer's work in the kitchen, Sarah was happy to see her go. If this woman had insisted on trying to compare the attributes of their households, Sarah was afraid she might be mean enough tonight to point out that the Robinsons' wall coverings looked shabby and faded enough to have withstood three presidential administrations. Lelia would never have forgiven her for that.

"So we've heard you're in the beauty business, Madam," Dr. Ward said. He was a round-faced man with a friendly twinkle in his eye that had a calming effect on Sarah. Somehow she knew already that he would not try to belittle her the way so many other "society" Negroes did, treating her as if she were inferior because she had come from humble beginnings. In some circles, she'd learned, just mentioning that she'd bought her home on Wylie Avenue was enough to wrinkle noses. "Madam C.J. Walker's Wonderful Hair Grower! We'll have to buy some, won't we, Zella?"

Dr. Ward's wife nodded eagerly. "Who wouldn't like to grow more hair?"

Mr. Parks, who was a large, blustering man with long gray sideburns, slapped C.J. on the back. "So how do you like being *Mister* Madam C.J. Walker, son?" he said, and Sarah thought C.J. would swallow his own tongue. His face burned red, the color of a brick.

Quickly Sarah took C.J.'s hand. "Oh, my husband has his own ventures. He's the company advertising director, and he's working right now on—"

"I can speak for myself, thank you, my darling," C.J. said sweetly enough, although Sarah knew how annoyed he must be. "I'll be selling C.J. Walker's Blood and Rheumatic Cure 'fore too long. Feeds the blood, makes you good as new. You'll see it soon enough."

"Well, if I can be of any assistance, Mr. Walker, you just let me know," Dr. Ward said. "I have a sanitorium and nursing school in Indianapolis, and I'm in support of any products to benefit the public health. So long as they're sound."

"Thank you kindly, Doctor, but I have years of training in pharmacy and such, so that won't be necessary," C.J. said, and Sarah's hand went cold inside her husband's. Such an outrageous lie! C.J. didn't know any more about pharmacy than she did. What was wrong with him? She'd been glad to hear Dr. Ward offer his help, since C.J. had been struggling to concoct a blood formula. A man like that could be of real service to both of them, and C.J. was feeding him nonsense like he was an ignorant customer being hustled on the street.

Sarah couldn't tell from the physician's expression, but she hoped he wasn't offended. She would talk to him later, she decided, to let him know they would be grateful for any help.

"Mr. Walker, I must say, now, that's a colorful suit you're wearing," Mr. Parks said, noticing C.J.'s cobalt blue pencil-striped linen suit. "I don't think I've seen anything like it."

C.J. stuck out his chest, hooking his thumbs behind his suspenders. "It's something else, huh? I had it made special, what they call Palm Beach style. Cost me twenty-five dollars. I know that's a lot to spend on a suit, but nothing's too much if you want it right. And this necktie is pure silk, you see. That alone was a good dollar."

Sarah glanced at Lelia in time to see her roll her eyes, and she understood why. How many times would they have to tell C.J. it wasn't polite to boast about how much he spent on his clothes? Sure enough, there was no mistaking the discomfort and amusement in the faces of the other guests. Sarah wondered if C.J. had nipped once too often at his whiskey flask before they left home. Lelia gave her a pleading look, and Sarah actually felt sorry for her daughter. C.J. was embarrassing them both.

As far as Sarah was concerned, the evening went worse than she'd feared. By the time she'd sat through dinner, bracing for inappropriate comments from C.J. or slights from her hosts, she had a headache and felt sick to her stomach. Dr. Ward and his wife had been wonderful, exchanging calling cards with her and C.J. so they could keep in touch, but Sarah thought it had been obvious that the Robinsons actually looked *down* on their family. And based on what? Sarah knew without asking that she earned far more than the Robinsons could dream of—the man was only a clerk, after all—so how dare they feel superior!

It was only as she prepared to leave that Sarah thought she discovered the true source of the family's pride: She saw rows of family photographs displayed on the foyer walls. The photographs pictured colored men and women of all complexions, from very dark to nearly white, all of them posing in fine, antiquated dress and stern expressions. Some of the photographs looked so old that they might date from before the Civil War, Sarah thought. The Robinsons had history, and that was more important than money to them. They had been free for generations, and they were proud of it.

No matter how much money she made, Sarah realized, she would never have that.

"You sure put on a show tonight," Sarah complained, climbing into bed beside C.J. He had disappeared beneath the bedsheets almost as soon as they got home, with his back turned away from her. She remembered a time when they used to cling to each other before going to sleep, especially during the months when they spent most of their time apart. Each night together had been a reunion of sorts. But no more.

"Thank you. I aim to please," C.J. muttered, more of his sarcasm. He always accused her of having an ugly side, but he had one, too. She'd never noticed his sarcasm when they were courting, or right after they were married. That, apparently, was his hidden weapon.

Sarah sighed. She was tempted to go on criticizing C.J., to ask him how much whiskey he'd had to drink before dinner, but what purpose would that serve? She was tired of arguments. All right, so she didn't like John Robinson or his family much. So what? Tomorrow morning, she decided, she would sit down to breakfast with Lelia and tell her, from her heart, that she wished her all the happiness in the world with her new husband.

And she wanted to make things right with C.J., too. Sarah gently rubbed C.J.'s bare shoulder. "You ain't been yourself, C.J. I can see it plain as day. What's wrong?"

C.J. half laughed, still not looking at her. "Now, what could be troubling Mr. Madam C.J. Walker? Not a thing I can think of, Sarah."

Sarah sighed again, curling up behind him, fitting herself to the shape of his body. She wrapped her arm around him and rested her chin on his shoulder. "That man was just rude, C.J."

"No . . ." C.J. said, and this time the sarcasm had left his voice bare. "He was tellin' the truth. I know I don't get no respect here."

"Oh, C.J., these OP Negroes don't—"

"It ain't just that," C.J. said. He paused, then rolled over to scoop her into his arms until their faces were nearly touching. At that instant she realized it had been a long time since C.J. had really held her. Too long. Their breathing rose and fell in unison as he pressed their chests together. "You wouldn't understand it, Sarah."

"Tell me," Sarah said softly, holding his eyes with hers. This close to him, she could smell the remnants of spirits on his breath.

"You know, I almost didn't leave Denver. I swear to God, I didn't want to lose you, but I didn't think I could go. Do you remember who I was in Denver? There wasn't *no place* C.J. Walker couldn't get an invitation. I was Johnny-on-the-spot. I'm nothing here, Sarah. I went and tried to join that Leondi Club I keep hearing about, thought I'd play some billiards with the fellas, but they didn't want to be bothered with me. To them, I'm just a man living off his wife's name. And I guess they're right at that."

How could he say that? C.J.'s words lanced Sarah, and she tightened her grip around him. "We're partners, C.J., just like you said you wanted. If it wasn't for you, I'd still be selling hair grease out of my kitchen in tin cups. You think I don't know what you've done for me?"

C.J. considered that a moment, then he moved a wisp of hair from her face with his index finger. "Maybe so, maybe not . . ." he said in a raw voice. "But I'll tell you one thing: You don't need me, woman. You're like one o' them Kentucky Derby thoroughbred horses. I just opened the gate, and out you went. I guess I thought you needed me, or maybe I just hoped you did . . . but a man can't be a man if he don't feel like he's of some use, Sarah."

C.J.'s words had robbed her mouth of its moisture. Yes, she knew why C.J. felt this way; their business had grown so fast that C.J. had reached the end of his areas of knowledge, constantly being forced to research questions of shipping, supplies, billing, and credit. Snags were common and frustrating. And Sarah was being forced to learn herself, monitoring the seemingly endless details about the activities of the agents who were selling Walker products all over the country. Soon there would be more than hundreds of Walker agents, she knew. Hundreds! Sometimes she was afraid her business was growing faster than she could learn, and she thought C.J. must feel the same way.

"I don't expect you to be an expert in every part of this thing, C.J.," Sarah said. "I know one day we'll have to hire folks to do what we can't. But I'll always need you. You can't see it, baby? I need you to watch over me. I need you to be my husband. And I need you to be proud of me wearing your name everyplace I go, because I'm sure proud to be wearin' it."

Sarah saw that C.J.'s eyes were glistening like new pennies, threatening tears. "I am proud," he said. "I'm proud every damn day, even when I'm too bullheaded to show it. You're about to be somethin', Sarah Walker. You hear me?" His voice became a hush, close to her ear. "I mean, you are about to be really *somethin'* like folks ain't never seen."

Then he kissed her with a hunger and urgency that Sarah had missed in C.J.'s kisses. *We're gonna make love tonight*, she realized, happy and surprised. With renewed vigor, C.J. raised himself high enough to reach for Sarah's wrists, pinning them on the mattress as he leaned over her and mashed his mouth over hers. His grip on her was so firm, and his mouth so intoxicating, that she couldn't have moved an inch even if she'd wanted to.

Chapter Twenty-six

INDIANAPOLIS
FEBRUARY 1910

MME. C.J. WALKER, of Pittsburgh, Pa.
THE NOTED HAIR CULTURIST
is in this city, at the residence of
Dr. J.H. Ward, 722 INDIANA AVENUE:
where she will demonstrate the art of growing hair.
Every woman of pride should see her during her stay in this city,
which is for a few days only.
DO NOT FAIL TO CALL AND SEE Mme. WALKER.
IT DOES NOT COST ANYTHING FOR CONSULTATION
Persons calling for treatment will kindly bring comb, brush, and two towels.

"Why do I use the term 'hair culturist'?" Sarah said.

There was no answer from the half dozen ladies who sat in Dr. Ward's parlor listening to her in the cozy heat from the physician's brick fireplace. All of them were sipping hot cider, their eyes watching her closely. "Because the Madam C.J. Walker method is not just about slappin' some grease on somebody's head, and I want that notion forgot from the start. My course teaches the totalment of colored womanhood, so anyone who sees you will know right off you are a woman of pride. We've all heard folks say colored women are unclean and lacking in virtue, and some of our own women have fallen to that idea and 'based themselves. You know it's true."

Entranced, the women nodded.

"Even before your customer comes, you have shown them you are a serious person. Your space is clean and swept up of dirt and hair. You have seen to it you're not carryin' no body odors, which is very simple to do by applying some zinc oxide powder to the right areas. You have sweetened your breath with mints. You have presented yourself in a professional way in your dress. And you keep your combs and other materials clean and sanitary. See, maybe your customers know some lady down the street that *does hair*, but you are a cut above the rest. You are a hair culturist who's studied the hair, the scalp, and the follicles, and who carries a proper attitude. And you are using only Walker products, which are science-proved and divinely inspired."

Sarah was tired, but no matter how often she repeated her ideas to new groups of potential customers and agents, she felt her blood coursing in her veins as if she were saying the words for the first time. She felt rejuvenated by their unblinking eyes, their flushes of excitement, their inspired smiles. One woman in today's group, a high-yellow woman in a very prim dress, was listening so eagerly that she was hunched forward, sitting so far at the edge of her seat that Sarah was afraid she would fall over. The woman's face was pure rapture, and that gave Sarah new energy even though it was evening, and she'd already had a long day.

So far the sales trip to Indianapolis was working out better than she and C.J. had hoped. After the Wards invited Sarah to the Midwestern city to sell her products, she and C.J. laid out plans for an advertising campaign in *The Indianapolis Recorder*, one of the city's colored newspapers. Of course, the ads included the photographs taken before and after her hair cure that had worked so well before. But this time they also devised a letter from her supporters so she would have a rousing introduction in the local press. The letter attesting to her product had been signed by friends, pastors, and customers from Pittsburgh and other cities she had visited. And if the hair grower didn't work after two months, they decided as part of their campaign, they would give any dissatisfied customer twenty-five dollars. *That* would catch people's attention!

And it had. Sarah had arrived in Indianapolis at the beginning of the month, and she'd already had a steady stream of customers for pressing, each willing to pay a dollar. And the hair grower, priced at fifty cents, was selling as fast as she could open new crates of it. This was a fertile town, all right! By the time the ad appeared saying she would be in Indianapolis only a few days, at the encouragement of Dr. and Mrs. Ward, Sarah had already decided to stay through the month, or perhaps longer. C.J. wouldn't like it much, she knew, but he would certainly be excited about how well sales were going after he received her letter with the news.

The women meeting with Sarah now were interested in being agents and beauty shop operators, hoping to take her beauty course. Like the students who came to Pittsburgh, these women were from every part of Negro society. One young girl here barely looked groomed, her gums caked with yellowish matter as if she hadn't seen a toothbrush and tooth powder in at least a month, which Sarah hoped to advise her about privately; but the woman at the edge of her seat looked as impeccable as a schoolmarm, her face virtually shining with her intelligence.

"I have heard it said by whites that Negro women in Africa mate with apes," Sarah went on, and the women's faces drew back with horror. "Now, we all know that's no more true of women in Africa than any of us here tonight, but the thinking about Negro women in America is not so different, in my book. And if the world sees us that way, ladies, then it is up to us to show different. We can do that through our beauty and the way we carry ourselves."

Sarah had a headache by the time she finished, although she ignored her discomfort as she graciously spoke to each woman privately, answering questions and accepting their praise. She stole a glance at the stately grandfather clock standing in the corner by the fireplace, and saw that it was already after nine o'clock. And she'd been pressing heads since eight that morning!

The last woman to approach her was the one who looked like a schoolmarm. The pale-skinned woman was nearly as tall as Lelia but looked like she must be exactly Sarah's age. She had piercing molasses-colored eyes that seemed to leap from her square-jawed face. Her hair, which was dark and fine-textured, was pinned into a bun on top of her head. *An old maid,* Sarah thought, noticing the woman's lack of a wedding ring.

But already there was something about this woman Sarah liked.

"Madam Walker," the woman said, squeezing Sarah's hand hard. "To me, this is a pleasure almost beyond expression. I am so overwhelmed to make your acquaintance. A friend of mine I've known since I was a girl is a Walker hair culturist in Philadelphia. She's a teacher by training, like myself, but there was so little work for her because Negroes cannot teach in those public schools, as you must know. Now she has her own shop, a good business, and her pride intact. To offer such a road of independence! You are a pillar of Negro womanhood, Madam."

Her speech! Sarah had almost stopped listening because she was savoring the lilt of this woman's words, which seemed to glide from her tongue. She had a deep timbre and the oddest accent, one Sarah didn't think she had ever heard before—not Southern, not Midwestern, and nothing like she would have expected from the lips of a Negro. The woman pronounced each word with loving care, making each sentence sound like a proclamation. Who could this woman be? This time it was Sarah who was spellbound.

The woman had not yet let go of Sarah's hand, and she squeezed more urgently. "This will hardly matter to you, but my name is Charlotte Ransaw. I'm also called Lottie."

"Where . . . are you from?" Sarah asked.

The woman's smile widened; she was obviously thrilled Sarah had asked. Finally she remembered to release Sarah's hand. "I was born in the South like you, Madam, in Selma. But I was fortunate, as a child, to be sent to live with a well-off uncle in Boston, where I attended preparatory schools that led me to Dartmouth College. That is where I took my degree."

Ordinarily Sarah would have felt defensive because she would have assumed this woman was being boastful, since so many elite folk in Denver and Pittsburgh trotted out their degrees to point out Sarah's deficiencies. But Charlotte Ransaw's eyes were genuine, and there was nothing at all boastful in her voice.

"I've had all the requisite classical training, Madam—I can read Greek and Latin, and I speak French quite well. I planned to teach, because that is my great love. But I must tell you, when it comes to Negroes, I think there is such a thing as *too* much preparation . . . because like my dear friend in Philadelphia, I have found few institutions to appreciate someone of my training. Presently I have taken up secretarial work." She stopped, taking a quick breath.

"Please forgive me if this inquiry is inappropriate, Madam, but I have to ask if you have any need for a personal secretary. I already have employment, but I am so taken with your work that I believe I could find a much greater sense of purpose working for you than anywhere else. You are building a Queendom, Madam Walker, and I could be of great help to you. I would take dictation, write out speeches, see to your needs while you travel, and the like. I have no family, so I am not bound to any geographical region. Are you familiar with Dr. Booker T. Washington's secretary, Mr. Emmett Scott . . . ?"

Again, Sarah's attention had drifted because she was so excited by this woman's careful speech patterns. There was a stodginess to her, no doubt, but words came to her with such ease and precision! *Wonder how long it would take me to learn to talk like that,* Sarah thought.

Then she realized the woman's glorious talking had stopped, and she was waiting for an answer to something. What had she just asked? Was she looking for some kind of job?

"I've never thought one way or the other about a personal secretary, Mrs. Ransaw," Sarah told her, recalling her words. "What would I do with one? We have a girl in Pittsburgh who writes letters on typing machines from time to time, but that's hardly any kind of work for you."

Mrs. Ransaw's face fell, and her lip sagged so low that Sarah feared she might cry. "Madam, there is never any work appropriate for me! I'm willing to start at the lowest office, if that's necessary, and I will prove my dedication to you."

Then an idea hit Sarah with such power that she literally felt as if she'd been tapped with a hammer between her eyes; her headache worsened, but her heart came to life. If this plan worked, she thought with wonder, it might be the most valuable purchase she could ever make.

"You say you wanted to teach, Mrs. Ransaw?"

"Yes, Madam. And it would give me great satisfaction if you simply called me Lottie."

"You know history and music, too, Lottie? An' you keep up with the magazines and papers, white and colored?"

"Yes, Madam, of course," she said, tilting her head curiously. "I take in *The Crisis* and the *Colored People's Magazine* from Atlanta, as well as—"

"Then you may have just got yourself a student," Sarah said. "But it's no regular job, Lottie. There's no set teaching hours, just whenever I have a minute to breathe. Maybe you can do some of that other stuff, too, the dictation and whatnot, but I really want a tutor. I didn't get but to the third-grade level in my schooling. I'm proud of where I've gotten to, but I want more. I want someone to read with me like my daughter used to, and teach me things I don't know. I want to learn French, too, hear? And I want to learn how to talk like you do."

Lottie's face was frozen. At first Sarah was afraid she'd insulted her. Then the woman's bottom lip began to quiver, and she lunged forward to give Sarah a hug.

"Oh, my goodness . . ." Sarah heard her murmuring, stunned. "My goodness gracious . . ."

Sarah laughed, patting the woman's back. What a gentle creature Lottie was, to have her talents so wasted! Sarah had heard of many Negroes from colleges like Dartmouth, Howard, Amherst, and Oberlin who had gone on to excel in law and education in their communities, but perhaps Lottie had been too fragile to fight the way she needed to. Perhaps one or two heartaches had made her give up and curse her skin color. Sarah knew plenty of folks who'd suffered that fate, too. *Like Etta,* Sarah thought sadly.

"You come back tomorrow, and we'll talk some more, Lottie," Sarah said. "My head's ailing me tonight. But I think we just found you a job you've got perfect trainin' for."

"Yes, ma'am," Lottie said, dabbing at her eyes. "Madam, you just don't know . . . Th-thank you so much. I'll be back tomorrow, Madam."

She was gazing at Sarah as if she had just saved her life.

Sarah hadn't asked him to examine her, but his wife had told him how often she got headaches. Dr. Ward had finally insisted she sit down and let him be a physician instead of just a friend. He had a small examining room in back of his house in case patients came to his residence instead of his office, just a table, two chairs, a desk with a lamp, and shelves of medical books. On his wall, he had his framed degree from the Physiomedical College of Indiana, which he'd received in 1900.

"When's the last time you saw a doctor, Madam Walker?" he asked, his brow furrowed.

"Well, since I'm a guest in your home, Dr. Ward, I see you most every day."

The doctor didn't smile at her joke. He didn't seem to like whatever his instrument reading was telling him. He gazed up at her and sighed. "You don't tend to your health, do you?" he said. "You probably haven't set foot in a doctor's office in years."

Shoot, maybe not ever, except to see after Lelia's burn that time, Sarah thought, but she kept that admission silent. She felt healthy, except for occasional bladder infections, headaches, and stomach cramps from her monthlies. But the problems never lasted long, and by the time she thought she might be able to fit in a doctor's appointment, her ailments were usually gone.

"What's this device telling you?" Sarah said.

"It's telling me your blood pressure. It's worth knowing, and I'm afraid it's not good."

Dr. Ward explained that the numbers he was reading were much higher than normal. Over time, he said, high blood pressure could be a serious ailment. Dr. Ward's eyes were no-nonsense as he told her the condition could lead to a stroke, a heart attack, or failure of her kidneys.

"I see the way you run around here, Madam Walker. You don't take any exercise, and I hardly see when you even have time to sleep. You need to take better care of yourself."

"Oh, Lord, now you sound like my husband. . . ."

"I'm glad someone is looking after you, then. You may be able to oversee a manufacturing business, Madam Walker, but I suspect you're not very good at looking after *you.* We'd like to have you with us a bit longer. George Knox would have a fit if you suffered a stroke now, you know. He's bent on having you move to Indianapolis."

"Who's George Knox again . . . ?" Sarah had met so many people during her visit that she was having trouble keeping the names straight in her mind.

"Publisher of the *Indianapolis Freeman* newspaper. The white-haired fellow you met the other day," Dr. Ward said.

Of course! She'd met him only once, but George Knox was quite a character; he'd been born a slave in Tennessee, run away during the Civil War, and learned the barbering trade. Now, in addition to the newspaper, he had fifty employees and barbershops all over town. He'd been insistent that Sarah move her plant to Indianapolis, and he'd promised to keep hounding her until she was convinced.

"Well, it's a nice change to have folks tryin' to bring me in instead of hopin' they can run me off," Sarah said, smiling. "I do appreciate all this kindness, Dr. Ward, and I appreciate your warning, too. But I don't think you need to worry about me having a stroke or moving here, neither. C.J. would have a bigger fit if we moved, and I have enough strife in my life already."

"Strife is your blood pressure's worst enemy," Dr. Ward said, wagging a finger at her.

"If that's true, then Lelia must have made those numbers go so high all by herself."

Dr. Ward's eyes shone with curiosity, but he was too polite to ask how Lelia was doing in her new marriage. Less than a year since her wedding in October, Lelia was already proclaiming to her mother that she had made a mistake. She traveled often, sometimes on Walker sales trips, but sometimes on expensive excursions with her St. Louis friend Hazel. Lelia complained to Sarah that her husband was too demanding, but Sarah was smart enough to figure out for herself that this boy probably only wanted a more traditional wife who would cook his meals and start a family. She supposed Lelia would not be carrying her husband's child anytime soon. *Mama, children are always underfoot!* Lelia complained to her once when she'd asked. *You've seen how horrible it is when families bring their babies on the trains and to moving pictures.*

And Sarah couldn't discuss her concerns about her daughter's marriage with C.J., because he only gave her a look that said, *What did you expect, Sarah? Like mother, like daughter.*

Like mother, like daughter.

The memory of C.J.'s silent accusations made Sarah's face tense. *C.J. better be glad I'm not home more,* she thought. *If I was, he couldn't be spendin' his nights runnin' around them saloons doin' God-knows-what.*

"Madam, I'm going to prescribe you some remedies, but the most important thing is this: From this day forth, you need to find ways to bring calm to your life," Dr. Ward said.

Sarah nearly laughed. With everything changing and growing so fast? He might as well have asked her to bring him the moon.

The Black Rose

There is no escape—
man drags man down,
or man lifts man up.

—BOOKER T. WASHINGTON

The seed waits for the garden where it will be sown.

—ZULU PROVERB

FEBRUARY 1919
VILLA LEWARO

*T*he new house girl, Laura, brought in the tea service Sarah had asked for;
with the apparent nervousness she always felt near Sarah, the girl set down
a sterling silver set with a steaming pot of tea and an assortment of sugar cookies.
"Madam . . . may I ask you . . . ?" Miss Long said when the girl had retreated
from the library. "How many employees do you have here?"

Sarah was amused by her curiosity, and she had to admit she felt pride at the
staff she'd assembled at her villa. "I guess it's eight, all told," she said. "My butler, houseman, cook, chauffeur, gardener, secretary, nurse, and now Laura.
They have rooms or apartments here."

"And . . . how many motorcars? You really don't mind me asking, do you?"

"No, that's all right," Sarah said. "I keep four. But my old electric Waverley
seems to be making its last gasps, so I'll be selling that one soon for another. I
leave driving the big cars to Lewis, but I really love having a little coupe for short
trips."

"Madam Walker, with all this . . ." Miss Long said, resting her hand on top
of Sarah's. "Do you have absolutely everything in the world you want?"

From her pleading eyes, Sarah figured Miss Long was hoping someone did.

Yes, Sarah could remember a time when she believed money solved everything, too. How much could Miss Long understand the things Sarah wanted that
had nothing to do with money? "Oh, no, not everything, in some ways," Sarah
said. "But in other ways I've been given a gift I could hardly have dreamed up.
Miss Long, God's grace astonishes me every time it comes to mind."

Chapter Twenty-seven

"Don't forget your *brake*, Sarah," C.J. said, holding his riding cap tight on his head.

"I don't need no brake yet," Sarah insisted with a laugh, steering her tiny box-shaped Waverley electric coupe around a mound of feed bags that seemed to have appeared from nowhere in the middle of the cobblestone roadway. The motorcar was speeding at more than twenty miles per hour, according to Sarah's gauge. The feeling of speed thrilled her, whisking her thoughts away from her troubles. Earlier, her afternoon drive with C.J. had been slow, subject to pedestrians, carriages, bicycles, streetcars, and uniformed traffic officers who clogged the business district near grand Monument Circle, with the towering Soldiers and Sailors Monument that stabbed the sky in the heart of the city. But now that she was closer to home, the street was much clearer, giving Sarah room to test her beloved car's speed. If only more roads in the countryside were paved and safe enough for driving! But she'd already learned the hard way that motorcars and mud were a cumbersome combination.

"Now I know why I keep hearin' them jokes about lady drivers," C.J. said as they sailed past a man on horseback, the car's tires jouncing across the cobblestones. "Woman, you need to sign up for that Indianapolis motorcar race if they do it again next year."

"Maybe I will, too!" When Sarah saw the street sign for Indiana Avenue, she made a sharp turn that tossed C.J. up against her in the tight body of the car as it veered around the corner. This time both of them laughed.

The laughter, to Sarah, was a good sound. C.J. hadn't wanted to move to Indianapolis from Pittsburgh, just as she'd thought, and she'd almost been sure the round of disagreements would destroy them. In some ways, their marriage for the past few months had been in name only, since C.J. had stayed behind to run the Pittsburgh office while she'd supervised the construction of the new Walker Manufacturing factory on North West Street.

The past few months had been so hard, Sarah hadn't thought she would have the inner strength to make it. Lelia's husband had vanished without warning—she'd simply come home from a sales trip and found that John R. Robinson had packed his things and left—and Lelia had been nearly inconsolable. Sarah had suggested that her daughter go away to college to take her mind off her heartache, so Lelia had spent the last year as a freshman at Knoxville College. But as much as Sarah wanted her daughter to finally get her schooling, she was torn; Lelia's absence meant it was that much harder to keep the operation running in Pittsburgh, especially with the Indianapolis move under way.

And C.J. had thought she was plain crazy. How could they maintain offices in both cities? Wasn't the expansion too quick? With the perpetual juggling act between accounts payable and accounts receivable—the money they were owed and the money coming in—was she trying to drive the company into the ground?

And Sarah knew there were ways in which C.J. was absolutely right. The Walker Company was in a delicate time, growing so fast daily that it was no longer simply exhausting to keep up, it was maddening. The number of agents had more than doubled in only a year, and she'd had to hastily add employees to take charge of shipping, billing, and teaching. Her dear friend Sadie had opened her own beauty shop in St. Louis using the Walker method, but Sarah had convinced Sadie to move to Pittsburgh with her family so she could teach at Lelia College and work in the beauty shop there. That offered some relief, at least, and Sarah was glad to have someone else in Pittsburgh she could completely trust, but that was only the beginning of the company's needs. The numbers in accounting never seemed to match up right, and she'd gone through three accountants in a year; they were always searching for the perfect supplier for the steel pressing combs, someone who was both good *and* reliable; and agents too often complained about receiving their supplies late. Since Walker products were sold only through the agents, not in drugstores, late shipments meant that customers weren't being satisfied and were probably turning to some other product, like Poro.

And with all that going on, Sarah had been building a warehouse and home in another city. *Either this is the end for us, or this is a beginning like nothing else,* Sarah often thought after her arguments with C.J. That could be true about her marriage or Walker Manufacturing, or both. In fact, in her mind, they were one and the same. If the marriage could last, she told herself, the company could last, and vice versa.

Now that C.J. had finally moved in with her in Indianapolis, she felt at ease with him again. She truly had a home for the first time since she'd begun living here.

And what a home! Their bank account was bursting, thanks to generous bank loans and mounting business, so Sarah had decided to use only top-notch furnishings for their twelve-room home at 640 North West Street in Indianapolis, which had twice the space of the one they'd just left in Pittsburgh. With help from Lottie, who had a glorious eye for decorative detail and recommended designers and artists they were not familiar with, she and C.J. were building a home that, in her mind, felt suitable for royalty. The construction and renovation seemed endless, but she knew it would be worth it. This would be *their* place, their reward for a long, hard struggle.

Sarah wanted long, airy walkways, so the hardwood floors seemed to stretch for miles. The drawing room was nearly finished—she called it the Gold Room—and its furniture was hued in old-rose and gold, with fine Oriental rugs across the floor and a golden curio cabinet that gleamed in the corner. She'd installed a Tiffany chandelier that reminded her of the one in the Denver ballroom, which cast the same ghostly, sparkling white light below. At the center of the room was a marvelous Mexican onyx table she'd found, its sides bound in gold. Sarah wanted Lottie to help her find the perfect Negro artist to display in this room; Lottie was investigating a young Indianapolis-born artist named William Edouard Scott she'd heard was making a sensation studying in Paris, and Sarah couldn't wait to buy his pieces. That would be the perfect touch.

Next, the library. The Robinsons thought Sarah should have a piano? Well, now she did—the Chickering baby grand piano that had just arrived was so new it shined, the library's showpiece. And Lottie had delighted in helping her fill the shelves of the library with books, along with etchings of poets Henry Wadsworth Longfellow and John Greenleaf Whittier she'd hung on the walls. An ebony bust of William Shakespeare was displayed in a corner. This was the room where Sarah took her lessons from Lottie in reading, history, French, and elocution for at least an hour every single day, even if her only free time was late at night or before dawn. Sarah savored the spirit of learning in her majestic library.

Oh, and the plans she had for the rest! She was ordering furnishings for all the guest and sleeping rooms, and Haviland china, special wall coverings, an oversize table with a Battenburg covering, and silver punch bowls and mugs for the dining room. Soon she planned to begin hosting eight- and ten-course dinners that would have tongues wagging for weeks.

The master bedroom was no less than sprawling, closer to the size of a living room than any bedroom she'd ever seen, but it was not yet furnished, except for her cherished photograph of her father and a massive canopied bed so high off the ground that she and C.J. needed foot ladders to climb onto it. *Like Miss Brown's bed,* she thought fondly, even though she knew the bed she had now was far more expensive than anything Miss Brown could have afforded.

Finally C.J. was here to share the bed with her. That was all that mattered. From now on, everything between them would be different, she'd decided. She would try to learn from what had happened to poor Lelia, and she would be more the wife C.J. wanted. *We have more supervisors and office help here, C.J.*, she'd told him, *so there won't be any reason we can't both travel together. When I have to go away, I want you with me.*

That was one of her wishes, in fact. In addition to newspaper articles about successful Negroes, Sarah had posted three new wishes on neat scraps of paper: *Five-thousand agents*, one said. *Larger manufacturing plant*, said another. The last read: *A happy Walker home.*

Sarah stared at the wishes each morning before she left the bedroom, until she could see her handwriting even with her eyes closed. And every time they reached or surpassed one of their goals, she and C.J. took the wish down and replaced it with another—but only after a special evening together, either a hot bubble bath or a private picnic or a long drive through the city.

So far, so good. C.J. had been more cheerful since his arrival in Indianapolis than he had been in months, and he'd taken a renewed interest in his role with the company. He was selling his Blood and Rheumatic Cure—which was prominently displayed on the company stationery—and he was calling himself a "scalp specialist," traveling on his own occasionally to consult with potential agents and customers. He seemed content, not so itchy and ill-tempered all the time.

Once again, C.J. was the man she'd had dinner with in St. Louis, full of ideas and dreams. And laughs! Sarah loved to hear C.J. laugh, that sound of warm honey.

When Sarah finally brought her car to a bucking stop at the curb in front of their house, C.J. was feigning a heart attack, clutching at his chest as he breathed hard. "Let me out of this monster!" he cried, scratching at the window. "I need to be drunk to ride with you, Sarah."

Sarah hated to hear him make a reference to drinking, since he was drinking much more whiskey now than he had when she first met him. But she didn't want to ruin their good mood. "I'm not that bad and you know it," she said, playfully slapping his shoulder.

As they climbed out of the motorcar, still laughing, Sarah noticed a young colored man in a slightly wrinkled suit and derby walking toward them on the sidewalk. He had been about to climb up their walkway to the front door, but he changed his course when he saw them.

"Madam Walker? Mr. Walker?" the man said, taking off his derby.

Once he was closer, Sarah recognized his clean-shaven face instantly; he'd aged in the two or three years since she'd seen him last, but this was Freeman Ransom, the porter! He looked so sober and sophisticated in a suit and tie, it was hard for her to imagine he'd been a porter at all.

Sarah invited him into the parlor, calling into the kitchen that she needed the new cook she'd hired to bring out cups of tea for her, C.J., and Freeman Ransom. "You sure I can't interest you in somethin' stronger than tea?" she heard C.J. ask the young man.

"Oh, no, sir. I don't drink," Mr. Ransom said pertly. "I took a vow when I was eighteen not to drink, dance, or gamble when I joined the YMCA. My vows are important to me, sir."

Sarah shared a look with C.J., and she had to struggle not to chuckle out loud. *Shoot, remind me not to join no damn YMCA,* Sarah knew her husband was thinking. But the young man's response impressed her. Once they were all sitting with cups of imported Japanese green tea, Lottie's newest discovery, Sarah asked Mr. Ransom how his schooling was going.

"I just received my law degree from Columbia University in New York," he said modestly. "And I've decided to make Indianapolis my home. I heard you had moved here, Madam Walker, and this city has so many opportunities for Negroes. Has your company hired a lawyer?"

"We used Robert L. Brokenburr once or twice. You know that name?" C.J. said. Sarah sensed her husband was trying to intimidate Mr. Ransom, testing him.

"Oh, yessir. Mr. Brokenburr is very well known. I've seen his name in the *Recorder*." Mr. Ransom looked disappointed. "Is he . . . er . . . is he your legal counsel, then?"

Sarah smiled at him. "We just use him now and again," she said. "We can always use more legal counsel, Mr. Ransom. I remember telling you I would keep my eye on you, didn't I?"

"Oh, yes, ma'am, but I wouldn't hold you to a promise so informal," Mr. Ransom said, his face earnest. "I have some ideas for you, and I hope you'll think I could be an asset to your corporation. I take it that Walker Manufacturing *is* a state-recognized corporation . . . ?"

Again Sarah glanced at C.J.; they'd talked about incorporating, but they'd never initiated the procedure. With so many details, it had just been left undone.

Mr. Ransom looked concerned at their silence. "Oh, my! Well, that's a piece of business you'll want to take care of, Madam and Mr. Walker, whether you decide to use my services or not. You'll want to establish a board of directors, a list of holdings. . . ."

Sarah's smile widened, and she experienced the same rush of warmth she'd felt for Mr. Ransom when she'd first seen him reading at Union Station in St. Louis. Such a serious young man! He was the sort of man who was a stickler for details, just like she was. She found herself wondering if he was married. He would be a much better husband for Lelia!

"How old are you, Mr. Ransom?" Sarah asked, out of curiosity. C.J. had fallen silent, as he usually did during these sorts of transactions lately, unless Sarah asked his opinion.

"I turned twenty-nine in July, Madam." Three years Lelia's senior. *Good*, Sarah thought.

"And if we were to decide that we'd be interested in your legal services . . . how much would that cost us?" Sarah said.

At that, Mr. Ransom looked uncomfortable for the first time. "Well, Madam . . . I've heard you take boarders here . . . and I'm new in town, you see, so"—he raised his eyebrows hopefully—"might I offer legal services in exchange for room and board?"

Sarah and C.J. glanced at each other, grinning. *Free* was their favorite price.

It was five-thirty A.M., nearly an hour before Lottie would be ready to begin tutoring her, but Sarah was already awake and fully dressed as she sat in the padded rocking chair on the front veranda of her house. She hadn't been able to sleep, so she'd risen early to mix ingredients in the warehouse in back of her home; she had women she'd hired who mixed portions and packaged the final product, but none of them knew all of the ingredients. That secret belonged to her, Lelia, and C.J., and Sarah wanted to keep it that way. She was terrified someone might steal her secret formula. *Guess this is how poor Annie Malone felt when I came along*, Sarah thought.

She'd heard from Sadie that some folks at the Poro Company had been saying she'd stolen Annie Malone's formula, which made Sarah angry, but she'd already decided not to answer those charges. C.J. had warned her long ago that she would become a target for jealousy. *You got to take the bad with the good, Sarah*, he'd said.

To seize her thoughts away from business, Sarah gazed at her peaceful, darkened street. Light was only beginning to creep at the edges of the sky, so the birds weren't even up yet; all she heard was the whirring and chirping of crickets.

But, no. In the distance Sarah made out the chugging and rattling of a motorcar, and soon she could see two glowing lamplights driving toward her on North West Street. The wooden-bodied Model T was driving at a fast clip until it neared Sarah's house, when it slowed and finally came to a stop. It was too dark for Sarah to see inside the car because the canopy was up, but she heard at least four men and women laughing softly.

"Good morrow to thee, A'Lelia," she heard a man's voice say in a mock English accent, and then the car filled with laughter again. Lelia was out this late?

After climbing out of the car with her skirt raised indelicately, Lelia waved the car off with her handkerchief as she stood at the curb. She was giggling to herself, and Sarah knew before her daughter even began walking toward the veranda in slightly lurching steps that she must have been drinking. She hadn't known Lelia to drink!

Seeing Sarah suddenly, Lelia gasped, clinging to the railing. "Mama!" she said.

"*Hush*, girl," Sarah said angrily. "You'll wake up the whole house."

"What 'chu doing out here so late?" Lelia said. Her words were slurred, though she had struggled to regain her composure by standing up straight without help from the railing.

Sarah's face felt hot. She'd been holding her temper in check, but her daughter's obvious intoxication made her long for the days when Lelia was small enough for a switch. "It's not late; it's *early*. It's morning, almost six A.M. Where have you been? Is this what you do at night? You stay out all hours like this, raisin' a ruckus—"

"Oh, Mama, nobody's raisin' a ruckus but you," Lelia said, plopping herself down on the top step of the veranda, near Sarah's feet. "I've just been out with some friends."

Sarah's hands were wrapped tightly around the rocking-chair armrests. "Well, ain't this is a sight! I'm hopin' you'll make some kind of impression on Mr. Ransom, and here you are—"

"On *who*?" Lelia said, her voice rising too loud again.

"On Mr. Freeman Briley Ransom. It should be plain to you he has a good future. It's long past time you divorced Mr. Robinson and started thinking about a better husband."

"Mr. Ransom!" Lelia laughed. "Mama, he's so stiff he must put starch in his drawers."

Sarah's face hardened. "You just can't rest until you've said at least one thing to try to shock me, can you? Like you were raised in an alley."

Lelia sighed, leaning back until her head rested against Sarah's knees. Sarah almost pulled her knees away, but she decided not to. Suddenly she was reminded of a time long ago, when Lelia had sat between her knees to have her hair combed and greased, just like Sarah's mama used to do to hers. Sarah suddenly felt sad, nearly lost, longing for something she couldn't name.

"I'm sorry, Mama," Lelia said, all mirth gone from her voice. "I've been drinkin', that's all, just goin' from house to house with some young folks. And playing some cards, too. They all like me. I feel like I'm having some fun for once, not just . . ." She didn't finish, only sighing.

Sarah stroked the top of Lelia's head. "Baby, I know your heart is just aching. But what you're doin' now won't bring us both nothin' but shame, hear? I was so glad you wanted to spend the summer here, but not for this. And how come you haven't said anything about going back to school? It'll be fall before you know it."

" 'Cause I don't wanna go," Lelia said, slurring again. She sounded younger now.

Sarah had suspected as much, although Lelia had never admitted it before. Still, Sarah had even thought of a plan, and she decided to suggest it now: "How 'bout you go back to Pittsburgh and take over the office there?"

Lelia didn't speak at first. "I thought you were gonna get somebody—"

"Who better than family? You know this business, Lelia—you grew up with it. If you don't like school, so be it. I'll give you Pittsburgh. My advice is yours for the asking, but do what you want with that office. The profits, everything. It's yours."

Lelia turned around to gaze upward at Sarah, her face slack-jawed. She was blinking fast. "You mean that, Mama? You really think I can do that? You . . . trust me to . . . ?"

Sarah squeezed her daughter's shoulders, leaning over her. "Course I trust you! If you wanted it, baby, you just had to ask me. This company ain't all mine and C.J.'s. It's yours, too. You think I'ma be here forever?"

"You better be!" Lelia said, smiling. She breathed sour liquor into Sarah's face. "I'm gonna make you proud, Mama."

Sarah stroked the side of her daughter's face. "You go on to bed, and try not to wake Mr. Ransom. Maybe there's hope for you two yet."

"No, he's not for me," Lelia said, shaking her head. "I'm a married woman, Mama."

Everybody's got to believe in somethin', Sarah thought, and gave her daughter a squeeze.

On the morning of September 19, five people stood over a desk in the office of Walker Manufacturing as a single electric lamp glowed bright above their heads. All of them were dressed smartly, so the occasion felt more like a ceremony than a business formality. Sarah thought Lelia looked breathtaking with her newly bobbed hair, neat turban, and matching tailored floor-length green suit. Lelia was a princess, she thought.

"These are the articles of incorporation for the Madam C.J. Walker Manufacturing Company of Indiana, which will manufacture and sell a hair-growing, beautifying, and scalp disease–curing preparation and clean scalps with the same," Mr. Ransom said, reading from the document on the desk before them. "The capital stock is ten thousand dollars, et cetera, with one thousand shares at ten dollars per share. The three members of the board of directors are Lelia McWilliams Robinson, Charles J. Walker, and Madam C.J. Walker, or Sarah B. Walker."

Sarah felt excitement trip up her spine, and she squeezed C.J.'s hand in one palm and Lelia's in the other. Lelia smiled at her, leaning over to kiss her cheek. "You did it, Mama," Lelia whispered to her. Sarah glanced at C.J., whose eyes were closed as he listened, which reminded Sarah of his serious concentration on their wedding day. *No, we did it*, Sarah thought, squeezing C.J.'s hand again. He opened his eyes and smiled at her, nodding. They knew each other's thoughts.

"All that's left, then, is for the new board of directors to sign," added Robert Brokenburr, who had assisted Mr. Ransom with the paperwork. "And we'll go file and make it official."

One by one, Lelia, C.J., and Sarah took turns writing their signatures with the fountain pen.

Sarah was surprised to notice that her hand was trembling slightly as she wrote. Damn! Her penmanship was poor enough already—that was one of the things Lottie had vowed to help her improve—but her signature looked worse than usual, and on such an important document!

She was afraid, she realized. Her heart's pounding had felt like exhilaration at first, but now there was no mistaking the nervousness she felt. What was she afraid of?

I don't want to lose this, she thought. They had made this company, and now she was daring to raise her hopes that *she*, of all people, could help build a company all Negroes in the country could be proud of. That was what Mr. Ransom said. But what if that wasn't what happened at all? What if they failed? Observers might say, *Well, what do you expect from Negroes?* Sometimes it all seemed to be held together by such a fragile thread.

"Once this is filed, I'll turn my attention to that other matter, Madam Walker," Mr. Ransom said quietly as he walked past Sarah, being ever so discreet. Sarah appreciated the young man's discretion. The other matter was her nephew, Willie Powell.

A month ago, Sarah had sent a train ticket and shipping money to Lou so she could move from Mississippi to Indianapolis and take a job with her company. Finally, after so many years, Sarah was ready to fully repay her sister for taking care of her all of those years after their parents died. She and Lou had their differences, all right, but that had nothing to do with the debt Sarah felt she owed her older sister.

Since neither of them thought it was a good idea to live in the same house—*Sarah, this ain't a house; it's a museum, girl*, Lou had complained. *I can't live someplace I have to stay so hushed an' be skeered I'll break somethin' on the floor*—Lou had found a suitable apartment nearby, which Sarah paid for. Lou also worked in the factory packaging hair grower, although early reports were coming to Sarah that her sister was far from industrious; she often arrived late and wanted to leave early. Frankly, Sarah thought, there were probably other problems her staff was afraid to report to her. Still, she decided, Lou would receive ten dollars a month from her regardless. She was going to take care of her sister.

And now that she had lawyers, she was going to try to get Willie out of prison. It was just too bad neither she nor Lou had been able to look into it properly before now, fifteen long years later. *But better late than never*, Sarah thought. *What good's money if you can't use it to make life better for your own family?*

Later that evening, after dressing for the planned dinner with her family at a local colored eating house called Gray's to celebrate the company's incorporation, Sarah stepped into the long hallway outside of her bedroom and saw C.J. and Lelia standing at the far end of the hall. They were nearly hidden in the shadows, but Sarah could tell there was something adversarial about their stance as they faced each other, so much so that she was startled. She ducked back into the doorway. The nervous feeling was back; her stomach felt tight.

"Well, it's done now," Sarah heard Lelia say. But she didn't sound happy.

"Yep, it's done."

"I'll tell you one thing, C.J. Walker," Lelia said in a hard voice Sarah had almost never heard from her daughter, "you may be on the board of directors, because that's what Mama wanted, but you wouldn't have been if it was up to me." The brashness of her words took Sarah aback.

"I'm sorry you feel that way, Miss A'Lelia. But I don't suppose it'd do much good for me to care too much 'bout what a spoiled li'l gal like you thinks of me. 'Specially since you don't mind none what the rest of the folks in this town think of *you*."

What in the world . . . ? Sarah thought. She knew C.J. and Lelia weren't close, but she hadn't realized so much open animosity had grown between them. It was as if she'd stepped backstage at a play production, catching a glimpse of actors who had taken off their costumes.

"If you keep trying to do the same mess like before, you better be concerned," Lelia said. "If I were you, I'd be *real* concerned. And you can take that exactly the way it sounds."

"Is that so?" The ugly sarcasm Sarah hated had returned to C.J.'s voice. "Yeah, maybe I should be downright scared of you, huh, A'Lelia? John Robinson must've been plenty scared of you, too, the way he lit out so quick. I figger he was just scared you'd shame him by drinkin' him under the ta—"

C.J. was cut off by a sharp snapping sound, flesh on flesh. Sarah knew her daughter must have just slapped C.J.'s face, and she didn't blame her. Shocked, Sarah raised both hands to her mouth, but she couldn't move otherwise. Her heart was thudding against her chest with something like real horror. What would make them say such hurtful things to each other? Sarah was outraged for both of them, and mortified. Lelia must be trying to protect her from something, or she would have confided what was troubling her about C.J. But what?

"You're one to talk about drinking," Lelia hissed, barely audible to Sarah. "And I wouldn't worry so much about my marriage if I were you. You best start worrying about yours. If something goes wrong with you and Mama, you just wait and see. The only time you'll set foot in a house like this again will be if someone hires you to come take out the trash."

Go out there right now and put a stop to this, Sarah told herself, her heart withering inside her. *Ask them to tell you what you don't know.* Tears of frustration and disgust welled in Sarah's eyes, but she couldn't make herself move from her hiding place.

If you keep trying to do that same mess like before, Lelia had said to C.J. Did that mean whatever she was talking about was over? Yes, it had to be! Maybe C.J. had taken a mistress in the months they'd been apart. Well, he was a man, wasn't he? Had she expected him to be a monk all the time she was away? She and C.J. were finally together, and with all they had to share now, what more could any man want? And once Lelia was away from her unseemly crowd in Indianapolis, with new responsibilities in Pittsburgh, she'd be forced to go back to her sober ways. She'd have to!

Sarah repeated those words to herself over and over, until she thought she believed them.

Chapter Twenty-eight

To Sarah, the new year was off to an unforgettable and promising start. She'd heard wonderful things about Dr. Booker T. Washington's Tuskegee Normal and Industrial Institute since he became principal of the Negro school in the 1880s; only six years back, in 1906, she'd read that President Roosevelt himself had attended the school's twenty-fifth anniversary celebration. Now, she, C.J., and Lottie were walking on the very grounds of the campus in Alabama's nippy winter air, past hilly acres of school buildings and majestic halls. Compared to the worn-down mansions nearby and the faded, bedraggled little town that shared its name, the school looked like a bustling city. There must be more than a hundred buildings, or even twice that! Sarah had decided to attend Tuskegee's annual Farmers' Conference to do hair demonstrations and recruit agents, and she was sorry she'd never come before now. Hundreds of farmers, ministers, teachers, and other tradesmen came to the conference each year to discuss practical ways to elevate the race, and Sarah planned to let everyone know colored women could elevate themselves by learning a well-paying trade as hair culturists.

"You'll find this hard to believe, Madam," Lottie said as they walked past a large building marked Andrew Carnegie Hall, "but I understand that Mr. Carnegie gave Dr. Washington a $600,000 contribution in oh three. Mr. Carnegie called Dr. Washington a 'modern Moses.' "

"Moses, huh? Does that mean Carnegie thinks he's God?" C.J. muttered.

"No, it sounds more like he thinks he's a good friend, C.J.," Sarah said, thinking to herself, *And that's the kind of friend I'd like to be someday*. She'd donated $1,000 to the building fund for Indianapolis's colored YMCA in October—if only there were an association for colored *girls*, too!—which had caused a stir in the press because no one could imagine that a colored woman could afford such a grand contribution. She would keep her word and make the payments, of course, but she'd had to measure them out; her company was worth $25,000, but she didn't yet have so much money that she could write out a thousand-dollar check without a blink. C.J. and Mr. Ransom thought the YMCA publicity was good for the company, but other "begging letters," as Sarah called them, were already pouring in. So many people in need!

What would she do if she could give money to anyone she chose?

Gazing at the Tuskegee campus, Sarah saw male and female students who were younger than Lelia wandering on the pathways, and others who were much older. They were studying subjects they could use to support their families, like mattress making, typesetting, horticulture, farming, masonry, blacksmithing, and sick care. Tuskegee students, she had learned, built furniture, carriages, and structures on the campus. And the students weren't all American Negroes, she noticed; some looked Chinese, others were East Indian, and the colorful costumes on some of the Negroes made Sarah think they must be from Africa. Students sought out this school from all over the world! Lottie had told Sarah that *Up from Slavery* had been translated into Zulu, Chinese, and other languages, so Dr. Washington's story was inspiring people worldwide.

Looking at them, Sarah vowed she'd give money toward education whenever she could. Lottie was a godsend in her life, but Sarah was forty-four years old, and learning was so much more of a chore than it would have been when she was younger. If only she and her parents could have gone to a school like Tuskegee . . .

As they walked into the Farmers' Conference meeting hall, Sarah was no less excited than she had been in St. Louis eight years before, when she'd gone to hear Dr. Washington at the World's Fair. But there was a difference this time, she noticed; the atmosphere was much more informal, and Dr. Washington was already greeting people in his simple gray wool suit and black bow tie as they walked through the door. Sarah couldn't believe how close she was standing to him. He was much more pale-skinned than she'd remembered, his skin a fainter brown than C.J.'s, and he wasn't much taller than she was. But she could already hear the rumbling of his voice and see his exuberant smile. Suddenly his eyes were on her. "Welcome to Tuskegee, ma'am," he said.

Sarah nearly forgot her words, but she thrust her hand out to him. "D-Dr. Washington, my husband and I are here representing the Madam C.J. Walker Manufacturing Company of Indianapolis, and we're here to do hair demonstrations—"

Sarah thought she recognized a slight flicker of impatience cross the educator's face, but his smile didn't waver. "God bless," he said, squeezing her hand. "Thank you so much."

There were many others waiting behind her, and Sarah felt the crowd surging forward slightly; others had come a long way for a chance to talk to Dr. Washington, too. Before Sarah knew it, he had stepped aside to greet someone else.

"You *talked* to him, Madam!" Lottie whispered, excited.

Yes, she had talked to him, but Sarah felt disappointment along with her giddiness. She'd wanted him to know what she was doing, that she'd come from meager beginnings just as he had, that she shared his passion for education. To him, she was just a stranger's face in a crowd.

"You talked to him, all right. You were 'bout to talk his ear off, Sarah," C.J. told her. "Shoot, the man was just sayin' hello. You can't expect to stand and have a conversation."

Sarah glanced over her shoulder, and Dr. Washington vanished inside the crowd of farmers dressed in drab suits and hats, probably the best they owned. For the first time in a long time, Sarah felt *overdressed* in her white, lacy shirtwaist and blue skirt. Here was a man who had dined with President Roosevelt and was consulted by President Taft on matters of race— though neither man was a true friend to the Negro, as far as Sarah was concerned, Taft even less than Roosevelt—and he apparently felt right at home in the midst of poor farmers.

But Sarah didn't know how much Dr. Washington felt at home until he walked to the podium. As he stood there before them, instead of opening the meeting with grand words as he had at the World's Fair, he simply began to hum. His throaty humming was the only sound in the hall, and the melody surrounded them, filling up the room.

Then Sarah recognized the song. She hadn't heard it since her parents sang it in the cotton fields, moving slowly through the rows. Sarah could almost hear her papa's voice:

There is a balm in Gilead,
To make the wounded whole,
There is a balm in Gilead,
To heal the sin-sick soul.
Sometimes I feel discouraged,
And think my work's in vain,
But then the Holy Spirit
Revives my soul again!

Soon other people in the room began to sing, and the hall became a chorus of rough, happy voices. Suddenly, her toes tingling, Sarah had never felt more at home herself.

Mrs. Dora Larrie. The woman had introduced herself to Sarah personally before the demonstration began, but it hadn't been necessary. Sarah would have noticed her regardless, the way she always noticed the most promising women who came to her. *Fire*, that was what Mrs. Larrie had. Sarah had seen it in Lottie, too; these women were so eager to change their lives, nearly desperate, that they would take up their new trade with the enthusiasm of converts to a religion. Mrs. Dora Larrie had that fire.

She was a tall young woman, about thirty, and Sarah liked the way she presented herself; her hair was neatly pinned, her clothes were modest despite her ample bustline, and she had a naturally pretty face, angular and bright-eyed. She looked exactly like one of those high-yellow women at the church picnic in St. Louis who'd turned their noses up at her, and Sarah couldn't help feeling a small glow of satisfaction that she'd come to *her* to learn.

The room assigned to Sarah was a cooking classroom, apparently, because it had a wood-burning cooking stove that she guessed was also used for heating. C.J. had lit a fire for her while Sarah selected one of the twenty-five women in the classroom to demonstrate her pressing comb. Dutifully, Lottie passed out yellow advertisements they had printed up about the company for their trip to the South, with testimonials from hair customers and agents from all over the country.

"As you'll see," Sarah said to the women, holding up her steel comb, "it's best to use two combs. In this way, one will heat while the other is in use, which will save you and your customers time. Efficiency is another watchword of the Walker method."

The women nodded, watching closely while Sarah parted her subject's hair; the woman was the wife of a farmer who had come to the demonstration purely out of curiosity, and Sarah had chosen her because she liked the natural length of her hair, which had been tied into two big braids. Sarah had already washed her hair and dried it carefully with towels, and now it was time to press. The results would be impressive, Sarah thought.

"Madam C.J. Walker's Glossine is a very important part of this process," Sarah said, as C.J. helpfully handed her an open jar of the pressing oil. "I've been told that some Walker culturists are substituting Vaseline and other products, but while that may save a few pennies, it is not in the best interests of your customer. Now, you place a small amount of Glossine with the index or middle finger of the right hand, using the fingertip along the part. You must apply the Glossine to *both* sides of the part. . . ."

Then Sarah asked the women to stand up and gather around her the best they could, because she wanted them to have a closer view of her work. The woman in her chair smiled, glad to be the center of so much attention. "You hold the comb in the right hand, like so, and a small portion of the hair between the thumb and first two fingers of the left hand. The teeth of the comb should be placed as close to the scalp as possible without touching it, and then turned so that the teeth face straight *up*. Pull the comb toward you, feeding hair through the fingertips to the very end of each strand. Then you pick up the same hair, insert the comb from the other side, and press *downward*. It's in this downward pressure, ladies, that you will get the desired result. . . ."

Mrs. Larrie raised her hand often, asking questions about the products. Sarah liked her persistence and her perceptiveness.

"Do you live right here in Tuskegee, Mrs. Larrie?"

"Yes, Madam," the woman said. "I'm from Indianapolis, but I live here now."

"Well, it sounds to me like you should be my first Tuskegee agent."

"Oh, yes, Madam, I sure would like that!" the woman said, her face flushed with excitement.

Some time later, Sarah noticed a regally dressed woman standing in her doorway, and she nearly lost her train of thought. It was Margaret Murray Washington, Dr. Washington's wife! Mrs. Washington smiled at her and nodded, and Sarah returned the gesture, feeling a rush of pleasure. Discreetly, Mrs. Washington motioned for Lottie to come to her. Sarah watched the two women talking quietly in the doorway, Lottie nodding as she listened, smiling widely. Then, just as quickly as she'd appeared, Mrs. Washington was gone.

Lottie walked up to Sarah and whispered the message: "She's having tea with a few ladies in a few minutes, and she would like you to come. One of Tuskegee's instructors, Dr. George Washington Carver, may also be there. . . ."

Sarah's heart leaped. She'd been invited to tea with Mrs. Washington! But how could she leave? Even though she'd nearly finished pressing her subject's head, she still needed time to talk to Dora Larrie about everything she would need to know about becoming a Walker agent. Sarah might need another half hour or more before she could even think of leaving.

C.J., who was standing close enough to have heard Lottie's words, also knew exactly what Sarah was thinking. He scribbled a note to her: *Go have your tea. That's not my liking, as you know. I'll see to the agent's needs.*

Sarah smiled at C.J., believing this must be one of the luckiest days of her life.

Chapter Twenty-nine

CHICAGO
AUGUST 1912
(SEVEN MONTHS LATER)

Sarah sweltered in the hard wooden pew of Dearborn Street's Institutional Church, which was a challenge to her stiff back. The National Negro Business League Convention had rolled on for two days of meetings, lectures, and debates. If C.J. were here, she thought, he would lean over and whisper his old joke, *Well, you know heat gathers wherever there's colored folks in numbers.*

She started to smile, but the smile itself brought discomfort. C.J. *wasn't* here, and she wasn't in the mood to consider the whys and wherefores of that. Not now.

It wasn't yet ten in the morning, and even this airy, grand structure with seating for hundreds was no sanctuary from the weight of the August sun outside. The room flurried with hand fans as the delegates tried to cool themselves. Sarah already felt the first prickles of moisture beneath her armpits, and she hoped she'd dusted her body with enough talcum powder under her velvet floor-length suit. The suit was businesslike, but too heavy for this oppressive weather. Still, heat or no heat, she wasn't going to take off her waist-length jacket or loosen the lace collar around her neck. Today was a special day. She would endure.

Sarah had attended the National Association of Colored Women's Clubs in Virginia last month, where she'd met Madam Mary McLeod Bethune, a dynamic and fiercely intelligent woman Sarah was quite certain would become a friend; Sarah had been so impressed with her that she'd vowed to lead a fund-raising campaign for Madam Bethune's school in Daytona. But this was the first time Sarah had attended a national meeting dedicated entirely to Negroes in business. Sarah's ears were filled with the hum of activity she'd come to expect at this NNBL event as delegates exchanged anecdotes, strategies, and solutions. These men were from all over the country, and Sarah could feel their expertise crackling in the air.

"Tell you what, though, if you start out with enough capital . . ."

"If I could find someone to map me out an advertising plan . . ."

". . . already seen what motorcars might mean to the future of blacksmithing . . ."

But Sarah felt slightly wistful: thus far, she was only a spectator. This was a club she didn't belong to—not yet, anyway. The only delegate she knew was George L. Knox from the *Indianapolis Freeman*, who had promised to introduce her today, and he had yet to arrive for this morning's session. As they had for the past two days, she and Lottie sat alone near the back of the church, simply listening to what was going on around them. Lottie had discreetly distributed yellow Walker Company advertisements throughout the pews on the session's opening day, but for once Sarah didn't have her demonstration kit with her; she was here to learn, not sell. Today she would be invisible until it was her time to speak.

Next year they'll all know who I am, Sarah promised herself. *Every single one*.

"It's a shame C.J. didn't come," Sarah said. "He'd be struttin' through this place like a rooster. I heard a man just now saying he wants better ads. C.J. would've talked his ear off."

Lottie nodded quiet agreement. After a moment she said, "What *was* his excuse for staying at home, Madam?" Her inflection was carefully neutral.

"C.J. said he had things to do," Sarah said, hating the defensiveness in her own voice.

C.J. had just shrugged and mumbled something about being tired, saying he was ready to stay at home a while. Granted, they'd already had an eventful year together; while they'd been staying in Jackson, Mississippi, for several months to train culturists and agents, C.J. had actually been *arrested* for selling products without a license. He and Sarah had been outraged about it, but Mr. Ransom had advised them to pay the fine and forget the matter, lest they be taxed in Mississippi. There were so many pitfalls to doing business! Besides, Sarah couldn't help feeling the law had been exercised so freely against C.J. simply because he was a Negro. *I'm 'bout done with bein' on the road, Sarah*, C.J. had said. Except she knew there was more to it than that.

C.J. had been tired a lot in the past five months, but when she tried to broach *that* subject he'd changed tactics, accusing her of chasing after Dr. Booker T. Washington's coattails. Well, perhaps that wasn't entirely wrong.

Sarah *had* been thrilled to meet Dr. Washington and his wife at Tuskegee in January. The great man, the league's president and founder, had sent her a gracious letter thanking her for her $40 contribution to the school, appropriately signing it *Principal*. But it had maddened Sarah to know that the best-known Negro in the country was going to be only a few hundred miles from Indianapolis for the NNBL Convention and would not come to town to see her company. She'd written him twice, first offering to pay his way to Indianapolis on his way *to* Chicago, then asking to host Dr. Washington on his way home. *Sorry, he's too busy.* Polite words on neatly folded sheets of fine paper, signed by Dr. Washington's secretary, Mr. Emmett J. Scott. In his second letter, Mr. Scott had said he admired her persistence, but she wondered if it amused him instead.

C.J. had cautioned her to stop pressuring the renowned educator everyone called the Wizard because of his power in building coalitions. *Lord have mercy, Sarah, he's got everybody and his mama running after him. Why you have to push so hard?* But that was always C.J.'s problem, not being able to put two and two together and see what it added up to. The way she saw it, if Dr. Washington was sufficiently impressed with the company, he might one day agree to offer the Walker method as a part of the *curriculum* at Tuskegee. And if that happened, Tuskegee itself would certify untold numbers of women in the use of Walker products and hair preparations. What a boon that would be!

Sarah had seen that potential as clear as day when she visited the Alabama school, but she couldn't approach Dr. Washington with such a proposition based on her mere say-so. For all she knew, the Washingtons might have viewed her as just another two-bit traveling salesman. No, Dr. Washington needed to see the company for himself. That would make all the difference.

And that was one of the biggest reasons Sarah was here.

Even though she hadn't yet been able to get close enough to Dr. Washington to even catch his eye or say hello, the NNBL convention itself had surpassed Sarah's wildest hopes. What a golden opportunity this was, hearing the stories of so many Negro businessmen! She wished Lelia had come, too. But Sarah had known full well from the nonchalance in her daughter's letter from Pittsburgh a week ago that Lelia had no interest in a business trip. *I'll think on it, Mama.* Not likely! Now, if Sarah had invited her to a *dance*, maybe . . .

"Morning, Madam Walker." Someone squeezed Sarah's shoulder warmly, and she turned to see George Knox behind her grinning, his wild tufts of white sideburns sticking out from the sides of his hat. He leaned over to give her cheek a peck, then he did the same for Lottie. His breath smelled of coffee. "You aren't nervous, now, are you, Madam?" He winked at her.

"Not until you said that, no."

"Don't mind me; that's just teasing. Why are you sitting way back here? How do you expect these folks to hear you?"

"Now, Mr. Knox, you should know me and my mouth better than that by now."

The newspaper publisher sat beside her with a chuckle. "Remember, you get only three minutes. Did you write out a speech like I told you?"

Lottie chimed in. "She sure didn't, Mr. Knox, even after I offered to help her by transcribing it. She seems to forget that's what I'm paid for."

"Well, I know sales, and sales is ninety percent mouth," Sarah said. "Don't you worry. You introduce me, Mr. Knox, and I'll do the rest."

"She will, too. This lady here is a constant marvel to me," Lottie said.

"*Marvel.* That's a beautiful word, Lottie—she'll be a marvel to this whole delegation. High time the world heard about the best-kept secret in Indianapolis!" George Knox said. "Just be patient and trust me, Madam. You're not on the program, so I have to find a way to work you in. I've sent a note up to the pulpit, but in case that's overlooked I'm ready to pick my own spot. When you're in the newspaper business, you have to know how to push."

Sarah felt a flutter of nerves in her stomach. The other delegates might not be nearly as impressed with her as George Knox was, she told herself. In the past two days, she'd heard remarkable addresses from bankers, publishers, and manufacturers who had been in serious business while she was still scrubbing clothes in a tin bucket. Why, Mr. Anthony Overton, who was based right here in Chicago, had a manufacturing business earning $117,000 a year! And her ears were still ringing with excitement from last night's address by a man named Bishop Scott, who'd talked about business opportunities in *Liberia*, of all places. Like everyone else, she'd leaped to her feet to applaud him at the close of his presentation.

By contrast, when a woman named Mrs. Coleman had spoken the first night about her hair-preparations business, Sarah thought the delegation's response had been only lukewarm. True, Mrs. Coleman's company wasn't as big as Sarah's, but she couldn't help thinking this mostly male organization might not support Negro business*women* as enthusiastically—or were they like so many others who didn't think beauty and hair products deserved their respect?

Well, she was about to find out.

"There he is," Lottie said. "There's Dr. Washington."

Sarah didn't need to glance in his direction to notice the respectful hush when the NNBL's distinguished president entered the room. He walked with a deliberateness Sarah admired, neither hurrying nor lagging, a sheaf of papers tucked neatly beneath his arm.

He was older than she was, she noticed, probably in his middle fifties. *A man, like my papa. Just a man*, she reminded herself. But she still felt light-headed, as if she were standing in the middle of a dream. "Mr. Knox, do you think you can bring us together at the end of the session? I'll go home happy if I can get his ear for just five minutes."

"I'll do my very best, Madam. Count on it."

"Oh! And Madam, I know how you like to say anything that comes to your mind . . ." Lottie leaned close to whisper, "but when you talk to him, please steer far away from politics. No matter how much you admire the NAACP and Mr. Du Bois's *Crisis* editorials, don't get mired in that bad blood between them."

The philosophical divide between these giants was well known: W.E.B. Du Bois believed Negroes should fight for every basic right, led by the black educated class; but Dr. Washington preached economic equality for the masses first, social integration second. Sarah didn't share all of Dr. Washington's conservatism, but she knew full well it was impossible to worry about fighting for seats at the opera when there wasn't enough food on the table. "Well, Lord, Lottie, I'm not a *complete* fool," Sarah whispered back.

"Madam, I was just trying to help—"

The gavel rang sharply against the podium, and the morning session was under way.

Most of the day was consumed with banking. Stocks. Deposits. Interest. Despite her excitement over the past days' sessions, Sarah found herself fidgeting like a schoolgirl, eager to stand up and tell the delegation about her own work. She watched George Knox's face in silence as long as she could, waiting for some sign of movement, but he seemed absorbed by everything he heard, constantly writing notes. Finally, at the end of a banker's address on how he gained the cooperation of his customer base, Sarah nudged Mr. Knox with her foot.

"Thought you'd have been called by now," he told her, speaking over the applause.

"Well, me, too, Mr. Knox. But it looks like no one's paying your note any nevermind."

The room once again fell silent. Dr. Washington gripped the side of the podium. "Now, then," he said, his voice reverberating through the packed hall. "Are there any further questions?"

After one sidelong glance from Sarah, George Knox rose to his feet and boomed: "I ask this convention for a few minutes of its time to hear a remarkable woman. She is Madam Walker, the manufacturer of hair goods and preparations."

Her heart thundering, confidence buoyed as hundreds of eyes turned toward her, Sarah stood up beside Mr. Knox. Finally her long wait was over. The stillness in the room felt like a precursor to pure magic.

But as Sarah cleared her throat to begin to introduce herself, her insides sank. Dr. Washington, at the podium, was not giving her the attention he had given all of the other speakers before her. He didn't even glance in her direction. Instead his eyes were fixed to the program in his hand, and then his voice filled the church: "Our *next* scheduled speaker . . ." He was speaking much more loudly than he had earlier, probably to drown her out, she realized.

Sarah was too confused to make out everything Dr. Washington was saying, but she heard him call on someone named Reverend E.M. Griggs. Helplessly, she watched as a man from the center of the room began to make his way up to the pulpit. The attention that had been focused on her wavered, and was gone.

She stood speechless, numb.

Urgently, George Knox tugged on the hem of her jacket. "You'd best sit down, Madam. He's going by the program," he said quietly.

Sarah sat. All of her enthusiasm drained quickly away, replaced with a deep and almost crippling humiliation. Dr. Washington had simply *ignored* her. Her ears began to burn hot, and in that flame C.J.'s words nattered at her. *Lord have mercy, Sarah, he's got everybody and his mama running after him. Why you have to push so hard?*

Lottie patted Sarah's wrist. "Don't you worry, Madam. He just doesn't want to break the order. I'm sure he'll call on you at the end."

Sarah barely heard Lottie's words. The Reverend Griggs's presentation was a blur. She felt as if she were sitting on a mountaintop, their voices and forms far away, the warmth of fellowship a pale and distant thing. Sarah had to fight to keep from leaping to her feet while Dr. Washington asked the banker a few leisurely questions. Every time she heard the delegation laugh and clap during the exchange, her ears burned again.

Why you have to push so hard?

Her chest hurt.

"Madam?" Lottie said. "Are you all right?"

Where was C.J.? Where was her husband while she was "pushing too hard," being shamed in public trying to build their common dream? Why wasn't someone here to grasp her hand in comfort now, when the simple, loving pressure of a caring hand would mean the world?

"Madam?"

". . . We thank Dr. Griggs for his splendid address," Dr. Washington said finally, the words Sarah had longed for, "and we hope that sick man who deposited eleven hundred dollars in his bank got well."

The audience laughed. The room rippled with applause.

Sarah stood, mindless of George Knox's alarmed expression, ignoring Lottie's touch on her arm. She pushed past them, into the center aisle, holding her chin high so her voice would bounce from the church's ceiling.

"Surely you are not going to shut the door in my face," Sarah said, even more loudly than she'd intended. Suddenly every eye in the room was on her again. Even Dr. Washington stared at her squarely from the podium, lines of displeasure drawn across his face. This time the silence was oppressive, as if Sarah had stolen all the joviality.

Sarah, why you have to push . . .
Because there's no one else, C.J.

Sarah swallowed hard, the pressure in her chest increasing. Everything inside her screamed to stop, to leave, to end this now before embarrassment and humiliation escalated into social ruin. But she had come too far.

Afraid of being interrupted or silenced, she hurried on, her words tumbling in a jumble. "I feel that I am in a business that is a credit to the womanhood of our race. I am a woman who started a business seven years ago with only a dollar-fifty. This year alone, I have earned over sixty-three thousand dollars."

A hush. But a different kind of silence this time. This was fascination. Respect. The pressure in her chest decreased, no longer a solid fist around her heart.

Confidence growing, she went on. "I went into a business that is despised, that is criticized and talked about by everybody—the business of growing hair. They did not believe such a thing could be done, but I have proven beyond the question of a doubt that *I do grow hair!*"

She paused, and realized that she was gulping for air, as if she had run a lone race carrying a desperate message. And just maybe she had. Suddenly the silence in the room was replaced by the friendly sound of laughter and clapping. She glanced at the strangers' faces turned nearest her, and she saw only smiles of encouragement. Lottie beamed at her.

With that, finally, Sarah relaxed. She told the audience about how her profits had grown from year to year, reciting the figures and details, names, history, and procedure from memory. No one interrupted. No eye left her, even Dr. Washington's, although his expression was unreadable. A warm wave of applause fell across her like a summer rain shower.

Sarah smiled widely, catching her breath. "I have been trying to get before you businesspeople and tell you what I am doing. I am a woman who came from the cotton fields of the South; I was promoted from there to the washtub . . ."—at this, her audience laughed—"then I was promoted to the cook kitchen, and from there I promoted *myself* into the business of manufacturing hair goods and preparations. Everybody told me I was making a mistake by going into this business, but I know how to grow hair as well as I know how to grow cotton, and I will state in addition that during the last seven years I have bought a piece of property valued at ten thousand dollars." The figure impressed them more than she'd expected, because that met applause, too.

By God. I have them!

"I have built my own factory on my ground, thirty-eight by two hundred eight feet; I employ in that factory seven people, including a bookkeeper, a stenographer, a cook, and a house girl." Laughing this time, the audience clapped again. "I own my own automobile and a runabout." The applause, this time, took so long that Sarah raised her hand slightly.

"Please don't applaud, just let me talk!" she begged them, and they laughed, but slowly grew silent.

"I am not ashamed of my past; I am not ashamed of my humble beginning. Don't think because you have to go down in a washtub, you are any less a lady!" Ignoring her earlier admonition, the audience exploded with applause again. But this time, instead of succumbing to frustration, Sarah felt a deep surge of pride that seemed to unburden a weary part of her soul.

"Now, my object in life is not simply to make money for myself or to spend it on myself in dressing or running around in an automobile, but to use part of what I make trying to help others. Perhaps many of you have heard of the real ambition of my life, the all-absorbing idea which I hope to accomplish, and when you have heard what it is, I hope you will catch the inspiration, grasp the opportunity to do something of far-reaching importance, and lend me your support."

This was the moment, and she plunged forward. "My ambition is to build an industrial school in Africa—by the help of God and the cooperation of my people in this country, I am going to build a Tuskegee Institute in Africa!"

Her voice rolled in the room, smothered only by the applause that followed.

George Knox was on his feet, his face lively with a joy that seemed to erase a decade from his features. His voice rose above the din. "I arise to attest to all that this good woman has said concerning her business in the progressive city of Indianapolis!" He nearly waved his hat in the air in his excitement. "You have heard only a part; the half has not been told of what she has accomplished. She is a generous-hearted lady of our town who gave *one thousand dollars* to the Young Men's Christian Association."

At the podium, Dr. Washington's face was still unreadable. Pleasure? Displeasure? Curiosity? She couldn't say. Once the applause had died to silence, he glanced at his program again. Without comment or questions, he called the next speaker, a banker from Birmingham.

But all around her, Sarah saw nothing but smiles.

The steamboat's lurching motion forced Sarah to cling to the rail, lest she lose her balance in her high-heeled, awkward shoes. The wind nearly took her hat, but she held it in place with her left hand and took a deep breath, enjoying the bracing mist as Lake Michigan's waters churned in the paddle wheeler's wake. The late-afternoon sun lit up the city in a stream of golden rays, displaying before her the grand structures and their shadows like an etching by a fine artist. Only the new seventeen-story Merchants Bank building in Indianapolis could rival these buildings. She could hardly believe most of Chicago had burned to rubble only forty-odd years ago.

As the steamboat began its journey along the lakeshore, dozens of passengers applauded. The hospitality banner from the church sessions had been strung across the railing, flapping in the breeze: WELCOME, NNBL. Sarah could also hear lively traces of string music being played from somewhere inside the boat's cabin. There must be musicians aboard!

"Now *this* is what I call style," Sarah said to Lottie, who nodded her agreement with a wary eye cast downward into the foaming waters.

At that instant, Dr. Booker T. Washington appeared on the deck, flanked by his secretary, Mr. Scott, and two other men Sarah didn't recognize. Dr. Washington's suit was still impeccable. With his hands clasped behind his back, he looked every bit the part of a solemn schoolmaster, his shoulders hanging slightly low, perhaps from weariness after the long convention. Dr. Washington's gaze swept across the deck without taking any notice of her, and his lanky form was soon hidden from her view by a huddle of delegates.

"I've seen that man smile only once in three days," Sarah mused.

"And when he does, it looks like it makes his face hurt," Lottie added, strictly within Sarah's hearing. Then her tone became more formal as she snapped to her official role: "Would you like an audience with him, Madam? After the way everyone crowded to you, surely he—"

"Oh, no. He heard what I have to say. I think I'd best leave it at that."

I've already pushed so hard. Maybe too hard, she thought. If that were true, she could forget about any dreams of having the Walker method taught at Tuskegee.

Sarah sighed, feeling out of sorts as she surveyed the lovely, calm lake from the boat's deck. Her fingers twitched instinctively, again yearning to be held. Many of the men at the conference had left their wives at home, including Dr. Washington, but she noticed that almost all of the women present stood contentedly on the arms of their mates. These women seemed to actually glow with pride, exactly the way she had once made C.J. glow. And hadn't she glowed for him, too? Every time she saw him dressed in his finest clothes, with his hair slicked back and his necktie looped into a crisp, perfect knot, C.J. made her glow. He could make her glow with the barest effort, just by noticing some crucial detail that had slipped her attention, or by squeezing her hand on a beautiful summer day like today.

But you know what, Sarah? she thought. *I think what really got your goat about the way Dr. Washington treated you today was how much it reminded you of C.J. acting like you ain't even breathing the same air as him no more.*

When she'd met Madam Bethune last month, the educator had told Sarah how lucky she was to have a husband who believed in her mission. (And *mission* was exactly the right word, Sarah thought; Madam C.J. Walker Manufacturing might have started as a business, but it had become something else to her.) *I'm afraid my dedication to my school became too much for my husband,* Madam Bethune had confided to her. *Albertus walked out in 1908 after ten years of marriage, and I haven't seen him since. Be glad Mr. Walker understands.*

But C.J. didn't understand, and lately he didn't seem to even want to.

Sarah barely noticed a young woman who came to stand at her elbow, bobbing up and down on the balls of her feet. "Now, Madam Walker, my husband is a delegate, and I liked what you said about promoting yourself from the cookhouse into business. But you must travel so much. My husband would turn me out if I did that. Your husband doesn't mind?"

For a moment Sarah was dumbstruck. Had this woman been reading her thoughts?

She collected herself. "My husband and I are building the Walker Company together. It's his name, after all," Sarah said, speaking the bald lie from habit. What should she have *really* said? Hell, yes, C.J. minded! If C.J. didn't mind, he would be standing at her side this very moment. If C.J. didn't mind, five months wouldn't have passed since they had last touched each other as man and wife, and she wouldn't have found that letter from Kansas City—

No. No. Don't think on that. Not now.

But the thoughts came anyway. Right in C.J.'s desk drawer, in plain sight, she'd noticed a feminine script on an open envelope from Kansas City. She'd thought it was related to business, or at least that was what she'd told herself as she started to read it, but inside she'd found a love note so familiar that she could have written it herself. There was no signature at the bottom, but someone—a woman, no doubt—had written saying how much she'd enjoyed her time with C.J., thanking him for his "sweet and kind letter." The correspondence had come in January, before the Tuskegee trip, but Sarah had found it only a few weeks ago. So he'd been running around with other women even during the time she'd thought everything was better between them, when they spent less time apart. He might still be running around now.

Lelia had warned Sarah before her very first supper with C.J. Walker, hadn't she? A woman in every city, she'd said. And Lelia had been right.

Sarah shook her head sharply, fighting off tears. The woman who'd sought her out was talking on about a business idea, but Sarah could no longer hear her. At that instant, she became fixated on the simple feeling of *knowing.* A clarity came to her that was different from the others that had visited her throughout her life and yet the same; gentler, somehow, but just as certain. She had to go home. If she cared about C.J. and she wanted her life with him to be the way it had been ever again, she had to go home *right now.*

But it's too late, said an even quieter, calmer voice in her head. *It's much too late.*

"Madam? You've made some more new friends," Lottie told her in a singsong voice, and a small congregation of wives enveloped Sarah in smiles and admiration.

"Madam Walker, I hope I can sign up my daughter to be one of your agents—"

"My husband and I enjoyed your speech today *soooo* much."

"—*love* your idea to open a school in Africa!"

Finally, the nagging voices in Sarah's head vanished, whisking away her anxieties, too. She took another deep breath, and she felt replenished. She touched something in strangers it was so difficult to touch in C.J., and it helped soothe the ache. But she had to remind herself it wasn't *her* these excited people loved so much—they were not "friends," as Lottie had called them—they didn't know her in flesh and blood, after all. They loved the *idea* of her. When they looked at her, they saw a future. For their daughters. For their race.

And why not? Anyone could do what she was doing, and maybe do it better. All they needed was to believe in it. Before she knew it, as usual, Sarah found herself speaking her thoughts aloud to her growing audience: "Sure the white folks have advantages, but we can't use that as an excuse not to do for ourselves. We don't need to start out with a lot of money. Don't even need to start out with a fancy education, although you always keep educating yourself along the way. I bet I don't have half the schooling most of you ladies have, but I try to learn something new every chance I get. This month my companion, Lottie, has been teaching me *Hamlet.* That's right! Do you think I'd ever studied any Shakespeare before? See, I'm not ashamed to say when I don't know something. How else would I ever learn it?"

Sarah's skin itched with adrenaline as she could feel the impact of her words coursing through the dozen attentive women, who looked so elegant in their brightly colored summer dresses, hats, and parasols. Sarah was very careful with her diction, still branded with the memory of how society ladies exactly like these had been so quick to dismiss her in Denver and Pittsburgh. She'd seen how quickly a single misplaced "ain't" could turn someone's face to stone.

"If I was afraid, I'd still be bent over a washtub. That's the biggest thing working against us, just being afraid. Afraid to look foolish. Afraid to try something new. Afraid to stand up. If we keep being afraid, our race will never have anything."

"Madam, tell them about the Isis," Lottie prompted gently, with pride.

"That's right!" Sarah said, and she told the women that she'd sued the Isis Theater in Indianapolis because of its policy of charging Negroes a higher price for tickets than whites. Sarah loved pictures, and she'd been so angry after seeing the price difference when she arrived at the theater with Lottie and her visiting niece Anjetta that she hadn't attended one since. "I won't be treated like I'm in a segregated Pullman train car every time I go to the movie house."

One dark, pretty young woman gasped aloud, then looked embarrassed that she'd drawn attention to herself. "Madam, down where I'm from, you'd get lynched for talking like that!"

"Well, some folks tried to say I'd get lynched in Indianapolis, too. But I tell you what, I'll see my moving pictures for a dime just like white folks, and not a penny more!"

The women laughed, and Sarah realized she had caught someone else's ear. The crowd around Dr. Washington had thinned enough for her to see his eyes, and they were resting on her like shining onyx stones, assessing her. When he began walking toward her, Sarah felt both nervous and electrified.

"Of course, there are times a little discrimination is *good*, Madam Walker," called an older, silver-haired woman who looked to be in her sixties. She spoke with great gentility, and Sarah hoped she wasn't about to be goaded into an argument with an old-timer who believed Negroes should be happy in their place. The woman went on: "What did the fighter Jack Johnson say? When he tried to board the *Titanic*, the steward told him, 'This ship doesn't haul coal!' That's the kind of discrimination against coloreds I don't mind one bit."

"Amen. And you see how it came out," said another woman. "Fifteen hundred dead!"

"Just goes to show, you don't tempt God," the older woman said again, with a prim nod.

The listeners agreed, making sympathetic sounds. The fascinating newspaper accounts of the *Titanic*'s survivors had helped Sarah and Lottie pass many hours on their train journeys since April. In fact, Sarah had wondered in the back of her mind if it might not be bad luck to take a steamboat tour so soon after that tragedy, but she'd dismissed that concern as pure superstition. Even if the boat sank, no one would freeze to death in *this* heat, that was for sure.

"I don't know if I believe Jack Johnson set foot anywhere *near* the *Titanic*," Dr. Washington spoke up, arresting the group's attention. His voice wasn't loud, but it was such a striking baritone that his words seemed to leap from his throat. "If Mr. Johnson tells you the time, I suggest you seek out a second opinion."

Everyone laughed, even though he'd spoken with a completely deadpan face. What was the word for him? *Stentorian.* Lottie had taught her that word, and it suited Dr. Washington perfectly. "Mr. Johnson likes to bring himself attention," Dr. Washington went on, his eyes still on Sarah. "But as I'm sure you can attest from your own experiences with your company, Madam Walker, excellence speaks far more eloquently than words."

Sarah felt a blush of pleasure at the compliment.

"Well, thank you, sir. I always tell my agents and culturists that exact thing! But sometimes excellence needs a little help, and a few words don't hurt."

"Well, I'm not at all surprised you started your business with so little and it grew so quickly each year, Madam," Dr. Washington remarked. "My wife has told me how energetic you were when you were at Tuskegee. All told, I'd say you're a perfect example of 'casting down your bucket where you are.' "

Sarah caught her breath, her heart dancing. She was ready to pour out her heart to Dr. Washington, to tell him how inspired she'd been to hear him say those words in St. Louis, how she'd been crossing the bridge with a load of laundry and decided to change her life. She was poised to frame the words when an unfamiliar hand touched her arm.

She turned to face a middle-aged white woman who had made her way through the crowd. Sarah recognized her as the wife of a man from the Chicago Association of Commerce who had welcomed the convention to town at the first session. Mrs. . . . Trask?

"Madam Walker? It's so fascinating to hear you say how we shouldn't be afraid, because I've been very interested in women's suffrage. May I ask you a question?"

Sarah looked down at the hand resting on her arm in a way that felt too familiar, like countless other white women who had felt free to touch her like property when she was washing their clothes. Lottie gave Sarah an irritated glance, and Sarah could almost hear her secretary's thoughts: *Just as soon as you have a chance to talk to Dr. Washington face-to-face, that white woman has the nerve to speak up and interrupt as if you're talking to any Joe Blow on the street.*

Mrs. Trask raised her voice slightly to be heard over the hissing steam engine. "Which has made your life more difficult, Madam Walker? Being Negro, or being a woman?"

The deck seemed to fall under a hush, except for the music and the boat's engine. Suddenly Sarah felt like a politician instead of a business-woman, searching for the right words. On the one hand, she could well understand why this woman would try to make a comparison. But on the other hand . . .

As Sarah noticed the diamond earrings dangling from Mrs. Trask's ears—earrings that had almost certainly been bought with her white hus-band's money—the question struck her as insulting. Had this woman ever lost a husband in a race riot? Had her parents ever been bought and sold? Would she ever live in fear that her son or brother might be lynched? Or that she might be casually raped by any drunken white man who consid-ered every Negro woman's private parts his own birthright? Lottie was breathing so loudly beside Sarah, bursting to speak, that she was afraid

Lottie would blurt out something that might not serve her well in the eyes of the Chicago Association of Commerce.

"Well, it's true both groups have had their cross to bear. I'd say all women deserve to vote every bit as much as Negroes do, and I'll be happy to see the day we can all cast our ballots freely," Sarah told Mrs. Trask in an even tone, holding her eyes. Sarah went on, as politely as she could muster: "But I sure hope you won't take offense if I speak frankly to you, ma'am. In my shoes, Mrs. Trask, it seems like only a white woman would even ask that question."

A collective sigh, nearly silent, rippled through her audience; Sarah had spoken their minds, men and women alike. The color seeped slightly from the woman's face, her lips thinning, and her fingers slipped away from Sarah's arm.

For only the second time Sarah had noticed in three days, Booker T. Washington's face had broadened with what was unmistakably a small smile.

Sarah grimaced as the train car bounced along the tracks. Thank goodness it was only a fairly short trip between Chicago and Indianapolis, but the hard wooden seat was already chafing her because the porter hadn't been able to find any spare pillows from the white sleeper cars, and the constant jouncing was irritating her ailment. As planned, she and Lottie had spent the day shopping with the wife of one of the delegates, who'd been so eager to show off the downtown department stores. But the adventure had tired her out, so Sarah had gracefully bowed out of their dinner plans with George Knox and the Newcombs. Despite the arguments from Lottie, who reminded her it was the first leisure time Sarah had spent in weeks, Sarah was ready to go home a day early. She couldn't wait to rest in her own bed again, at last.

Besides, the knowing voice in her mind had come back, urging her to go to C.J.

Sarah had relieved herself at the hotel before she left, her stream burning in a way she'd learned to recognize as trouble—and she hadn't been able to find any cranberries to help ease it before she and Lottie caught the train. The last thing she wanted was to have to relieve herself on the train, which would be that much worse with the bright, stinging pain. She hoped the tracks would smooth out and stop worrying her bladder.

To keep from thinking about her body's complaints, Sarah tried to concentrate on Lottie's soothing tones as she read to her from the Shakespeare volume. Sarah could read it for herself if she wanted to by now, even if it might be a struggle at points, but Lottie insisted Shakespeare was meant to be *heard*, not read. And despite the difficult language of

Shakespeare's time, Lottie's inflections were so true that Sarah rarely had problems following the story lines as she had when the lessons first began; the meaning was crystal-clear in Lottie's recitation, even if Sarah sometimes didn't recognize the words.

The play was nearing its end, Sarah knew, and Hamlet had some important decisions to make. She had a feeling the poor tortured boy was about to get himself killed.

"... 'Sir, in my heart, there was a kind of fighting that would not let me sleep. ...' "

Lottie was speaking Hamlet's lines, and Sarah understood exactly. Even after such a long day yesterday, between the session, the steamboat tour, and the lengthy evening banquet, she'd barely slept at all last night. But for once she hadn't been thinking about the company. She hadn't even been awake relishing the memory of how Booker T. Washington had promised to try to visit her headquarters someday, perhaps if he came to Indianapolis for the dedication ceremony for the YMCA. Even *that* wasn't what had kept her awake.

This time thoughts of C.J. had stolen her sleep.

"Did you have any questions about that passage, Madam?" Sarah said, pausing.

"I have a question, but not about *Hamlet*," Sarah said, barely recognizing the thick hollow of her own voice. She gazed solemnly at the flat prairie land passing by the window, streaked in fiery shades of gold and orange by the twilight sky. The train felt like a hotbox.

"What about, then?"

"What time do they expect this train to get us home tonight, Lottie?"

"It'll pull into the station by ten o'clock, if it's on time. Eleven at the latest."

All the moisture seemed to have been sucked from Sarah's mouth. "At eleven o'clock on a Saturday night, if C.J. isn't at home when I get there, where do you think I would find him?"

Sarah could see Lottie's reflection in the glass, and her secretary's face seemed to sag. Her perfectly painted lips fell open slightly. She didn't make a sound.

"You understand what I'm asking you, Lottie."

"Yes . . ." Lottie was looking at her lap.

"That's why you looked so scared when I said I wanted to leave early. Isn't it?"

Lottie's reflection didn't move or answer.

Not for the first time, Sarah longed for real *friendship* from Lottie, not just loyalty. This woman's reticence had been such an appealing quality before, giving Lottie an air of refinement and accomplishment Sarah had longed to adopt as her own, but now Sarah needed to communicate with the *person* underneath. Lottie and Mr. Ransom spent so much time trying to protect her that Sarah had lulled her own self into thinking there was nothing to be protected from. They'd all begun treating her as if she were some kind of fragile object in a curio cabinet. And she'd liked it, too. She'd liked having so many people standing between her and the truth.

"I think," Lottie began finally, "it's best you're going home tonight."

Sarah closed her eyes for a moment as part of her winced. But she had to push on. "Go on and tell me, Lottie."

"If he's at home, it would be the first Saturday night in a long time. So people say."

People? Sarah cringed to imagine how many people might already know what she was apparently to be the last to hear. But she *had* heard before, hadn't she?

"Tell me where I can find him," Sarah said.

At this, Lottie sighed so hard that Sarah could feel the other woman's breath puff against the back of her neck. "Are you really certain about that, Madam?"

"That's right, Lottie, I'm sure as death. Now speak up."

"The Hopkins Hotel on Indiana Avenue," Lottie said, then added in barely a whisper: "Room ten."

At that, Sarah whirled around to look at Lottie with wide eyes. Lottie had spoken those words as *fact*, not gossip, the sort of fact she had verified on her own—or that she'd heard from someone else who had. Had someone followed C.J.? Lottie herself? Mr. Ransom?

"How long?" Sarah breathed, her heart flipping.

Lottie cast her eyes down toward the book, which she had closed in her lap. "I think . . . some time after you and Mr. Walker came back from Jackson. Her name is Dora, an Indianapolis girl. She's one of your agents, Madam. You met her at Tuskegee—"

An agent! Weakly, Sarah held up her trembling palm in a silent plea for Lottie to hush.

Oh, Lord Jesus, help your child. As soon as Lottie said the girl's name, she'd roared to life in Sarah's memory. Dora. Dora Larrie. And her face came to her, too: so young! She'd had the sweetest girlish smile, and eyes so hungry with ambition. Sarah had liked those eyes, which had so mirrored her own, reminding her of how she had been hungry to build her life, too.

C.J. with Dora Larrie? How could anyone be so shameless? And right under her nose!

It couldn't be an accident, Sarah realized. Oh, God, it was painful enough to imagine C.J. filling his nights in a hotel with any random high-yellow who caught his eye . . . but Dora Larrie! That must mean there was more to it. A hungry woman like Dora was after something else from C.J., and either he was too stupid to see it or—

Sarah fought not to bring the next thought to her consciousness, but it bubbled up all the same. *Or C.J. is up to something. C.J. is with her right now, plotting against you.*

Then, like a voice from a nightmare, Lottie spoke Sarah's darkest fears aloud: "Madam, Mr. Ransom has been worried because Mr. Walker knows your formula. This all came to his attention by accident, because there is some money missing Mr. Walker could not account for. Mr. Ransom believes Mr. Walker may be planning a venture of some sort with this woman. He had Mr. Walker followed, and he and the woman have been to Atlanta more than once—"

Sarah let out a loud choking sound as she forced herself to swallow a sob back into her tight throat. She would not cry. Not here. Not on this train, where strangers would hear her.

Sarah had never fainted in her life, even the night she'd lost Moses, but now she could feel her body melting away from her as the train bumped along the tracks. Her stomach surged, then lay as still as a rock. And her face seemed to burst into flames that sent a feverish sensation all the way to her toes. She sat as still as a statue, unable to move.

Unexpectedly, Lottie clasped Sarah's hand and pulled it to her breast. Sarah could feel the racing of Lottie's own heart. "Madam, I've prayed so much over it. I wouldn't know anything at all of this matter, except I over-heard a conversation between Mr. Ransom and Mr. Walker. I wanted to say something, I swear to you. It broke my heart to have to keep silent—"

Sarah thought her words would tumble out of her mouth as screams, but instead she could barely hear herself over the whine of the train. "You should have told. Something like this? How could you . . . ?"

"Mr. Ransom wanted to choose the time, Madam. He forbade me. He'll be angry I said anything now. He was trying to handle it, and he said he didn't want to disrupt—"

"You should have told," Sarah hissed. Those were the only words that came to Sarah's mind, churning around in her head like the name Dora Larrie. "You should have . . . told."

"Oh, my goodness," Lottie said, her face wrenching with grief. "Madam, I'm s-sorry."

With a blind flash of anger, Sarah yanked her hand away from Lottie's grasp. As many times as she'd argued with Lelia and her wild-mouthed niece, Anjetta, she didn't think she'd wanted to strike anyone as much as she did right now. Not poor Lottie, but someone, anyone. The emotions swamping her were alien to her, stealing her breath and nearly dimming her vision. How could a day that had begun with a routine train ride have turned into this awful moment? Sarah stared at her trembling hand, momentarily not recognizing her own flesh. She would faint now, that was all. She would faint and wake up.

"Should I call a porter to bring you some water—"

"Get up," Sarah said, still little more than hissing. She already regretted her harsh tones, but she couldn't help herself. "I said *git*. Don't even *look* at me."

Her mouth fixed in an agonized O, Lottie frantically gathered her book and handbag together. "Oh, I told Mr. Ransom he was wrong, I swear I did. I told him not to keep it from you. He made me promise. . . ." Lottie tried to explain, even as she parted the blanket the porter had hung to give them privacy and scurried from her seat.

Something between Sarah's temples seemed to pop, and her crown suddenly felt weighed down by the worst headache she had ever known. As the train rocked its way toward Indianapolis, Sarah sat rigid in her seat, on the verge of nausea, waiting to faint.

But she never did.

After she walked through her front door, Sarah didn't bother to turn on any lights in the house, relying on the moonlight streaming through the windows to illuminate her way through the wide hallways. Even in the darkness, her wooden floors gleamed like smoked glass.

Oh, she loved this place! She loved its contours, its shadows, its scents of fresh paint and polished wood and new Oriental rugs. To her, this house always smelled like a new beginning, like the promise of everything she'd spent her life trying to build. But tonight the satisfaction she usually felt when she walked into her home had been smothered by a dread that made her entire frame feel stiff. She didn't even have to call out to know that no one was home except boarders.

Anjetta had been staying with her, but she remembered her niece was visiting friends in St. Louis this month. And C.J.? Well, she knew better than to expect him to be here. She knew by more than the darkness and quiet.

"C.J.?" she called out nonetheless, still hoping.

She thought she saw a movement, a phantomlike white shirt appearing in the doorway to her office at the end of the hall, but when she blinked she realized it was only a trick of the darkness. There was no one here except her. Sarah's legs carried her past the Gold Room and the library through the empty doorway that had fooled her. There, in nearly pitch black, she felt her way to the large mahogany rolltop desk where she kept her papers and letters. She opened the bottom drawer on the left side, a drawer she had opened only once, quite accidentally, and never again. This was C.J.'s drawer. Inside that drawer, her fingers were drawn to the metallic cold of the gun's nozzle. C.J.'s beloved derringer was still here.

She had to find him, and the Hopkins Hotel was in a bad part of town. She might very well need protection.

Without allowing herself to think, Sarah slid the gun into her purse.

She bounced it once, enjoying the unfamiliar metallic weight inside. She'd begun to breathe in rasps deep from her chest. It was so hot in here, too, she realized. It felt like none of the windows had been opened in days. A tomb, she thought. That was the word. Her house felt like a tomb.

Sarah went outside to get her automobile.

It didn't occur to her even once how much she hated to drive herself at night. As she got closer to her destination, navigating her Waverley toward Indiana Avenue, she even forgot to be worried about possibly being recognized by folks who would consider her a strange sight. The woman she was now—with a gun in her purse and a plan in her head that she'd hidden from herself in a darkness not unlike the stifling dark back at her house—couldn't care less about what such-and-such or so-and-so would think about seeing Madam C.J. Walker tooling around a questionable section of town at this time of night. All she saw were the dim pools of light from her car's driving lamps and the passing patterns of crushed stone and gravel on the roadway as she drove, her hands tight on the steering wheel. She pressed her foot harder against the stiff pedal, taking the car a hair above the twenty-mile speed limit.

The deserted pharmacies, cafés, law offices, and general stores on Indiana Avenue began to give way to the unseemlier businesses crowded on the opposite end. And the streets, which had been mostly deserted, began to crawl to life. Clumps of colored men, and a few women, appeared on the sidewalks, laughing, chatting, and walking jauntily. More than once Sarah thought she saw C.J. among them. A certain manner of dress. A special tilt of the head. But she stared hard at the faces each time, and as the features came into focus, they were always wrong.

She passed Mooney's Bar. Avenue Billiards. Then the Liza Hotel, which everyone knew was just a sporting house the law turned a blind eye to, men pooled in a raucous, eager overflow line outside its doors. Another block farther, with a boldly painted red sign, sat a squat brick building called the Hopkins Hotel. There, at the empty curb, Sarah brought her car to a stop. Her engine rumbled and ticked, then died.

Sarah's breathing had evened out during the drive, but her headache was back.

What am I doing out here? a faint voice in her brain wondered. But then the name Dora Larrie tightened around Sarah's chest like a vise, and she stumbled out of her car, giving the door a hard slam behind her. She walked past the faceless stream of cologne scents and perspiration-stained shirts to cross the hotel's threshold.

Inside, the spare, clean hotel was quiet. The only person in sight was the thin counter attendant, who looked so young that Sarah doubted if he was yet a man. The boy had a brush of facial hair above his lip so thin that it was nearly invisible. He raised his head from a magazine, startled to see Sarah. Maybe he recognized her, she thought.

"Is there a Mr. Walker in room ten?" she asked quickly.

"Uhm . . ." The boy paused, running his index finger across his register. "Ma'am, see, there might be a Mr. Walker in that room, see . . . but I ain't sure if . . ."

"Give me a key. Right now."

The boy eyed her as if he wanted to protest. She opened her handbag and pulled a five-dollar bill from inside. His eyes widened. Even after she extended the money, he still stared into the handbag. When he looked up at her, he looked as if he were going to be ill.

Taking the money, the boy turned and found a large brass key on one of the hooks hanging on the wall behind his desk. His fingers shook as he gave it to her. "Now, see, this here is a legitimate 'stablishment, and we don't want no . . ."

But Sarah had already whirled away from him, and she didn't hear his words. In fact, she couldn't hear anything. Her head felt puffed up, and the only thing in her ears was the sound of the blood rushing through her head, welling up from her furiously beating heart. Instinctively, she ignored the hallway on the lower floor and began to climb the hotel's wooden stairs. She felt as if she knew exactly where the room was, as if she had lived this moment before. With each clumping step on the staircase, her head whirled.

". . . Hear that? We don't want no trouble!" the boy shouted after her.

Well, if I find what I think I'ma find up there, you got some trouble whether you want it or not, Sarah thought. Or maybe she said it aloud. She didn't know.

Room ten was the third door on her right, at the end of the second-floor hallway. There, as if frozen by the sight of the black number painted in the center of the door, she stopped and caught her breath. Her chest heaved. Then, with her head strangely silent, she wrapped her hand around the butt of the gun, gingerly massaging the trigger with her index finger.

The whole thing was simple, really. If it was the wrong room—and it could be, really, her brain rattled, because there was a chance this was all one big mistake, that it wasn't *Charles* Walker in this room but someone else entirely—she would apologize to the occupant, make her way back down to her car, and go home to bed. But if she opened this door and saw C.J. inside, and if he was in there with that scheming little Tuskegee whore, well, she would—

Sarah's stomach dropped as she heard a low laugh float from beneath the doorway. Warm honey. Like a memory from a dead woman's life, she heard the sound of her very own warm honey, and yet it wasn't meant for her ears this time. That laugh had been for Dora.

Just go, a voice inside her pleaded. *Stop this foolishness and go back home.* She didn't want to fit the key into the lock and open the door. She didn't want to see the lamplit, startled faces in the bed, or the quiver of the woman's plump, bare breast before she flung the bedsheet over her naked-ness. She didn't want to see C.J.'s shamed, trapped eyes. And she didn't want to inhale the stench of their mingled sweat.

But she did. In one swift motion, as her body defied what was left of her mind, Sarah walked into that room and saw exactly what she didn't want to see. A glimpse of the skin she had caressed. A flash of his sloe-eyed tramp's perfect, heavy breasts, the slender waist that had never borne a child. She didn't even remember why Dora was cowering behind C.J. with a fit of screams until she looked down at her own hand and saw the gun.

"Now b-baby . . . what you gon' do with that?" C.J. said, his voice weighted down with fright. He held both palms out toward her as if to push the sight of her away. "What you bring that here for? Huh?" His voice was part cooing and coaxing, part panic. His handsomeness slapped her face, and in that instant she truly hated him.

"Why you look so surprised, C.J.?" Every word tore a hole in Sarah's throat. "Look like you must've wanted me to know. Didn't you? You got it so everybody in town knows. Well, ain't this what you wanted? You wanted me to find you with your yellow bitch. Ain't that right?" She prod-ded at him with the gun, and he flinched back. "Ain't that why you made it so easy for me? *Ain't* it?"

Struck dumb, C.J. could only shake his head back and forth. He mouthed the words *No, Sarah,* and tears sprang to his eyes.

"You're a goddamn liar!" she screamed at him. "You *know* you did!"

At that moment, C.J. uttered what Sarah would later remember as both the most courageous and damnable words she had ever heard come from his lips. Not blinking despite his tears, he lowered his chin and met her gaze dead-on. "Woman," he said in a soft, shaking voice, "since when do you care what the hell I want?"

Dora screamed again, as if she was certain C.J. had just become a con-spirator in her murder. "This ain't nothin'!" she cried through her screams. "M-madam, this ain't n-nothin'!"

Sarah's finger tightened on the trigger.

Since when do you care what the hell I want?

Once again, as she had on the train earlier, Sarah felt something in her head go *pop.* But this time it wasn't the prelude to a headache—although her headache was alive and well. This time she felt as if she'd suddenly snapped back into herself, and she could see the scene in the hotel room from a detached place high above. C.J. was lying in this tiny bed with some ninny. And Sarah Breedlove Walker was standing before them with a gun in her hand, aching to end his life and her own by firing it.

It was a sad, absurd sight. *Almost like something from Shakespeare him-self, ain't it?* Look at that fine woman, *the* Madam C.J. Walker, so exquis-itely dressed, about to throw away her own name and anything good that had come to be associated with it. Her company. Her freedom. Her whole life, potentially. What would Booker T. Washington say? Or Mary McLeod Bethune? *It's such a shock! I'd just met Madam C.J. Walker, and I thought she was a fine example for the race!*

And over what? Sarah suddenly realized that this man with a laugh like warm honey lying in this strange bed had nothing at all to do with her and her name. Madam C.J. Walker belonged to her now. Only her.

Sarah gasped as her rage gave way to anguish. She could barely breathe. "Nigger," she said, the hated word like poison in her mouth, "you ain't even worth this bullet. Y'all go on and do what you want. I'll pay you back every cent you ever lent me, plus interest, but if I find out you've stolen any money, you won't get nothin' else from me except another trip to jail, hear? I don't care if you live or die, C.J., so long as you stay away from my company. And God help you if you don't." Still watching the scene from above, Sarah saw Madam C.J. Walker turn around and walk briskly away through the open door. She came to the stairs so quickly that she nearly stumbled as she descended. For the first time all day, tears streamed freely down her face and she didn't give a damn who heard her sobs.

You were wrong. You were so wrong, she thought as she wove in near-blindness through the carefree Saturday-night streets. A sob pitched so loudly from her throat that it sounded exactly like one of Dora Larrie's begging screams.

Chicago and the National Negro Business League meeting seemed almost imaginary now, but Sarah suddenly remembered how the white woman, with the presumptuousness of wealth and racial privilege, had asked her whether it was more difficult to be a woman or a Negro. Like a fool, Sarah had been nearly rude to her, telling her the worst kind of flippant, awful lie to try to impress Booker T. Washington and all those fine colored folks. But Sarah hadn't known any better then. She just hadn't known. That night, driving away from her husband and his mistress with a fresh and bleeding wound in her soul, Sarah Breedlove Walker realized that being a woman was the hardest thing of all.

Chapter Thirty

OCTOBER 1912
(TWO MONTHS LATER)

"Mama?" Lelia called softly through Sarah's door. "It's official! Can we come in?"

Sarah's room was nearly dark, as she'd kept it purposely in the weeks since she'd been at home. Her heavy curtains were always drawn, blotting out any light that tried to reach inside. Sarah had never been in such a strange state; she felt as if she were nursing a long fever, even though Dr. Ward assured her that her temperature was normal and she didn't seem to be ill except for her blood pressure, which remained high. Often Sarah woke from naps in her grand bedroom and blinked several times as she glanced around the room and its regal furnishings, forgetting where she was. Then her eyes would find her father's photograph staring at her from its frame on her nightstand, and she would remember: *Yes, I live here. This is all mine.*

"Come in," Sarah said, her voice sounding thin. When the door opened, Lelia walked in with her arm resting on the child's shoulder. Mae was thirteen, and such a *lovely* child; she had a shy manner, a very pleasing brown face, and jet-black hair that grew so long she could actually sit on it. She'd been a Walker Company model for nearly a year, supplementing her impoverished mother's meager income. Mae and her siblings practically lived on the streets.

But that had all changed for Mae now.

"Here she is, Mama, your new grandbaby!" Lelia said, clapping her hands together.

"All the paperwork's done?" Sarah said.

"Yep! It's all legal in the courts. This is Mae Bryant Robinson, my own little girl. And I made a change for me, too, Mama—I'm A'Lelia *Walker* Robinson now, named for my mama."

Sarah sat up in bed, where she'd been reclining in her elegant robe.

Again, she felt distant from herself, as though her daughter's words were part of a misty dream. So Lelia had a child now, and Sarah had a granddaughter. Part of her must be overjoyed, she knew, but instead she still felt hollowed out. Another piece of paperwork had become final this month, too—her divorce from C.J. had been finalized as of October 5, only a few days before. Mr. Ransom, himself a newlywed, had helped her file for divorce in September. The court had finally made it real.

C.J. had been gone in spirit for months, and he'd been gone in the flesh ever since that last day she'd seen him at that hotel. But now he was gone by law. And she was still carrying his name, which sometimes felt like a wound, other times like a trophy. But Sarah's moods didn't matter; Madam C.J. Walker was the name people knew her company by, and it was a little too late to change it now, since the company had nearly 1,600 agents, and made weekly revenues close to one thousand dollars. The name had its own life, even on the days when Sarah went to bed with cramps simply after anyone uttered the word *C.J.* within her hearing, when her head whipped around, and she still expected to see him walk into the room.

"Come here, pumpkin," Sarah said to Mae, extending her arms. The petite child walked slowly toward her with a shy smile across her face, hardly looking Sarah in the eye. When she was close enough, Sarah leaned down to give her a warm hug. "Welcome to the family, child."

"Yes, Madam Walker," she said, nearly whispering.

"Don't you call me Madam now. You can call me Grandmother."

Mae was silent. Sarah glanced up at Lelia's beaming face, then back at Mae's. The sadness in this child's eyes was unmistakable. What was wrong? Was she sad her mother had agreed to give her up? Or had she carried this sadness her entire hard life? Gazing into Mae's eyes, Sarah remembered well how it felt to be tossed to and fro as a child, helpless. But Mae would be better off as part of the Walker family, Sarah knew. God willing, Lelia would begin setting a better example and try to be a good mother.

"Why don't you run down to the kitchen, Mae?" Sarah said. "There's fresh biscuits in the kitchen, and I'm sure there's one with jam waiting for you."

"Yes'm!"

Once Mae had marched out of the room, Lelia twirled around, giggling. "Mama, isn't it *great?* I'm a mother! And that hair of hers is so pretty, folks go wild for her. Wish mine grew that long! I can't wait to take her for demonstrations down in—"

"Did you really adopt that child, Lelia? Or did you adopt her head of hair?"

Lelia's face fell. "Well, that question's an insult, Mama. But I guess if you're feeling well enough to insult me, you must be back to your old self. I should think you'd be more grateful—"

"Oh, Lelia, please hush, child," Sarah said, weary. She patted the bed, and Lelia climbed up to sit next to her. Sarah leaned against her daughter. "Don't go having a fit. No, I'm not back to my old self. I can't hardly get out of bed one day to the next. And I *am* grateful, baby—I don't know where I'd be without you. I'd have cried myself to the grave, I expect."

"No, you wouldn't have, Mama," Lelia said, kissing her cheek. "I know you better."

For a moment Sarah just enjoyed the feeling of resting her head on her daughter's firm shoulder. Lelia had been such a big help these past two months! Sarah had been so humiliated by the disaster with C.J. that she'd nearly felt ashamed to show her face in her new city. Just as she'd begun to make inroads into the colored social circles, her personal life had overshadowed her; now, she heard, many of the monied families had dismissed her as trash. And could she blame them? It was all so torrid! C.J. had cashed some checks made out to the Walker Company and pocketed more than a thousand dollars of company funds he'd planned to use to start his own company with Dora Larrie. Mrs. Larrie, apparently, had plans to divorce her husband so she could marry C.J. Vaguely, Sarah wondered if C.J. still had his little honey up in Kansas City, too.

Well, that was Dora Larrie's problem now, not hers. Sarah shook her head, sighing.

"I thought having a granddaughter would cheer you up," Lelia said, stroking Sarah's head.

"Oh, it does, Lelia. I just worry, that's all," Sarah said. "It's a big responsibility, raising a child. And that one's so reserved, like she was born grown!"

"She'll get warmer toward us, Mama. It's a big change for her."

"Don't I know it!" Sarah said. She'd married Moses when she was just a little older than Mae, she remembered. "You take care to give that girl lots of love, and don't just put her to work. It's a blessing to raise a child, Lelia, but it's not a substitute for a man."

"Mama, I'm surprised at you! After the horror you've just been through . . ."

"Yes, that's right. Just because . . . I feel like I do about C.J. doesn't mean I expect you to give up on marrying, too. I made mistakes, Lelia. I had a hand in this thing, just like you had a hand in what happened with John Robinson. So it's not sour just on the men's side. That girl Mae should have a papa, too. I'd give anything to have had mine for even a year or two longer. And God knows I think you'd be better for it if you'd had Moses. . . ."

Cheerfully, Lelia pinched her mother's cheek. "But I didn't, Mama, and I turned out fine! So let's stop all this talk about marriage. I don't think matrimony agrees with either one of us, and we'd better just accept that fact. Any men we meet now would just be sniffing after our money anyway. You know that, don't you?"

Sniffing after her money! Sarah paused, momentarily struck by the truth of her daughter's words. She'd never thought of it before now, and it was so hard to believe! She, Sarah Breedlove, had enough money to draw undesirable men who preyed on women with fortunes. After C.J., she'd begun to fear that perhaps a woman could have *too* much money!

"We're rich, Lelia," Sarah said softly, as if realizing it for the first time.

"Awfully, terribly rich!" Lelia said, squeezing her mother's hand hard. "And now we have someone to pass it to when we're gone, Mama. The Walkers have an *heiress*. Don't you see?"

Sarah raised her head, searching her daughter's eyes. "Is that why you did it, Lelia? Is that why you adopted that child?"

Lelia smiled sadly. "She was living on the streets, and I can give her anything she wants. I want her to love me," Lelia said, her eyes earnest. "Is that really so selfish?"

Looking into Lelia's eyes, Sarah couldn't bring herself to say a word against it.

Sarah couldn't remember the last time she'd walked through the arched doorway of Bethel AME Church in Indianapolis, the church she'd adopted after her move to the city. It had been a cruel trick of God's, she thought, to give her everything she'd dreamed of in exchange for yet another husband. Besides, she couldn't bear the thought of the staring eyes of people who would have heard the stories about her. That was her own fault, wasn't it? She'd made herself so famous here now that her very bedroom was fodder for the gossip of strangers.

Take the good with the bad, C.J. had said. Words from the best friend she'd ever known.

You stupid fool, C.J., Sarah thought, gazing at the large brick church's entrance with a pounding heart. *Why'd you have to try so hard to make me hate you? Is that the only way you knew I'd let you go?*

"Come on, Mama," Lelia urged softly, hooking her arm inside Sarah's. Her entire family was assembled outside of the church to go with her today: Mae, Anjetta, and even Lou. It was time she got out of the house, they'd all decided. It was time for her to go on with her life. Already, as worshipers walked past them to go inside, Sarah saw the curious eyes, a few discreet whispers. But mostly she saw smiles. And something else, she realized . . . Respect.

A young man tipped his hat, stepping aside so she could walk in before him. "Morning, Madam Walker," he said. As Sarah walked into the sanctuary with her family, heads swiveled around to follow them. Sarah paused as she stood in the center of the aisle, humbled by the sight of the massive pipe organ directly in her path, behind the pulpit; the brass pipes reached the ceiling, framed between two carved pillars and the blue-and-rose-tinted stained-glass windows.

"You 'member you saw that lady, hear?" Sarah heard a mother whisper to a young child. "That's Madam C.J. Walker. She's the richest colored lady in the world. You can get anything you want in life, if you just pray and work hard, just like her."

The richest colored lady in the world. Mr. Ransom always told her she was well on her way to earning that place. She *could* be someday, couldn't she? She'd found herself a miracle, and there was no telling where it would end. She could be *great* just like Booker T. Washington, a beacon for her race. All she had to do was try!

"Come on, Mama. You can do it," Lelia urged quietly, believing she'd lost her nerve. In truth, Sarah had just regained it like never before.

Chapter Thirty-one

February 4, 1913

Mother,

    I am so excited to hear you have changed your mind about helping me move to New York. I promise you'll never have reason to regret it. New York is the place to be, Mother. There are so many Negroes coming to Harlem now, and I am convinced we can build a Walker parlor there that would put us on par with anyone, white or colored. I know you are worried about the Pittsburgh office, but I will find a suitable forelady to help Sadie before I move. I've grown too bored and wretched in this place, which reminds me of John. In New York I am a new person. Once you spend more time there, you'll want to move, too. You'll see!

    Love,

    Lelia

    P.S. Mae and Sadie both send you their love. I have heard from Mr. Ransom's wife, Nettie. They seem the perfect couple to me. How nice to have married a college sweetheart! I'm happy there is still some romance left in this age.

May 27, 1913

Mrs. Lelia W. Robinson
592 Lenox Avenue, Apt. 12
New York City

My Dear Mrs. Robinson:

I hope it will not be long before I am able to enjoy a long-
overdue visit to your new home. Madam has completed
her real estate purchases in Gary, and is now the proud
owner of a 13-passenger Cole Motor Car. The car is quite
a sight, sure to turn heads, so I know you will admire it.
Given these purchases, however, I wish you would help
me encourage Madam to bank as much money as possible
so it can draw interest and protect you against unforeseen
hard times. Madam could soon be the wealthiest colored
person in America, and I would like to help her reach
that goal. Can I depend on your help?

Respectfully,
F.B. Ransom

September 1, 1913

Dearest Lelia,

*Well, you are the only one who thinks it's a good idea for me to go overseas
now to make a name, but you always give me a boost when everyone else says
"Don't." I'm just sorry your hands are so full building the house in New York.
This trip is shaping up so nicely in a short time! I am taking my touring car, and
we would have had so many nice hours together. I'll be leaving next month,
visiting Jamaica, Costa Rica, Haiti, and the Panama Canal Zone. Lottie speaks
French and a little Spanish, so she will get plenty of practice. Yes, I'll take care
not to get sick near the canal. I have heard those stories, too.*

*Now, Lela, I've already told you I don't want Mae to miss so much school.
I agree that travel is a good education, and Mae is a wonderful model when she
travels with me, but I think she is too young for this overseas trip. As for you
wanting more time to yourself—now you know how taxing motherhood can be!*

Love,

Mother

*P.S. No, my penmanship has not improved this much. I dictated this note
to Lottie. She says hello!*

Lelia College　　　　　　**Walker's Hair Parlor**
New York City　　　　　　　Brooklyn office
108 West 136th Street　　　　300 Bridge Street

December 7, 1913

My Dear Mr. Ransom:

Am writing you to do a friendly turn for me, am dodging behind you to keep the bullets from hitting me. I have never told Mother the final outcome of this house. I thought somehow or other I could come out of it without bothering her again. I am enclosing the estimates.

Now I know, Mr. Ransom, Mother has been wonderful to me. She has been so good until I know it seems an imposition, and so it is, for me to say money to her again. That is why I am getting behind you. If Mother was only here on the job. She could see and know; that is why I want her to come on over to New York. You can trust me when I say the home is wonderful!

Whatever you do, don't let her get sore at me and bawl me out, for I am certainly one nervous child. Am expecting house to be complete enough for us to move into it in the next two weeks so I will have to have the money right away.

Give my love to Nettie and kiss babies for me. I realize I have certainly imposed some task on you but you'll have to be to me what the Carpathia was to the Titanic.

Anxiously awaiting your answer.
Sincerely,
Lelia W.R.

INDIANAPOLIS RECORDER
Weekly Newspaper Devoted to the Best Interests of the Negroes of Indiana

SATURDAY, MARCH 21, 1914

C.J. WALKER SAYS: "As You Reap So Shall You Sow"
FORMER HUSBAND OF WELL-KNOWN HAIR
MANUFACTURER REGRETS PAST LIFE

To the Freeman:
Dear Sirs: Will you give me space in your valuable paper to warn men against the use of strong drink and women?

I had the best, purest, and noblest woman Christ ever died for, but I let drink and this designing evil woman come between us and now I am a wreck on life's great sea, with no hope of anchoring. She made me believe I was being treated badly by Mme. Walker because she did not let me handle all the money, not withstanding the fact I had no responsibility, not even my clothes to buy and with $10.00 per week to spend as I pleased.

I was foolish enough to let her persuade me to leave the woman I still love better than life.

By making me believe, with my knowledge of making the goods, and her ability to do the work, and talk, we could make thousands of dollars, and I would be master of the situation. She closed her work at Tuskegee and came to me. We did not do so well under the name of the "Walker-Larrie Co.," so she planned to get a divorce so we might marry, which she did, and on March 4th, we were married by Rev. Jackson. We were not married long before I discovered she did not love me, but that she only wanted the title Mme. and the formula. The latter, I refused absolutely to give.

My life has been a hell since she went so far as to have me put in jail, said I was interfering with her business, when in truth, the business was my own, a thing Mme. Walker would never have done. She also tied up what little mail there was coming in, so I could not get a cent. All I got was ten cents on Sunday for paper and shoe shine. I left her but she threatened to have me arrested for wife abandonment, so I had to stay and try to get enough money to get out of Louisville, which I found impossible to do as everyone was so prejudiced against us, so I had to appeal to my sister for help. Had it not been for her, and her dear husband, I would have been crazy by this time.

I am here in a strange land, among strangers, broken in health and spirit, but happier than I have been for months. If I get well I mean to start life anew.

I don't ever want to see Dora Larrie's face in life, as she is the cause of all my sorrow. Our lives together have been a complete failure.

—C.J. WALKER

June 5, 1914

Dear Mr. Walker:

I assure you, I have passed your letters on to Madam Walker. You may have heard that she is currently on a

very busy tour of the Northeast, so she has been unable to
provide a response. She is very sorry you have been ill,
and we both wish you a speedy recovery. I hope in the
future, however, you will refrain from any mention of
reconciliation with Mme. Walker, as she becomes very
irate when you speak along that line. She has made her
thoughts on this matter very clear, I think. In the future, I
would suggest you limit your inquiries to business.

Respectfully,
F.B. Ransom

July 31, 1915

Dear Mr. Ransom,
    *Am writing to let you know I have given a check for $1,381.50 to the
Cadillac Motor Co. Won't you see to it that the check is cashed. If there isn't
enough in the bank place it in there out of your reserves. I guess you think I am
crazy but I had a chance to get just what Lelia wanted in a car that had been used
a little. It was worth $2,650 and I got it for $1,381.50. Since I was going to
give her one for Xmas I thought I had better snatch her one, as it would save me
money. Just received a letter from Willie and he can't find any work to do.
Would you think about me letting him come there? He could work for me and he
and his mother live in the house, since I am not going to be in Indianapolis. I
would rather that than always sending him money, as it makes him so dependent.*
    *Write me how everything is getting along. Also what my balance is. Love to
Nettie and babies. Best regards for yourself. Am leaving today for Colorado
Springs.*
    Yours,
    Madam

August 2, 1915

Madam C.J. Walker
Salt Lake City, Utah

Dear Madam,

To answer your question, I don't fear for your sanity, but I
do worry about your bank balance. My only consolation is
the knowledge that you cannot possibly find anything else
left to buy! Ha, ha.

Regarding your nephew Willie, I share your relief that he
is finally free, but I do not believe you should invite him
to have such close contact with you. His mother is
already behaving as if your home is her palace, and I fear
Willie would adopt the same attitude. He is an adult, and
he should find a job on his own. If he's having difficulties
where he is, then he should move. There is no good
reason he can't support himself. I know you will act as
you see fit, but I felt it was only fair to warn you.
Sometimes, Madam, your heart is too kind.

Nettie wanted me to let you know she is bored silly when
you go traveling. Frank B., who is proud to remind
anyone who will listen that he is your godson, hardly
opens his mouth without mentioning "Ma Walkie's giant
car." And your gift to your daughter will make her look
exactly like the heiress she is! We all send our love.

Respectfully,
F.B. Ransom

September 1, 1915

Dearest Mother,
I am thrilled to hear your news! You seem to have had so much fun
entertaining and showing slide presentations of your travels that I feared you
would never want to leave Indianapolis. I hoped you would finally see the
difference in people for yourself and decide to come here. All other cities are so
backward compared to New York. I am already spreading word that you will
make your home here, and you should see the excitement! Many people find it
hard to believe you have 20,000 agents making a good living, all due to your
hard work, but we both know it is the truth. How many others can say the same
thing?
I still laugh when I imagine us frantically mixing up the formula in your
kitchen. It is all so long ago, and yet not long ago at all. There are many days I
want to pinch myself to make sure it is not just a dream. Money comes and goes
so fast, it's almost like it isn't real at all. Yes, I am trying to be careful. And with
you here to watch over me, I will have no choice!
Love,
Lelia
P.S. Enclosed are details of further expenses. I need the money
right away.

LELIA COLLEGE
FOR
TREATING AND TEACHING
MME. WALKER'S
METHOD OF
HAIR GROWING

The Mme. C.J. Walker Mfg. Co.
640 N. West Street
Indianapolis, Ind.
New Phone. 5232-K
Old Main 7256

MANUFACTURING OF
Mme. Walker
Wonderful Hair Grower

BRANCH OFFICES
New York City
108 West 136th Street
Phone. Morningside 7883

Pittsburgh, Pa.
6258 Frankstown Ave.
East End
Phone. Hiland 5409

1449 West 35th Place
Los Angeles, Calif.
September 9, 1915

My Dear Mr. Ransom:
All of your letters received. Thank you very much for your prompt attention. I also received Nettie's letter yesterday; also from F.B. Jr. Bless his little heart. I am so anxious to see him; but I fear I will not be able to reach home before the latter part of November, as there is a great demand for my work throughout the West.

My sister-in-law and the girls accepted the offer, and Anjetta and Mattie are here now; the other girls will come later with their mother. I just sent them their fare. I know you think I am awful, but this has cost me more than I planned; yet, I think it best as I have to help them, and I had just as well put them upon their feet so they can make good for themselves.

Just had a letter from Lela and she has informed me that she found that her renovation will cost ten thousand dollars. She has asked for an additional loan of four thousand. I have sent her the check. Will you kindly go to the bank and get my balance; see if there is sufficient amount to cover the same? If not, you make arrangements so they will honor my check.

Concerning loans, I am glad you notified all persons against whom I am holding notes, and I do want you to enforce payments. At the rate Lela is going, I won't be able to build my house this year, unless I have the money.

I am sure that this trip is going to add two or three thousand per month to my income. I am getting invitations from many of the ministers of the surrounding towns, asking me to come give lectures. I am succeeding in making agents wherever I go.

I leave Saturday night for San Diego; then will come back here after a week, and will then make two or three other little towns before leaving for Frisco.

With best regards to Nettie and Frank, and all the home crew, I am:
Respectfully yours,
Madam

October 24, 1915

Now, Madam, I know you are still sore but that is no reason to pretend you do not care if I live or die. I am hurt you have not written me back even once to ask after how I have been doing. I hope you will let the past be the past and still be a friend in my life, which is nothing without you. You are still my Black Rose. Every time I read notices about you in the papers I puff up with pride. And I know you still care for me, too. Just thinking of you.

Yours,
C.J.
P.S.—I am four months sober.

LELIA COLLEGE
FOR
TREATING AND TEACHING
MME. WALKER'S
METHOD OF
HAIR GROWING

The Mme. C.J. Walker Mfg. Co.
640 N. West Street
Indianapolis, Ind.
New Phone. 5232-K
Old Main 7256

MANUFACTURING OF
Mme. Walker
Wonderful Hair Grower

BRANCH OFFICES
New York City
108 West 136th Street
Phone. Morningside 7883

Pittsburgh, Pa.
6258 Frankstown Ave.
East End
Phone. Hiland 5409

November 1915

Dear Mr. Ransom,

Your letter containing the report of Booker T. Washington's funeral received. So glad you were able to get there in time. I knew if anyone cared it would be you.

It gave me much pleasure to know even though I was so far away I was represented so beautifully. His death touched me so forcibly that I am sure or I fear that I would have acted unwomanly at the funeral. I have never lost anyone, not even one of my own family, that I regret more than I do the loss of this great and good man, for he is not only a loss to his immediate relations but to the race and the world. Even yet I can't picture him dead. And to think he was a young man, only fifty-eight, with so much yet to accomplish, but God knows best and we must bow our heads in humble submission to his will. Peace be unto his ashes.

Yes, I, too, will miss Thanksgiving dinner with you and your family. I guess it will be a long day before we have another Thanksgiving dinner together again since I am going to be so far away. Thank you very much for having sister over for dinner. Give Nettie and the babies my love. Tell little Frank I will soon be home.

I am suffering now with a dreadful cold, the first I have had since leaving home. I have been in bed two days. I had a lecture last night. Tried to get out of it, but the minister would not hear of it. He said if I would only put in an appearance he would be satisfied, for the people were so very anxious to see me.

Love to you, Nettie, and babies from Mae and I.

Sincerely,

Madam

September 1, 1916

Dear Lelia:

Really! What's all this I hear about your being in debt and unable to pay? I would have thought that by now you would be better able to balance what you spend with what you owe. You really do have to learn to be more responsible! You did so well with Pittsburgh for a while that I had started to think you had finally matured, but these reports from New York are disappointing to me. Tell me how much is still owed and I will pay it, but after this I want to take control of your mail-order business and begin processing ALL orders through Indianapolis. This is much easier for me to keep track of and will be less of a hardship for you. I am thinking the house in New York must be too much of a burden to you. Have your brains been addled by too much drink?

Not much time to write now, but we will discuss later.

Mother

Headquarters, Indianapolis, Ind.

WALKER'S HAIR PARLOR

New York City
110 West 136th Street
Phone. Morningside 7883

Brooklyn office
782 Fulton Street
Phone. Prospect 9410

LELIA COLLEGE

November 16, 1916

Mr. F.B. Ransom
19 E. Market St.
Indianapolis, Indiana

My very dearest Friend:

Your consoling letter received just this minute, and I am answering immediately. Mother reminds me of the story of the cow who gives the good pail of milk and then kicks it over. If I am to be confronted with this house or threatened with the loss of it every time it pleases Mother I cannot enjoy it and would rather not have it. Mother is just like an impulsive baby. I am no Breedlove. I am a McWilliams and that impulsiveness does not run in my blood.

I do not want to be dependent on anyone. Whenever I am entirely dependent upon Mother, as you say, there will certainly be a clash. Mother rules with an iron hand and forces her opinion on me regardless of what I may think, and if Mother and I should have any controversy I would far rather move away to some little Western town, Oakland, Calif., for instance, open a hair parlor there and buy my preparations from Mother and have peace of mind and freedom.

I have never sauced Mother in my life and I did not want to have a long argument about anything. She does not know she has made me so angry about it, but her letter has made me do some tall thinking. Contentment in a two-room flat beats being pulled around by the nape of the neck, whether it be sister, brother, husband, or mother.

Tell Nettie I am sending her a fur coat. I hope it will fit her. My love to the babies and kiss them for me.

With love I am,
Sincerely,
Lelia

November 20, 1916

Dearest Lelia,

Excuse hand writing. Lottie is asleep and I am writing this myself. I have been thinking over my last note and I think I have been to hard on you. I am so happy this is my last tour in the south becuase I cannot stand the strain even in my own car instead of those awful railroad cars. There is so much hard ship and poverty every where and so many bad memories. I am gratefull I can give a trade, but no matter how many new agents I sign there are all ways so many people who seem helpless and hopeless.

I am not feeling well at all but I will go to Hot Springs to rest in a few weeks. Could you join me for the holidays?

I was in a bad spirit when I wrote you, my darling but it was not your fault. Some days I think you should be happy you never had a sister! After all I have done for Lou and Willie you would think she would be more gratefull. I have told Mr. Ransom I wish I could send them both to a small farm somwhere to raise chickens and pigs and be on there own. The more I do the more people want from me. Some days I wish I had less, except for the good I can do with the money.

I know you are not like Lou, dear Lelia, so let me take back my harsh words. I am only afraid you do not relize how easy we could lose everything we have worked so hard for. There are many more hair formulas being sold than when we started, and I fear it will only get worse.

And you would be horified by the reports I am hearing about the treatment of Negroes in the south. We had word of another lynching only yesterday. No wonder so many Negroes are fleeing to northern cities! I am treated like a queen during my lectures and then like a vermin when I want to take a room, find a meal, or have a bath. I can never forget that for all the good luck for Walker Co. there is so much hardship for all the Negroes in these times. So many things your father gave his life for are still held from us. I think sometimes I can hear his sad angry voice in my ear.

With the talk of joining the war my spirits are gloomier still. But the one good thing would be if Negro soldiers could fight and prove how brave and patriotic I know we can be. Then the whites would have no choice but to give us our respect at least that is what I pray. I miss you, my darling daughter.

With much love,

Mother

P.S. I did not want to be so mean when I wrote you about drink. But we have both seen the result on C.J. and I would hate to see you fall the same way. I want to write him but when ever I begin the words turn sour and I crumble up the notes. I feel the C.J. I married is dead. I wish nights were not so long and I did not have so much time to think. As usual I can't sleep for thinking!

Chapter Thirty-two

*T*he train.

Sarah's eyes flew open and she heard herself gasping as she sat up in her bed. The image that had roused her from sleep was still as distinct as a photograph: the rear of a train car backing toward her, ready to crush her with its great weight and speed. She could feel her pulse fluttering in her neck, making it hard to breathe. *Just a dream. It's just a dream, Sarah.*

But it wasn't really just a dream, was it? The train had nearly taken her, and the image of the day still haunted her even all these weeks later. She'd just finished her engagement at a Clarksdale church, stirring the women in the congregation up into an enthusiastic fury, and she'd been looking forward to a home-cooked dinner that had been promised to her by a deacon's wife. Her driver, Lewis, was taking a leisurely pace as he drove them across the railroad tracks, toward their host's home. Then Lottie had heard a frantic shout. *Get out the way!*

Sarah saw Lottie's head turn suddenly, and so she followed her gaze, whipping her head around in time to see the terrifying sight: A train was backing toward them at a good clip, ready to snuff out all of them. She could see the flaking paint on the rear railing, the coarseness of the train's wooden car, even a lone white ribbon someone had tied to the railing dangling limply. Sarah would never forget those details. She'd memorized that moment because it was the exact moment she had believed to her soul that she was about to die. She'd felt a certainty like none she'd ever known, even when she'd had her premonition that she had finally lost C.J. for good.

Thank goodness for Lewis's quick reflexes! He sped the car forward, and Sarah's eyes were riveted as that white ribbon on the train railing seemed to graze her nose just before the car flung her to safety. It had been hours before Sarah could stop shaking, and even the lure of the meal she'd been looking forward to couldn't urge her from her room that night. To think that a train would have been at that precise spot when her car was crossing the tracks, without even so much as a bell to warn drivers to stay clear. Sarah couldn't help feeling the train *had* been meant to take her that day, and only grace had saved her. Had she done enough to deserve her reprieve?

Sarah turned on her electric bedside lamp and reflected on everything she had done and still had left to do. Her business, it seemed, was charmed; every time Sarah thought the explosive growth might bury them all, good and competent workers came to her to help carry the weight. There were so many good women—Lottie, Sadie, Indianapolis forelady Alice Kelly, secretary Violet Davis Reynolds, bookkeepers Marie Overstreet and Mary Flint—and they had become a close team. Like any team, they had their quarrels, but all of them worked hard for Walker Manufacturing Co. And where would she be without Mr. Ransom and his family? Despite the formality of their address, since he always called her *Madam* and she never used his Christian name even though they had long become good friends, she knew they loved each other as well as any family members. Many days, in fact, Mr. Ransom's family felt better suited to her than her own; Frankie, her godson, seemed more like a grandchild. And Mr. Ransom's wife, Nettie, was more a sister than Lou could ever hope to be.

Together they had all created something that felt more and more like destiny. Walker Manufacturing Co. had a life all its own. That life was waiting for her in the little towns she visited, when people gathered so eagerly to see her and hear her speak. That life was pulsing in home beauty salons, where so many women were supporting their whole families because of *her* guidance, *her* inspiration. Oh, there were frustrations and occasional disputes with her agents—and some mean-hearted person had even begun circulating rumors that she'd made her fortune as the madam of a sporting house in Pittsburgh, such an outrageous lie that Sarah had cried when she first heard some people close to her actually *believed* it—but at the root of it all, the life was always there. She knew there were people now who looked at her with an admiration much like she'd felt for Booker T. Washington. And although she didn't believe she deserved as much credit as he did, she'd grown to understand that people were desperate to have someone to believe in because that belief alone could stir up all the hard work and innovation inside *them*.

So Sarah had tried to do her part. And she'd had her fun along the way, too. In New York she didn't seem to carry any of the stigmas that had followed her in Denver, Pittsburgh, and Indianapolis; at her beautiful town house on 136th Street, Sarah was considered among Harlem's elite, and her dinner invitations were eagerly accepted. Sarah knew there was no black leader she could not reach if she wanted to; her days of desperately trying to get the attention of the likes of Booker T. Washington were over. Her money had bought her access anywhere she wanted.

And look at her now! Here she was at a resort frequented mostly by wealthy whites, living in luxury accommodations so generously provided to her by the Negro organization Knights of Pythias, which kept a bath-house for its members. She, Lottie, and Lelia all had their own rooms, with fresh sheets, towels, gourmet meals, and the intoxicating hot mineral waters of the resort at their disposal.

But the price!

At that, Sarah sighed deeply, and she could feel weariness weighing down her bones even now, after a long night's sleep. A kindly doctor in Mississippi had warned her before she came to Hot Springs that she was on the verge of a nervous breakdown, and she didn't doubt it. Even after all the soaking she could stand, sometimes she felt her breakdown was only biding its time. She barely recognized herself when she caught her reflection in her bathroom mirror; she seemed to have aged years in only a short time, and her tailored clothes sometimes struck her as so odd and different from the clothes she'd worn all the earlier years of her life, as if she'd borrowed them from someone else. Half the time she still expected to see herself wearing a rag on her head. She felt as if she were dreaming, and she was so easily confused now. She'd just complained to Lelia that she hadn't received an expected letter from Mr. Ransom, but Lelia had patiently pointed out that she'd read a letter from him just the day before! What was wrong with her?

Sarah had felt tired before, but nothing to rival what she felt now. She sometimes felt so bored in this sedate place that she wanted to scream, but at the same time she was usually too weary to ask Lottie to dictate any letters for her. The minute details of her business that usually fueled her imagination now seemed to be clogging it, choking it. She was hungry for news from the outside—it seemed it would be only a matter of time before the U.S. would join the war in Europe—but any news she read always left her feeling low and empty. The world was marching on outside without her, and she was too tired to walk, much less march.

And each day felt like every other, with dreams of the train almost every night.

Later that day, sharing a hot bath with Lelia amidst clouds of steam in a private area of the resort, Sarah shared her thoughts with her daughter. "I just don't know, child. . . ." Sarah sighed. "Your mama's a mess."

Lelia had taken to wealth like a duck to water. With her head wrapped tightly in a towel, she leaned against the tiles with the utter serenity of a woman who had been frequenting spas her entire life. "We told you about all this running around, didn't we, Mama?" Lelia said. "My doctor says

I need to get more rest too, but I know how to sit still more than you ever did."

"Well, I'll tell you the truth, Lela. . . . Some days I feel like I ain't done a damn thing."

Alone with her daughter, far from the watchful eyes and ears of Lottie and the expectations of the crowds she spoke to, Sarah felt at ease lapsing into her less practiced ways of speaking, softening her enunciations, no longer monitoring herself for poor grammar. In her mind now, it was almost as if Madam C.J. Walker was someone wholly separate from Sarah Breedlove. She loved both sides of herself, but lately she was grateful she could be Sarah for a while. Madam C.J. Walker carried a weight on her shoulders that was harder for Sarah to bear.

Sarah admired the palm plants lining the baths in their colorful ceramic pots, creating the tropical feel she'd enjoyed so much while she was traveling in the Caribbean. Now *there* was a place that knew how to slow down and relax, Sarah thought. As hard as she'd been working during those months overseas, a part of her had still felt like she was on a glorious vacation. Those incredible beaches . . . and the pure ocean water, like liquid sky . . .

"You still having bad dreams, Mama?" Lelia asked her suddenly.

"I just look at those dreams as messages, Lela," Sarah said. "Now that I think on it, I'm glad about what happened in Clarksdale. Helped wake me up. I won't be here forever."

All of the doctors were wrong about her, she decided. It wasn't that she didn't *believe* Dr. Ward and her other physician friends when they told her she would die if she didn't keep her blood pressure down. She could feel differences in her body already: she urinated more often, but her stream was sometimes only a dribble and had an unusual foamy quality; she battled headaches and awful sore throats; and then there was this strange, new brand of fatigue, which was the scariest part of all. No, she believed them, all right. Perhaps she just didn't believe she could help it, with so much left to be done.

Lelia had dark spots under her eyes, too, Sarah noticed, probably from the strain of trying to combine her business life and social life in New York. More social than business, according to Nettie and others who visited. Lelia liked entertaining a certain set of artists and writers, folks who lived fast lives and kept strange hours. Some days, she'd been told, Lelia didn't climb out of bed until past noon. Sarah traveled too much to observe Lelia as much as she thought she should, but she didn't doubt that her daughter's perpetual debt problems were because she spent too much time playing.

Suddenly a concern loomed large in Sarah's mind: What would happen to the company if she left it in Lelia's hands? Mae already seemed much more prim and responsible than her mother, but she was only eighteen, and she'd just gone away to school at Spelman. Mae was too young to take over such a responsibility.

"Mama, you're only forty-nine. Through pure stubbornness, you'll be here longer than anybody I know," Lelia said, smiling, as she took a sip from her tall glass of lemonade. The dripping glass suddenly made an image flash across Sarah's mind, a longing for lemonade she'd felt as a child. She couldn't remember the details, but she knew it had been an awful, hopeless time. The memory of that time felt so powerful, in that instant, that it seemed as if it could peel away Sarah's new life and reappear at will.

Sarah shook her head. "No, child. You're wrong. That train was a sign, and it's just up to me to see how to use it. You know what? We need to start building on that property I bought north of New York, in Irvington by the Hudson River. We need to talk to Mr. Tandy, that colored architect, and build the most beautiful home Negroes have ever owned."

The water splashed as Lelia sat up straight, her eyes full of joy and astonishment. "Yes, Mama! With thirty rooms, at least, in a grand Italian style—"

"Yes, but it's not just that I want such a fancy place for us, Lelia. It's for the *race*. It's something folks can be proud of, something we ain't never had before now. And I know Mr. Ransom gets nervous when I bring up politics, but I can't keep silent on that end either. God rest Booker T. Washington's soul, but I think Mr. Du Bois and William Monroe Trotter and the rest of them are right—the time to be quiet and keep working hard is over, Lelia. It's like your daddy used to tell me, it ain't enough to work hard. I'm real proud Mr. Asa Philip Randolph's wife is using her Walker hair parlor to keep up her husband's political newspaper, or they'd have been in the poorhouse by now for sure, but that ain't all I can do. I need to raise up my voice. I have money now, so my voice is louder. Maybe folks will listen. Maybe this is the time for us, Lela."

Just that quickly, Lelia's expression seemed to deflate. Politics, apparently, didn't inspire her as much as the talk of building a mansion. "Oh, Mama . . . isn't it enough you work yourself half to death without trying to save the whole race, too?"

In her mind, once again, Sarah saw that train backing toward her in Clarksdale.

No, child, it ain't nearly enough for me, she thought. *The good Lord saw fit to give me a pulpit, and now it's time to preach.*

Chapter Thirty-three

Sarah had known simultaneous gloom and exultation in her life many times, because she'd learned that her waves of sorrow and joy flowed over her in currents, one after the other. As she stood in front of the White House gate under the heat of the summer sun, gazing at the majestic white columns she had seen many times in photographs, she felt her heart swelling with both excitement and grief. She was grateful to be here, especially in her present company, but the reason they had all come made her stomach ache. She'd been on the verge of tears for weeks.

What was happening to her people?

Of all the places Sarah had lived, St. Louis had felt most like home. That was where all the seeds for where she was now seemed to have been planted. And East St. Louis, Illinois, right across the bridge, was as familiar to her as any city in America. She'd had customers there.

It was bad enough that the United States had entered the war overseas in April, a war with proportions that baffled and terrified Sarah. She couldn't guess how many young men would die in this Great War in foreign lands. But now a war had been declared at home: In July a melee had broken out in East St. Louis that newspapers were touting as the worst race riot in American history. More than one hundred men, women, and children dead. Six thousand people displaced from their homes because of fires set by a mob of three thousand whites who destroyed houses, churches, and businesses. She'd heard reports from people she knew in St. Louis—Rosetta, for example, and Jessie Robinson, wife of St. Louis printer C.K. Robinson, whom she'd known from church when she was a washerwoman and who had since become a good friend—that the police and National Guard had stood by and done nothing while buildings were torched and people were beaten and lynched. Negroes had been shot as they fled their burning homes. Even a child had been shot and then thrown into a burning building to be roasted alive, she'd heard. *Negroes ain't people to them*, Rosetta had written her. How well Sarah knew!

They done kilt him. I seen it. Oh, you poor girl, your man is dead.

The memory of losing Moses on that rainy day in Vicksburg was like a brand to Sarah, and it had been seared anew since the riot. The anti-lynching march called the Negro Silent Protest Parade in Harlem three weeks after the riot had helped her pain some, although Sarah had felt that same bittersweet mingling of exhilaration and sorrow. With the women and children wearing bright white and the men clad in dignified mourning clothes, ten thousand Negroes had marched in stark silence along Fifth Avenue; the only sound had been the muffled beat of a mournful drum. Sarah had never experienced anything like it; to be swallowed in the midst of her people, unified in purpose, demonstrating their undeniable humanity to all who watched them pass. Even the children's faces had been set in sad determination as they marched for their futures under a mammoth streamer behind the American flag that read YOUR HANDS ARE FULL OF BLOOD.

Was it too much to ask to be allowed to live in peace and freedom in a nation that was sending its young men overseas to fight for it elsewhere? Was it too much to ask that lynching be made a federal crime, since states were none too interested in putting a stop to it? Two years ago, D.W. Griffith's film *Birth of a Nation* had portrayed Negroes as clowns and schemers and the Ku Klux Klan as heroes instead of terrormongers. And while Negroes and fair-minded whites had protested the film, President Woodrow Wilson, a Southerner, had endorsed it.

That fact, almost more than any other, kept Sarah's heart from rejoicing as she stood in front of the White House with an assemblage of colored leaders. The man inside this White House, who publicly supported segregation, was not a friend to Negroes. He had agreed to see them—*And that's a start; it has to mean something*, Sarah tried to convince herself—but the meeting probably would not bear fruit. Margaret Murray Washington had confided to Sarah how frustrated and disappointed her husband had felt in his role as a racial adviser to Presidents Roosevelt and Taft. *Just because they ask your advice doesn't mean they'll take it*, she'd told Sarah, *and you can find yourself wondering why they asked in the first place.*

But maybe it would be different this time, Sarah thought. So many people dead! She and other colored leaders in Harlem had brought a petition to President Wilson asking that lynching and mob violence be made a national crime. Leadership had to begin at the highest level, and at least it would be a start. How could anyone fail to condemn murder, even against Negroes?

She'd *make* him care, Sarah decided. She'd talk from the heart, as she always did in her speaking engagements. She would tell him about Moses. She would use the same persuasive powers she'd been practicing all these years to sell Walker products and inspire women to try to change the mind of a president.

James Weldon Johnson, who stood beside Sarah, let out a long sigh as he stared at the impressive building before them. The writer and NAACP activist had pleasant features and perfect diction. Sarah loved the stirring song he had written, "Lift Ev'ry Voice and Sing," which his brother J. Rosamond Johnson had composed the music for, and she'd had the piece performed on her organ at social gatherings at her home on 136th Street. The Johnson brothers were refined, intelligent men who sparked everyone who met them, and Sarah was proud to know them.

"Well ... Here goes nothing, I'm afraid," Mr. Johnson said in a flat tone.

"And nothing's exactly what he'll give," someone else in the party muttered, either *New York Age* publisher Fred Moore or Reverend Adam Clayton Powell, pastor of the Abyssinian Baptist Church in Harlem. Sarah didn't see which of them had spoken.

"At least he said he'd listen," Sarah said earnestly. "That's how anything gets started."

"Well, let's pray you're right about that, Madam Walker," said W.E.B. Du Bois, who stood at the head of the group. Sarah was convinced the Harvard-educated leader was the most poetic and intelligent man she had ever had the pleasure of meeting, with enough fire to match his intellect. The slender man dabbed perspiration from his dramatically receding hairline before slipping his handkerchief back into his coat pocket. His beard was neatly trimmed, and his mustache curled upward at both ends without a stray hair out of place. "I say we go on inside to the battlefront, then, gentlemen ... and *lady*," Mr. Du Bois said, recognizing Sarah with a nod of his head. "Our appointment is at noon, and we don't want to keep the president waiting."

After Reverend Powell suggested they bow their heads in a prayer, they formed a small processional past the gate, telling the guards in their dress military uniforms that President Wilson was expecting them. Only then did Sarah's heart begin to pound in anticipation.

Although Sarah kept her eyes straight ahead, she could feel heavy stares following them through the immaculately polished hallways of the White House. Some of the stares were merely curious, she knew, and some were probably outright hostile. Negroes were rarely considered a welcome sight in such august surroundings. They traveled through several passages, past colorful portraits of past presidents, banners, and patriotic memorabilia. The building was blanketed in a respectful hush, except for the sound of their shoes on the floors.

According to a handsome grandfather clock, it was ten minutes to noon when they reached a fair-size room they were told was the executive waiting room, with plush antique chairs and a small conference table. All of them took their seats in thoughtful silence. The room also doubled as a library, apparently, with glass-enclosed shelves of books with worn spines. Had Thomas Jefferson read any of these books? Or Abraham Lincoln?

At noon, when the silence of the room was broken by the resounding bells of the grandfather clock, the double doors opened. Instinctively, they all rose to their feet, but the man who entered the room was not the president. He was a mousy, dark-haired man with tortoiseshell eyeglasses and a nervous smile. "Ah, Mr. Du Bois," the man said, reaching out to shake their leader's hand. "I'm Joseph Tumulty, the president's secretary. After so much correspondence, it's good to meet you in person. We appreciate your making this journey."

They all nodded and shook his hand as they were introduced, then found themselves in the midst of an awkward silence. Mr. Tumulty cleared his throat. "I'm afraid I bring bad news, which isn't unusual during these times, as you might imagine. We're happy to read your petition and give it utmost consideration, but the president is unable to meet with you."

Sarah's breath died in her throat. Glancing at the eyes of the other men in her group, she saw them exchange knowing gazes. They looked disappointed, but not surprised.

"It would only take a moment," Mr. Du Bois said calmly. "He needs to know—"

Mr. Tumulty shrugged, his voice becoming curt. "I'm sorry. A meeting is impossible."

"War business?" Reverend Powell said, his hands behind his back.

At that, Mr. Tumulty's face began to flush red. "No . . . not that . . . but he's signing an important bill. It has to do with . . . farming. The animal feed supply . . ." His voice trailed off.

None of them said a word. If the president was more concerned about animal feed than lynching, they knew there were no words they could utter that could possibly matter to his ears.

Only two weeks later, Sarah was able to shake off the growing sense of frustration she'd felt in the wake of the East St. Louis riot and her disappointing visit to the White House. That feeling had grown worse a week after the visit, when she heard dreadful news about Negro soldiers rioting and shooting white residents in Houston. The incident was apparently sparked by a Negro soldier's beating after he complained to a police officer who slapped a Negro woman, but it was still a horrible mark against Negro enlisted men.

But now, if anything, Sarah felt a sense of rebirth.

Sarah had created the Madam C.J. Walker Hair Culturists Union of America in April of 1916, hoping to contribute to good causes and protect her agents from competitors who might infringe on their prices. The

union's first convention was scheduled to be held in Philadelphia beginning August 30. As much as Sarah wanted to look forward to the first national gathering of her agents, she arrived in the city with a nagging dread
about the event. The local organizers had assured her and Mr. Ransom
that the convention would be a rousing success, but Sarah wasn't so sure.
As the ranks of her agents had swelled in the past few years, so had countless incidents of mismanagement, misrepresentation, and all sorts of petty
complaints. As if she didn't have enough to worry about with shipping and
suppliers, every time she turned around, she seemed to hear reports about
agents removing labels from her products to sell as their own, performing
poorly, or criticizing her publicly. And these were the same people who
owed their livelihoods to her! Philadelphia's branch of the union was
growing quickly, but Sarah recently had learned from the organization's
president that Walker agents were supplying white drugstores in Philadelphia that were not authorized to carry her products. The agents knew
Sarah's rules and standards, and yet too many were willing to ignore both.
Didn't people have any loyalty? What was wrong with these Negroes? *You
can lead a horse to water*, Sarah often thought, shaking her head, *but Lord
knows you can't make some of 'em drink.*

Growing pains, Lottie called it. All the nonsense put Sarah in a foul
mood, so she was braced for controversy when she went to Philadelphia.

The meeting convened at Union Baptist Church on Fitzwater Street,
and Sarah realized right away that her mood would improve drastically as
she sat beside Mr. Ransom and the other union officers, including Sadie, at
the pulpit. Sadie looked *so* good in her businesslike white linen suit and
fashionable ostrich-feather hat; and Mr. Ransom looked proper as always
in his gray suit, bow tie, and finely shined black leather shoes. All morning they watched women stream steadily into the church in growing numbers, their voices rising from soft murmurs to a powerful din. There were
many faces she knew, of course—Sadie was there, and tireless little Lizette
from Pittsburgh, and scores of others—but there were also many agents she
did not know, women who had completed the correspondence course
or had been trained by others. And, exactly as she had wanted to impart to
them, these women were the perfect advertisement for the products and
method they sold; some of the women were wearing hats, but she could see
that their hair was shiny and healthy, and many of them sported tight,
lovely curls. Walker Company truly had taken on its own life with a sister-
hood of well-coiffed, dignified Negro women of all skin shades, educa-
tional levels, and ages who had come to take care of business. As the
church filled, Sarah felt her heart rejoicing.

"You're a long way from lettin' your hair down at the church picnic,
huh, girl?" Sadie murmured to Sarah with a low, warm laugh during Sarah's
lengthy introduction. Sadie, like the other agents, usually called Sarah
Madam now—and only half in jest—so Sarah felt a rush of affection for

her longtime friend to hear her call her *girl*. She squeezed Sadie's hand tightly. Nowadays Sadie owned a large Walker hair parlor in Pittsburgh and occasionally wrote Sarah about her headaches, but both of them had discovered that their new lives didn't leave much time for old friends. Sarah missed Sadie terribly, but the only thing that mattered to her at that instant was knowing how far they had come. Together.

"Yes, Lord," Sarah answered softly, marveling at the church filled with women. Swept away by the sight, Sarah momentarily didn't realize her name had been called.

"Madam?" Mr. Ransom prompted her, smiling. "I think they'd like to hear you speak."

When Sarah stood up, applause exploded from the church's pews.

A few women near the front rose to their feet instantly, led by Lizette, and then the women stood in waves until the entire room was giving her a standing ovation with smiling faces. Their applause grew louder, until it was almost deafening to Sarah. They reminded her of the image she'd seen in her dream so long ago, the field of black roses. *Her* roses. Her children, almost.

Sarah walked slowly to the pulpit, basking in their applause. Her face was shining with a large grin, her eyes moist. There were days when Sarah had forgotten what was at stake in her work, when she'd wondered why she was traveling so much that she barely had time to spend in her own home, but not today. Today she understood exactly what she'd been working toward all along—not just building a life for herself, but helping to build a nation of colored womanhood.

"Good ladies," Sarah said, her voice quavering with emotion once the applause had died. "There are no words for how proud I am as I stand before all of you. A good friend of mine, Dr. Mary McLeod Bethune, has agreed to begin teaching the Walker method at her school for girls in Daytona, Florida. She and her students have been using Walker products for four years, and she believes beauty culture will be a valuable course of study for those young ladies. Now, Dr. Bethune likes to say that the world better get used to seeing a black rose, and that is exactly what each of you is to me. Anyone who does not respect Negro womanhood has never *seen* Negro womanhood as I am seeing it now."

The group applauded again, and Sarah could see the pride in Lizette's eyes.

"We are more than hair culturists, ladies. And sales is much of what we do, but we are more than saleswomen. As women, we have duties to each other and our race. To my mind, it is a sacred duty, and that duty is to use our *power*. This is a time in our nation like no other. America is facing a terrible war overseas. I tremble with pride every time I think of my good friend from Indianapolis, Dr. Joseph H. Ward, who has enlisted in the army to serve his country. Ladies, we *must* remain loyal to our homes, our country, and our flag. This is the greatest country under the sun. But we must not let our love of country, our patriotic loyalty, cause us to abate one whit in our protest against wrong and injustice. We should protest until the American sense of justice is so aroused that such affairs as the East St. Louis riot be forever impossible."

Sarah's voice had risen to a near shout, and her words were smothered by applause. She paused, inhaling. "Today we have a new challenge: We must learn the ways of politics. And if we believe lynching and discrimination are wrong, then we must raise all of our voices as one. We must become lobbyists to try to influence those who make our nation's laws. We must never, ever be afraid to stand up. We cannot leave it to anyone else. If it is to be done, then it is to be done by *us*."

Again the agents were on their feet and Sarah fell silent. She had nearly lost her voice with the strain she experienced more and more when she spoke, but her heart was booming loudly in her chest, her blood hot and excited in her veins. She was holding tightly to the pulpit as she leaned forward to speak, clinging so tightly that it hurt, almost as if some part of her believed she was in danger of floating away from joy.

Chapter Thirty-four

"How long have you been in practice, Dr. Kennedy?" Sarah asked her handsome young guest as they wound their way through the 136th Street salon, past pleated velvet curtains and shiny parquet floors. The protégé of Dr. Ward's was visiting from Chicago, and he had asked to give Sarah a medical examination as part of his promise to Dr. Ward that he would help keep an eye on her while his mentor was in the service. As it turned out, this young man had just enlisted himself and would be leaving soon for his basic training down South. Sarah liked the young physician's manner so much that she'd insisted on giving him a personal tour of her salon. She also hoped he would have a chance to meet Lelia. Dr. Jack Kennedy was dark and well built, and something about him told Sarah that he was of solid character. He would be such an improvement over the men her daughter kept company with!

"Not very long, to be honest, Madam. I only opened my practice in Chicago this year. But wartime makes no accommodations for the plans of one man."

"That's the truth, all right," Sarah said. American soldiers had yet to suffer any major losses in the war, but she was fearful of what would happen to the enlisted men when they met up with those horrible German gas canisters. People like Dr. Ward and Dr. Kennedy would be very valuable overseas, and they could show their superiors that Negroes could be heroes, too.

Dr. Kennedy glanced around the plushly decorated parlor, which was bustling with activity. The decor was matching pearl gray, from the walls to the cushioned seats for waiting customers, and the room smelled of brewing coffee, since customers were free to sip tea and coffee while they waited. There were at least six women in chairs having their hair treated, all attended by solemn-faced culturists in standard white dresses and aprons who were no doubt nervous to have Sarah standing over them.

And with good reason, Sarah realized as she glanced at the tiled floor. What was the name of this broad-shouldered girl again . . . ? "What's your name? Miss Sneed?"

"Miss *Reed*, Madam," the girl said. Her comb froze in her customer's head.

"Miss Reed, I'm sure you've heard me tell you ladies time and again to sweep up the floor after each customer. Why is there so much hair under this chair? This is our showcase parlor, and this floor looks like a barnyard."

Miss Reed glanced at the other women, who were all gazing at her dolefully, as if to say, *Why are you making us look bad?* Nervously, the woman put down her comb and wiped her hands on her apron. Sarah thought she might be about to burst into tears. "I'm s-sorry, Madam, I'll sweep up right away."

"It doesn't look like a barnyard to me, Madam Walker," Dr. Kennedy said as Sarah steered him out of the room. "Far from it."

"I just don't have patience for it," Sarah said. "People come here to feel special, and that's exactly what I aim to provide. Too many of our people are just accustomed to any old thing. Sometimes we forget to have higher standards."

"Yes, ma'am."

At that, Lelia appeared in the doorway in front of them. Although it was still only late afternoon, Lelia was dressed in a black silk dress and a black-and-gold turban with a single feather above her forehead. Lelia grinned. "Mother!" she said, eagerly taking Sarah's arm and giving her a whiff of flowery toilet water. "There's someone you *must* meet."

Sarah was ready to scold Lelia for ignoring Dr. Kennedy's presence, but she kept quiet when she saw a robust white man standing just behind Lelia in a tuxedo, top hat, and full-length black coat. Seeing Sarah, the man extended one arm with a flair and gave a low bow. "Ah! Madam Walker," the man said, taking Sarah's hand to kiss. "This pleasure is all mine, you see." The middle-aged man's accent was so thick that Sarah could barely understand his words. Was he Spanish? Italian?

"Mother, you'll never guess who this is." Lelia always called Sarah *Mama* in private, but she used the more formal *Mother* in public and in her letters. "Who is the most famous opera singer in the entire world?"

Sarah knew that, of course, because Lottie had tutored her in opera by using the tenor's recordings, which she played on the gold-leaf Victrola in her drawing room. But before she could give the name, the ruddy-faced man spoke: "*Mi chiamo* Enrico Caruso, Madam—and proud to make your acquaintance!" he boomed. "Everyone is talking of the famous Madam C.J. Walker."

"Well, I'll be," Sarah said, smiling. "How very nice to meet you, sir."

The man made a dismissive gesture. "Ack! Me, I see every day. There is no joy to see this old face. The joy in this world is to meet beautiful women and make new friends. Especially when they have built a salon as fine as any in Rome."

Lelia spoke breathlessly. "Mr. Caruso performs at the Metropolitan Opera, and he and his wife have friends in common with me. I've invited him for tea, and then we're all going to have drinks. I was telling him all about the mansion we're building, Mother. If it fits his schedule, wouldn't it be wonderful to invite him to give us a private concert once it's finished?"

Sarah's eyes shined. She could only imagine Lottie's face when she heard! She was also glad Mr. Caruso had a wife, because she didn't like the familiar way Lelia had hooked her arm around the arm of this man who was old enough to be her father. "Well, that's a fine idea—"

"This villa you are building, what is it called?" Mr. Caruso asked.

"Called . . . ?" Sarah said, puzzled.

"Yes, yes. You see, a fine villa must have a name, just as a child. Remember this!"

Sarah laughed. "Well, Mr. Caruso, we have a saying in this country—we'll cross that bridge when we come to it." Suddenly Sarah remembered her manners. "Oh, this is Dr. Jack Kennedy. Dr. Ward is his mentor, Lelia, and he's on his way to his military training."

Lelia's grin widened. Somehow she looked energized despite the pronounced bags under her eyes. "Wonderful! Then you must join us, Dr. Kennedy. I would ask Mother to come, but I know she won't want to stay out so late."

"Yes, Dr. Kennedy, you should go," Sarah urged him.

Dr. Kennedy shook his head, although his eyes lingered on Lelia. "Thank you for the invitation, but I'm not staying long. I have to keep a promise to a friend, and then I have to go."

"A promise?" Lelia asked, curious.

At that, Dr. Kennedy glanced at Sarah. "Yes. I promised Dr. Ward I would do my best to keep your mother in good health."

"Good health! That blessed beast we all seek that eludes us," Mr. Caruso said. "In that case, Doctor, your invitation is taken away. *Ciao!*" His hearty laugh rang throughout the salon.

"You have a busy life, Madam Walker," Dr. Kennedy said, once Sarah's examination in her mahogany-furnished bedroom was complete. He spoke over the melodic strains of "Mighty Lak' a Rose" bursting from the ceiling-high player organ in her main hallway. Dr. Kennedy had checked her heart rate, looked at her throat, and listened to her breathing. He had also asked her a series of questions: Did she suffer from thirst and a frequent need to pass water? Had her stream diminished? Did she have swelling of her hands or feet? Did she often suffer from a lack of appetite or fatigue? Had she noticed strange rashes or a fruity smell to her breath? The answer to most of his questions was yes. He hadn't commented yet, but he looked very somber as he took notes.

"Well, I guess you saw a piece of my life today," Sarah said from where she sat on her canopied bed. "There's always somebody coming through here. I'm home to rest, but . . ."

At that, the doctor met her eyes. "But you don't know how to rest, do you?"

"You can tell that about me already? Usually folks need to know me longer." As she said those words, Sarah thought sadly of C.J. She was still getting letters from him, asking her for either money or employment. She'd prayed he would have gotten his life on better track by now with nothing to do with her, but he seemed to have lost everything of the confident, creative man he'd been when she met him. *My habits are better. My heart has changed*, he'd written in his last letter. *I am writing these lines with tears dripping from my eyes.* There was a time she would have gloated over his words, but no more. Now, despite the wall she'd built around her own heart, she felt sorry for this pathetic man she had once loved.

"Dr. Ward told me about your work habits," Dr. Kennedy went on. "And I don't want to alarm you, Madam Walker, but I think I should be frank instead of pulling punches. Especially when a situation is serious."

At the word *serious*, all thoughts of C.J. vanished. "Go on, then," she said softly.

Dr. Kennedy exhaled slowly, searching for words. "Madam Walker, you probably travel on trains a lot. Imagine you're a train conductor—and as a doctor, I'm a bridge engineer who's seen what's ahead on the tracks. Now, if I somehow managed to reach your train in time and I told you the bridge ahead won't hold you, and that the whole train was going to fly into a ravine in a short time, what would you do?"

Sarah's heart pounded with dread. She hadn't expected a good report, but she hadn't expected one to begin so gravely, either. "I'd . . . stop the train," she said slowly.

Dr. Kennedy nodded. "That's right. That's what common sense would tell you to do. But for some reason, when it comes to health, a lot of folks have trouble living by common sense. I hope you won't take offense. . . ."

"Go on, Dr. Kennedy. Just say what you need to say."

Dr. Kennedy tapped his pencil against his notebook. "Dr. Ward wrote me you have high blood pressure, and he advised you years ago to slow down. Instead you've kept that train going full steam, and he's been worried about you. Well . . . I think there's a good chance now you might have a kidney inflammation, what we call nephritis. I can't say for certain in an exam like this—you'll need to see another doctor. But when kidneys don't work the way they should, they slowly poison your blood and cause the symptoms you've been experiencing. There may be a day when we'll have a pill to cure it, but for now the only weapon you have is to start taking very special care of yourself. First, I'm going to recommend you spend some time at the Battle Creek Sanitorium in Michigan and see a doctor there. Booker T. Washington used to spend time at Battle Creek. I'm afraid he was probably given much the same advice I'm giving you . . . but he couldn't make himself stop that train."

Sarah glanced quickly at her bedroom window to make sure it wasn't open, because she suddenly felt as if a cold wind were blowing across her face. In her mind she could see that white ribbon tied to the back of the train car that had grazed past her in Clarksdale. Hearing Dr. Kennedy's words, she felt as if the bad omen were finally coming to pass.

"I can stop it," Sarah said firmly, genuinely frightened.

"Even if it means giving up control of your business to someone else?"

Sarah sank back against the wall, stunned. Everyone from Lelia to Lottie to Mr. Ransom had advised her over the years to delegate more responsibility, but to give up control entirely? That thought had never occurred to her. *It won't survive without me,* she thought.

"Pardon me if it isn't my place to say . . . but you have a lovely and lively daughter, Madam Walker. And she's certainly of an age to take the business from your shoulders."

Sarah was shaking her head before he finished his sentence. Lelia in control! That fickle child couldn't be trusted to take control. Lelia had flourished for three years in Pittsburgh and then lost interest suddenly; now she put her mind on business only when the mood struck her. The rest of the time she seemed to be dazzled by Harlem's social life. To Sarah's mind, any existence built on pure socializing was fragile and temporary. Sarah loved parties, too, but she wasn't afraid of work. That, more and more, seemed to be the biggest difference between her and her daughter. And she sure as hell hadn't worked so tirelessly all these years just so Lelia could spend the company's hard-won money on champagne and jewelry.

"Lelia's interests don't lie in that direction," Sarah said simply.

Dr. Kennedy patted her hand. "Well, Madam Walker, I'm no expert in business, but I'm almost sure your business can live without you—and I'm very sure that the only way *you* can live is without so much worry over your business. Dr. Ward has told me about the Wish Board you have and how you make those wishes come to pass. It must be mighty powerful if it's brought you this far, and now it's time you put up a wish for yourself and your health. I'm just trying to wave you down on those train tracks. I can't make you stop, but I have to try. Dr. Ward gave me direct orders."

Sarah nodded again, her throat suddenly feeling clogged. For once, someone was telling her the stark and utter truth instead of only what they thought she wanted to hear, and he was a virtual stranger. Or had she just refused to listen to everyone's warnings before now? Even back in Denver and Pittsburgh, C.J. used to warn her she'd ruin her health by working so hard. She'd thought he was lazy and lacking in vision, when maybe he'd only been trying to save her life.

"You're a good young man," Sarah said. "It takes courage to talk to a person like you just did to me. I don't like what you said, but I sure appreciate you saying it."

For the first time since the examination, Dr. Kennedy grinned. "Well . . . I'm just working up my mettle for war, Madam Walker. See, I figure that if I have the nerve to try to tell *the* Madam C.J. Walker how to run her own business, those Germans won't scare me at all."

Sarah took his hand and squeezed it tight. "Come back and see Lelia one day," she said quietly. "I'd like both of us to know you better."

Dr. Kennedy smiled boyishly. "Yes, ma'am, I'd like that, too."

Sarah knew, once again, that he was telling her the truth.

Chapter Thirty-five

APRIL 1918
FIVE MONTHS LATER

Even though the door was closed, Sarah heard the raucous laughter of men and women floating from inside Lelia's card room on the upper floor of the town house as she stood in the carpeted hallway in her robe, her breathing strained from her exhaustion and anger. "I said a *straight!*" she heard a man inside the room shout, but his voice was swallowed by a chorus of taunts. Even from several feet away, the scent of tobacco wafting underneath the door was so strong that Sarah felt a sudden headache. And how could she mistake the sweet, sharp smell of whiskey? She could also hear the player piano in the room playing a roll of James Scott's rags. It was three A.M. on a Sunday night, and Sarah's home sounded like a barrelhouse.

Sarah was so tired she could barely stand up without leaning against the wall, but she was wide awake. She wasn't feeling the kind of tired that came from not getting enough sleep, she knew. This kind of tired went to the bones, winnowing them out and then filling them up with lead. It was a tired that seeped from the body into the mind, or maybe it was the other way around, she mused. The kind of tired she remembered seeing on her papa's face when he sat down at the table for supper.

Without knocking, Sarah flung the door open, and the room fell into silence. Sarah had prepared herself to see anything, but she still found herself shocked: There were at least ten young people in the room. A few were at the card table, but many of them were sprawled on the sofas. One young man was bare-chested, sitting on the floor between the knees of another man who had his arms draped across the half-naked man's shoulders. And Lelia sat beside them, resting her head in the lap of a tall, lovely young woman Sarah had seen her daughter with many times before. The woman reminded Sarah of Hazel, her daughter's friend from St. Louis, except that this woman looked more refined and glamorous—and dangerous, somehow. Her hair was bobbed almost as short as a man's, and the playful smile didn't vanish from her lips even as her eyes met Sarah's with a heavy gaze. The woman was wearing a string of pearls that dangled down near Lelia, and Lelia's hand was wrapped inside them. The bare-chested man beside Lelia was massaging her stocking feet.

"Mother!" Startled, Lelia sat up straight, nearly tangling herself in the woman's pearls.

Seeing Sarah in the doorway, the bare-chested man quickly found his jacket on the floor and covered himself, and his friend jerked his hands away from him as if his skin had suddenly turned to fire. Most of the others looked like guilty children caught sneaking puffs of cigarettes or sips of gin behind the schoolhouse. Why, one of the boys here looked barely eighteen!

"I need to talk to you, Mrs. Robinson," Sarah said to Lelia in a dull tone, not blinking or pausing. "Right this minute."

After a quick look of irritation, Lelia sighed and stood up. She slipped her feet into her high-heeled shoes and mashed out a cigarette she'd had in one hand, which Sarah hadn't noticed before. Since when did Lelia smoke? "Y'all count me out in the next hand," Lelia said to the group, and then she closed the door behind them.

"We'll go to your room," Sarah said, not able to meet her daughter's eyes.

"Mama, what's this about?" Lelia said, trailing after her. She spoke with a slight slur. "Were we too loud? I can turn that piano off. I didn't know you could hear it—"

As she walked toward Lelia's bedroom, Sarah's breathing felt more and more difficult, as if she were climbing a steep flight of stairs. She didn't know if fatigue or rage was responsible for making it so hard to draw air into her lungs. "Who was that man touching your feet?" Sarah said at last, unable to contain herself. "I thought you were exchanging letters with Dr. Kennedy."

"Oh, Lord, Mama, you sound like you did when I was sixteen years old. A few letters don't mean we're engaged. That man in there is just a friend, a poet. Believe me, he's nobody for you to concern yourself with." Then she laughed to herself, a laugh that sounded dark and salacious to Sarah, as though Lelia had told a private joke she didn't believe Sarah would understand. But Sarah understood, all right. Ever since she'd come to New York, she'd heard rumors that her daughter kept company with men who were *that way*, who preferred their own kind to women. She'd heard other whispers, too.

"And that woman you were falling all over?" Sarah said. "She ain't nobody for me to concern myself with neither?"

At that, Lelia stopped laughing. "Just tell me why you're pulling me away from my own party at this time of night, Mama. It's late and I've had a little bit to drink, so I don't want to say anything improper. If you just need to yell at somebody about something, go on and yell. But you need to start minding your own business."

Minding her business! That almost made Sarah laugh herself.

"Oh, I'm mindin' my business," Sarah said. "There's nobody but me to mind it."

Lelia was silent for the rest of their walk. By the time they got to Lelia's bedroom, Sarah's fingers were trembling. She virtually collapsed in Lelia's bedside chair, her chest heaving noticeably. Her breath rasped in her throat.

"Mama, you know what . . . ?" Lelia said, more gently this time. "It sounds to me like you need to be in bed. The doctors at Battle Creek told you to rest, and then you turned right around doing all those NAACP speeches in one city to the next. It's no wonder you're not feeling well. You need to leave those people alone and just sit still like the doctors said."

"You're one to give anybody advice," Sarah said. Now, finally, she did gaze directly at Lelia, and she lodged her gaze like a weapon. "You're a goddamn disgrace."

Lelia stared at Sarah impassively. Lelia's face became stony whenever she tried to hide her feelings from her mother, and it had certainly turned to stone now. Whether it was shame, guilt, or anger, Lelia's face was always the same. "What now?" Lelia said, sitting on her bed.

"Alice Tisem," Sarah said simply, and Lelia's mask melted. Now she knew.

Alice Tisem was an agent in Pittsburgh, someone Lelia had hired years ago, and now she was raising a stink about Madam C.J. Walker products, claiming the quality had diminished since Sarah had moved to New York because she was partying and allowing anyone to mix her ingredients in Indianapolis. In fact, now Tisem was marketing her own product, and some of the other Walker agents had begun using that instead. But the worst rumor was that *Lelia* had revealed the Walker Hair Grower formula to Tisem. She hadn't wanted to believe it was true, but she could see it plainly in her daughter's eyes.

"M-Mama, I . . ."

"You *what?*" Sarah said. "You were drunk? That's the story. Is that your excuse?"

Lelia blinked hard. "No . . . it's no excuse, Mama, but it's the truth. She tricked me! I didn't know she—"

"She tricked you?" Sarah said, mimicking her daughter's whiny voice. "I'm sick and tired of hearing about gettin' tricked! C.J.'s out there whining now 'bout how he was tricked, a full-grown man. But at least C.J. had the good sense not to tell that Larrie bitch my formula."

"Oh, Mama, don't make such a fuss—"

"It's *my name!*" Sarah roared, suddenly overcome with emotion that surprised even her. She shook violently in the chair, her hands clenched into fists. "I been all over this country to make my name, and now you're out there *throwing it away* like it's one of your empty goddamn whiskey bottles! Don't you have even a *lick* of sense, Lelia? You ain't learned even *one* thing?"

Hurriedly, Lelia wiped away tears that had sprung to her eyes. "That's not fair, Mama. I've worked myself silly for you! I admit it, I made a mistake with Alice. But—"

"But, but, but," Sarah cut her off. "I'm so sick and tired of *but*. You always got some kind of excuse, always running to Mr. Ransom to cover your tail. Mae had more sense than you when she was just thirteen and you were grown! And don't think she don't know it, too. Everybody knows it, hear? *Everybody!*"

Sarah gathered a ragged, scrappy breath, speaking in nearly a wheeze. "And . . . as if . . . that ain't bad enough . . . then you got to be bringin' those kind of people in this house, shaming me on my own doorstep. Playing poker all hours, sleeping all day, when you could be helping me build something that can last . . . forever . . ." Sarah couldn't go on. Her words were stolen from her.

"Everybody can't be you, Mama," Lelia said in a clear voice, tears still shimmering in her eyes. "It's about time you figured that out."

Sarah heaved a few more breaths, and found her voice again. "Mr. Ransom is—"

"He's just out to build his own name, Mama. Don't be so blind."

"You know that's not true. And even if it was, at least he wants to build *something*," Sarah said. "What do you want to build, Lela? Just tell me that. What do you want anybody to remember about you? You threw a good party?"

"We both want to throw parties, Mama. You're spending a quarter-million dollars building that mansion so you can throw parties and show folks you're somebody. You know the only difference between my parties and yours? You invite politicians, and I invite poets."

"You think . . . that's all I want?"

At that, Lelia's face and voice softened. She sighed again. "I don't know what you want, Mama," she said, her voice aching with sincerity. "At first I thought you wanted to have a business, and you got it. Then I thought you wanted to get rich, and you got that, too. Now it seems like you want to be like Booker T. Washington, and I guess you'll get that, too. You always get what you want. But I don't want the same thing! Does that make me some kind of family disgrace, just because I don't want the same thing?"

"I still don't know what you *do* want."

"I just want to live, Mama! What's so god-awful about that? All you and Mr. Ransom ever talk about is the business. I can talk about it sometimes, but that's not all I am! You think I want to end up like you? You—" But Lelia stopped herself, shaking her head. "Never mind."

"No, you finish," Sarah said, her bottom lip trembling. "Like me how?"

Lelia gazed at Sarah directly. "It seems like you don't have nothing to say to me anymore if it isn't about Walker Manufacturing. And no matter how much I do, it's not enough for you 'cause I don't do it like you. So I give up! I can't be you, so I'm just gonna be me. And that goes for courting, too! I already told you how I feel about Wiley Wilson—I know you don't like him, but he's the first man I've thought about like this since John—and if I even look a man's way, all I hear about is Dr. Kennedy. Dr. Kennedy is nice, Mama, but you don't control my heart, too!"

"I don't want . . . control. . . ."

"Oh, Mama, please!" Lelia said, exasperated. "You think I don't know you? That's *all* you want! And anybody who tries to go against you knows that."

Was that all Lelia thought of her, that she was some kind of monster? Sarah's heart plunged. "Did you give Alice Tisem the formula on purpose, Lela?" Sarah asked, suddenly suspicious. "Did you do it to hurt me and the company? Tell me the truth."

A light seemed to go out in Lelia's eyes. The stony mask did not return, but Lelia was gazing at Sarah the same way she would at a stranger. Her jaw shook. "Everything I have is because of you and the company, and I love you both," she said. "If you don't know that, then you don't know me, and you sure as hell don't think anything of me. So if you don't mind, I have some friends waiting who know me and like me just fine."

Lelia got up and walked across the room in sweeping steps, then slammed the door hard behind her. Anyone who had slept during their shouting match would have certainly heard it.

With the door closed, there was suddenly no light in the room, and Sarah sat in the chair in an overpowering darkness. She heard a low moan from deep in her belly, and suddenly the sound had filled up the room. She was cramping, and she hugged herself, doubled over.

Madam Walker, the situation is very simple.

Lelia was right, she realized. She could not force her daughter to become someone she was not. Lelia would not sacrifice as much as she had. If she didn't try to accept Lelia for who she was, she would push her daughter away. Who would she truly have left in her life, then?

Your blood pressure is quite high and your kidneys are probably failing.

So she would have to try to hold on to the Walker Company as long as she could. Mae was so much more serious than Lelia; maybe in a few years, when Mae was older . . .

It's very good you came here to Battle Creek for some rest, but your situation calls for more than a visit. Do you understand my point?

But there was so much more to do now! Why had she been cheated for so many years, when she'd been in better health but powerless to do anything even for herself? Now she was gaining the power to help her entire race! The African students she'd been sponsoring at Tuskegee were only the beginning. Her visit to the White House was only a start.

As a physician, I'm afraid there's only one way to phrase this question, Madam: Do you want to live, or do you want to die?

"I want to live," Sarah whispered in the darkness, answering her Battle Creek physician's question exactly as she had in November, during her monthlong stay at the Michigan sanitorium. But this time, instead of the false hopefulness she'd felt at Battle Creek, her voice was laden with a wellspring of despair she felt growing in her soul.

"Oh, dear Lord, please let me live. I want to live. I can do so much for my race, Lord. Don't give all this to me and then take it away. *I want to live.*" But for the first time in her life, Sarah felt like her prayer was falling on no one's ears but her own.

Chapter Thirty-six

Villa Lewaro.

When Sarah repeated the name of her new home in her mind, she could hear the Italian tenor uttering the name with his delightful accent: *Lee-Waaa-Ro.* When Lelia brought Caruso and his wife up to the property to visit last week, he toured the house and thought of the name as soon as he sat in the sunken Italian garden to drink iced tea with Lelia and Sarah, gazing out at the fountain and swimming pool. He'd been awestruck.

This place already has its name, and it has whispered it to me, Madam— LeeWaaaRo. Did I not say a fine home is the same as a child? It has named itself after lovely Lelia. L-E for Lelia, W-A for Walker, and R-O for Robinson. Villa Lewaro!

Caruso was right, she knew. Villa Lewaro had been the mansion's name all along, even before she knew it.

In the five A.M. darkness, Sarah allowed herself to enjoy the immensity and serenity of her home in a way she'd rarely been able to since she'd moved in amidst its boxes and clutter in June. She was the only one awake now. The servants were asleep, and there were no guests at this hour. She could enjoy Villa Lewaro for herself.

Thirty-four rooms. Three stories. *I want it to look like a palace in a story-book,* Sarah had told her talented Negro architect, and he had built her an Italian Renaissance–style palace fit for nobility. After making so many visits to monitor its progress, noticing so many dissatisfactory details and then suffering the endless unpacking and decorating, Sarah had never viewed her home with the real pleasure of a newcomer. Walking gingerly in her slippers because of her badly swollen feet, Sarah traveled from one end of her house to the other, turning on her beautiful green and white Chinese jade lamps as she moved, taking in the sights that would meet her party guests when they arrived for the villa's opening gala later today.

What she saw made her cling to her satin robe with gratitude. Her home was a vision!

As a child visiting Missus Anna's grand home in Delta, she'd thought there must be some invisible dividing line between Missus Anna's life and hers because Missus Anna had a fine house and she lived in a leaky cabin; and Missus Anna was white, while she was colored. But that line had been only in her imagination, hadn't it? It might have *seemed* so—and maybe, until the end of slavery, it had truly been so for most of her people—but that line was gone. Negroes still had more than their share of unfair obstacles, but it *was* possible to get around them. She'd built her house with money she'd made from Negroes, and many of those Negroes in turn earned their living from other Negroes. And she'd built the house with Vertner Woodson Tandy, a Negro architect, to further make her point. *This* was her monument to Negro achievement.

Sarah opened one of her double doors on the ground floor and began outside, walking to what she still thought of as her front porch, but which the architect called her *portico*, where six stately columns proclaimed her home to all who passed it. After she turned to face her marble entrance hall, Sarah's eyes became tearful as she climbed the marble steps to her living room. Gazing at the living room before her, she imagined the hotel ballroom in Denver where she and C.J. had danced their first waltz. That ballroom would look plain and uninteresting to her now, no doubt, but back then it had symbolized a brand-new beginning. And C.J. had been her shining prince, come to take her to the Promised Land. Or so she'd thought, anyway. *Too bad you ain't here to see it, C.J. You talk about a room to dance in!*

She had hired an Italian artist to decorate the walls and paint the ceiling by hand, and the room had exquisite Italian furnishings. Two hundred twenty feet ahead of her, she admired the gold bough over the doorway that led to the dining room, then she turned to gaze at the shimmering gold detail on the massive entrance hall's fireplace, which was the showpiece of the west wall. Her feet sank into the Tabriz rug, which had cost $13,000 and covered a large portion of the room. Sarah walked past the fireplace into the music room—the new, larger Gold Room—where her massive glistening chandeliers hung, reflecting the gold leaf that trimmed the room's walls and ceiling. The draperies, too, were gold-trimmed.

And here was her precious $25,000 Estey organ—which seemed to always be in disrepair, but luckily was ready to play music for the party—and her 24-carat gold leaf–trimmed grand piano, which she'd lacked in Pittsburgh but had more than compensated for now. Her gold-leaf Victrola was positioned nicely on its own table, more art than machinery, and the chairs seated before the phonograph in a half circle had been designed to look like pure gold themselves. The music room was narrow, but it was the length of both her living and dining rooms, so it was truly palatial, with French doors at either end. Since her music was here, with the organ chiming each quarter hour and built to pipe music to every corner of the house, this was one of Sarah's favorite rooms. This room, to her, seemed nearly blessed.

Sarah stopped to rest her hand on the smooth marble statuette of Romeo and Juliet that adorned one corner of the Gold Room. The tragic heroes' youthful faces moved her just the way she imagined the artist had intended. She had so much art, and so little time to actually appreciate it. And what about this large bronze statue of an old woman Lottie had told her was an original piece by a very famous sculptor named Rodin? And more paintings than she could count. She liked ivory so much that she collected small ivory pieces whenever she could, but now they sat in a display case virtually ignored.

And there were so many rooms to choose from! Sarah realized just how massive the home was as she made her trek from one end to the other, her feet complaining the entire way. She couldn't neglect to admire the dining room, as expensive as it had been to furnish it. The first thing she noted, as everyone did, was the large tapestry hanging on her wall, several feet long and several feet tall, woven of silk and wool. The $3,500 Aubusson tapestry, which overlooked her extensive mahogany dining set, depicted six hounds cornering a wild boar during a hunt. *The Boar at Bay*, it was titled. The piece made Sarah smile; she liked the brotherhood of the hounds, their dedication to the hunt. One of the dogs, in fact, reminded her of the stray dog that had adopted their family in Delta soon before her parents died.

The organ chime told Sarah it was already five-fifteen, and she had admired only the first floor so far. Thank goodness for the elevator, she thought as she took the contraption down to the basement. Of all of her floors, she spent the least time here. The basement housed her gymnasium, which she didn't visit nearly as much as she'd planned, to make use of the rowing machine, climbing bars, and electric baths the way her nurse advised. Even now, she only glanced into the gymnasium before doubling back toward the kitchen. Her days in the kitchen were long gone, and she had a cook to prepare her meals that weren't catered, so unless she ate a meal at the long kitchen table, this elegant part of her home was the domain of others, not her. The kitchen floor was so clean that it gleamed, and there were cabinets to spare, enough to store food for a year, it seemed.

The servants had their own dining area at one end of the kitchen, with an adjoining shower room and toilet, and Sarah noticed that the servants' table was spotless except for a newspaper someone had left behind. Imagine, she'd once had to tramp outside in the rain just to travel back and forth between her kitchen and her home in Vicksburg! That little kitchen had probably been about as big as her servants' shower room today, she mused, and she felt a tingle across the back of her neck.

She was tiring already, she realized with dismay.

With a determined sigh, Sarah found the elevator again and took it to the third floor, which had guest rooms, servants' rooms, and Lelia's favorite—the billiard room. Sarah walked into the dark, richly hued billiard room and gazed with satisfaction at the large Flemish oak billiard table and ten matching high-backed armchairs. *A gentleman's billiard room*, Sarah thought, imagining that some of her guests today might slip up here for a friendly game.

Sarah knew the second floor very well; this was where her bedroom and sitting room were, along with four other bedrooms, all with their own bathrooms. The private passageway between her sitting room and bedroom had large mirrored closets on either side. Sarah's bed was still rumpled from where she'd left it not long ago beneath its red canopy, but she gazed at it as if it were a new discovery, imagining the dear little wooden bed Moses had built for them with his own hands after they were married. One entire wall of her bedroom was a large picture window displaying the landscaped grounds outside, including the $10,000 Japanese prayer tree she'd had imported, with an adjoining door leading to her enclosed porch. Beyond that, there was the beautiful expanse of the Hudson River and the dramatic cliffs of the New Jersey Palisades on the other side. The entire room was kept cozy by her bedroom's fireplace.

And, of course, there was one item on Sarah's nightstand that had kept its place her entire life, following her to Vicksburg, St. Louis, then Denver, then Pittsburgh, then to Harlem, and now here: the photograph of her father. It had a much more regal gold frame now, but the photograph was unchanged from the time she'd first found it as a girl. Gazing at the photo, Sarah heard herself speak aloud: "You proud of me, Papa?"

Of course he was, he and Mama both. And Moses, too. And C.J.?

Suddenly Sarah felt a fist in her chest. The feeling frightened her—all sudden pains or sensations now startled her, making her fear her doctors' warnings were coming to pass—until she realized it was only a keen, sharp loneliness. Grief, really.

Sarah felt utterly absurd for a moment. Here was Sarah Breedlove in this big house stuffed with treasures, all of it worth probably half a million dollars, and she still felt a longing for something else. *I don't know what you want, Mama,* Lelia had said during their last horrible fight, one that still seemed to linger between them even though neither of them had brought it up since.

God help her, she didn't know herself.

More than twenty thousand agents. A full-fledged factory with three hundred employees. A thriving business. Real estate holdings around the country. A palace. Four automobiles. Eight servants, even a butler and chauffeur. A tutor. A nurse. In all, she thought, she might be worth a million dollars, as all the newspapers kept claiming about her. There were only two wishes still posted on her Wish Board: *Rest*, one said. The other: *Justice for Negroes.*

Yet she was here in her bedroom on her most triumphant day with an ache in her chest that felt very much like a real hole that she could touch if she tried. Sarah's eyes traveled back to her nightstand, and her eyes found the tiny porcelain black rose C.J. had given her on their wedding day. It had been slightly chipped somehow, but she still kept it. Was *he* the reason for the hole? *God help me if that's true*, Sarah thought.

She had not talked to C.J. since his betrayal. She'd finally relented and told Mr. Ransom to allow C.J. to set up an agency to sell Walker goods—that, in her mind, was only fair—but she did not want to think about him. His sister Agnes Prosser, who was a wonderful woman and remained a friend of hers and the Ransoms, told her how C.J. was doing from time to time, but even Agnes knew better than to bring up her brother's name unless she was asked.

She didn't need him. She was doing better than ever without C.J. Walker.

But the phantom pain in the middle of Sarah's chest, right between her breastbone, told her clearly that she wanted something she did not have, and she was beginning to realize that even a trunkful of money couldn't begin to buy it for her.

The doorbell chimed endlessly, and the butler dutifully announced all newcomers in a stentorian tone that could be heard throughout the entrance hall over the organ music.

"Mrs. Margaret Murray Washington!"

"Mrs. Ida B. Wells-Barnett!"

"Mr. and Mrs. A. Philip Randolph!"

"Mr. Arthur Schomburg!"

"Mr. and Mrs. James Weldon Johnson!"

"Mr. and Mrs. Rosamond Johnson!"

"Mr. Carter G. Woodson!"

The house swelled with guests, and soon it was filled with the din of conversation and clinking glasses as the guests enjoyed fruit punch and each other's company. Sarah and Lelia flitted between them, greeting them all and accepting their compliments with grace and modesty.

"My only reason to have the villa is to share it," Sarah told everyone who expressed astonishment at its opulence. "It belongs to the race."

Sarah was so proud of Lelia; she'd outdone herself today, dressed in a glittering ivory-colored dress more striking than anything she had ever seen her daughter wear. It lacked ruffles and frills, and it was simple in its elegance of design, reaching only just above her ankles. Dresses were certainly getting shorter, Sarah realized. It wouldn't be long before women would be wearing dresses above their shins. And nothing could have suited Lelia's figure more.

"I think we should all do our part in the war effort," Lelia was saying to Emmett Scott, Booker T. Washington's former secretary, who was now a special assistant to the Secretary of War. "Mother has addressed our troops to uplift them, as you know, and she sells war bonds as well as she does Walker products. We haven't forgotten the unfortunate ones, either—so I take great pride in my work to provide first-aid supplies for the Circle of Negroes' War Relief."

"Your help is much needed," Mr. Scott said, nodding.

Listening to her daughter, Sarah found it impossible to believe that this was the same Lelia she had pulled from her card room that awful night a few months ago. How could Lelia be so wanton and still so poised? "Very soon I'm going to start meeting returning soldiers who have been maimed and injured," Lelia went on. "I'm trying to start a Colored Women's Motor Corps in Harlem, you see, so we can drive ambulances. Mother sits on the board for the Motor Corps of America, and I want to take part in my own way. But I'd better take driving lessons first!"

Later, in the drawing room, Sarah found herself flanked by Margaret Murray Washington and Ida B. Wells-Barnett, who were admiring the same art pieces she'd been gazing at in privacy before dawn. "No, let me tell *you*," Mrs. Wells-Barnett said to Mrs. Washington, pulling on Sarah's arm. "You should have seen her when she first started out. I'll tell you one thing, I thought she was talking a whole lot of nonsense. Hair grower! Isn't that the truth, Madam?"

"You and a whole lot of other folks," Sarah said.

Mrs. Washington's eyes shone warmly, although Sarah also recognized the sadness there. Of all the people still reeling from the loss of Booker T. Washington, this woman and his children must feel it the most, Sarah thought. "She made a real impression on me at Tuskegee, I'll say that," Mrs. Washington said. "But still, I never expected anything like this!"

"Well, I'm not one for a whole lot of social affairs," Mrs. Wells-Barnett said, "but today, I think a true monument has been unveiled."

Sarah attended her own gathering in a daze, sometimes giddy, sometimes feeling as if she were sleepwalking. She quietly reacquainted herself with people she knew: NAACP board chairman Joel Springarn, who thanked her for her fund-raising speeches; the treasurer, Oswald Garrison Villard, editor of the *New York Evening Post*; assistant secretary Walter White; and a stream of others who had entered her life suddenly since her move to New York. Some she knew fairly well; some she knew barely at all. But most of them met her with smiles that were nearly gushing, as if they were just the slightest bit intimidated by her.

How in the world did you do this? The unspoken question was obvious in their eyes.

She remembered how self-conscious she'd felt at that first formal gathering with C.J. in Denver, and she had to smile. None of those snitty folks even warranted an invitation to her party today. From city to city, the local elite had never wanted much to do with her, so she'd become a darling of the *national* elite instead, the folks who really mattered. No one in this room saw a washerwoman when they looked at her. No one.

"Mother Walker!"

A familiar child's voice made Sarah's head whirl around with joy. Little Frank Ransom, wearing short pants and an adorable coat and tie, lifted his arms upward to Sarah as he bounced in front of her feet, excited. His baby teeth were displayed in a wide, dimpled grin. Sarah knew his parents must be not far behind, and she was glad. She'd missed Nettie and the boys horribly, and she had business to discuss with Mr. Ransom. Nettie had just given birth to her fourth child—a daughter, at last!—so she'd been afraid they might not make it to the event.

"Ooh—just lookit my godbaby!" Sarah said, leaning down to give Frank a hug. "Don't you know you're too big for me to lift you up like before? Why do you keep growing? Huh?"

The boy giggled. "Is this your great big house, Mother Walker?"

"It sure is! Wait until you and your brothers see the nursery upstairs."

Soon the other boys crowded noisily around her, expecting their hugs, too, while their parents tried to hush them. Freeman Ransom's hair was shaved much closer to his head than it had been the last time she'd seen her attorney, and he seemed just a few pounds stockier, too. But otherwise this man seemed to change less than anyone Sarah had ever known. He gave her a warm smile. The love and admiration he felt for her seemed to glow from his skin, and Sarah understood how he felt. In some ways Mr. Ransom had been more a partner than C.J. And Nettie seemed to be recuperating well from the birth, if she looked a little tired.

"Madam," Mr. Ransom said, squeezing her hand. "I'm speechless today."

"Not you, Mr. Ransom. As soon as you take a walk around, you'll start scolding me for the cost," Sarah said. "Let me see the baby!"

The tiny newborn swathed in a blanket in Nettie's arms looked like she'd just left the womb, she was so small. Her brown eyes squinted at Sarah. "Oh, Nettie . . . she's a little *wonder*! You have to find Lelia to show her," Sarah said. Her daughter would be especially thrilled to see this baby, since she was the child's namesake: A'Lelia Emma Ransom.

"I will, but I just can't get over this house! You've really done it this time, Sarah," said Nettie, who was wearing a lilac-colored summer gown and matching hat. It had taken Nettie a long time to finally agree to call Sarah by her Christian name instead of *Madam*, but Sarah was grateful Nettie had made the transition. She had few true friends in the room today. "I do believe you finally have everything in the world."

Her words, to Sarah, felt like a bolt of lightning. Jarred, she glanced at the Ransom children, then at her huddles of guests, before returning her gaze to Nettie's smile. In that instant she forgot the strange sense of sorrow she'd felt before dawn. "You know something, Nettie . . . ?" Sarah said with wonderment. "I do believe you're right. And I've had it a long time, long before I built this house. How have I been so blessed?"

"You know how, Sarah—*work*," Nettie said.

She raised her index finger to Sarah's chin to stroke it before giving her a long, warm hug with her free arm. Sarah hugged her back tightly, careful not to press against the baby.

"You go find Lelia and get the boys some of that punch, Nettie," Sarah said, pulling away. "I need to talk to Mr. Ransom."

Sarah took Mr. Ransom through the Gold Room to the balcony outside, closing the French doors behind them. She could hear some of the din from inside, but she could also hear her fountain's gurgling and the calls of nearby birds. Without meeting Mr. Ransom's eyes, she gazed out at the trees and shrubbery lining her lovely property, feeling a growing sense of peace.

"I'm a better gardener now than I was as a girl, that's for sure," Sarah said. "I should take you down to see my roses and vegetables. I must have gained a magic touch."

"You've always had that, Madam," Mr. Ransom said, standing beside her. He rested his hands on the balcony, leaning forward. "That's apparent here today. You've shown yourself to be a true woman of standing with this occasion. And I only want to caution you not to spoil it."

"Spoil it how?" Sarah said, confused. Then, before Mr. Ransom could answer, Sarah knew his concern: He thought she was becoming too heavily involved in politics, consorting with activists like William Monroe Trotter, who was considered a radical. There had been a vicious political rivalry between Mr. Trotter and Booker T. Washington before Dr. Washington died, to the point where Mr. Trotter had hampered the deceased leader's speaking engagements; but although Sarah didn't always like Mr. Trotter's tactics, she believed he had the best interests of the race at heart. Perhaps Negroes had been *too* conservative until now, Sarah thought.

"I know you can't help yourself, but I'm not in the mood for a lecture just now, Mr. Ransom," Sarah said. "I'd much rather hear if you've thought about what I've offered you."

Freeman Ransom sighed. "I've thought about little else, Madam," he said.

"Then I hope you'll say yes."

He paused. "I talked to Nettie first, and then I talked it over with God. I think they're both trying to push me in the same direction. But sometimes I think it's men who are the weaker sex. I'm afraid I still have doubts, Madam."

"Good," Sarah said, looking at him with a smile. "I'd be scared if you didn't."

"How will A'Lelia like it?" Mr. Ransom asked solemnly.

"Maybe not much at all. But in her heart, she knows what's best."

Sarah turned around because she felt someone watching her through the window. Sure enough, as if she'd known they were talking about her, Sarah saw her daughter standing there staring. There was a hardness in Lelia's face, but also resignation. Quickly, Lelia cast her eyes down and moved away. A piece of Sarah's heart seemed to follow her daughter.

"So, Mr. Ransom . . . will you be the lifetime general manager of the Madam C.J. Walker Manufacturing Company? We need you. I want it specified in the will I'm drawing up that the *ownership* always has to be in the hands of women, and Lelia will be the president. That's the only thing that feels right. I'll make it clear that she can't dispose of the company. And in terms of running it, Mr. Ransom, there's no one better than you. If I don't hand it over to you right now, I don't see how I or this company can go on. And that's the truth."

There was something in Mr. Ransom's eyes too large for words. He looked humbled, saddened, and the slightest bit awestruck. But slowly, at last, he nodded.

"I'll draw up . . . the papers. . . ." Mr. Ransom said, mumbling.

Quickly, Sarah took her attorney's hand and gave it a firm, definite shake. Their hands did not part for a long time.

Chapter Thirty-seven

December 21, 1918

Madam C.J. Walker
Villa Lewaro
Irvington, New York

Dear Madam:

When Christmas comes around, I am always reminded of
the number of years that I have known you and, looking
back over your remarkable career, I take a peculiar pride
in the fact that I have had the pleasure of watching you
develop in business and also broadening along all lines,
and then I congratulate myself on having the honor of
knowing you and representing you in some small way. I,
of course, am writing in the hope that God will continue
to smile on you and that you will continue to bless and
help the less fortunate. Villa Lewaro will always stand as a
monument to your business ability and foresight as well as
a milestone in the remarkable advance of a people.

Our little token will be completely lost among finer
surroundings and more appropriate remembrances.
However, you will please accept same as an expression of
our love and affection.

Frank and your sister-in-law, Mrs. Prosser, will leave
tomorrow morning and will arrive in New York Monday.
Will wire you as to the exact time.

Again wishing you a Merry Christmas in which my whole family joins me, I am

Respectfully,
F.B. Ransom

January 11, 1919

Dear Madam:

Frank is telling wonders about New York, saying that you took him to halls, moving picture shows, theaters, etc., and he is telling of some of the great things he saw in these halls and places, all of which I take are figments of his rather vivid imagination. He said he slept with you and that every morning you and he would wake up and talk. I asked him what you talked about and he said, "We talked business."

I note what you say about Mr. Trotter's National Equal Rights League, and the only thing I am concerned with is the danger of your becoming identified with some person or persons whose acts will hurt your future in this country. You are traveling in the right direction, and I do not want to see anything occur to hamper or lessen your influence in this country.

Respectfully,
F.B. Ransom

VILLA LEWARO
IRVINGTON-ON-HUDSON

February 4, 1919

Dear Mr. Ransom:
   Your arguments have been passionate indeed against my participation in the Paris peace conference meetings planned by Mr. Trotter. I agree it is best to try to change a system from within, but I thought Mrs. Ida Wells-Barnett and

myself would have represented our race well in the talks overseas. My great fear is that the world will finally forge its peace treaties, but Negroes will be left out entirely.

But do not think your pleas have fallen on deaf ears! I do understand I must be concerned for my business and future too, so I will separate myself from those radical elements you feel would be harmful to me and the company.

All this talk of Paris has made me very excited at the prospect of traveling abroad, however, and Lelia shares my excitement. She is making plans to take Mae on a sales trip to South America, but we have already decided that we would like to spend some time in Paris together afterward—perhaps even up to a year! I am pursuing plans to secure a passport. I'm pleased to say that the Long family has been very helpful in establishing my birthplace, as you know I have no proper birth records owing to my family's condition when I was born.

Thank you again for your very thoughtful advice.

Sincerely,

Madam

P.S. There are so many heroes among us! Dr. Ward is back visiting me with Zella. I think my schedule still alarms him, though he is glad to see me calmly tending my garden. I have become a real "farmerette." Roses abound! He is now Major Ward, you know—and he commanded a base hospital in Paris! And Dr. Kennedy has written to Lelia that he is very likely to receive a Croix de Guerre for his bravery overseas. Negroes certainly represented our race well in this unfortunate war.

The Madam C.J. Walker Mfg. Company

640 NORTH WEST STREET
INDIANAPOLIS, INDIANA

F.B. Ransom
Atty. & Mgr.

March 20, 1919

Dear Madam:

I do look forward to seeing you! I am in receipt of your note mentioning that you will leave Irvington on or about the 26th of the month. I was reasonably sure that this would be the time of your leaving, as I heard you were going to speak in Wilmington. And while Dr. Ward advises against speaking dates, I am sure that it will not

hurt you to make this meeting and then come on to
Indianapolis.

I am glad to know that you are resting.

Respectfully,
F.B. Ransom

The Madam C.J. Walker Mfg. Company
640 NORTH WEST STREET
INDIANAPOLIS, INDIANA

F.B. Ransom
Atty. & Mgr.

March 22, 1919

Dear Madam:

Enclosed are samples of the new literature. I am aware
that you requested me when in New York to go ahead
with these things, relieving you as much as possible of any
such business details, but I have gotten in the habit of
consulting you, so you will pardon me at this time. In all
seriousness, however, I consult you in this respect as I do
not wish to make such change, necessitating a slight
additional cost, without first securing your approval.

Lottie stated that you are suffering from a severe cold. I
hope this will find you feeling much better, as I want you
to be in your best health during your travels.

Respectfully,

F.B. Ransom

P.S. Nettie and the boys are on their heads to see you! We
hope you will be able to stay with us a few days before you
move on to St. Louis to help launch the new products
line. After that, please take Dr. Ward's advice and stay at
home to rest.

Chapter Thirty-eight

It's a cold. Just a very bad cold, Sarah repeated to herself as she sat in the empty back office of St. Paul AME church holding a cold, damp cloth to her feverish head. A fan gently stirred the papers stacked on the pastor's rolltop desk, and she could hear the distant voices of choir members rehearsing in one of the wings. She'd asked to sit alone for a few minutes, hoping she would feel better before services started. Her skin was burning, but she could hear her teeth chattering. Oh, she hated to be sick! She'd hoped to shake this cold weeks ago, but it had refused to leave her. She'd felt all right in Indianapolis, but she'd felt steadily worse since her arrival in St. Louis. *Oh, I should have just gone on back to New York like Lottie said.*

Her hosts, Jessie and C.K. Robinson, had suggested she stay in bed at their home that day, offering to miss the Easter service themselves to nurse her, but Sarah had been sure she could bear to at least sit through the service. She wouldn't address the congregation, she knew—she'd save her strength for her speech at the Coliseum in a few days—but she'd wanted to at least make an appearance. There were so many old friends at the church, so many people who had known her as Sarah McWilliams. She might not have the chance to come back soon. . . .

Sarah coughed, and she was dismayed to feel her entire chest constrict painfully.

It's a cold, Sarah. Just a cold.

The voice in her head continued to coo its assurances, but Sarah believed that voice less and less. She'd never had a cold that made her feel like her body was hardening to rock, as if it would take more strength than she'd ever had just to stand up and make her way back into the sanctuary where the Robinsons were waiting for her. Lottie or Jessie would come back here looking after her soon, she knew, and she wanted to put on a good face. If she sat perfectly still during services, she might be all right.

And even if she wasn't all right, she'd *look* as though she were. Then she'd go right to bed just as they had suggested in the first place. Maybe she would have to cancel her Coliseum speaking engagement. She'd been looking forward to it, but enough was enough. *This is what you get for being stubborn,* she thought. *You shouldn't be here at all.*

Sarah heard uneven footsteps approaching the pastor's doorway, so she forced herself to sit up straight. She removed the damp cloth from her forehead, holding it in her lap. She didn't know how her face looked, but she hoped she'd managed something at least resembling a smile.

When the shadow in the doorway finally took its human shape, Sarah held her breath and forgot her ailments: It was a man, but it wasn't the pastor or Mr. Robinson. An old man who looked familiar and yet unfamiliar stood there with a walking stick and a slightly rumpled brown suit. He kept glancing down from her eyes, clearly nervous. But wait . . .

It *wasn't* an old man, Sarah realized. The man's hair and mustache were graying and his posture was poor, making his bones look frail, but this man was hardly any older than she was. Then she allowed herself to recognize what she'd known from the moment she'd seen him.

This man was C.J. Walker.

"I, uh . . ." C.J. cleared his throat, wiping the side of his mouth with a white kerchief he'd crumpled in one hand. "I know I shouldn't have come back here . . . but I saw 'em bring you back, and . . . well, I . . ." Sarah noticed that C.J.'s hand was trembling on his walking stick. He was putting most of his weight on it, and it was a struggle for him. The sight of the shaking hand transfixed her. How could this be . . . ?

"I know you're sore, Sa— Madam. And not in a million years did I ever think I'd be standing in front of you like this. But I couldn't help myself. When I was passing outside and saw you walk inside this church, it brought a whole lot to mind. A whole lot."

Ordinarily, Sarah thought, she'd probably have leaped to her feet and screamed every epithet she could think of at C.J., or else wrested that walking stick away to knock him in the head. Or would she have leaped to her feet to hug him . . . ? She honestly didn't know. But it didn't matter now, because any leaping was out of the question. She wondered if she could really speak a word to him, even if she wanted to. She was using all of her concentration to listen to him, and she had to ask herself in all honesty if he might be only a hallucination. The way she was feeling, a hallucination wouldn't surprise her at all.

But no. She never would have imagined him like this. His skin, which she'd always remembered as so fine and smooth, looked thin and dry, nearly leathery. Had his drinking altered him so horribly? Or was it the rheumatism he'd always complained about in his letters? It was hard for her to imagine there was a time when he'd been neatly dressed and handsome. He didn't look quite like a hobo, but his clothes hadn't been given the same care and attention C.J. used to be so proud of, and his shoes were scuffed.

Finally Sarah felt an emotion; it was neither anger nor love, just pity.

And C.J. must have recognized it in her eyes the way she'd always been able to recognize it in the eyes of others. He tried to straighten his shoulders some, but the effort didn't help much.

"I know," he said, nodding slowly. "I must be a real sight to you. I told my sister she better never say a word to you 'bout it. If you asked, I told her she should just say, 'He's gettin' by.' But she say you don't hardly ask, and I've been glad about that. After you told Mr. Ransom I could start selling the Walker goods again, I figured that's about all I could hope for. But I guess I ain't completely lost my selfish streak, Madam. I didn't know how bad I needed to say some words to you until I saw you today."

He blinked fast, fighting tears. It was a long fight; apparently C.J. was determined not to cry in front of her. When he'd finally composed himself, he took in a deep breath and went on: "Thank you for givin' me this chance, Madam. I won't forget it to my dying day. This will sound strange to you from the likes of me, but you'll have to forgive me if my tongue gets tied up. I've had a long time to think on this, what I've done. Pride and envy's the only reasons I can think of to explain it, but even that ain't enough. I didn't pay no mind to folks sayin' 'The devil made me do it' until that ol' devil got into me, and now I think maybe he does more mischief than we know about. That's not an *excuse*, now—it's just my way of explaining. But I tell you what, that still don't go far to explaining why a man would give up everything any sane man in the world could want. See, Madam, I think I done sold my soul when I met up with that woman. That's why you see me this way now. I ain't never been the same after what I did, and I expect I never will."

He paused, his breathing heavier. He leaned on the doorjamb for support, taking some of his weight off the walking stick. "Now, you notice I ain't never asked you to forgive me in those letters I wrote. I don't see as I have a right to ask that. Besides, I know you too well: I remember you tellin' me a story once about a friend who did you wrong—I think her name was Etta—and how you closed up your heart and never saw her again. That's why I knew better. You're one of those folks who can't open her heart once it's been shut. But I am sorry, Madam. Sorry don't even begin to sum it up. If I have one thing to feel good about, it's knowing that I never gave her your hair formula, just like I said in the paper. Oh, she wanted it, all right, but I never would say. That's the gospel truth, or lightning can strike me where I stand."

Sarah believed that. She and Mr. Ransom had kept careful track of Dora Larrie's movements, and Larrie had never had any success in business even when she tried to use the name *Madam C.J. Walker*. She'd once had the nerve to try to threaten Sarah with legal action if she wouldn't give up the name she believed now belonged to *her*, before Mr. Ransom put her in her place. Mr. Ransom had even paid someone to send Sarah a sample of the woman's product once, and Sarah knew just by looking at that mess in the jar that Dora Larrie was fumbling in the dark. And Sarah didn't think C.J. would have revealed the formula to anyone else. She'd known him that well, at least.

"Now, whatever happens to me, that's just my lot, and I ain't even worried 'bout it," C.J. said. "But one thing does worry me: I put a wrong idea in your head. The way I acted, I left you to believe there was ever a day I thought I didn't love you." After his voice cracked, C.J. took a deep breath. "And even though I know it doesn't seem like it to you, that's just a damn lie. I always did, Madam. I loved you the first day I took you out to supper over to the Rosebud Bar, and I loved you when you were pointing that gun at my heart. I half hoped you'd pull that trigger. Maybe even more than half."

C.J. bit his bottom lip, again valiantly fighting an emotional display. He gazed up toward the ceiling, away from Sarah's eyes. "So maybe it ain't fair, Madam, but that's the one thing I wanted to come here and tell you. And you don't have to say nothin' else to me, but I just wish you'd tell me you believe I loved you, and that I've never stopped. Do you believe me, Madam?"

Sarah's mind and heart felt stripped. C.J. had broken himself because of her. She would never fully understand why, but he'd broken every part of himself. She could do nothing except slowly nod her head *yes*. C.J. grinned when he saw her affirmation. He smiled a sickly smile.

"You look like I feel, C.J.," Sarah said in a thin, raspy voice.

"That may be, but I sure wish I felt as good as you look, Sarah," he said. Then, with obvious discomfort in his joints, he reached up for his lopsided hat and tipped it. "Madam."

Somehow Sarah managed to smile at him, and the smile stayed on her lips as she watched C.J. Walker turn around and walk away with painstakingly careful steps as he leaned on his walking stick. She heard his footsteps retreat to the end of the hall, and then they disappeared behind a click of the basement door. In the instant before the door closed, she'd heard a motorcar horn sound from outside. She should have known C.J. wasn't about to sit through a church service unless he was trying to make a sale. He hadn't changed *that* much, then. Sarah shook her head.

"Good-bye, C.J. Walker," Sarah said to the silence. "You poor fool."

Then Sarah closed her eyes and tried to steel herself for church.

By the time the shouts of affirmation had died down after the choir's spirited rendition of "Were You There When They Crucified My Lord?," Sarah was shaking in her seat. But despite the electricity in the room, with lingering cries of "*Yes, Lord!*" and "*Amen!*" still issuing from the lips of excited worshipers in the midst of sporadic clapping and dramatic organ chords, Sarah knew her shaking had nothing to do with the Holy Spirit sweeping her neighbors. She felt as cold to the bone as she might on any winter's day, but her underclothes were drenched in perspiration. Her entire body was wet. For all she knew, she'd lost control of her bladder.

I'm really sick, she thought, as if amazed. *I've never been sick as this.*

The Robinsons had not yet noticed her sudden decline, but Lottie had. Sarah's tutor was holding her hand tightly, her eyes pinned to her. "Madam?" she said into Sarah's ear. "We can't wait for the end. We have to get you to bed. I want to call Dr. Ward."

"But I have to *speak*, Lottie!" Sarah said sharply, too loudly. Jessie and C.K. Robinson glanced at her that time, as did several people in the nearby pews. The room seemed to stand still only for small instants, then it swam into an indecipherable blur. Sarah swayed in her seat without realizing it, her weight resting against Lottie. "Where'd C.J. go? Do you see him anyplace?"

The words tumbled out of her mouth from nowhere. Sarah had never mentioned to her companions that C.J. had met her in the pastor's office, and she hadn't meant to. Why had she said that? "Oh, Lord—what's wrong with her?" Jessie whispered, touching Sarah's forehead.

But Sarah forgot them both, because she could hear the pastor's voice in front of her, and it seemed to her that he must be talking about her. Yes, he was!

A daughter of St. Louis. Fourteen years as a washerwoman. Hair formula in a dream.

Suddenly Sarah could hear the man's voice clearly, not just in snatches: ". . . She isn't scheduled to make an address here today, but she is right here in our midst, and I was hoping she could stand and say just a few words to inspire us all—Madam C.J. Walker!"

All around her, Sarah heard gasps of surprise and delight, then applause that sounded to her like the hooves of a wild stampede across a plain. The sound seemed to shake the floor and rattle her teeth. What a humbling sound! It was a gift she could never repay.

"*No*, Madam," Lottie begged, tugging on her. "You're not well."

But somehow, in a single lurch, Sarah managed to free herself from her tutor's grasp and found herself standing on her feet. She had to lean on the pew in front of her with both hands for support, but her stance was triumphant. She'd done it! She'd stood up by herself.

Nearly rocking, Sarah looked around her at the faces in the room. Beaming, expectant faces. Many of the women in this room were Walker agents, Sarah knew, because Jessie Robinson had already introduced her to several agents in the congregation. Mr. Ransom had told her he'd seen a Walker parlor on every corner when he was visiting Chicago, just like in

Harlem, and she'd seen for herself that St. Louis had its proud share, too. And look at all of these women! Most of them were wearing their Easter white, and they were a portrait of dignity with their lacy dresses and fresh-cut white flowers in their hats, with their men proudly at their sides.

We're all makin' it, and we're doin' it together. Ain't none of us washing no damn clothes. Them days is gone.

"I'm so happy to see you," Sarah said, and they smothered her in applause. "I'm . . . not well today. I'm not feeling my best. But when I see you . . . when I see how beautiful we can be . . ."

Her heart was full of sentiment that helped calm the strange racing of her heart, but suddenly Sarah couldn't think of words. Her mouth was dry, empty. She'd made many speeches when she wasn't feeling well in the past year, but the sight of the crowds had always given her new strength to go on. Not today. She struggled to find one inspirational word, but nothing came from her mouth except the sound of her harsh, ragged breathing.

Who in the world was that screaming in her ear? Was it Lottie?

Before Sarah even realized she was falling, she had already collapsed to the church floor. *I must look like a heap of wash down here*, she thought, still lucid enough to feel mortified.

But soon, even that worry was gone.

Chapter Thirty-nine

VILLA LEWARO
MAY 1919

Sarah still thought about her ride on the train.

She and her employees had used first-class Pullman cars for years, especially when she wasn't traveling in the South, but the train that had brought her home must have set tongues wagging all the way from St. Louis to New York. The Robinsons had chartered her a private railroad car on the lightning-quick 20th Century Limited, with plenty of room for her bed, Dr. Ward, her nurse, and Lottie. There'd been so many flowers in the train car's windows, it had been no wonder Lottie reported curious, wondering faces along the way. She herself had heard someone say: "Who's that in there, the King of England?"

No one had seen anything like it. Now, that had been something, all right.

And it was while she was on that train—not *enjoying* the ride, exactly, but tolerating it in the highest spirits she could muster—that Sarah had her inspiration: It was time to give away more of her money. She'd always given away bits here and there, but now it was time to truly give. Mr. Ransom was always cautioning her to be thrifty, but suddenly she realized that she had to indulge herself in one last spending spree. Not on her homes or cars this time, but on her people.

If she'd had her way, Sarah would have traveled from place to place presenting the checks herself, but she knew that wouldn't happen now. No, even if she did recover, she wasn't going to be able to do that. She'd finally understood what Dr. Ward and Dr. Kennedy meant about not exerting herself, and she only hoped she hadn't pushed herself too far. The one and only thing she wanted to save her strength for now was a trip to Paris with Lelia this summer. If she couldn't go this year, she'd rest until she was ready to go next year. And if she died in Paris, then so be it. *We all have to go somewhere, sometime,* Sarah thought. And she couldn't take her money with her, whenever she died, so she might as well put it to use now.

"Where were we, Lottie?" Sarah asked from her bed, sipping from a glass of tepid orange juice. The organ downstairs was playing a beautiful piece entitled *Communion in G,* which Sarah never tired of hearing. That organ had given her plenty of trouble, but it was finally working. Her music was often interrupted by the endless ringing of her telephone as people from all over the country called to inquire about her condition (Lottie brought her an armful of new telegrams and letters each day, and there were so many flowers that they had filled the villa with a sweet smell), but Sarah knew better than to take any calls, no matter how much she was tempted. She needed all of her energy to keep her mind clear and her strength up. By the time Lelia came back from Central America in August, she wanted to surprise her daughter by being out of bed and healthy once again, never mind what Dr. Ward had said about her poor body's ailments.

"Five thousand dollars to the NAACP Anti-Lynching fund," Lottie read from her notes. "That's a wonderful gift, Madam. I'm sure they've never had one so big."

"Good . . ." Sarah said. She coughed, then cleared her throat. "Let's see . . . there are so many. . . . Oh! Don't forget Mary Bethune. Put down the Daytona school for a contribution, too. Make sure she knows right away."

"Yes, Madam. This brings your total to . . . twenty-five thousand dollars in contributions," Lottie said, tallying up the figure. Lottie's expression was dutiful enough, but Sarah could hear the unhappiness in her tutor's voice. Lottie looked uncharacteristically disheveled, as if she hadn't slept in days. Maybe she hadn't, bless her.

Dr. Ward might be right about her, then. That was why it was more and more difficult to speak, and why her vision seemed to be dimming. Everything was blurry now; she couldn't deny that. She'd hoped her vision would improve, but it hadn't. Maybe it would get worse. Dr. Ward hadn't admitted it outright, but she'd known from his voice when she complained about her eyesight that he expected she might well go blind.

Sarah felt a stab of alarm. There was no more money to give, not if she wanted to leave enough for her company to run. She'd bequeathed $10,000 to establish an industrial and mission school in Africa, and her will provided for her little godson, for Lottie, for Nettie, for Lou, for Willie. And Lelia, of course. She'd even bequeathed a thousand dollars to C.J.'s sister, Agnes; she had looked out for C.J. before, and Sarah knew she would look out for him now.

She had nothing left to give, she realized. Nothing.

"Lottie . . . can you write a letter to Lelia for me? I'd write this one myself, but . . ."

"Of course, Madam," Lottie said, pulling her chair closer to the bed as if Sarah were a fire she hoped to warm herself by.

Sarah sighed, suddenly allowing herself to realize how awful it felt to have Lelia so far away from her now, a yawning chasm between them. It was just so much harder this way! She often woke up at night with a feeling of searing panic, knowing something was undone, and she guessed it was Lelia's absence. She'd never have imagined even going to Paris without her daughter, and where was she going now?

But it was all right. Lelia was making better choices in her life, so at least Sarah didn't have to worry about her anymore. Because Lottie's features were so blurry to her, Sarah tried to imagine that Lelia was here beside her now, and she began to speak:

"My Darling Baby," she began. "Lottie just read me your letters, and you made me very happy to know that at last you have decided to marry Kennedy. I never thought Wiley would make you happy, but I do believe Kennedy will. Let me know what time in August you will return and at what time you will marry. If you think it best, I will announce the engagement while you are away." She paused a moment to catch her breath, as she was often forced to now. Her lungs, like everything else, were in rebellion. "My wish is for you to have a very quiet wedding out here and leave shortly afterward for France. You may get your château and I will follow. Then I will take my contemplated trip around the world. Let Kennedy study abroad for a year. I will make France my headquarters. I never want you to leave me this far again."

Sarah sensed that Lottie was looking at her now with some surprise, but she didn't care. She would move to France, if it came to that. The villa didn't matter—all that mattered was being with her baby. Somehow Sarah had felt from the first time she'd walked through the doors of Villa Lewaro that she had not been meant to live here long.

And if Dr. Ward was right, she would not live anywhere long.

"Nettie is here with Frank and your little namesake," Sarah went on. "You will love seeing her. She is too sweet and dear for anything. I am so happy having them with me. Nettie and the girls join me in love to you and Mae, and I send my love, kisses and kisses and kisses. Your Devoted, Mother."

Sarah stopped, and there was a stark silence in the room except for the scribbling of Lottie's pen. Even the organ had stopped momentarily. Sarah could hear the erratic rhythm of her own breathing and the clumsy beating of her heart.

"Madam . . ." Lottie said suddenly. "You should tell her to come home now. Don't let her stay away until August."

Sarah pursed her lips defiantly. *She's right, Sarah,* the voice in her mind railed, the inner voice that had tried to steer her all her life. *You know what's happening to you. Don't pretend.*

But Sarah shook her head firmly. "I'm getting better, Lottie. Lelia once told me I get everything I want, and she's right. I'm getting better every day."

Sarah couldn't see Lottie's face clearly, but she could feel the grief bubbling from her bedside. Now, at last, Sarah understood the determination she'd seen on her father's face as he'd dragged himself out to their front porch right before he'd died. He hadn't wanted to let death take him, not willingly, at least. Maybe fighting was in the Breedlove blood.

"Madam, I have something I must say to you," Lottie began. "I know I am not entitled to speak for any woman but myself, but I've had such an extraordinary vantage point these past years, watching you. And learning."

"Learning . . . ?" Sarah said, chuckling. The chuckle ignited a small coughing fit, and she swallowed more juice to calm it. "There was nothing left to teach you, Lottie Ransaw."

"Yes, *learning*," Lottie said, helping Sarah steady her glass. "You've made my life rich beyond compare, and not just mine. You've given us all so much, at such a price. And in case I haven't said it properly before, I wanted to tell you . . . what you did will never be forgotten. I'm going to tell my nieces and nephews about you, and their children after that. I'm going to tell them about a woman who began life with much less than they will have, and how you achieved more than anyone could have reasonably expected. Watching you has taught me how to believe in the impossible, how to believe in a better day, and I will always be grateful to you for that. What you have done has truly mattered, Madam. You have mattered."

For the briefest instant, the room seemed to lose its air, but then Sarah realized she was holding her breath as if Lottie were threatening to strike her. There was no other way to look at it; Lottie had just given her a deathbed speech. Suddenly, with frightening clarity, Sarah knew why she didn't want to summon Lelia home: There was no time. She would die, and she would never see her daughter again. She couldn't change that. Of all the cold facts Sarah had been forced to accept her entire life, maybe this last one was the hardest. Oh, yes. Sarah's fingers trembled uncontrollably around the glass, and Lottie helped her lower it to her nightstand.

"Dr. Kennedy . . . will be good for Lelia, won't he?" Sarah said.

"Oh, yes. He's a very accomplished young man."

"And . . . you and Mr. Ransom will keep her out of trouble, won't you?"

"You know we'll always do our best, Madam." Lottie's eyes shone.

Sarah nodded, testing her emotions. She'd expected to feel more afraid when she came right out and admitted she was dying. But instead, since there was nothing else to do or change, the idea filled her with a strange calm. She relaxed, letting her head sink back into the pillow. As soon as she did, the bedroom door burst open, startling her because everyone usually trod so gently and quietly in her presence now. She looked up and saw the blurry figure of Lou lumbering toward her.

"Sarah, those nieces we got are 'bout the dullest bunch of folk anyone could stand," Lou said, exasperated. "Girl, I'm goin' out my head in this place, an' I git lost jus' goin' to my room an' the kitchen an' back—not that you *got* any food I like to eat. I know why you're sick, Sarah, 'cause you're *bored.* Now, let's get Nettie in here and all of us play some whist."

Lottie's mouth dropped open. "Whist! Most certainly not, Mrs. Powell. You—"

But Sarah laughed softly. Lou was contrary as always, but she had a point. If Lelia had been here, she might have said the same thing.

"She's right, Lottie," Sarah rasped. "I may not make it to Paris, but I still know how to play me some cards. Go make sure Dr. Kennedy is comfortable in his room, and tell him I'll talk to him more about Lelia tomorrow. Don't let on we're in here playing, and *please* don't say anything to Dr. Ward. Now hurry up and bring Nettie in here. You'll have to be on my team, Lottie, because I won't be able to see a single card face."

Lottie stood stock-still for a moment. Then, only vaguely, Sarah saw her grin. "Yes, Madam!" Lottie said, sounding happy for the first time since Sarah's collapse.

With the bedroom door firmly closed to keep out intruders and physicians, and the window open to let in the spring breeze, the four women played cards all afternoon at Sarah's bedside between fits of irreverent laughter. The organ downstairs played without a flaw, and none of them paid any mind to the ringing telephone.

Sarah figured if she didn't live another day, she was having one last day worth living for.

Epilogue

*Madam C.J. Walker's life was the clearest demonstration I
know of a Negro woman's ability recorded in history. She has
gone, but her work still lives and shall live as an inspiration to
not only her race, but to the world.*

—MARY MCLEOD BETHUNE

There was so much traffic, the Irvington village police chief himself was
posted in the middle of the road on Broadway, outside stately Villa
Lewaro. He directed the cavalcade of cars and large autobuses while birds
chirped merrily in the trees on that sunny afternoon, but the birdsong was
the only merriment as perfectly groomed men and women in muted
mourning colors filed past him for the funeral of Madam C.J. Walker. The
police chief was keeping a tally of people in his head with mounting disbelief: First there had been two hundred, then three hundred, then four hundred. And that had been an hour ago. Now, he realized, the number of
arrivals must have reached one thousand, and most of them were Negroes.
He had never seen so many Negroes in his life, and certainly not like
this: erect, self-possessed, dignified. Although lines of sadness creased their
faces, their manner bespoke a roiling sense of purpose. As long as he lived,
he never forgot the sight of them.

It was Friday, and Sarah had died on Sunday after spending three days
in a coma. Her nurse said that Sarah's final coherent words had been that
she wanted to live to help her race.

Inside the grand mansion, the grief was so pervasive it seemed to have
its own breath, despite the explosion of springtime colors in the flower
arrangements lining every inch of the living room walls. Women clad in
white, representing the Motor Corps of America, helped usher the atten-

dees as the crowd inside swelled. Where so recently the halls had been filled with laughter and celebration, Villa Lewaro had become a cheerless shrine, suddenly robbed of its hostess. The guests greeted each other with heartfelt handshakes and lingering, silent hugs. They passed their hushed recollections back and forth like precious trinkets.

"I was just here for her Christmas party, and I never imagined I'd be back like this. . . ."

"I saw her not even a month ago, over in Indianapolis. . . ."

"We had dinner in March, and I knew she wasn't well, but she was so lively. . . . ."

Fifty-one years old. The mantra came from all their lips, adding further confusion to the sudden turn of events. Madam C.J. Walker, as most of them knew her—or Sarah Breedlove, as a select few of them did—had died when she should have had so many useful years ahead. Losing her was tragedy enough, but to lose her so soon . . . And there was another pained whisper, a pervasive hope that flowed through the mourners: *Has A'Lelia made it back yet?*

A'Lelia and her daughter, Mae, were probably still at sea, they had been told. A'Lelia had learned of her mother's death on an ocean liner on its way back to the United States from Panama, but there had been no more word of her arrival. Each time the massive doors opened to let in new mourners, heads swiveled in search of A'Lelia's face. As more time passed, it grew more and more likely that A'Lelia would miss her own mother's funeral.

Another sadness, when there was already so much.

Lottie Ransaw, in the same dreamy haze she'd been in since Madam first collapsed in St. Louis, wove her way through the mourners to go to the organ her employer had loved so much. She did not glance inside the open bronze casket gleaming in the center of the drawing room because she had already had too long to study the vacant face of the lifeless woman who now had a wreath of orchids across her still breast; she *resembled* Madam, but that was only her body, after all. Instead Lottie's fingers settled across the organ's keys, sure and ready. After a deep breath she began to play, and the music gave her relief. Lottie knew Madam must be watching her from above with a smile: She was playing *Communion in G*, one of Madam's favorite pieces. Lottie smiled a little bit herself as the organ's majestic notes flowed throughout the house. It was the first time she had smiled in days.

Freeman Ransom heard the music, and he smiled a bittersweet smile, too, from where he stood on the marble staircase, holding his son Frankie's hand. That music was worthy of a queen, he thought, and Sarah Walker had been just that. Gazing at the gathered mourners, he couldn't help thinking of Booker T. Washington's funeral four years ago, when dignitaries and simple folk alike had poured onto the Tuskegee campus to bury the great leader. That had been a sad day for him, but also a proud day; and his pride swelled even more today, outpacing his sadness. Death was never easy—the Wards, who were here, had lost their only son last year, and it rocked that poor family to its core—but losses forced such simple, powerful reflection on how valuable the life of the loved one had been.

All Ransom had to do was look out at the faces here today to feel Madam C.J. Walker's lasting value in a way he never had before. Just last night, consoling each other, he and Nettie had marveled at how lucky they had been to know her. She had been a true race woman, a woman who had had a role in delivering her people from slavery's legacy as surely as Harriet Tubman or Sojourner Truth, and he hoped his children, and their children after that, would grow up to follow her example. God had seen fit to bring her into his life when he was a train porter, and now He had seen fit to set her free. The awfulness of losing her only made his luck, and his gratitude, feel that much more keen.

"Daddy . . ." young Frankie whispered up to him. "Is Ma Walkie gone now?" He'd been very concerned about the moment when she would be buried, when her body would be *gone*.

Slowly Ransom shook his head and gazed down at his son. "Not at all. There's a piece of your godmother inside every person in this room."

The funeral had begun with the reading of the twenty-third Psalm, and after Lottie finished playing *Communion in G*, the telegrams of well-wishers from all corners were read, including those from Mrs. Booker T. Washington; Robert Russa Moton, the new principal of Tuskegee Institute; and Dr. Mary McLeod Bethune. Then J. Rosamond Johnson graced the room with an original song he'd written on the occasion of Madam's passing, "Since You Went Away," and his sweet voice caused a flurry of white handkerchiefs as the mourners were brought to fresh tears. There was a long, reverent silence after he finished. Then Reverend Adam Clayton Powell walked forward to begin his scheduled remarks.

Sadie Jackson was among the mourners, sitting near the rear, with a contingent of other Walker culturists and agents who had made the trip to the funeral. A woman named Lizette Simons, who had apparently known "Madam Sarah" since she lived in Denver, sat beside Sadie with a lanky young man she'd introduced as her son. They had briefly exchanged proud motherhood stories before the services began; Sadie's sons had both graduated from college, and one was now a lawyer. And Lizette's son was in his second year at Howard University, studying pharmacy. What was most obvious need not be stated between them: They had both financed their children's education through money they'd made as Walker culturists. Sarah, in following her own dream, had helped them secure their families' future generations.

But that wasn't the real reason Sadie had come to the funeral. She'd come because of the letter she still carried in her hand, and she glanced at it every few moments so she could feel a sense of communion with her friend. *Please come say a few words about me when I'm gone*, Sarah had written her in a letter, which had arrived the same day her death was announced in the newspapers. *You may know me best of all.*

Now, after watching the pomp and circumstance of this opulent funeral, Sadie knew exactly what her friend had meant in her letter. She and Sarah had grown so far apart in the last few years, Sadie could barely remember when they'd last shared a quiet evening together, but theirs wasn't the sort of friendship that needed constant tending. Their friendship had been sealed long ago, and nothing in the past few years could have faded it.

A man named Reverend Brooks was delivering a sweeping eulogy, but Sadie barely heard it because of the pounding of her heart. She'd done very well for herself in business—she owned two Walker beauty parlors in Pittsburgh, and she was thinking about opening a third—but she had never cared for the social circles that seemed to accompany success. She hadn't come up that way, and she'd never yearned for acceptance in those circles the way Sarah always had. She'd congratulated Sarah when she moved into her mansion, but she would have felt out of place at its official opening, and she'd declined Sarah's invitation. So today Sadie felt pangs of discomfort as she realized she was about to be called on to address this impressive roomful of folks. She hadn't been able to think of a speech to put on paper, and what could she add to so much praise about how important Sarah had been to the race?

Sadie decided just to stand up and speak whatever came to her mind. That was what Sarah would want, she thought. In fact, she knew that was exactly what Sarah would *do*.

Sadie's heart thumped when she heard her name called. Lizette squeezed her hand, and Sadie began to walk to the head of the room as all of the faces watched her, wondering who she was. She wasn't wearing any finery today; instead, she was dressed exactly as Sarah had always urged her representatives, in a white blouse and simple skirt, a uniform she was proud of.

"Afternoon, y'all," Sadie greeted the group nervously. "My name is Sadie Jackson, and I'm nobody special. I knew Sarah Breedlove McWilliams Walker before she was special to anybody except her friends. We used to wash clothes together in St. Louis, right in her yard, back when she used to count her little pennies in a mason jar." Sadie took a deep breath, fighting a stone in her throat from the sudden vivid memory of her friend's face.

"In some ways, it hardly seems real for me to be standing here in

Sarah's big grand house with all the newspapers talking about her passing, and with all you folks come to honor her. But then I guess I just always expected it somehow. Sarah had a belief all along, you see, that she could do whatever she put a mind to. And if you knew Sarah like I did, you know she had a *strong* mind—not just smart, which she was, but ornery, too. It could be raining buckets outside, but if Sarah thought it was sunny, you couldn't say a word to change her mind."

At that many people in the room laughed aloud, even as they dabbed their eyes.

"Sarah liked what she liked, too. She liked that pork, one thing. No matter how much money Sarah had, she was never too proud to find some pigs' feet. And she *loved* to work. She didn't always love the work she was doing, I can tell you that, but she had something inside of her that made her want to do her best. And that was all she ever tried to give anybody—her best. When she gave her best, it made you want to give your best. That was all her company was supposed to stand for, to my thinking; she was giving her best, and she expected the same from all of us. She cared about how we looked to the outside world, because she saw something beautiful in us. She told me once she had a dream about a field of black roses—and I think Sarah was really just a gardener. That's how she saw herself. She was trying to get those roses to grow."

Sadie paused, rocking on her heels. She felt a growing sense of serenity as she spoke about her friend. "Do I think Sarah would have wanted to live a few more years? Well, I guess we all would. But even though I wasn't here at the end, I think I know what was in Sarah's mind. There was one day back in St. Louis, we were all sitting around the kitchen table, reading the newspaper— I think, in fact, Sarah had just put on a pot of coffee— and we came across an article about *Plessy versus Ferguson* and separate but equal, and we all talked about how there didn't seem to be a good future ahead for Negroes. It's the only time I ever saw Sarah look scared a day in her life. But I can tell you one thing. . . ."

Sadie paused, gazing at Lizette in her white hat and lovely dress, and her tall son beside her, and F.B. Ransom on the stairs with his young son on his arm, and the scores of other women who represented Sarah's company, as well as the dignitaries who had come to honor her. Somewhere a baby was crying—and Sadie guessed it was the infant she'd seen that someone told her was named A'Lelia. So A'Lelia was here today after all, wasn't she?

"Sarah wasn't scared anymore," Sadie went on. "We may still be in some dark days, but the future is right in this room, and she knew it. I think if she was standing here, she'd see all these sad faces and say, 'Y'all just hush. There ain't nothin' to be cryin' about. This room was built for dancing, not cryin'. I've worked hard, and my work is done. I saw my roses grow.' "

For years afterward, those who heard Sadie speak that day would tell her she'd looked and sounded so much like Sarah at the funeral that they had wondered in their hearts if it wasn't possible that Madam C.J. Walker had come back to life.

Sadie never believed her friend had left at all.

AUTHOR'S NOTE

Historical note: A'Lelia Walker Robinson reached home the day after her mother's funeral; she privately visited the Woodlawn Cemetery vault where her mother's casket had been kept for her. Almost immediately, A'Lelia married not Dr. Kennedy, but Dr. Wiley Wilson. She soon divorced Dr. Wilson and married Dr. Kennedy, but they, too, divorced in a short time.

A'Lelia, who was instrumental in the construction of the historic Walker Theatre, still located in Indianapolis, became one of the most visible personalities of the Harlem Renaissance. She was known for her literary salon, called Dark Tower, where she entertained figures such as poets Countee Cullen and Langston Hughes. Hughes wrote a poem for her, "To A'Lelia." She died at the age of forty-six in 1931. There were 11,000 mourners at her funeral.

Soon after Madam C.J. Walker died, her former husband, C.J., wrote to F.B. Ransom to ask whether or not he was listed in her will. Mr. Ransom told C.J. he recalled hearing Madam say that she intended to include C.J. in the will—but apparently she did not. F.B. Ransom's parting line to C.J.: "You, I think, will admit, however, that whatever you lost, you have no one to blame but yourself for it."

The Madam C.J. Walker Manufacturing Company thrived for decades after her death, celebrating its sixtieth anniversary in 1960. F.B. Ransom was general manager until his death in 1947. Madam Walker's adopted granddaughter, Mae Bryant Perry, eventually served as company president, as did F.B. Ransom's daughter, A'Lelia Emma Ransom Nelson.

I have tried to be faithful to the *spirit* of Madam C.J. Walker in this book, but *The Black Rose* is a work of fiction. Aspects of Madam's life have been presented slightly out of sequence or fictionalized, including the creation of composite characters like Lottie Ransaw. Ultimately, no one knows how Madam devised her modification of the steel comb or created her hair formula. She consistently said in interviews and advertisements that the formula came in a dream, which might well be true. One source interviewed for this book believed that a St. Louis physician had given her the formula, and that could also be true. In fact, her secret was so well kept that I do not even know what her hair formula was, except that it probably contained sulfur.

The interviews, documents, and publications included in the boxes of research I received from the Alex Haley Estate are too numerous to mention, but they were invaluable in the writing of this book. Here are a few additional titles I discovered that were helpful:

Madam C.J. Walker, by A'Lelia Perry Bundles; Slave Songs of the United States, edited by William Francis Allen, Charles Pickard Ware, and Lucy McKim Garrison; Booker T. Washington: The Wizard of Tuskegee, 1901–1915, by Louis R. Harlan; Aristocrats of Color: The Black Elite, 1880–1920, by Willard B. Gatewood; To 'Joy My Freedom: Southern Black Women's Lives and Labors After the Civil War, by Tera W. Hunter; Stolen Childhood: Slave Youth in Nineteenth-Century America, by Wilma King; Ain't but a Place: An Anthology of African American Writings About St. Louis, edited by Gerald Early; When Harlem Was in Vogue, by David Levering Lewis; The Great Cyclone at St. Louis and East St. Louis, May 27, 1896, compiled and edited by Julian Curzon; The World Came to St. Louis: A Visit to the 1904 World's Fair, by Dorothy Daniels Birk; Paths of Resistance: Tradition and Dignity in Industrializing Missouri, by David P. Thelen; Victorian America: Transformations in Everyday Life, 1876–1915, by Thomas J. Schlereth; and Africana: The Encyclopedia of the African and African American Experience, edited by Kwame Anthony Appiah and Henry Louis Gates Jr.